Treasure of Sherwood

A ROBIN HOOD MYSTERY

Novels by Jay Ruud

THE MERLIN MYSTERIES:

Fatal Feast

The Knight's Riddle

Lost in the Quagmire

The Bleak and Empty Sea

The Knight of the Cart

To the Great Deep

THE ROBIN HOOD MYSTERIES:

Sleuth of Sherwood

Ghoul of Sherwood

Treasure of Sherwood

Treasure of Sherwood

A ROBIN HOOD MYSTERY

JAY RUUD

Encircle Publications
Farmington, Maine, U.S.A.

Paperback ISBN 13: 978-1-64599-540-1
Hardcover ISBN 13: 978-1-64599-541-8
E-book ISBN 13: 978-1-64599-542-5

Library of Congress Control Number: 2024936663

Encircle editor: Cynthia Brackett-Vincent

Cover illustration by Isabella Gifford
Cover and book design by Deirdre Wait

Published by:

Encircle Publications
PO Box 187
Farmington, ME 04938

http://encirclepub.com
info@encirclepub.com

PROLOGUE

The white-bearded man walked through the old oak trees into a clearing in the forest. He took a handkerchief from the sleeve of his tunic and wiped his brow, which was wet with perspiration after his long hike. The sun to his left, which had kept him unseasonably warm all through his walk, was beginning to sink below the horizon. Breathing heavily, he continued up the gentle slope to its highest point.

This hillock was about twenty-five feet across and raised ten feet or so above the surrounding forest floor, so that it could not even be seen from any distance because of the thick trees blocking the view. But the old man knew that at one time this spot had been a meeting place for representatives from all the neighboring farms and villages. That had been in pagan times, though. In fact, some believed that this was an old heathen burial mound from many centuries earlier. Well, he thought, if there are pagan spirits lurking in these woods, they would no longer congregate here after he had done what he had come to do.

The old man was accoutered like a knight, dressed in a well-worn habergeon of rusty chainmail, over which he wore a green surcoat with a brown lion rampant, the blazon of his house. A short arming sword hung from a sash around his waist, and he bore on his back a sturdy shovel and a pick. In addition, he carried a deerskin bag within which was a box he highly prized.

1

At one corner of the clearing a small boundary stone marked with a "W" poked out from the ground. The old crusader knelt by the stone and laid his shovel down, the end of the handle pointing due west to where the sun was setting. He used the spade's handle to make a line running west to east, then took his sword and placed it precisely vertical to the shovel, the two instruments intersecting at the stone. Then he marked a spot on his right-hand side that he judged was precisely midway between the horizontal and vertical lines, and began a line in the sand, moving his sword now to lay it at a precise forty-five-degree angle, directly northeast of the stone. He carried this line out two sword lengths, which was exactly six feet. At that point he began to dig.

As he dug, he told himself he was glad the light was fading. It lessened the possibility that anyone would see him by chance digging in this mound. He also planned how he would record all of these steps in Latin on a map he would draw—he'd had a good deal of experience reading battlefield maps in the Holy Land, and was skilled in their use. And he planned how once his eldest son was old enough, he would share the secret with the lad, so that his family could depend on the treasure held within this box in coming years. It was, he thought, the future of his house.

Precisely three feet deep, he placed the box, tenderly as if it were a child. He filled in the hole by moonlight, and packed the earth down with his feet, finally drawing a branch across the whole area to disguise the fact that someone had been digging there recently. Then he gathered up his tools, heaved a sigh of relief, and started to make his way back through the oaks, to the tree where he had left his horse. He had wanted no horse tracks left where some tracker of the forest might follow them to his hiding place. He smiled as he made his way slowly back through the dark forest. He had insured his family's security, he was now confident, for generations to come.

CHAPTER ONE

The mighty gyrfalcon was barely a speck in the sky as the small wedge of barnacle geese flew beneath it. When she judged the time was right, the great bird of prey tucked in her mighty wings and began a powerful drive aimed unerringly at the small, weak goose that trailed the others. The falcon struck hard, tearing the weaker goose with her powerful talons and curved beak while yet in full flight. Still clutching her prey in those formidable talons, the meticulously trained bird slowed, dropped the goose to the ground, and landed gracefully on the thick leather glove that protected the fist of Lord William Randal.

Lord Randal, astride the chestnut palfrey he saved for hunting, smiled at the great bird and spoke lovingly to her as he stroked her head with his other gloved hand. "That's my pretty one! Best hunter in the mews, aren't you my great Xenobia? Isn't she, Dap?" This last he said as he leaned down to allow his falconer to take the gyrfalcon from him and to place the leather hood over her eyes, tying her then to the leash or creance and placing her in her cadge, the padded wooden frame she was carried in. She was a beautiful bird, with snow-white feathers. Powerfully built, she weighed nearly five pounds and had a wingspread of close to five feet. Lord Randal had paid dearly for her when she was brought from Iceland a few years earlier, and was justly proud of her.

3

"Best hunter in the whole shire, m'lord, by my reckoning," Dap answered gruffly, the early morning damp graveling his voice. "But let's see if this here new little runt can hold a candle to her, or if we should chop him up and feed him to Xenobia for dinner!" Despite his dry humor, Dap's sun-browned features, sharp and expressionless as if carved from stone, betrayed no flicker of amusement as he removed the hood from his master's newly acquired peregrine.

This new bird was a good deal smaller that the great gyrfalcon, at about two pounds, and his blue-grey wings spanned perhaps three feet, but as Lord Randal held out a small shred of meat to entice the shy young peregrine onto his gloved fist, he said, "Just wait, Dap. You're going to be astounded when you see how fast this new fellow can fly. I've seen peregrines strike so fast, a young duck in flight never knew what hit him. I think I'll name him Mercury, what do you think?" He stroked the nervous bird gently with his free hand and called over to his other servant, the dog boy, who stood at the edge of the clearing holding Troilus and Cresseid, Randal's two greyhounds, by the leash. "What do you think, Wulf, ever seen a peregrine falcon in flight?" Wulf, a thin slouching lad of nineteen or so, with a long hanging face and ears and nose, had been gazing at the ground as if looking for something, and surprised out of his reverie by his master's question, looked up and shook his head indifferently. Like his older fellow Dap, he was dressed in a simple brown tunic with a green hood, that being the livery of Lord Randal's house. But he filled it out far less well than the stocky, muscular Dap.

"Well," Randal told both of them as he scanned the sky from the back of his horse. "Let another wedge of geese fly by and I'll loose him, and then you're going to see something awe-inspiring, let me tell you!" The nobleman shook his wavy brown locks out of his face as he gazed upwards, shading his dark eyes with his gauntleted right hand as he held the peregrine on his left, and his smile revealed a full set of teeth still white enough after twenty-three years' regular use.

Perhaps it was because he and both his servants were carefully scanning the sky that they did not notice the half-dozen men in Lincoln green garb silently emerging from the trees that surrounded the clearing, moving cautiously forward with arrows notched in their longbows and the bows held at the ready. What those men saw were two unarmed servants, one with a pair of dogs and the other with a cadge for hunting birds, their two palfreys tied to a tree, and an imposing young nobleman mounted and dressed in a fine brocade surcoat embroidered with flowers, and dark blue cloak and hood of fine woolen tiretaine. Hanging from his leather belt, this young fellow did have a short sword, but more importantly he also had a fat purse dangling there, and that is what had drawn the intense interest of the men in green.

"Now, now, go quite easy there," a good-humored nasal voice suddenly startled the three men in the clearing. "Move slow, or one of my boys might get excited and send an arrow in yer direction, and I'd hate to ruin that lovely embroidery on yer surcoat, m'lord. Must 'ave took some poor girl weeks o' work makin' it. I'd hate to have her work go to naught. Now get that bird calmed down and put away first, slow and careful now."

The peregrine was squawking and fluttering his wings nervously, spooked when Randal had started at the sudden interruption. Fortunately, he was still on his leather leash, or Lord Randal would have lost his latest acquisition. He lowered the bird slowly to Dap's hands, and the careful falconer replaced the bird's hood and gently placed him back in the cadge.

The speaker, whom Randal assumed must be the leader of the group, was clad in green with a brown hood that lay across his back so that his wild brown hair hung free. He had a wide friendly-looking smile that revealed perhaps half of his original teeth. The pug nose was sprinkled with freckles and the brown eyes twinkled with mischievous—though not, Randal judged, with evil—intent.

Lord Randal spread his hands in a calming gesture and addressed the speaker in what he thought was a conciliatory tone. "Be calm yourself young man. You are royal foresters of Sherwood, I am assuming? Well, I think you will want to stand down when you hear who I am. I am called Lord Randal of Halloughton, because I have a great manor house there, two miles from Southwell. I am not poaching here—I'll have you know I have written authorization signed by the king himself to hunt in his royal forest. I appreciate your doing your duty, but you need not threaten me with arrest. My hunting here has royal sanction." With that last word Lord Randal's right hand moved unconsciously toward the hilt of his sword.

"Na, na, na, none of that my lord," the speaker cautioned. "Put that hand in the air, won't you? Skipper, slip over there and take that sword out of our new friend's scabbard will you?" At that, one of the others put down his bow—he had seemed ill at ease with the weapon anyway, Randal had noted—and stepped to the horse, relieving Randal of his sword. This fellow was a strange looking woodsman, with long blond hair braided down his back, and a battle axe stuck into his belt: a weapon, Randal had no difficulty imagining, with which the muscular blond was probably far more comfortable than his bow.

With Lord William now unarmed, the group's spokesman let his own bow dip and his arms relax. "Now as to arresting you, we've no such intention. You mistake us, my lord. We don't care about yer poaching. We do enough of that ourselves. We're certainly no royal foresters. Let me introduce myself: they call me Much, the miller's son. And frankly, my lord, we're not impressed wi' yer king's permit. I mean, who's the king these days anyway? Nobody around here has seen such a person. Fact is, it's our captain who happens to be Master of Sherwood Forest. And he doesn't want us to arrest you. He wants us to invite you to dinner." And with that Much gave the nobleman a gap-toothed grin.

Lord Randal found Much's grin almost irresistible, and couldn't help grinning back. With a confident nod to his two servants, he replied, "Well then, Much the miller's son, lead us on! I've a notion I'd like to meet this captain of yours! And to repay his courtesy, we've got two fat geese and a couple of nice rabbits my hounds tracked down in the game bag Wulf is holding over there. I'd like to contribute those, and the one my gyrfalcon has just killed, to pay for my share of the dinner."

"Well…" Much's grin grew broader as he looked down at the earth and rubbed the back of his neck, and his five companions stifled their laughter. "Yer share might end up costing you a bit more than that. And by the by, we're going to have to bring you hooded like yer hawks there, since we can't let anybody see how to get to our camp, ya see. So if yer two men will mount their horses, my friend John here will supply the masks."

Intrigued but not alarmed by the woodsman's curious words, Randal nodded to his men, and Dap, carrying the cadge, mounted his grey palfrey. Wulf first picked up the newly slain goose and bagged it before mounting his own dark brown rouncey. John the cook's son handed a black hood to each of them and made sure they drew it over their faces, and Much took the reins of Lord Randal's horse to lead the whole party through the woods. "Just a reminder, my lord," Much whispered confidentially. "I wouldn't try to sneak a peek from under that hood. Or try to break away with yer horse. My men have still got their bows. And trust me, they're crack shots."

* * *

After an hour or so of tramping through the woods, listening to the clomps of the horse hooves on the forest floor and the songs of those birds that still remained in Sherwood in early October, along with the occasional remarks the outlaws made quietly to one another, Lord Randal was thoroughly confused. He had tried to remember which direction his horse had been turned, and to guess how far it was between turns, but after the first quarter hour he was so completely turned around, what with Much's constant changes of direction and retracing of steps, that he gave up any thought of remembering how he had come.

At length Lord Randal began to hear voices, many jolly voices that seemed to be bantering with one another as a group of people went about their mid-day tasks, and he smelled the smoke of a good sized campfire, and felt full sunlight on his face, suggesting they had come out of the deep woods. Then he felt a tug at his belt and realized some hand had reached up and snatched his purse away. That annoyed him somewhat, and he recalled what Much had said about his paying for his meal. But immediately thereafter someone yanked the hood from his head and, blinking a bit in the sun, he looked around at a boisterous encampment, with at least fifteen more Lincoln-clad foresters, some bustling, some lounging, within a wide clearing around the largest oak tree Randal had ever seen.

Now a group of half a dozen outlaws came forward to meet the new arrivals. They were led by a suntanned mountain of a man who gave Lord William quite a start. The man was at least six and a half feet tall, with broad shoulders and bulging biceps and a bulk that must have weighed a good twenty stone. He approached Randal with his right hand extended, and the lord was struck by the giant's sharp blue eyes, his ruggedly handsome face, his blond hair and well-trimmed beard.

"Welcome, my lord," the fellow said, taking Randal's hand and helping him from his horse. "I see our friend Much has invited you to dine. I'm John Naylor, though folk hereabout call me 'Little John,' obviously because of my puny size. And you are?"

At the name "Little John," Lord Randal's eyes grew large. Of course, waylaid in Sherwood these days? Who else could it be but that band of outlaws known to be led by Little John and the notorious Robin Hood. He let out an inarticulate "Ah!" and shook his head as if to shake the cobwebs from the corners of his brain. "So this is the camp of the infamous Robin Hood, is it? Despoiler of the king's deer? The thief that terrorizes all the folk who enter Sherwood?"

"Well, not *all* the folk," Little John corrected him. "Just the rich ones. They're the ones need terrorizing."

"Well now, that's putting it a bit crudely John, don't you think?" A freckled, handsome youth at John's side interrupted. "My lord, what my friend means to say is that it is only rich nobles or prelates that we invite to dinner, and we do ask of them a small contribution to help pay for their entertainment. To the common folk we do no harm. In fact, we often share our pickings with the poor folk of the forest—talk to any of them and you'll hear us spoken of more fairly."

"Oh, our guest is quite ready to contribute to the feast," Much said. "In fact, if you take the game bag from that scrawny slouching brute on the brown horse, you'll find a brace of geese and rabbits he's pledged to give us."

"Is that so?" Little John said. "Scarlet, why don't you grab that bag and take it to Ellen there at the cooking spit? She's just about to start the meal, I would think!"

At that one of his other companions, one with laughing blue eyes and a great mane of blond hair that was covered by a bright red hood worn over his Lincoln green tunic, took the bag from Wulf and flashed Lord William a wide smile before dashing toward the cooking fire.

"That's Will Scarlet," Little John told the lord. "And this other young scamp you've been talking to is my own personal thorn in the flesh, Will Stutely. But you ain't answered my first question, my lord. Who are *you*?"

"My apologies, my good man, I was so taken aback by being here at the camp of the Sherwood outlaws I quite forgot my courtesy. But he is one Will" (Randal nodded at Scarlet's retreating back), "*he* is another (and with that he nodded at Stutely), "and I must make a third. William Randal is my name, Lord of Halloughton. I hunt in these woods with the king's sanction. But I am told I'd much better have the consent of Master Robin Hood, de facto Lord of Sherwood." At that the corner of Randal's mouth twisted upward slightly to match his mocking tone.

"Who exactly the king is anymore we're hard put to say here in the north," Stutely continued in a mock-serious vein. "But we do know that the representative of royal power here in Nottinghamshire—one Sir Guy of Gisbourne—far more resembles the arse end of your horse than he does the arm of a king."

Lord Randal cocked his head. "Do I detect some bitterness there in your voice, young Stutely?"

"I was entertained in Sir Guy's dungeon for about twenty years one night," Stutely answered, then pointed to the scar over his left eye. "He left me this to remember him by."

Randal looked thoughtful a moment and then mused, "Yes,

well, Gisbourne—he *is* one of those who characterized your whole band as thieves and poachers deserving to be hanged." But then after another brief moment's thought, he added, "Of course my neighbor, Sir Richard of the Lee, says those claims are nonsense—that you are a generous and kindly crew who exact a toll only on those who can afford to pay it."

"You know Sir Richard, then?" came a voice from behind. When Randal turned around, he was face to face with another sturdy, well-built yeoman in the Lincoln green livery of the outlaws, standing with hands on his hips and flashing a most mischievous grin. While not so striking as Little John, this fellow had an easy air of confidence and authority about him, from his blond hair and shrewd blue eyes to his soft deerskin boots. "Well any friend of Sir Richard's is a friend of ours! But let me ask you this, my lord: are *you* one who can afford to pay our toll?"

"Once we weigh this purse we'll know the answer to that, Robin!" Much held up the purse he'd snatched from Lord Randal's belt, and he tossed it to Robin, who tested it in his palm and whistled.

"Quite a fat purse you've got there, my lord," Robin said, jiggling the bag and looking thoughtful. "Perhaps it needs to miss a meal or two. Thorvald!" he called. "We need a reckoning here!"

From the group of men that had now begun to crowd around the cook fire to watch a young woman spitting Randal's geese and begin roasting them over the open flames, a little fellow emerged and made his way as quickly as he could to Robin's side. He was a grizzled old dwarf with white hair and beard, and a face that seemed perpetually angry, but his voice was pleasant enough as he took the purse from Robin's hand and said, "I'll 'ave them figgers fer ya by the time the meal is done, Robin!" And off he went, back into the crowd.

Lord Randal gawked at Robin as if he'd met the pope, "You…you're…Robin Hood, then, the notorious outlaw?"

"At your service," Robin answered with an ironic bow. "Though of course, as you have said, Sir Richard would not label us so. Now, my lord, let Much and Will make you and your servants comfortable, and to help you wile away the time till dinner, those geese you brought us will make a tasty meal, but we can give you some cheese and nuts and a splash of ale while you're waiting, right lads?"

Stutely and the miller's son showed their guests to a comfortable bed of grass at the foot of the Great Oak, and left them alone while they visited the stores being doled out by another of the young women of the group, and secured three cups of ale, three wedges of cheddar, and a small pewter bowl of nuts, which they brought back to the guests under the tree. In the meantime, Lord Randal looked around at his leisure. He saw a small group of men playing at Hazzards on the other side of the tree. And further off three or four others were playing what looked to be a version of Nine Men's Morris with black and white pebbles and a playing surface scratched into the forest floor. But by far the greatest number of men were crowding about the fire where, like Will and Much, they could pick up a bite or two to quiet their bellies while they waited for the main course of fowl.

Randal lounged in the moss enjoying the coloring leaves of early autumn, the yellows of the sturdy oaks, interspersed with the deep reds of the ash and the gold of the beech trees scattered among the oak. Vouchsafed a serving of the outlaws' cheese, nuts and ale, Lord Randal and the chiseled-faced Dap sat comfortably munching their snack, while the surly Wulf wandered unobtrusively around the edge of the camp, still apparently searching the forest floor as he had done before.

But Randal paid his sulking servant little heed, as he noticed a young man with a lute moving toward the center of the clearing. What, he thought, are we about to get some kind of entertainment? The young minstrel was of an age with Randal, and he wore a bright blue hood over his uniform green tunic, and wore hosen of the same color as his hood. A bit of a dandy, Randal thought as the fellow listened to his lute and adjusted a few strings. And why not? He was a handsome enough lad, with short-cropped sandy hair and a thin goatee to match, and he swaggered a bit as he took up his instrument.

For a time, Randal was all but mesmerized by the fellow's fine tenor, and enthralled by the tale he sung, a ballad Randal had not heard before, about a young girl called Meggie and her lover, Sweet William, who leaves his beloved and is murdered on his way home. And his grisly head is hung from the beams of the church ceiling the next day, right over poor Meggie's own accustomed place.

When the song was ended, Randal felt a bit of a letdown, as if returning home after a bracing gallop on his favorite horse, or winding down after a rollicking dance with his own beloved lady. He clapped his hands to show the minstrel his appreciation, and the singer turned toward him, raising his eyebrows in surprise at such a reception from one of the company's generally unwilling guests. And, swinging his lute onto his back, he began to saunter over to Lord Randal, flopping himself next to the nobleman with a friendly air.

"So, my lord," the minstrel began, his hazel eyes dancing with delight. "I see you appreciate good music!"

"With all my heart," the lord exclaimed. "And that was some of the finest singing and playing I've heard, in hall or tavern or in the greenwood itself. What is your name, fellow?"

"I am called Alan a Dale, my lord. And you, I understand,

are Lord Randal of Halloughton. And it's pleased I am you enjoyed my music so."

"I cannot say how much," the lord replied. Then, growing animated, he burst out, "I must have you come and be a part of my household in Halloughton! What would you take for it? I'll grant you an annuity that will certainly exceed your share of booty with this lot," and he gestured around the clearing. "And a new set of clothes every Michaelmas. What say you?"

Alan's eyebrows shot up again, and he scratched his beard thoughtfully. "Well, it's terribly generous, my lord. But of course, it's not just me. I've got a wife to consider." He turned toward the cooking fire, at the hardy young woman turning the spit. "That's her there," he gestured. "That's my Ellen. There'd have to be a place for her, too in your house."

"Absolutely!" Lord Randal agreed. "We'll definitely find a position for her. Perhaps an attendant on my wife—when I do marry, which I plan on soon. And I'll add a pitcher of wine a day for your family as well. Come, come, what say you?"

Alan continued scratching his beard. "I admit your offer is awfully tempting. Of course, you don't know how much my share actually *is* here in the greenwood. I suspect it's a good deal larger than you think. And then there's the freedom. No offense, my lord, but there's a lot to be said for being my own man. I'm servant to nobody, and I don't have to do anything I don't want to do. I've no *master*, you see—only a *leader* in Robin—and that, let me tell you, is worth more than gold. I don't expect you to understand, never having been in servitude yourself, but freedom is a sumptuous commodity."

Lord Randal would have answered, but he was interrupted by Will Stutely bringing him and his companion Dap a bread trencher heaped with roast goose. At that Alan hopped up and dashed to the cook fire to get some for himself, with Randal calling after him, "Bring something back for my boy Wulf, will you?" The lad was hanging back, leaning against an oak at the edge of the clearing, but he looked up with anticipation at the promise of roast goose.

"So, my lord," Stutely asked, inclining his head courteously as he stood over the nobleman. "Are you satisfied with the feast so far?"

Sir William seemed about to reply when he caught sight of something that made his jaw remain motionlessly hanging. From amongst the crowd around the cook fire where his eyes had followed Alan, there emerged a figure who wore no Lincoln green. He was tall and erect, with the bearing of a knight, and he was dressed in a tunic of blue samite and fine leather boots, and wore a finely woven black surcoat, though all of his clothing seemed somewhat the worse for wear, as if he'd been a nobleman in his time, but had gone several years without a new set of rich raiment. But more startling than that, the man's visage was a dark mahogany color.

After a moment Stutely asked, with some concern, "Are you all right, my lord? Did your dinner not agree with you?"

Lord Randal, shaken out of his reverie, replied, "No, no, sirrah, my, uh, digestion is quite fine. I was just taken aback by that man there, walking toward the center of the circle. He's...he seems to be dressed as a knight. Why...?"

Stutely waited a moment, but when it became obvious that Randal was not about to elaborate his question, he responded, "Why is he dressed like a knight? Because he *is* a knight." On seeing Randal's skeptical reaction, Stutely continued: "That's Sir Palomides. He was in fact a knight in the court of the old king. When most of his brethren were wiped out in the king's last war, Palomides became a knight errant, but kept searching for a new lord that would have him."

"But…he's…he's a Moor, or am I mistaken?" Randal had heard enough about Moors from acquaintances who had been off to fight in one of the Holy Crusades that seemed to go on perpetually in the Holy Land and in Spain, though he had never seen one in the flesh. Returning crusaders had described the Muslim enemy as skillful and mighty warriors, who fought with the strength and guile of the devil himself. Was it any wonder that Randal would have expected some outward manifestation of this rendering, like fiery eyes or demonic horns? It was a bit of a disappointment to him that Palomides looked not unlike other men. Except, of course, for the tone of his skin. Well, Randal thought, perhaps those fine leather boots concealed some cloven hooves below.

"Well of course he's a Moor," Stutely said. "He's no infidel, though. He has been baptized. But that was of no account to the great lords he sought service with. Finally, he decided to give up the life of the court and come into the greenwood and join with his friend from the old king's castle."

"Robin Hood you mean?" Again Lord Randal was surprised and amused by the things he was learning about the Sherwood outlaws. "Robin Hood was a member of the old king's court?"

Stutely shook his head. "Oh no, Robin is a freeborn yeoman and prouder of that than if he'd been one of your ilk, my lord. But he was captain of the of king's guard, and took to the forest here when that kingdom fell. But Palomides is definitely a knight, with all the martial skills and with his own great war horse. And with the courtly skills as well, including the skills of the troubadour. Look, he's going to regale us with a song!"

"Right, you're in for a treat now," Alan a Dale said, returning to Randal's side with his own trencher of fowl, having delivered one to the sullen Wulf before returning. Randal, seeing Sir Palomides unsling a small gittern he had flung across his back, settled back to be entertained again by these happy woodsmen. "Palomides is no wandering minstrel like me. He's his own composer as well as singer, just like your old troubadours. Though I'm pretty sure he's written a ballad he's going to sing now."

"So you're saying..." Randal began.

"Shush!" He was shut down by both Alan and Will. "He's about to begin!"

Sir Palomides stood in the midst of the clearing and stared about him until all was quiet. Then in his sonorous baritone he introduced his theme: "Men and women of the forest, comrades and special guests," and with this he nodded courteously to Lord Randal and his companions. "You have heard my friend Alan a Dale sing a merry ballad of the death of Sweet Willie." There were a few guffaws at his characterization of the grizzly story as "merry." "And he told that story well, my friends. But I have a story to tell you now that might make you see our pleasant minstrel in a different light. It's a ballad I've just composed, and I like to call it "Robin Hood and Alan a Dale." Here's how it goes:

As Robin Hood in the forest stood,
Amongst the leaves so gay,
There espied a brave young man
Come drooping along the way.

And when he came bold Robin before,
Robin asked him courteously,
"O hast thou any money to spare
For my merry men and me?"

"I have no money," the young man said,
"But five shillings and a ring;
And that I have kept this seven long years,
To have it at my wedding."

"Yesterday I should have married a maid,
But she now is from me ta'en,
And chosen to be an old knight's delight,
Whereby my poor heart is slain."

"What is thy name?" then said Robin Hood,
"Come tell me, without any fail,"
"By the faith of my body," said the young man then,
"My name it is Alan a Dale."

"What wilt thou give me," said Robin Hood,
"In ready gold or fee,
To help thee to thy true-love again,
And deliver her unto thee?"

"I have no money," then quoth the young man,
"No ready gold nor fee,
But I will swear upon a book
Thy true servant for to be."

Then Robin he hasted over the plain,
He neither shirked nor stayed,
Until he came unto the church
Where Alan should be wed.

"What dost thou do here?" the bishop he said,
"I prithee now tell to me:"
"I am a bold harper," quoth Robin Hood,
"And the best in the north country."

"O welcome, O welcome," the bishop he said,
"That music best pleaseth me;'"

"You shall have no music," quoth Robin Hood,
"Till the bride and the bridegroom I see."

With that came in a wealthy knight,
Who was both grave and old,
And after him a dainty lass,
Who shone like glistering gold.

"This is no fit match," quoth bold Robin Hood,
"That you seem to make here;
For since we are come unto the church,
The bride she shall choose her own dear."

Then Robin Hood put his horn to his mouth,
And blew blasts two or three;
When four and twenty bowmen bold
Came leaping over the lee.

And when they came into the church-yard,
Marching all on a row,
The first man was Alan a Dale,
To give bold Robin his bow.

"This is thy true-love," Robin he said,
"Young Alan, as I hear say;
And you shall be married at this same time,
Before we depart away."

"That shall not be," the bishop he said,
"For thy word will not stand;
They shall be three times asked in the church,
As the law is of our land."

Robin Hood pulled off the bishop's coat,
And put it upon Little John;
"By the faith of my body," then Robin said,
"This cloth doth make thee a man."

When Little John went into the quire,
The people began for to laugh;
He asked them seven times in the church,
Lest three times should not be enough.

"Who gives me this maid," then said Little John;
Quoth Robin, "That do I,
And any that take her from Alan a Dale
Full dearly he shall her buy."

And thus having ended this merry wedding,
The bride looked as fresh as a queen,
And so they returned to the merry green wood,
Amongst the leaves so green.

There was raucous laughter and applause all around the clearing when Palomides had finished his song, and Lord Randal, quite taken out of himself with joy at the performance, applauded louder than any of the others. "By Gemini and the little fish," he exclaimed. "Is this company filled with nothing but fine musicians? I swear by the five wounds of Christ, if you won't come and serve as my household minstrel, I'll talk this Sir Palomides into coming. No one would take him as knight you say? I'll make him my own household knight, Moor or no, so long as he plays for me every night."

Alan a Dale raised his eyebrows and looked seriously at the nobleman. "If you're serious about that, my lord, you may have better luck with Palomides. It's a different proposition to come to you as servant to master than to come as vassal to liege lord. It may be just the sort of thing Sir Palomides has been looking for, for such a long time. I urge you to speak to him before Much or some of the others escort you back to where you were picked up."

"I will, Alan, be sure of that. But tell me, this story he told of you and your wife—how much truth is there in it?"

"More than a little, I can tell you that," came a gentle alto voice from the woman who was coming up to them just now. She was the youngest of the few women Randal could see about the campsite, but she had a casual air about her that implied she was in her element and had as much a right here as any of these men. She was dressed in a simple blue belted shift that reached to her ankles, and though she was married, her blonde hair tumbled down her back like a young maiden's. "It's true I was pledged to Alan, but that my father had contrived to marry me to a man old enough to be my grandfather. And Alan, well, he wasn't sure what to do till he ran into Robin Hood here in Sherwood." She flashed her blue eyes at Alan's hazel ones and smirked, but it was Will Stutely who continued the story.

"Robin was going to help him no matter what," Will confided, "but he teased Alan first. You know, trying to keep up his reputation as an audacious thief. So knowing full well Alan is poor as a widow without a mite, he says, 'What'll ya give me if I help you get your woman out of this?' and Alan, falling right into it with both feet, says, 'Oh, I'll swear to be your man from this time on.' And so we snatched Ellen right from the altar."

"But was the bishop truly shoved aside, and Little John performed the wedding ceremony?" Randal asked, with real concern. "I mean, doesn't that mean the marriage isn't really a true one in the eyes of the church, or of the realm?"

"Oh, that story just tells how Ellen was saved from the altar.

But she'd not have moved here with me without a true church-sanctioned marriage. Fortunately, our band has got our own spiritual leader, our good Friar Tuck. See him there with the flagon of ale?" Alan pointed to a jolly-looking tonsured fellow with a round belly and a short threadbare grey habit, who was toasting Sir Palomides among a ring of Lincoln-green clad woodsmen gathered around him. "Tuck married us that same day, and we moved into our own tent here at the camp that very night. And by the way, Will Stutely," he finished on a mock-serious note. "I swore fealty to Robin Hood then, and I've never had reason to regret that promise. He's as good and true a man as any in England."

"Amen and amen," Ellen concluded, lounging next to her husband and draining her own flagon of ale.

"Well, I can see how you would be reluctant to quit your place here—go back on your promise—and come serve me in my household. But your story means a great deal to me…"

This took Alan aback, and he asked, "But why? How so?"

"Because," Randal began slowly, not sure how deeply to go into his own history with these complete strangers, but finally deciding, why not? It would probably go no further. "I see in it a mirror of my own situation. I have a paramour, you see, my own beloved Eleanor. You see, miss Ellen, even the name mirrors you. My Eleanor is the daughter of a small landowning freeman, one Edward Franklin, whose property borders some of my own lands. She's a quite respectable lady. Even had a smattering of education—her father sent her to be tutored by a resident from the Minster School in Southwell in a bit of grammar and logic. I think at the time he believed she might have a vocation, and convinced one of the scholars there to give her private lessons.

"Still, my mother, Lady Joan, wants to find me a richer bride, who would bring more to the family. My sister and brother are in agreement with her. And so my love and I have been unable to plan seriously for our future. We have even talked of marrying secretly—perhaps with the blessing of Father Timothy, the local parish priest, or of some mendicant friar—and thereby thwart the whole pressure of the family."

"But you're your own man," Alan objected. "You're of age, and you are lord of your own lands. Who can tell you what to do?"

Randal rolled his eyes. "In theory that's true. In practice—it's not that simple…"

"My lord, something is happening," the falconer Dap spoke for the first time, nodding toward the center of the circle, where Robin Hood looked toward the dwarf Thorvald, who was standing on a tree stump that raised him higher than anyone else in the camp. In his right hand he held aloft the leather purse Much had snatched from Lord Randal's belt.

"Our guests seem to have been pleasantly accommodated," Robin was calling out in a voice that carried through the clearing. "So Thorvald, can you give us an assessment of the charges for their meal and entertainment?"

Lord William snickered at what he assumed was a little charade played for his benefit, fully expecting his assessment to be the full value of his purse, and congratulating himself that he had not been carrying a much larger sum—as well he might have.

"Men, the purse contains a total of sixty gold nobles!" Thorvald called out in a strong clear voice. There was a small cheer that went up from the assembled crowd. "Which means, by my calc'alations, that twenty o' those gold pieces will go direct into our own coffers!" Now there was a much louder cheer that arose, as each man calculated his own share of those twenty gold pieces—that is, nearly a noble per man. Randal, somewhat confused, wondered why on earth the outlaws were taking only a small portion of his money, which lay completely in their hands. Thorvald held up his hand for silence and then continued. "It also means that, as usual, another twenty nobles'll be goin' to feed the 'ungry an' care for the sick among the poor of the neighbor'ood!" And that pronouncement elicited the loudest cheer of all from the group in the campsite. And with that word Friar Tuck put down his flagon and began making his way quickly to Thorvald's side, to take charge of the twenty gold pieces for charity. Thorvald's next announcement astonished Randal most of all. "And o' course, that means Lord Randal leaves 'ere with twenty gold pieces of 'is own, and good luck to 'im!"

Even that last declaration received a bit of a cheer from the outlaw band, though a less enthusiastic one than those earlier. But Randal looked toward Alan a Dale with a puzzled expression. "You mean…I'm keeping a third of my purse? And a third is going to the poor? And this is your common practice is it?"

Alan shrugged. "Well, sure," he answered. "What do you think we are, common criminals?"

No, Lord Randal said to himself. Criminals you may be, but not of the common variety. And he kept this thought through the rest of his ordeal—the re-hooding (not before he'd had a quick word with Sir Palomides), and the ride back hither and yon toward the clearing he'd been picked up in. And all the time he was considering what Alan had said to him. Perhaps there was a way to simply take his Eleanor in spite of all objections. But there were so many other things to consider. Perhaps he should ride to see her right now and have it all out with her. He must take time by the forelock, or lose it all.

CHAPTER TWO

Thorvald the dwarf, Will Scarlet, and young David of Doncaster, concealed at separate points in the forest, were watching the Great North Road, the highway that led from London all the way to York. It was the main road north and south through Sherwood, and it was the road that most often yielded travelers with fat purses that might fill the outlaws' coffers—or, as Robin Hood preferred to put it, guests that might be invited to a fine dinner in the greenwood. Will, mindful of the need for camouflage, had tucked his red hood away in a pouch at his side, and was crouched behind one of the oaks that lined the side of the road. Thorvald, for his part, stood behind a beech tree on the other side, directly across from Will, while David, the youngest and nimblest of the three, was perched on a thick branch of Will's oak that slanted across the road so that, hidden in the foliage and lying along the branch, he could peer directly down the road in either direction, and would be the first to see when anyone approached. And just now someone did.

"Rider coming on a fine horse, some two furlongs off. There's an attendant. Looks like a knight!" David spoke in a voice barely audible to his companions.

"Right!" both of them replied. Will nocked his arrow and stood ready to loose the bolt if he had to. If it was an experienced knight, and if his companion was doughty, it could be very difficult for the three woodsmen to bring them to bay, unless they could surprise their quarry with bows drawn before those victims had a chance to arm themselves. David sat up on the branch of the tree and carefully brought his own bow to the ready, nocking his arrow on the string. Thorvald, unable to use a longbow effectively because of his height, drew out his short sword and prepared for a possible skirmish.

As quiet as death the three outlaws awaited their prey. He was certainly a knight. That much was evidenced by his great destrier or war horse—tall and muscular and chestnut brown. His white beard marked him as a man past middle age, but he sat erect in the saddle and wore a short arming sword in a scabbard hanging from his leather belt. That belt encircled a rich surcoat with his family crest embroidered on it—a red (or in heraldic terms *gules*) lion *couchant* (that is, supine with head raised) on a black or *sable* field. Over his surcoat was a fine woolen cloak and hood of black, and under it a rich blue linen tunic, green hosen and fine leather boots. He wore no armor but the gold chain around his neck tokened at least moderate wealth. Thorvald could make out no purse yet but was sure this fellow would be carrying an ample one. There was something familiar about that coat of arms, though, the dwarf was thinking.

His companion wore only a simple brown tunic with a green hood. He rode a grey palfrey and, as far as the outlaws could tell, was completely unarmed. Perhaps this wouldn't be so difficult after all, Thorvald thought. An old man with an unarmed servant—they could easily surprise the two long before the old fellow had a chance to draw his weapon.

So it was with some confidence that, after nodding quietly to his friends, Thorvald stepped quickly out into the road just as the two riders were coming into range, and held up his left hand, brandishing his sword in the other. "Your pardon, good sir," Thorvald shouted.

"But I 'ave the duty to inform you that at this very moment, two of my fellows are 'idden in these trees with arrows aimed directly at you. We are 'ere to enforce a toll that my master, the good Robin 'ood of Sherwood, 'as imposed on any as use this 'ere road through the forest. In return for which 'e invites you to a fine dinner of roasted venison, to be eaten with a very 'andsome an' merry band of foresters. What is your answer, m'lord? Will ya come quietly, or are you of a mind to make a fuss?"

To Thorvald's great surprise, the only answer he received from the old knight was a peal of laughter, at which Thorvald, abashed and waxing a bit angry, shielded his eyes and looked up into the knight's face, ready to change his courteous tone to a more menacing one. But then he too began to laugh.

"Why Thorvald, old sot, has it been so long that you don't recognize your old friend Sir Richard at the Lee, Lord of Verysdale? You don't seem to have changed much yourself. Have I aged so quickly?"

"No, no sir, not at all," Thorvald said through his own mirth. "I just saw a rich nobleman on a fine steed and stopped 'im, never looking into your face, my lord. Just thinkin' o' robbin' *what* you are, my lord, if ya follow me, and not payin' attention to 'oo ya were. But now as I think on it, I *knew* that crouching lion on yer surcoat was familiar!"

By now David had climbed down from his branch, and Scarlet had come out of the trees, and both drew around Sir Richard with cries of friendly welcome. It was only after a few moments of this that Will glanced over at Sir Richard's companion, who was sitting immobile as a stone, quietly taking in the welcoming scene. With a start, Will recognized the stony visage of Sir Richard's attendant.

"Why you're the fellow called Dap, Lord Randal's falconer," Will exclaimed. It had been only five days since the outlaws had shared a meal with him. "So have you changed masters so quickly, Dap, or did you find our cooking and company so pleasant that you took this opportunity to dine with us once more?"

Dap sat unmoved, and looked rather coldly at Will, but Sir Richard answered for him.

"These are things I must discuss with Robin, Will. I would prefer not to tell the story now only to repeat it again and again. Bring us, if you please, to Robin Hood, and you shall know all our business. It is a serious affair, I'm afraid, and could not wait."

"Right away, then!" Will announced, and had just taken Sir Richard's horse by the bridle to lead him, when David of Doncaster piped up.

"The hoods, Will. You know Robin's rule that nobody from outside come to the camp without being masked."

"Now, Davy, this 'ere's Richard at the Lee, ya daft ninny! 'E's a great friend o' Robin and Little John. We don't need no..."

"No, no, it's quite right," Sir Richard interceded. "Neither I nor my companion should see the way to your campsite. Only then can we honestly tell the Sheriff or any other authorities that we do not know where your camp *is*. It's all right."

And so it was that the three outlaws walked into Robin's camp an hour later with two friendly blindfolded prisoners.

* * *

Robin had been overjoyed to see his good friend Sir Richard again, and Little John pounded the old fellow's back so boisterously that he was nearly knocked off his feet. But on learning that the knight had come deliberately to see him about some urgent business, indeed had taken the Great North Road knowing that Robin's men would waylay him there, the outlaws led Sir Richard and the attending Dap over to the Great Oak. Here they seated them on the soft moss, and gathered close about them to hear the news. Robin, John, Thorvald, the Wills Stutely and Scarlet, Alan a Dale, and Friar Tuck all leaned in, forming a ring around their guests, while David of Doncaster and Much the miller's son joined Ellen in making up trenchers of venison to entertain the guests.

"So what's this story so extraordinary you must needs relate it only to our Robin's ears?" Scarlet began.

"What I hear must be open to my men as well," Robin declared. "Whatever it is, if it concerns me it must also concern them."

"It concerns you chiefly, Robin," Sir Richard affirmed, "but the others by association. If you insist on all hearing the news at once, then let me begin by telling you that the Sheriff of Nottingham has issued a warrant for your arrest…"

Robin laughed. "He issues a new warrant for us every week. Thieves we are and poachers, and disturbers of the king's peace. There's nothing new in this and nobody's caught us and dragged us into his jail yet."

As most of Robin's men laughed with him, Will Stutely pursed his lips. He, of course, *had* been dragged to jail, and narrowly escaped with his life, so he took the possibility much more seriously now. Sir Richard looked down and shook his head, and Dap's stony expression showed no sign of change. "No, no, Robin, you misunderstand," the old knight said. "It's none of those usual crimes this time. The Sheriff now wants you on a charge of murder."

A hush fell upon the gathered outlaws, as they all looked at each other with shock and dismay, just as Much ran up with two trenchers ready to serve the guests. He glanced around the circle and gingerly handed the guests their dinner, then asked cautiously, "Did I miss something?"

Finally Friar Tuck broke the silence. "Now Richard, you know, we all of us know, that Robin is dead opposed to the taking of a life, due to his special devotion to the Blessed Virgin. And none in his band is ever to kill another person except in self-defense— no, not even the Sheriff's deputy or Sir Guy of Gisbourne's guards, though they have no such direction regarding ourselves. So you know as well as we do how absurd this charge is. As the scripture says, 'the voice of thy brother's blood crieth unto me from the ground.' We have no such blood on our hands. What's the source of this absurd charge?"

Sir Richard glanced to his right where Dap sat immobile and quiet. "My companion can tell you more about it than I can. But as you have observed, Dap here visited you five days ago with my neighbor and friend, Lord William Randal."

Sir Richard paused a moment while Robin and his men nodded and after a moment Thorvald urged him on. "I may be old as Cain 'imself, as the friar hints, but my memory ain't yet *that* short. But go on, tell us what's this got ta do with Lord Randal an' 'is falconer?"

"It has everything to do with it, Thorvald my friend," Sir Richard said, finally getting to the painful point he'd been dancing around. "It's Lord Randal's murder you're charged with."

After a collective gasp from the listeners, Alan a Dale took up the questioning. "Lord Randal? But he was young and strong. And he was rich and powerful. And he was about to get married! How… how could this have happened?"

Sir Richard nodded in agreement with Alan's objections, then answered, "I assure you, it is true. Here's the man that can tell you more." And he nodded in the direction of Dap, who, on cue, broke his silence and began a narration of events in his flat, unemotional voice.

"When my master and we two servants were directed from

here back to the clearing where we'd been hawking last Friday," he began, "Lord Randal was morose. You would know more about his mood than I," Dap said, nodding his head toward Alan a Dale, who lowered his eyes and tried to remember the conversation. Dap continued, "He decided that he must visit his beloved, the lady Eleanor. He did not reveal his plans to me or his reasons for that visit. She lives in a small manor house on a plot of land adjoining my master's own holdings. When we stopped there, Lady Eleanor seemed very pleased to see him. She insisted that he stay a while and said that he must dine with her. He objected that he had already eaten quite well—in fact, he was referring to his meal here in the greenwood."

"Yes," Little John prompted. "I think we all realized that."

Dap went on undeterred. "But the lady Eleanor would have her way. She insisted that Lord Randal sit down and eat the dinner she was cooking, a dinner of fried eels. It was Friday, she insisted, so the meal must be fish."

"Indeed," Friar Tuck agreed, though he and the Sherwood outlaws seldom kept that fast. "Fried, you say?"

"Yes, she'd cut them into small pieces and coated them with flour, and set them to fry in a standing pan over her kitchen fire. Her household servants were involved in other duties about the manor, so my companion Wulf and I were pressed into service for the meal. We set it before Lord Randal, and he did eat, though not so hungrily as Lady Eleanor would have liked."

"I daresay not," Alan a Dale ventured. "He did eat quite hungrily when he was here. But did you hear what it was they talked about? Why was Lord Randal so intent on seeing her that day? What did he ask her?"

Dap gave a short sigh, which seemed to be his way of expressing exasperation. "I was in and out of the kitchen and am not given to eavesdropping. I will say, though, that the subject of marriage was being discussed. Lord Randal seemed in favor of marrying in secret, if at all. Lady Eleanor seemed reluctant. And I know that there were raised voices and some kind of argument while we were plating the food in the kitchen. They were both sullen and silent when we brought the meal in to them. That is all I can say."

"That says a great deal," Robin remarked thoughtfully. "But I'm at a loss at to what all this has to do with our—that is, *my*—being wanted for murder."

"Patience, lad," the old knight told him. "Let Dap get on with the story and it will be clear to you soon enough."

Robin made a gesture of capitulation and the falconer went on. "Lord Randal was unable to finish the meal, though he tried gallantly to do so. And I myself was still quite full from our lunch here, so I declined when he offered me his leavings. Wulf would have nothing to do with it, but did feed a few pieces of eel to Lord Randal's greyhounds, Troilus and Cresseid, waiting outside. That gave me the idea to feed the remaining scraps to the two hawks I carried in the cadge. When that was done, Wulf and I waited outside while Lord Randal made his farewells to the lady Eleanor. I don't know whether they had come to any final agreement about an elopement. I'm sure Lord Randal never shared that information with me, and when he emerged his face was unreadable. But we left Lady Eleanor's and started home to the lord's own manor house."

"I still don't see..." Robin began, but Dap raised his voice and talked over the interruption.

"It's an hour's ride through the forest from Lady Eleanor's manor house to Lord Randal's. But we'd barely ridden a furlong way or two when the two greyhounds began to act strangely."

"Strangely how?" Friar Tuck, less anxious and more coaxing than Robin, took over the questioning.

"They seemed confused at first. Sitting down on the path. Unsure where they should be going. Wulf got them up and moving forward, but it was as if they were dizzy or perhaps giddy. But before long they began vomiting. First one, then the other, then the first one again. They were weak and could barely walk. We urged them on, but they had become too weak to stand. They lay down and shivered, and Lord Randal was beside himself, exhorting Wulf to do something, anything, to save his hounds. But the boy was as much at a loss as he and I were, and the dogs died within the hour."

"Poison then?" Alan a Dale ventured. The others looked at him with some irony, as if congratulating him on his distinct grasp of the obvious.

"My master was grieved at the loss of his hounds, who were as dear to him as if they'd been his own children. He made us take the time to build a simple litter to lay the dogs on, and tied it behind his horse, so to bring Troilus and Cresseid home to be buried in his own chapel yard. But no sooner had we started off again towards his home than he stopped again and in a kind of panic had me look into the cadge to see how his hawks were faring."

"And?" Friar Tuck prompted him.

Dap looked down and pursed his lips. "Dead. Both of them. Lord Randal flew into a wild frenzy of rage and grief. He cursed God and Nature and all the pagan gods of the forest. I looked at Wulf and he at me, and he seemed to be thinking just what I was—Randal was cursing everyone but the one person he ought to curse: Lady Eleanor. Where else could those animals have been poisoned but Eleanor's dinner? And if it was the fried eels that had poisoned them, then what was going to happen to our master? So far he was showing no symptoms, but I knew we had better get him home quickly. He was larger in bulk than his beasts, and so the poison may take longer to work on him, and perhaps a leech could be called for at his manor house who might save him from the same fate. And so I urged him to ride on."

"I take it your efforts were unsuccessful," Friar Tuck murmured.

"There was no saving him. We reached his manor house, and his mother took him in, seeing how pale and bilious he had grown, and made haste to get him to bed. But he died before ever a leech could be found."

"But I still don't see," Robin burst in, unable to restrain himself any longer, "what this has to do with me? With us? Seems to me pretty evident that this Lady Eleanor poisoned him. Who knows why? Lover's quarrel of some sort I suppose. Why come after the men of the greenwood?"

"This is the part concerns you now," Sir Richard assured him. "Go ahead Dap—tell him what happened next day."

Dap breathed a heavy sigh and continued his narrative. "Next morning Lady Randal, the lord's mother, determined to ride into Nottingham town to see the Sheriff and report the murder of her son. She took young Wulf with her as a witness to all that had occurred leading up to the murder. I had other things to do at the manor house—I set two of Lady Randal's maids to prepare the lord's body for burial. And I paid a visit to the parish church in Halloughton and brought back Father Timothy, the rector there. It was far too late to administer last rites, Father Timothy told me, since these must include confession and communion. But he came to the house and he prayed with me for Lord Randal's soul, and assured me that Lord Randal would be safe from the fires of Hell, assuming he died in a state of grace. I thought on how he had cursed God and all that was holy when his dogs died, and bit my lips. Perhaps Randal's last words had been more to the point. At least I hoped so.

"Meanwhile, in Nottingham Lady Randal had met with the Sheriff, and Wulf had given him a thorough report on how we had spent that previous day, and when he heard that we had dined in the forest with you before visiting Lady Eleanor, he snatched at that point before any other. Clearly, he concluded, Lord Randal was poisoned in the greenwood by Robin Hood and his men, who bore an unregenerate hatred for all the gentry in the land. Lady Randal was more of a mind to blame Lady Eleanor—apparently before he died her son had suspected he was poisoned at her house—but Wulf apparently was convinced by the Sheriff's certainty, and Lady Randal eventually agreed that it was perhaps the likelier explanation. Why, after all, would Lady Eleanor suddenly take a notion to destroy her lover? And so word went forth from Nottingham that Robin Hood was to be arrested for murder."

Friar Tuck shook his head in disbelief. "But how could they explain away the fact that the dogs and the hawks were killed by the same poison, and they had eaten nothing during your dinner here? And how explain the fact that neither you nor this Wulf suffered any effects of poison when you ate the same things as your master when you dined here? How can any judge condemn Robin on such flimsy evidence?"

"It's nothing to do with truth or with evidence," Little John remarked, putting into words what everyone was thinking. "The Sheriff is not interested in finding the murderer of Lord Randal. He just wants an excuse to hang Robin. As for a judge, look no further than Sir Guy of Gisbourne. He is officially the king's representative in Nottingham. In the absence of any other magistrate, Gisbourne could easily be drafted as presiding judge in this case. He's not even likely to try to give the appearance of impartiality. The case will be over before it begins."

"Right," Robin said thoughtfully. "Seems to me there's only

one thing to do: find the true killer and expose him—or her—so that it's obvious the blame can't be laid at my door."

"Yes, well, you might have noticed that you don't actually *have* a door, my captain," said Friar Tuck, gazing around at their forest home. "But I agree with you in sentiment. Of course, from what Dap here has told us, it seems pretty clear that it's at this Lady Elanor's door we should start. It's her dinner of eels that most certainly destroyed the hounds and the hawks, and so must have poisoned Lord Randal as well. And it seems that Lady Randal for one also believed in Eleanor's guilt."

"Unless somebody else tampered with the meal in Eleanor's kitchen," Will Stutely speculated. "I mean, we really need to be absolutely certain of our proof."

Dap bristled at that, though his expression did not alter. "No one else was about while we were there. It was only Eleanor, Randal, Wulf and me. And if Lord Randal were here, he would swear to my own fidelity."

Will held up a hand. "I have no doubt of your honesty, fellow. You would hardly have come to warn us of this false charge if you were guilty of it yourself. But I don't think we can simply assume the guilt of the woman."

"Indeed not," Friar Tuck agreed. "We would need to uncover a sufficient motive first, I believe. If we can find that, then the more circumstantial evidence of Randal's dying after eating her food will be enough to hang her, and to set Robin free."

"If I may," Alan a Dale cut in at this point. "I want to say one thing. This Lord Randal spoke me fair when he was our guest. He praised my music and he offered to take me on as his household jongleur." There were gasps and raised eyebrows all around the circle. "It was a high honor to be paid, and though yes, I declined it—I can never leave the greenwood," and with that he gave Robin a slight bow, which the outlaw chief acknowledged and returned, "I feel I owe Lord Randal…something, in gratitude for his friendship and good will. I would feel something of a scoundrel if I didn't put everything I have into finding out his killer, as if I really had been in his service. I swear here and now before you all as witnesses, that I will not rest until I've caught the killer and exposed him."

"Good," Robin agreed. "Let's start right now. When did you say Lord Randal's funeral will take place?"

"It's to be held tomorrow," Sir Richard said. "At the parish church in Halloughton, with this same Father Timothy officiating. Why do you want to know?"

"Seems to me," Robin said, scratching his right ear thoughtfully, "that most of the people we might want to talk to ought to be there: Lord Randal's mother and his sweetheart too, and who else in the family?"

"He had a brother, Geoffrey Randal—he that's now Lord Randal, as it happens, on his brother's death," Dap informed him. "And a sister, Lady Anne Randal."

"Unmarried?" Robin asked.

"A maiden living at home, some sixteen years old," Dap said.

"Marriageable age," Sir Richard added. "In fact, being our neighbor, there had been occasional speculation that my son, Sir Peter, might be a good match for her. But the family was never forthcoming about a dowry for the girl."

"Then we must be at this funeral, and we must take the chance to talk with all four of those mourners," Robin declared.

"It must be done tactfully," Friar Tuck cautioned. "You don't just walk up to people at a funeral and start badgering them. These things must be done delicately."

"I can be delicate," Robin insisted. "When have I not been delicate?"

Little John cleared his throat and, rather than answer that

question, posed another. "Is it wise to show yourself at that funeral, when you're already charged with the murder of the corpse? It seems clear that someone other than you ought to be there to do the questioning."

"I want to be there," Alan a Dale insisted. "I insist on going. I can talk tactfully to those people."

Sir Richard shook his head. "But you are, pardon me, a jongleur and a yeoman. These are four nobles burying their noble son and paramour. They will be affronted if you begin questioning them, however tactfully, and will think you are forgetting your place. Let me make this suggestion: I shall certainly be attending the funeral—I'll be expected to as Lord Randal's friend and neighbor. My son will most likely accompany me. Alan, you shall come with us and I will introduce you as a member of my household—my household minstrel as Lord Randal wanted you to be his. It should be easy enough to converse with the Randals if we do so together."

Alan bowed in deference to Sir Richard's wisdom. "Very sensible," he said.

"And I think that, as a religious, it may not be amiss for me to attend the rites as well," Friar Tuck added. "There are four people to interview there, which could be a large number for just the three of you as a team to approach. No one will be wondering why I am there, and if I can give comfort I will. And if I can get some information out of these people while I'm giving comfort, I will do that as well."

"And if I may add one more thing," Sir Richard said, "Dap here is, I am sure, planning on attending the service as well. He will be expected to be there. As a servant, he can go almost anywhere unobtrusively. If he is willing, I suggest that he watch and listen, and report to us anything that might seem remarkable or out of place. Are you willing to do that, Dap?"

Dap, man of few words, merely nodded without changing expression.

"Then that's settled," Sir Richard said. "Now listen: The funeral is scheduled for sext tomorrow, and it's a long morning's ride from here. So Alan, Tuck, and you too Dap, why don't you all return with me to my castle at Lee, and we'll only have a short five-mile trek in the morning to get to Halloughton for the service."

The others all nodded, but Robin stood with his arms folded, his face twisted in disapproval. He could see the wisdom in this approach, but felt restless and impotent being left out of the first efforts to exonerate his own alleged guilt. Then he had an idea, and smiled. "It's the perfect plan," he said. "but it occurs to me that we ought to be looking elsewhere as well: This whole thing is the Sheriff of Nottingham's trumped up case. We ought to try to find out just how he's planning to proceed."

"That would mean going undercover to Nottingham itself," Little John said. "And who's crazy enough for that assignment?" Robin grinned suggestively. "Oh, of course," the big man finished. "Silly question."

"Besides, I've got a reliable connection in the Sheriff's own house," Robin continued.

"His wife?" Little John asked.

"Got it in one," Robin replied, smiling. Looking around, he noticed that his guests had not touched their dinner, and he clapped his hands and said, "So it's begun! Some will be off to Halloughton, some for Nottingham. But before you go, my friends, please eat your venison, so the poor hart may not have died in vain. Eat up! I assure you it isn't poisoned!"

And so, with a bit of uncomfortable laughter, the colloquium ended.

CHAPTER THREE

The church of Saint James in Halloughton was a small stone parish church without a bell tower or other elaborate external features. It would have been difficult for a stranger even to recognize it as a church if it weren't for the arched entryway on the south side. The interior was quite modest as well. There were windows, but not many. The two tall lancet windows on the east wall were the chief source of light in the morning, and at the hour of sext the sun was high enough so as not to blind parishioners looking toward the chancel at that end of the building, where stood an altar with a hanging crucifix above. A simple pine coffin lay closed before the altar.

Father Timothy had prepared for the service by having a dozen or so wooden stools placed in the nave three at a time, with a wide aisle between. When Alan and Sir Richard walked in, trailed by Richard's son Sir Peter, the front chairs on the north side were filled by a mature woman, a weeping maid of sixteen or so, and a tall grim looking young man, all garbed in rich mourning weeds. Alone on the south side of the aisle was a young woman of petite proportions whose face was veiled. Alan assumed that these were the surviving Randal family—mother, daughter, and son—and the Lady Eleanor, sitting alone. There were no other visitors sitting, but several servants stood in the rear of the small nave, and with them one hooded friar in the black habit of a Dominican, whose face was shadowed by his hood so that Alan could make out only a pair of very dark, very bushy eyebrows. Among these servants Dap took his place and stood impassively, his arms folded across his chest. Alan did not see Wulf anywhere among the group. He and Sir Richard, having decided to disturb no one before the service, took seats in the second row behind the family. Friar Tuck came in minutes later, and seated himself behind Lady Eleanor. Sir Peter joined him there.

On the south wall of the sanctuary, four memorial tablets were embedded in the stone wall. Alan wondered whether Lady Randal was planning to mount another for her son. Lord William's final resting place, in any case, was not to be in some vault beneath the church floor, but in the small churchyard, where his body would be interred following the service.

Father Timothy was a small, fidgety priest, with a black robe that had seen better days. Halloughton was a small country parish and not a profitable one, Alan concluded, and Father Timothy, a young priest of not more than twenty-five, was probably hoping for some more lucrative appointment from the bishop if he served this parish well for a few years. With that end in view, a supportive comment in the bishop's ear from Lady Randal or the newly titled Lord Geoffrey Randal would go far in smoothing Father Timothy's way, and so he was particularly concerned that everything go as desired on this mournful but most important occasion for the family. He had hoped, he told Friar Tuck later, to have performed a different ceremony for Lord William: apparently Lady Eleanor had already talked to him about wedding her lover in secret, and he had agreed to perform the service if they were agreed upon it. But that was not to be now.

And so Father Timothy began, in as sonorous a voice as his

diminutive frame could produce, to recite the introit to the requiem mass.

"*Requiem aeternam dona eis Domine, et lux perpetua luceat eis,*" he began. Eternal rest give to them, Oh Lord, and let perpetual light shine upon them. Alan did not understand the Latin, but knew in general the intent of the words. When he'd attended funeral masses before, there were always a bevy of lesser clergy to support the presiding priest in performing the long ritual. In particular there was generally a choir to chant some of the passages. In this small corner of Christendom, only Father Timothy stood between the departed and the road to hell.

But why Father Timothy? Surely as the Lord of Halloughton and a respected member of the aristocracy of Nottinghamshire, Lord Randal might have been expected to receive his funereal rites in one of the great churches in the county. Why was this mass not being performed at the Church of Saint Mary the Virgin in Nottingham city? The monks of Lenton Priory, which owned the church, would have had a complete choir out to sing Lord Randal's mass. In fact, William's father, Lord Stephen, was interred there. Whose idea had it been to give William Randal so little ceremony at his sendoff?

"*Kyrie, eleison,*" Father Timothy intoned. "*Christie, eleison! Kyrie eleison!*" Lord have mercy on us. Christ have mercy on us. Lord have mercy on us. The thinness of Father Timothy's voice had begun to annoy Alan. He had his small gittern shoved into the sack he had flung across his back, and toyed with the idea of producing it to accompany the priest in his chanting. But he thought better of it, guessing that the family might see such an impulse as lacking the proper dignity for the proceedings.

By now Father Timothy had reached the *Dies irae*, the most somber moment of the service, and Alan's head jerked up as he heard a second rich tenor voice take up the chant and sing along with Father Timothy. Timothy himself started for a moment at what seemed an intrusion, but then gently settled in with the duet with Friar Tuck, who had noted a slight tremor in Father Timothy's voice as he reached this point and had given his voice to bolster the priest.

"*Dies irae, dies illa*," sang the two of them together. "*Solvet saeclum in favilla, teste David cum Sybilla.*" Day of wrath, day that will dissolve the world into burning coals, as David bore witness with the Sibyl. Alan had a vague notion of what these words were about, and was personally glad that no one other than Friar Tuck and Father Timothy himself knew the precise import of those fiery words. He glanced over to where Lady Eleanor sat, her head bent and shoulders heaving with sobs as the ceremony drew toward its conclusion. While he had been virtually certain upon entering the church that the only obvious suspect in Lord Randal's murder was his own dear lady, seeing her like this at her lover's funeral made him a good deal less certain. Was there another possibility after all? Other than, of course, Robin Hood himself?

Timothy and Tuck chanted the conclusion of the mass, as six of the servants who had been standing in the back, including Dap, came forward and lifted the coffin from where it rested before the altar. "May the angels lead thee into paradise: may the martyrs receive thee at thy coming and lead thee into the holy city of Jerusalem." Alan recognized the allusion to the Heavenly Jerusalem, and imagined the grave into which Lord Randal's body was to be laid as the vehicle by which his short-lived friend would be carried into that glorious city. Or at least into Purgatory, from where, eventually, he might work his way in.

"*Chorus Angelorum te suscipiat, et cum Lazaro quondam paupere æternam habeas requiem,*" the priest and friar concluded the mass as the coffin reached the open grave in the small churchyard. May the choir of Angels receive thee, and with <u>Lazarus</u>, who once was poor, mayest thou have eternal rest. At the graveside, the six pallbearers stood, prepared to lower the heavy casket into the earth, while the church's sextant, a spade in his hand, waited to fill in the hole with the pile of newly dug earth at the side of the grave. On the narrow end of the grave at the coffin's head Father Timothy stood, with Friar Tuck on the opposite side at the feet. On the long side of the grave opposite the pile of earth stood Lady Randal with her daughter and Lord Geoffrey. After some space but still uncomfortably close, Lady Eleanor stood directly beside the priest. Sir Richard, Peter, and Alan stood behind that initial group and, again, several servants stood behind them.

The service at the graveside was quite brief compared with the full funeral mass. Father Timothy began by chanting the antiphon "I am the Resurrection and the Life," and when he'd finished, the coffin was lowered into the grave, while Friar Tuck joined Father Timothy in chanting the Canticle Benedictus, the Song of Zechariah: At this point, one of the servants, paired with the hooded Dominican, came forward with the bodies of the greyhounds, Troilus and Creseid, wrapped in burial shrouds, and placed them in the grave atop the coffin. They were followed immediately by Dap, carrying the cadge in which lay the poisoned falcons, Xenobia and Mercury. That was the point at which Alan was overcome. Head bent, he left the graveside and wandered away, tears welling in his eyes. If there was hunting or hawking in heaven, he mused, Lord Randal would be well prepared.

Father Timothy repeated the antiphon again, and then, as he sprinkled the coffin and shrouded animals with holy water, the assembled congregation repeated the Lord's Prayer. Timothy recited one final ancient prayer, then closed the service with the petition, "May his soul and the souls of all the faithful departed through the mercy of God rest in peace. Amen." And that "Amen" was the signal that the service had concluded.

As the assembled folk began to turn slowly away from the grave, each now turning his or her thoughts homeward, they were startled by a loud introductory chord being struck upon a gittern, and a strong pleasing tenor voice rising above them in the air from where Alan a Dale had set himself up on a slight rise some twenty yards from the grave site.

> *Lully, lullay, lully, lullay,*
> *The falcon has borne my mate away.*
>
> *He bore him up, he bore him down,*
> *He bore him into an orchard brown.*
>
> *In that orchard there was a hall*
> *That was hanged with purple and with pall.*
>
> *And in that hall there was a bed.*
> *It was hanged about with gold so red.*
>
> *And in that bed there lay a knight,*
> *His wounds a-bleeding day and night.*
>
> *By that bed's side there knelt a maid,*
> *And sore she wept both night and day.*
>
> *And by that bed's side there stood a stone—*
> *With "Corpus Christi" writ thereon.*

When the chords of Alan's song ceased, a stillness fell upon the churchyard, and all those within the sound of his voice stood motionless in a stunned silence as the words and melody of his song washed over them. Then, shaking off the spell, they continued their departure from the yard.

Alan knew, of course, that the song was a crucifixion lyric, the last line identifying the bleeding corpse as *Corpus Christi*, the body of Christ. But he figured that was what made it appropriate for a church service. But the falcon carrying the body away and the identification of the body as a slain knight, as well as the weeping beloved kneeling by the bier, all brought Lord Randal into Alan's mind. And he had finally felt that Lord Randal deserved some true music in his ceremony, beyond the priest's thin chanting. His own performance was, he thought, the next best thing to a full choir. And by the looks on their faces, he felt that the congregation at the service agreed and felt satisfaction with his tribute. He had never actually had the chance to become Lord Randal's resident minstrel, Alan thought, but at least he had been able to perform this small last service.

Returning his giterne gingerly to its sack, Alan made his way toward the departing guests. He noticed that Friar Tuck had been immediately approached by Father Timothy, who had a hand on the shoulder of the friar's gray robe and was clearly thanking him for his contribution for the day's service. Alan let them be, assuming they'd be discussing the finer points of the funeral mass, perhaps even in Latin. The young Lady Anne, wiping away tears, was being consoled by her neighbor Sir Peter of Verysdale. He was a handsome young man whom Alan knew a little from an earlier adventure, and had once been romantically linked with Countess Lydia Peveril, but that had never blossomed. And as Sir Richard had hinted, there had more recently been some thought of a connection between him and this Lady Anne. That too had apparently fizzled, but at least he was available now to speak to her courteously and with some sympathy.

On the other side of the churchyard, Sir Richard was conversing with Lady Randal, and was surreptitiously beckoning to Alan to come join them. As Alan approached, he heard Sir Richard telling the lady how very sorry he was for her loss. "And to lose him so suddenly, and in such a dreadful manner, why, it's a wonder you can still function."

"Sir Richard, you are the only one of our neighbors that has made the effort to come to this, admittedly, out-of-the-way place to attend this funeral, and so have shown yourself to be our true friend. But to answer your concern—I've lost children before," the matron confided, her jaw protruding determinedly. "Two of my daughters died before reaching the age of reason, their seventh birthday. But William was my eldest, and I'd had him with me many a year. I'll miss him more than the others, and that's the truth."

"Lady Joan Randal," Richard said, reaching out to place a hand on Alan's shoulder and turn him toward the matron. "Permit me to present Alan a Dale, resident minstrel of my household at Lee. He had met and admired your son, and would not be left behind when he learned I was coming here today for Lord William's funeral mass."

"And was it not a godsend that he came?" the lady gushed. She looked at Alan with gratitude in her hazel eyes, and he could see that the careworn face had once been quite beautiful, and would be so still if it could be drained of its sorrow. The streaks of gray in her auburn hair and the crows' feet in the corners of her eyes did nothing to lessen the effect of her large eyes, high cheekbones and strong chin. "Sirrah," she addressed Alan, "your beautiful voice and that moving song made this day more precious to me than it could have possibly been otherwise. I must thank you for it."

Alan hadn't considered it, but it seemed his spontaneous tribute to the lord he hardly knew had made his presence welcome and had given him an entry into conversation with the lord's noble family. "My Lady," he began, with as much courtesy as he could muster, "I barely knew your son, but he did treat me with such kindly deference that last time we met" (Alan thought this phrasing was more likely to win over the lady than the more accurate "the only time we met"), "that I was moved to sing that dirge for him. He did tell me that he admired my singing. But my Lady, if I may be so bold as to ask, is it known who is responsible for your son's so untimely demise?"

Lady Randal's hazel eyes flashed fire at the question, but it was not for anger at the questioner, lowly commoner though he was. Her ire had much higher targets. "That bumbling nincompoop John of Oxenford, who styles himself Sheriff of Nottingham, would pay no attention to my pleading. He determined, on the very mention of his name, to lay this crime at the door of that Sherwood bandit Robin Hood. Why the whole thing is absurd when you follow the evidence." There was that imaginary door in the forest again, Alan couldn't help thinking. "Yes, my son had an early dinner with the outlaws, as his servants told me, but it was only after he'd eaten with that hussy 'Lady' Eleanor—and I say 'Lady' advisedly—that his animals died and, soon after, he himself. When he was dying at home, *he* even suggested that his lady love may have poisoned him. This all would have been clear to that pitiful excuse for a Sheriff if he'd only listened carefully and not jumped to conclusions at the very mention of the outlaw's name. And then the wretched girl has the effrontery—indeed the *brazenness!*—to *show her face here at his funeral, when everyone knows she fed him his death...*" (these last phrases the lady virtually screeched, so that no one in the churchyard, no one within the sound of her voice, could have failed to hear her). "Why," Lady Randal concluded, "it's unconscionable, that's what it is. There's no other word for it.

"But I'm afraid I am being discourteous, Sir Richard," the lady continued.

"Not at all, not at all," the old knight demurred. "Your emotions do you credit. You want to find the true murderer of your son, and to bring him to justice."

"Bring *her* to justice," the lady corrected.

"Yes, yes, well, to punish the true killer, in any case," Sir Richard agreed. "But tell me, my friend, why do you balk at giving the lady Eleanor that title of 'lady'?"

"Hmmph," Lady Joan scoffed. "I said I use the term advisedly. I know of no ceremony in which her father, or any of his forebears, was ever knighted. They were simply freedmen who had a piece of land that they were able to turn into a bigger piece of land by their hoarding and saving, and ultimately gave themselves the appellations 'Lord' and 'Lady' solely on the basis of their having a bit of land to call their own. But he's still only plain Edward Franklin to my mind. And I know of late that their stores have been less full than formerly due to poorer crops the past few years. And yet she used her feminine wiles on my poor unsuspecting son and entangled him in her web, seeking to get him to marry her. Over my dead body, I told him."

"Rather over his," Alan muttered under his breath. But the lady continued, unhearing.

"I told William that she was not of his class and that he was not to consider her of marriageable quality. Now I don't know exactly what he went to see her about that last day—his servants were not in the room with them and did not hear what he had to say to her. But it's my belief that he went there to break off his relationship with her, and that when he did so, she poisoned his dinner to spite him."

From what Lord Randal had confided to Alan that morning in the forest, he was sure the lord's meeting with Eleanor bore no resemblance to the one Lady Randal was imagining. But what did happen in that dining room, he wondered, that could possibly have given Lady Eleanor motive to murder her lover, as she almost certainly had?

"So many eligible young women of good families in the area," Lady Randal was now sighing over imagined and lost opportunities. "Why, I understand that the Countess of Chesterfield, the enormously wealthy heiress, remains husbandless, and is forced to govern her lands alone, without the strong right arm of any male consort. The idea is absurd! What a brilliant match that would have been for my son. Well..." and now she looked thoughtful. "Geoffrey is still unmarried. Perhaps we can arrange a match with her for *him*."

Alan's head was spinning at the quick changes in the direction of Lady Randal's thoughts. And her turning to the topic of the Sherwood outlaws' most ardent defender among the nobility, the woman who was, at least formally, Robin Hood's own liege, made Alan quite nervous. But Sir Richard answered her with a polite check to her ambitions. "As you may have heard," he began, "my own son, Sir Peter, was a suitor for the Countess's hand—as in fact was his old foster brother, Sir Walter of Horsley. The Countess Lydia rejected them both, and soundly, declaring her intent to rule in her own right. She has no intention of changing her resolve."

Lady Joan shrugged. "Well," she said, "that's what she says now. Let her see how truly difficult it is for a woman to be her own man," and with that she smiled at her own cleverness, "and she will sing a different tune. I still think my Geoffrey may stand a chance down the line. But now, Sir Richard, will you join the family for a mild repast in the narthex of the church? We knew it would make little sense to make attendees at the funeral travel all the way back to our manor to partake of the funeral meats, but could not let lord William go without some such show of respect. Come join us in the church for some refreshment before you leave this place, won't you? And bring your servant with you."

With that the lady turned and began to stride toward the church door, and Sir Richard, not willing to lose his access to her, quickly moved ahead to catch her up. But Alan had noticed the quiet, unobtrusive form of Lady Eleanor moving furtively around the edge of the churchyard, apparently not willing to leave the grave site and equally unwilling to join the other mourners for the funeral meats. Alan could not imagine a better time to speak with the bereaved lover alone, and so made his excuse to Sir Richard. "I'll meet you inside in a quarter of an hour or so," he told the knight, motioning with his eyes toward the solitary Eleanor.

Sir Richard and Lady Randal made their way, now arm in arm, toward the church door, where Alan could see the others disappearing, including Friar Tuck and Father Timothy, still in close conversation. Alan took the opportunity to approach the fragile-seeming form of Lady Eleanor, distracted and weeping softly as she made her hesitant way, head down, along the edge of the forest that bordered the churchyard. After Lady Randal's description of the young woman, Alan thought it worth taking the chance that she would not spurn his questions as coming from a lowly peasant. She, it seemed, was closer to his own state than she had really been to Lord Randal's.

That she had heard nothing of his approach was apparent in the way she jumped when Alan finally addressed her. "Please excuse my rudeness in interrupting your reverie, my Lady," Alan began. "But I was wondering if you were planning to come in for the funeral banquet, or whether you intend to stay out here in the churchyard while the others feast?"

To his surprise Eleanor gave a grim laugh in response. "Banquet? Funeral feast? You're dressing a pig in a bridal gown when you say such things. This funeral is a travesty. I call it an insult to the memory of my dear William," and with that her voice cracked and she sobbed again. With frustrated ire she yanked the wimple and veil from her face, and Alan now saw the tears still standing in her deep brown eyes. Her matching russet hair cascaded around her shoulders, and Alan could see that there was a feisty pertness in her small features, puckered as they were in her sorrow and resentment. "These Randals are rich as Croesus, you know. Heirs to a secret fortune William's father brought home from the crusade."

"You're...certain of that?" Alan wondered, taken slightly aback.

"Of course," the lady answered. "And yet instead of burying their lord in some great basilica, with a choir and a bishop to preside, they choose this out of the way parish on their lands—and instead of a fine banquet for the many guests who'd have come to see my poor boy off to his heavenly reward in a cathedral, they put out a few cold slices of mutton and some fruit and nuts, with one small cask of wine, to feed the handful of mourners willing to come to this obscure corner of Nottinghamshire. Why is this? Are they simply not willing to spend the fortune he left them? Or are they trying to sweep his murder under the rug, so people won't be talking about his death, or how he died? It's awfully fishy, if you ask me."

Alan, overwhelmed at first by the lady's vehement objections, had been wondering the same things himself. But he still wanted to talk to Lady Eleanor about her own connection to the murder, and thought he would bring up the fried eels while Eleanor seemed ready and willing to share just about anything. "Speaking of fishy," he began, "I understand you served…"

"So you can just go ahead and tell your masters…" Lady Eleanor continued, ignoring his stammering and finally taking a good look at Alan's face, at which she stopped short. "Oh!" she exclaimed. "I thought you were just another one of the Randals' servants. But you're not, are you? You're that minstrel who came here with Sir Richard at the Lee, the one who sang that haunting lyric at the end of the service. I want to thank you for that. Especially the verse about the maiden weeping at the bier of her fallen beloved. I mean, I *know* it's supposed to be the Blessed Virgin and all, but for the duration of that song I saw myself, and felt one with the maiden in the poem. You have a true gift, sirrah…what shall I call you? You have a name, I suppose."

Quite a change had come over the lady, and with that last comment she'd become almost sprightly. Alan was happy that conversing with him had taken her out of her own misery. But he still needed to broach the subject of her involvement in William's murder. He owed it to his true master, Robin Hood, and he owed it to Lord Randal himself. "Indeed, my Lady," he said, "my name is Alan a Dale, and I am pleased to have given you some small comfort in this time of tribulation for you. If you will forgive me, though, I think that most people here will interpret your not partaking of the funeral meats as an expression of your not being willing to face the family, because of your own involvement in Sir William's death scene. Indeed, some may go so far as to interpret it as a feeling of guilt and shame over your part in the murder." As a new cloud of anger descended on Lady Eleanor's brow, Alan made an attempt to deflect her anger from himself and to qualify his assertion.

"That, at least, is what some are saying, my Lady. For my own part, I am only too happy to hear what you have to say to exonerate yourself from these rash insinuations."

Now Lady Eleanor laughed again, not so grimly this time, at Alan's defensiveness. "The Sheriff is blaming the death on this Robin Hood, the bandit of the forest." At that the lady shrugged. "Who knows? He may be right. All I know is that that plate of eels I served him was…was nothing but eels. I set them to fry in the pan and they were never out of my sight until they were cooked and I called his own servants in to serve them to us. I had nothing to do with poisoning my beloved William. Why would I? We were going to be married."

"Truly?" Alan questioned. "I've heard it said that Lord Randal had come to your manor to break things off with you, and had done so just before he was served that meal. That would have been enough reason for you to think of murdering him—those people are saying. One of the servants even claimed to have heard the two of you quarrelling."

"I'm the only one alive who knows what was said in that room," Eleanor asserted. "Not Lady Randal, or Lady Anne, or bloody Lord Geoffrey." She scoffed. "They all hated me. Didn't want their precious lands and riches coming into my hands instead of their own when William married me rather than some rich tart of their own choosing. So they'll say anything about me. But I know what William said to me, and if this whole Robin Hood thing turns out to be a false lead, I'll still tell the truth before the Sheriff or anybody else who comes to my door. We were to be married. And I can prove it."

With that Lady Eleanor reached into her bosom and pulled out a ring, hanging from a thin leather string round her neck. She held the ring out for Alan to examine, and he saw a carved falcon on the ring's face, flanked by a W and an R. "The falcon is—was—his crest. The W and R stand for William Randal. This was his own signet ring. He gave it to me that day as a pledge of his undying love, after we had agreed to wed." Now she snatched the ring again and tucked it back where it had been lodged in her bosom. "If Dap or Wulf claims to have heard some kind of argument, it was about the ring. He insisted I take it, and I said I needed no proof of his love, especially one his mother or brother would accuse me of stealing or cajoling out of him by guile."

Alan, less convinced than ever of Eleanor's guilt, asked her one more thing: "So in your opinion, this Robin Hood fellow is the one who really killed Lord Randal? But why would he?"

"Why *wouldn't* he? If he'd robbed my poor boy, doing away with him would prevent him from reporting the outlaw's treachery to the authorities, wouldn't it? And he'd no doubt used some very slow acting poison, so that it would be harder to connect him with the crime, so that my own dinner of the eels, since it came closer before the death, seemed suspicious."

Turning it over in his mind, Alan had to admit that Lady Eleanor's explanation did make some sense, looking at things from a certain point of view. Of course, it still didn't explain the deaths of the hounds and the hawks by the same poison. Although Eleanor could as easily have claimed that the four animals must have been tossed scraps from the feast in the forest, and the poison had acted just as slowly on them. And so he decided to drop the questions for now.

"Well," Alan said lamely, "I'm very sorry for your loss. I met Lord William only once, but he was very kind to me and flattered me that he admired my singing and playing a great deal. That is why I was compelled to sing for him one last time at his graveside service."

Lady Eleanor smiled wanly. "He always did like music," she

said softly. Then she perked up, as if trying to adjust herself into a more courteous affect, she asked, "And what is your name sirrah? You never mentioned it."

Alan bowed politely, not bothering to point out he'd already told her once. She has a good deal else her mind he reasoned, and said, "I am called Alan a Dale, my Lady. I am at your service. You only need send for me if you are ever in need." This last was perhaps a bit too large of a gesture, but Alan was carried away by the moment. If this lady is guilty of killing her lover, Alan reasoned to himself, then I'm a hedge-born fopdoodle.

With a light laugh, Lady Eleanor brushed him off. "And how would your master Sir Richard like that?" she teased. Then, giving him no time to answer, she concluded their conversation. "Well, Alan a Dale, if I ever am in dire need of a song, I'll send for you. In the meantime, I need to be alone right now. Return to your master, and leave me to my own thoughts and tears, I bid you. Adieu, courteous minstrel." And with that she wandered off, Alan following in her wake, before he turned and made his way toward the church door, where the rest of the mourners had disappeared.

* * *

Lady Eleanor had not misspoken about the funeral meats laid out in the church. There were truly only a few choices available: a plate of cheese, a bowl of fruit—just a few apples and pears and two plums that looked like they'd seen better days, another bowl with a small assortment of hazelnuts, chestnuts and walnuts, and what passed as a "main course"—a few thin slices of roasted chicken and, ironically, some filets of fried eel.

There were no bread trenchers to hold the food, so that guests were forced to simply move back to the long table on which the items were spread and to eat while standing there. There had been little thought and less expense given to the board, and certainly it had not been prepared by any cook worth the name. The cooks of Lord William's own estate had apparently not been troubled to prepare anything remotely appropriate for the feast and, as Alan learned later from Friar Tuck, who had it from Father Timothy himself, the onus of putting something together for the funeral feast had fallen on a few of the parish women whose task it was to keep the church building in order. The Randal family, it appeared, had not even paid for the dismal fare there was.

Alan, picking up an apple and moving on, began to polish it on his tunic sleeve as he drew close to Sir Richard who was now deep in conversation with the sister, Lady Anne, and the new Lord Randal, the brother Geoffrey. Sir Peter had clearly excused himself from his conversation with Anne and was walking by himself in the churchyard, and the teenaged girl was chatting away as Alan drew nearer, munching his apple. He noticed that she'd quite recovered herself after having wept so deeply at her brother's funeral mass. Wearing neither hood nor veil, her ginger hair was pulled back on her head and hung down her back between her shoulder blades. Her green eyes darted from her brother's face to Sir Richard's, and now to Alan's as he came up, catching her in mid-sentence.

"And mama was so devastated by the whole thing, well, she was in no fit condition to plan anything like this funeral. And so Geoffrey said have it at Saint James' and mama said anyplace was fine she just wanted it over with, and so he contacted Father Timothy and that was that. I took charge of the arrangements and Father Timothy said some of the matrons in the church would lay out a few items for after, and that was fine. I suppose we could have had the thing at some cathedral in Nottingham town, as we did with father, but the fact is that Saint James is our home parish. Father had quarreled with the old priest here, and refused to give them any kind of endowment when he died, and so we didn't bury him here. We didn't tell a lot of people about the mass and so there aren't many who came anyway, so we didn't need a large feast. Only the family and the servants and our closest neighbor. We're so happy you were able to come, Sir Richard…"

"I only heard about the service by chance myself," Sir Richard shrugged. "One of Lord William's servants, Dap his falconer, happened to see me and told me the sad news. I was only just able to get away with my court musician, Alan here, who had met Lord William and admired him." Alan bowed like a good servant first to Lord Geoffrey and then to Lady Anne, who wrinkled her freckled nose up in a surprised delight.

"You're the one with the song!" she exclaimed with a childish giggle, grabbing Alan by his elbow in her rapture. "What an inspired thought that was, to end the graveside service with such a haunting tune. Well good for you, minstrel, is all I can say."

Alan was pretty certain it was not all she could say, since she hadn't stopped speaking since he'd arrived in the narthex. But she was interrupted now by her brother, who was not at all of the same opinion. "Nothing but vanity," Lord Geoffrey growled. His voice was low and somber, and his face a mask of melancholy. It was an unfortunate face, Alan thought, red as a cherubim's with blemishes of the skin, framed by a thin black beard that matched his stringy hair. His eyes were black as charcoal and seemed to pierce Alan's soul. "Strutting like a peacock with your songs and fiddles. My brother is dead. It's nothing to sing about."

Sir Richard stepped in to save Alan from an embarrassing situation. "Lord Geoffrey, my servant acts under my direction. If you are unhappy with his performance today, you may address yourself to me, I assure you it was not intended to diminish your brother's obsequies."

Lord Geoffrey drew himself up to his full height, which was not negligible, as he towered at least three inches over Richard himself, despite his skeletal frame. "I stand corrected Sir Richard. I shall then think of the act as you say it was intended, rather than as I experienced it. Now, if you will excuse me," and with that the young lord stalked off, clearly still not mollified.

Alan, abashed now by the lord's rebuff, turned to his sister and expressed what regrets he could. "My Lady, if my song did not please, I do apologize. I admired your late brother a great deal, and was moved to eulogize him as I could…"

Lady Anne wrinkled her nose again and waved off Alan's contrition. "Don't mind Geoffrey," she said. "He's got a lot on his mind, you know, having all of a sudden been made the new lord of the Randal estates, and there's quite a bit of land and peasants that go with those estates, I can tell you, so anybody would be overwhelmed, I should think. And Geoffrey's never been the gregarious sort, you know, not like me, who get along with everybody and can fit in anywhere. Never at a loss for words, that's me."

Alan felt he did not have to be told that last bit, but did raise a provocative question, just to see how the girl would respond. "So Lord Geoffrey actually is much better off, though doubtless grieved, now that his brother is dead. Lord of all the estates. Lord William's was a fortuitous death for him, I suppose, made him rich as a king with lands and cattle."

Sir Richard threw Alan a look that seemed to say, "you're going too far, fool!" but Alan just looked at Lady Anne innocently and the girl seemed oblivious to the hint. "Oh, he's got a lot of new lands, for sure," she said. "But William left his cattle to Mama, I suppose to make her independent so as not to need help from

Geoffrey to get by. As for all his gold and silver, William left all that to me, you see. Wanted me to have a decent dowry, you know, so I can marry well. Yes, some people might think that Lady Eleanor did us all a great favor when she killed our William. Made us all rich. But I suppose that wasn't her intent, was it? Anyway, we're not so rich after all. We're just finding out how little there really was. But maybe there's a fortune hidden somewhere that we'll find yet. Ha! Well, I've got to run and see if mama needs anything. Help yourselves to whatever you can eat that's still here. And thank you again for coming. Adieu."

Left to themselves as the Randal family emptied out of the church, Sir Richard shrugged at Alan and put his hand on the minstrel's shoulder. "There's an interesting pair," the knight said. "Neither one seems terribly grieved over their brother's death."

"Oh, I don't know," Alan mused. "The girl seemed honestly mourning during the mass. But she's a teenager. Her emotions come and go quickly. And she does seem rather happy to have inherited a dowry in silver and gold. Lord Geoffrey? He is more disgruntled, it seems, by his new duties than truly mourning his brother, if we can believe Lady Anne. But that's mainly distracting him, and keeps him from showing his true sorrow at Lord William's demise. At least for now."

"But he's done pretty well also," Sir Richard commented, "inheriting a bit of wealth in land and the power that comes with it. But did you learn anything by talking to the girlfriend? Everyone does seem to think she's the guilty party."

"Well, everyone but me, I suppose," Alan admitted. And to Sir Richard's suggestively raised eyebrows, he added, "She's the only one who seems sincerely distraught by Lord William's death. And, moreover, the only one who seems to resent the lack of pomp and ceremony in these funeral rites. If she poisoned William, it was a complete accident."

Sir Richard looked doubtful but before he could make further comment, they were distracted by the figure of Friar Tuck, panting loudly as he came rushing toward them, his face a picture of excitement and his bald tonsure glistening with beads of sweat. "Good friar," Sir Richard greeted him. "You spent the entire time talking with Father Timothy, did you?"

"Indeed," the friar agreed still huffing, but silently impelling the two of them toward the church door. Finally recovering his breath, he looked about to ensure they were the only ones in hearing distance, Then he said in a voice just above a whisper: "Wait until you hear what Father Timothy just told me. Guess how Lord Randal's father died?" When Alan and Richard looked blank, Tuck answered, "Murdered. The case was never solved. Rumor had it that the mother did it—Lady Randal murdered her own husband!"

CHAPTER FOUR

When Robin Hood awoke that same morning, he had rolled out of his tent and stretched, peering upward with one eye as the sun shone brightly down from just above the eastern horizon. He twisted his mouth a bit in thought. A gloomy day would have been better for his purposes. Slinking about Nottingham town all bundled in a dark hood might look a bit suspicious in the bright sunshine of this day. But there was nothing for it. He couldn't very well go undisguised to the Sheriff's door. Oh well, he thought at least he'd taken the time to darken his blond hair a bit last night with the juice of blackberries. Though how he was going to keep the waxwings out of his hair he didn't know.

Then he thought of one more thing, and ducked back into his tent to grab the eyepatch he occasionally used as a part of more elaborate disguises. When he came back out, there were a few others stirring in the camp, and he noticed Ellen, Alan a Dale's wife, was already building a cooking fire, planning, he assumed, to boil some water to mix with rolled oats to make a breakfast porridge for herself and some of the other women. Most of the men were more interested in eggs and bacon when they could get it in the morning, but Robin's band had never taken to raising chickens—it would be too likely to give the location of their camp away if a flock of hens were found to be brooding in the wild greenwood. Robin turned up his nose at the idea of porridge, but approached Ellen anyway.

"Morning Ellen. And how'd you sleep last night, with your lord and master away from your tent?"

"Got the best night's sleep I've had in *yeeears*," Ellen said, drawing out the long *e*, "without Alan's great snoring honker of a nose in my ear. And I see you're all painted up to fool the burghers of Nottingham. And I suppose you're dawdling here instead of starting out for the city because you think I'm going to be talked into giving you some breakfast to fuel you on your journey?"

Robin looked at her sheepishly and admitted, "The thought had crossed my mind, my pretty Nell."

Ellen, who'd been stirring oats on a pot over the stove with a long wooden spoon, now brought the spoon down on Robin's head with enough force to make the point that she was not joking. "Now, Robin Kempe, alias Robin Hood, don't you try using your sweet talking charms on me. I'll have my Alan put an arrow right through your Lincoln green hosen and then I'd probably end up being the one to sew them up, so don't make more work for me, see? Anyway, this porridge won't be ready for a while so if you're hoping to get off soon I'll give you a piece of bread and some cheese and you'll have to make do with that."

"And so I shall, good lady Ellen," Robin said, accepting the mild reprimand and taking the light breakfast from the woman's hands. "And tell Little John I expect to be back by nightfall, if you would please." Ellen, looking back down at her pot, waved the spoon at him as a sign of agreement and returned to her task.

Robin pulled on his dark woolen cloak and hood and checked to make sure his short sword was in easy reach in its scabbard in case he needed it. He'd have been more comfortable if he'd been able to bring along his bow and a quiver of arrows, but he knew carrying that weapon into Nottingham would be far too conspicuous. Then, munching his bread and cheese, he moved to the smaller clearing away from the camp where the outlaws kept their horses. Here he put a saddle and harness on Daisy, his favorite mount, and climbed on her back, turning her head toward the Great North Road where he would turn her south for Nottingham.

* * *

Lady Maude Peveril—distant cousin to Lady Lydia Peveril, Countess of Chesterfield; discontented wife of John of Oxenford, Sheriff of Nottingham; and occasional bedfellow of the outlaw Robin Hood of Sherwood—sat in the comfortable chair in her closet in the Sheriff's large manor house. She had brought out the portable writing desk she kept under the chair, and placed a clean sheet of parchment on its angled surface. Dipping her feather quill into the black ink she held on the surface of the desk, she began a long overdue letter. As it happened, she was writing to the Countess. She had begun by thanking her cousin for the annuity Lady Lydia had granted her, the second payment of which had just arrived from the Countess's steward.

Those necessary courtesies paid, Maude now wrinkled her brow and clenched her jaw as she moved into the true purpose of her missive: She needed to tell her cousin of the difficulties their mutual friend, Robin Hood, had gotten himself into this time.

Wanted for murder, of all things, Maude tsked. Biting the feather end of the quill, she contemplated just how she might break the news to the Countess without making the poor girl swoon dead away. After some thought, she decided to address her cousin in the most intimate terms, and to present the present crisis as a plea for the Countess to take some decisive action, rather than as cause for lamentation.

And now, dearest coz, she wrote, *I come to the most distressing part of this letter. Our mutual friend, whose name all the denizens of Sherwood know, has landed in a new predicament. He and his meinie recently detained a minor nobleman of this area, one Lord Randal, and that young worthy died at his home later that same day! Now the authorities (you know who I mean) are saying that the young man died of poisoning, and that our friend is to blame. He is, consequently, accused of murder, and all the forces of Royal authority are arrayed against him, to track him down, apprehend him, and bring him back to Nottingham to be hanged for murder. I know, my dear, that such an outcome must be as distressing to you as it is to me, and implore you to use whatever force and influence you have to protect our friend from the dire consequences of this no doubt mistaken accusation. I send this by the speediest messenger I can find, and look forward hourly to your response.*

Lady Maude closed the letter with a flourish about her signature, and then waved it in the air a bit to dry the ink before she folded it and sealed it with candle wax and her Peveril family signet ring. Now, she thought, just who was the fastest messenger she could find who might deliver this epistle to her cousin? There was a certain Brother Philip, connected to the Church of Saint Mary the Virgin, who regularly made the journey from Nottingham to Peveril Castle: Lenton Priory, the Cluniac house that owned the church, had been founded decades earlier by William Peveril, ancestor of both Maude and Countess Lydia, and therefore Lydia, current holder of Sir William's former titles, felt herself obligated to contribute regularly to the upkeep of the Priory and the great Nottingham Church.

Maude had not used Robin's name, or that of her husband the Sheriff, but had referred to them obliquely, on the chance that the messenger could be waylaid en route to Lady Lydia's castle and the letter confiscated. Of course, her euphemisms would not fool someone already familiar with the situation, but they were enough to confound local authorities on the road. And she knew that Brother Philip would be cautious, and at the same time would certainly be more than willing to make the two-day trip to the fortress of his house's benefactor. Maude could only hope the Countess would respond with equal dispatch.

But she could not calm her anxiety. Again she chewed on her quill, her indomitable jaw moving methodically as she bit up and down on the feather. Her dark eyes stared ahead, focused on nothing in the room but on the terrible image in her imagination that featured Robin Hood hanging by the neck on a scaffold erected before Nottingham Castle. Her head, bound up with a linen veil and pearl-embroidered fillet over a thin barbette that circled her chin, nodded limply. She slumped forward, wrinkling her simple blue linen gown with the unfashionable sleeves that hugged her wrists rather than hanging down to her waist—a current trend she thought of as frivolous and impractical. It was in this posture that the face, popping up over windowsill of her private second-floor chamber, observed her.

That visage, framed by a dark gray woolen hood, had dark hair, mustache and goatee smelling faintly of blackberries, and it was peering at her with one eye, the other being obscured by a black eyepatch. It continued to observe her for several moments before Maude's eyes finally focused on what was before her and noticed the face in her window. And at that she jumped.

"Robin!" she exclaimed, undeceived by his thin disguise. "What on earth are you doing here? Get up here into my bedroom immediately!"

"Now that's an invitation I hope never to decline," the outlaw quipped, pulling himself over the windowsill and into Maude's waiting arms. He dropped his woolen cloak to the floor and, as Maude pulled him into her room, she noticed he had found the small ladder her superannuated servant Giles kept behind the house for emergencies, and used it to climb to her window. Quickly she closed the shutters and shoved the outlaw onto the curtained bed. Her impassioned angst, met by Robin's sudden arrival and the bawdy suggestiveness of his greeting, had been channeled into a different kind of tension, and she raised her skirts up to her waist while Robin, barely quick enough on the uptake, lowered his hosen just in time for her to settle herself upon his rising flesh. Robin reached up to yank off the barbette and fillet that constricted Maude's beautiful auburn locks, and let the hair tumble free in a swirl of waves, clutching it in his hands as Maude moved hotly against him.

* * *

Some forty or forty-five minutes later, all passion spent, Robin lay on his back in Maude's curtained bed, the lady's auburn head on his right shoulder, her face turned to his chest, her body curved around his with her left leg lying across his thighs as if pinning him down. The only item of clothing remaining on Robin's body was his eyepatch, which for some reason Maude had found particularly erotic. As for Maude herself, she had not a stitch left. Try as he might Robin could not recall when in the process this had actually happened. But as he lay there, he was assailed with feelings of contrition or, at least, liability. When he thought about Maid Marion, his one true love, as he had begun to consider her, he could not help feeling he had betrayed her. Of course, she was not called *Maid* Marion for nothing, and he could not foresee any time when that designation was likely to change, at least as far as he was concerned. Yeoman class did not marry noble class, and Marion was not a woman to bestow her favors outside of wedlock. As for Maude—well, how was it he could never spend any time in Maude Peveril's company without joining her in making the Beast with Two Backs? Ah, it was such a well-worn path by now, and she was so willing, that it seemed second nature.

But lying there with his mind now clear, Robin began to think more prudently about where he was and how to proceed. He thought first about the floor plan of the Sheriff's home: He knew there was one other sleeping room here on the second floor of the large waddle-and-daub manor house, which was the Sheriff's private solar. Like this one, it had a window looking to the rear of the house—the Sheriff knew how to avoid the window tax that imposed a levy on every window that faced the street. His own house had none at all. Therefore Robin did not think anybody could have seen him come through the lady's shutters. On the ground floor he knew there was a kitchen, hall, buttery, and storage area, with the door facing the street. This was the domain of Anna, Lady Maude's maid. But Robin had heard no sound from that part of the house since arriving. Of course, he hadn't really been listening. But now he concentrated and heard nothing.

"Maudie?" Robin whispered to her, twitching his shoulder slightly to rouse her, since she'd nodded off after her exertions of the afternoon. "Maudie, I assume that Anna is not at home just now, am I right?"

"Right," Maude replied groggily, blinking her eyes and raising her head slightly before letting it fall back on Robin's shoulder with a slight sigh. "She's gone to market and to meet James the journeyman cobbler, but she thinks I don't know about that. So she won't be back for a good hour yet."

"How about Giles?" Robin asked, remembering the old

handyman servant who took care of the garden and the horses and any odd jobs that needed doing around the house. Giles lived in his own small hovel behind the house, preferring it that way for privacy's sake. But it had occurred to Robin that Giles might well have seen him climb in the window.

"Oh this is the time of day when he usually makes his way to the Blue Boar Inn for his mid-day libations. We won't be seeing him for a few hours anyway. And before you ask, my husband is in his office in the castle, as he always is until dinnertime. So unless you left your horse outside my door, we're safe as houses for the moment."

"Oh no, I left Daisy at the blacksmith's near the city gate. Thought I'd be less conspicuous on foot, as long as I kept on my long cape and hood."

At that point Maude, who'd been half asleep from the beginning of this conversation, suddenly punched Robin's shoulder with all her strength, snapping, "Conspicuous? Yes, you bloody coxcomb, what are you doing in Nottingham?"

"Ow!" Robin responded, rubbing his shoulder. "Now I'll probably have a bruise there. What are you so riled up about?"

"Bruise? Bruise? I'll bruise you!" And with that she punched him again, this time in his chest, which made him sit up himself and hold out his hands in self-defense. "But bruises are going to be the least of your worries if my husband catches you in Nottingham. You do know that you're now wanted for murder, don't you?"

"Yes, yes," Robin said in a mollifying tone.

"And he means to hang you in the town square when he catches you?"

"Yes, yes," Robin repeated. "But how is that different? He's been threatening to hang me if he caught me for years. And he hasn't caught me. In years."

"But he's more determined than ever this time, and has hired more deputies, and has got Sir Guy of Gisbourne's men all searching Sherwood for your camp. I mean it, they're serious. And they're doing it very methodically. Gisbourne's got some new learned cleric called Friar Bungay who's what they call a cartographer, who maps out small patches of Sherwood and records what's in those places, I don't understand how he does it, but he keeps track of every section of the forest searched by these forty or fifty men, and then they know just exactly where they've been searching and what's there and where they need to search next. I mean it, they can't help but find you. What can you do?"

Robin pursed his lips and pondered the matter. Gisbourne's men had found the outlaws' winter camp at Creswell Crags just last year, luckily immediately after they had abandoned it. They could not move the camp back there—that would make it too easy for Gisbourne and the Sheriff to find them. But if they stayed where they were, they were just asking to be found eventually. This would need some solemn thought, and more heads than his.

"Well Maudie," he sighed. "You asked me what I was doing here, and the fact is I was planning to pump you…for information I mean. And what you've just told me is exactly what I need to know. And hearing what you say, I'd say first of all that you're right, I should get myself back to Sherwood, which is still probably safer for me than Nottingham. But listen, answer me this: You know I didn't kill Lord Randal, don't you."

"Of course," Maude cooed. "I know you wouldn't hurt a fly. A deer, sure, but not a fly. You're no murderer. Just a thief and a kidnapper and a blasphemer. Oh, and a fornicator, of course, and guilty of coveting your neighbor's wife. But no murderer."

Robin shrugged. "I am unquestionably all those things," he answered her. "But I do some good as well…"

"Oh, I never said your fornicating was *bad*," Maude said. "And the common people, they do love you for your charity. So yes, there's a bit of something to balance the scales."

"Well, let me ask you one more thing. If I could prove that somebody else did this murder, that I and my men are completely innocent of it, wouldn't the Sheriff have to back down from this current obsession with catching me?"

Maude twisted up her face as if Robin had uttered complete and utter nonsense, "Of course he's not going to back down. He doesn't care whether you're guilty of this murder or not. He's just using it as an excuse to chase you down. He's *going* to hang you if he catches you, guilty or not. And he'll excuse it by calling you a thief and a poacher."

"But there must be a trial, mustn't there? I mean, that's common law."

Maude shrugged. "He'll have Gisbourne judge the case, and Gisbourne will find you guilty. You'll probably not even know when this so-called trial takes place."

"And this will be fine with the burghers of Nottingham?" Robin asked, becoming frustrated. "Shouldn't the trial be public? Shouldn't there be a jury?"

"No one has complained before," Maude replied. "And it's happened more times than I can remember." But then she pouted, and tilted her head in thought. "But the truth is, in the past the trials and subsequent hangings have been of unknown common criminals, men nobody in Nottingham knew or cared about. But you're a different kettle of fish."

"Long as it's not eels," Robin said under his breath, then asked aloud, "How do you mean?"

"I mean everybody knows the charitable bandit of Sherwood: He entertains his victims with meat and song. He venerates the Blessed Virgin on every conceivable holiday. He robs from the rich! He gives to the poor! And believe me, my dear, there are a lot more poor than rich. Many of the poor of Nottingham have been on the receiving end of Friar Tuck's charity. These are people who are not going to sit quietly by if you are brought to the dock." Maude stroked her chin as she thought about the situation. "There would have to be a public trial, or the outcry would be too great even for them. So yes," she concluded, now smiling with a touch of relief. "I think you may have a chance at a public trial, and if that's the case then proving somebody else guilty of this murder might very well save you."

Robin jumped out of the bed and began quickly to gather his clothes around him. "Maudie," he said, "you've raised my spirits once again, as you always do!" Pulling on his hosen, his tunic and his boots, he continued to speak so rapidly she could barely keep up. "Tuck and Alan a Dale and Richard at the Lee are already on this case and were to be at Lord Randal's funeral today. I'll get with the rest of the boys and we'll have this case solved in no time. We're good at that!" And now he grinned and donned his gray cloak and hood, after first securing his short sword in its scabbard along his thigh. Bending over, he gave Maude one last kiss as she settled back in her bed, then with a cry of "Adieu, my pet!" he threw open the shutters and scrambled over the window sill.

"Farewell, you fool," she called after him. "Don't get caught!"

* * *

Robin strode purposefully along the streets of Nottingham. It was still sunny, though moving on toward later afternoon, and he tried to stay in the shadows as far as possible, without appearing to skulk. He'd dawdled later than he'd intended with Lady Maude, and now feared that he would not get back to camp before dark, and would worry Little John and the others. But it couldn't be helped. And he'd learned exactly what he'd wanted to know from the Sheriff's wife. The cartographer's plan to comb every inch of Sherwood was troubling, but if he, John, Tuck, Alan and Will Stutely could put their heads together, he was confident they could find a way around this new trouble. He was beginning to feel a bit vulnerable here in the Sheriff's own city, and would feel much better when he was back on his own ground in Sherwood and on his way back to the outlaw camp. He was glad he'd left Daisy at the sign of the Prancing Pony, the blacksmith and livery stable just inside the city gates. He could hop on Daisy and be out the gate in no time at all.

What Robin had not figured on was the Sheriff's ancient handyman and factotum Giles. Too elderly to keep awake if he had his pint of ale after sundown, Giles was in the habit of taking his afternoon respite and lunch break at the Blue Boar Inn, which was located outside the Nottingham gates about a furlong north on the Great North Road. And he was just coming back through those gates on his way back to the Sheriff's house when he happened to glance through the door of the livery stable and his eyes fell upon Daisy. Now Giles had served the Sheriff for more years than either of them could remember, and he had looked after Daisy in the Sheriff's stable from the time she was a foal to the day Robin Hood had stolen her from the Sheriff's own stalls. He recognized the chestnut colored rouncey at first sight. The ale—which had turned into several pints before Giles decided to make his way home—had not muddled his wits so much that he didn't immediately realize that Robin Hood was in Nottingham. And he stepped into the stable to warn the blacksmith of the notorious bandit whose horse he was harboring.

Word had spread immediately. The smith had sent his apprentice running to the castle, where he'd burst in upon the

Sheriff and Sir Guy of Gisbourne in consultation and blurted out the news, after which Gisbourne and the Sheriff had rounded up all the deputies and guards in easy reach—more than a dozen of them—and set out in quick march to surround the stable, and to wait until the rider, surely to be in disguise, arrived to claim the horse. All of this was happening while Robin was listening to Lady Maude's explanation of the Sheriff's new plan to capture the outlaws.

So it was that when the dark hooded figure approached the livery through the shadows and made his way to the door, he was surprised by the sharp point of a cold steel blade that suddenly pricked the side of his neck while a low guttural voice commanded, "Don't move or you're a dead man."

Quick as lightening Robin jerked his head to the side as his hands grasped for his own short sword. But he'd barely begun his move when he felt a set of strong arms imprison each of his own, while another sword point touched his back. Another figure approached him from the front, sword pointed toward his heart, and growled, "Master Robin Hood, I presume. You are under arrest by order of the Sheriff, for the murder of Lord William Randal. I advise you not to struggle, or you won't live to see the inside of your jail cell."

CHAPTER FIVE

Sir Richard and Dap returned with Alan and Friar Tuck to the outlaws' camp, and were welcomed enthusiastically by Little John, Will Stutely and Scarlet, Sir Palomides, and Much the miller's son. Several of the other men were out hunting and a few were patrolling the Great North Road for possible dinner guests, but when Ellen saw Alan return she rushed to meet him, to learn whether his attendance at Lord Randal's services had purged some of the anxious sorrow he'd been feeling since hearing of the nobleman's murder. He smiled wanly when he saw her and closed his eyes as he held her close, whispering "Only more mystery" when he saw her questioning eyes.

"Well," Sir Richard began as the woodsmen pressed around him for news. "I'm not sure we found out anything that could possibly prove Robin innocent. But there were a lot of curious things going on at that funeral."

"And the family, were they convinced the girlfriend did it?" Little John asked, and the returning group all nodded.

"Oh, they're all quite certain," Sir Richard answered. "Of course, nobody had any evidence that could possibly prove it. And the girlfriend—surprise surprise—says she thinks Robin Hood is behind it."

"Well, she would, wouldn't she?" Will Stutely said. "Gets her off the hook, eh? To have the Sheriff himself throw suspicion on somebody else when you're the prime suspect? She couldn't have planned it better if she'd planned it," he concluded, relishing the tautology.

"But what's her motive?" Alan addressed them all. "I mean, sure, she had the means, the fried eels themselves. And she had the opportunity, Lord Randal was at her house eating them. But we've gotta have a motive if we're going to convict her."

"Lover's quarrel?" Will Scarlet ventured. "He tells her it's all over, he can't marry her after all, and she counters with, 'Oh yeah? Well chew on this for a while then, ya blighter!'"

But Ellen, cuddled into her husband's side as he sat on the green turf and curling one of her long blonde locks thoughtfully around her index finger, pursed her lips and shook her head. "Iii…don't see it," she said, drawing out the long vowel. "I agree with my handsome and clever husband," and with that she patted Alan's cheek. "The woman loves him, and she's already made the dinner. He tells her they're through and she runs into the kitchen, quickly douses the fried eels with some poison she just happens to have lying by for just such occasions, and sits there while he eats it? No, no. It's too convenient. If I'm a young lass who's been waiting for her true love to come by and have a meal I've cooked, and instead he turns up and breaks my heart, my reaction's going to be some angry hurt tears, and a command to him to leave my home and get out of my sight immediately if not sooner. There's too much, what do you call it, *premeditation* involved for her to be the killer."

At that Dap broke his stony silence to second Ellen's assessment. "I was there. Not in the room with them when he arrived, but outside the door. There were a few exclamations. I didn't hear what about. But when we served the meal, they were quiet, like they'd been discussing something they didn't want us to hear about. But they didn't seem ready to kill each other."

"I can well believe it," Alan continued. "Lady Eleanor showed me the ring that Lord William had given her with his family crest on it. She says it was his pledge to marry her, and I believe her. The exclamation Dap heard was most likely a shout of joy when he presented her with that token. I see no reason to believe she murdered him."

"No reason other than the fact that he died after he ate her cooking," Will Scarlet said drily. "Maybe she's just a terrible cook?"

At that Ellen picked up a pebble and tossed it at Scarlet, who ducked and grinned at her. And Alan went on, "The fact that Lord William's family hated the lady and discouraged their marriage explains why they would automatically assume that Lady Eleanor's the guilty party. But it's prejudice, not evidence. No, I talked to the lady for some time, and I'm convinced she didn't kill her lover. Besides, Friar Tuck did learn some interesting news about the mother, Lady Randal, didn't you Tuck?"

The good friar nodded and bowed his head for a moment. He was either silently praying or considering just how to approach the subject. Then he began, "The state of holy matrimony is a sacred tie by which God intends to bind together two loving souls. The sacredness of love, any sort of love" (and at that word he glanced momentarily at Little John and Will Stutely) "is a lesson I have only recently had brought home to me. But it is also true that human failings will sometimes make a marriage a tool of the devil rather than a glorification of Love Divine. In my own life, I've had to face the truth of my own parents' hellish marriage, and can readily sympathize with those in such a relationship. Oh, I know the Church demands that those married remain so forever. They will point to the text in Genesis that says, 'Therefore shall a man leave his father and his mother, and shall cleave to his wife: and they shall be one flesh'; or to our Lord's words in Matthew's gospel that read, 'What therefore God hath joined together, let not man put asunder.' And they are right if they are discussing marriage in the Kingdom of God. But life in the kingdom of this world often falls short of the heavenly realm."

"What is this, friar, a sermon?" Sir Richard interrupted, triggering a few chuckles from some of the other listeners. "Tell us what you need to about Lady Randal, before Christmas is upon us!"

Tuck closed his eyes as if reluctant to continue, but decided to give up trying to put his remarks into a wider context and simply blurted out, as he had earlier, "It seems that Lady Randal is suspected of having murdered her husband. There it is."

There were audible gasps from the circle around him, and Sir Richard encouraged the friar to go on. "Go ahead, explain it as you explained it to us earlier."

"Well, you should all know that I heard these things from the local parish priest, Father Timothy, who I have every reason to believe is a good and pious man, who would not lightly engage in malicious gossip. Although he did say that he'd got these rumors from his predecessor, the old priest Father Mark, whom he says Lord William's father had had a falling out with over some trifle. The old Lord Randal made no gift to Saint James in his will, so the old priest might have been willing to listen to a good deal of gossip, But for what it's worth, it seems that Lord William's father, Lord Stephen, *also* died in mysterious circumstances. He was found in his bedchamber at the Randal estate one morning with his throat slit from ear to ear. The two old family servants who found him testified they had been in the house all night, sleeping in the great hall on the ground floor. No one could have come in or left by the door to the manor house without their knowledge. The three children—William, Geoffrey and the girl,

Lady Anne, who was but a toddler at the time, were all out of the house and visiting their mother's parents in Sheffield when the murder took place. So the only person on the second floor of the house was Lady Randal herself. She and her husband slept in separate quarters, so when the servants found the body in the morning, they had to rouse her from where she lay sound asleep in her own bed. And what was especially damning, there were bloody handprints on the outside of her door."

"But none on her hands or her clothing?" Will Stutely immediately probed. "If she'd cut his throat in that manner, she could not have kept the blood from splashing onto her clothes, or staining her hands."

"She could have washed her hands and changed her clothes during the night. No search was ever done of her own solar—she was the lady of the house and the discoverers of the body merely her servants. She could have easily disposed of the water she'd used to wash her hands, and perhaps even burned the clothes she wore, and never allowed her servants to see the telltale signs. When the local magistrate was finally informed of the crime, there were strong suspicions concerning Lady Randal, but nothing anyone could prove. There remained strong suspicions of the lady, and the killer was never caught, but no one could prove anything against her."

"And the point here is what?" Little John demanded. "That the lady is an experienced killer? That she killed her husband and then went on to kill her son fifteen years later? Even granting that she might have killed the husband, what was her motive? And more to the point, what could her motive possibly be in killing her own son?"

Friar Tuck heaved a sigh. "First, let me say that the evidence against her in the case of her husband is not proof, but it is compelling. Who else would have known that the children would all be gone that night? Who could have gotten past the servants sleeping on the ground floor? Who else had the power to cover up any evidence and the status to squelch any further inquiry into the matter?"

"But again, what about the motive?" Little John persisted. "Did your Father Timothy say why she might have killed this husband of hers? This old Lord Stephen?"

"There were different rumors, apparently," Tuck explained. "One rumor said that the lady had taken a lover, and took this opportunity to get rid of her husband so that she could be with her paramour. But when no lover appeared to fill the husband's place after the murder, that rumor died down—though some of that theory's more devoted adherents claimed that the lover had deserted her once he learned she had done away with her spouse. A second rumor was that Lord Stephen regularly brutalized his wife, beating her for the slightest offense, and that in the end she had had enough of that treatment and killed her tormentor in his sleep. Still another rumor, which seems to me pretty far-fetched, claimed that the husband knew of an immense treasure, one he'd brought home from the crusades and hidden away, but that he refused to divulge its secret hiding place to his wife, and made her live in modest circumstances that she resented fiercely."

"Well if you ask me," Ellen volunteered, "as the only woman present, it seems to me that the first possibility is highly unlikely. Lady Randal has had no known lovers since her husband's death, correct?"

"As far as anyone knows, that is so," Tuck answered.

"It is certainly so," Dap interjected. "Such an affair cannot be kept from the servants of the household, and I would have been aware of it. I was not a member of the household at the time of Lord Stephen's murder, but took service there five years later, and no one ever suggested the hint of immodesty on the lady's part."

"There!" Ellen said. "Definitive proof. As for the third rumor, you're right, it seems far-fetched, and even more unlikely that Lady Randal would have killed her husband in that case. After all, even if she was angry at being deprived of riches, it's a poor reason for murder, and besides, if she wanted her husband to share the wealth, why kill his secret along with him? She'd *never* have a share in the treasure then. No, if she killed her husband, and I say if, because it's not at all certain that she did, then she did it because he beat her and she would no longer tolerate it."

Friar Tuck sighed. "I'm afraid I agree with you. My own experience has shown me that, pushed to such extremes, women may act in such a manner. Saint Paul says, 'husbands, love your wives as Christ loved the church.' And if you don't, watch out for the consequences!"

"I don't know if Paul said that last part," Alan a Dale said. "But why keep speculating about this? We have one of the household servants here with us. Dap, can you shed any light on this? Were there rumors of Lord Stephen's mistreatment of the lady among the servants you knew who were in the household at the time?"

"Well, let me see," Dap replied in his restrained tone. "When I started service with the Randals, Lord William was just thirteen. I was taken on because I knew something about hawks and hawking, which as a young nobleman he was expected to embrace. He'd begun hunting with hounds a few years earlier. It was just a year earlier that Wulf had been employed, to take care of the hounds. You remember him from that morning you detained us. Wulf was the only servant there younger than I was at that time. The others were quite a bit older. There was the children's old nurse, Sarah, who still had charge of Master Geoffrey and little Anne. And there was the mistress's ladies maid, Margery, who was quite old at the time. She's dead now."

Now Dap began to count on his fingers. "The cook Robert. The groom Thomas. And the huntsman and general factotum Francis. They're all dead. And oh, there'd been another servant, the huntsman that Francis had had to replace, while keeping the rest of his duties. He'd left the service several years before I started, but apparently he was a bit younger than the others. Now what was his name, anyhow?" Dap rubbed his chin and furrowed his brow a moment before he said, "David, that was it. From somewhere in East Anglia, as I understand it. Mind you, I never met the fellow. But they said he'd left to go join some holy order someplace. Must have been a little higher born than the others."

Alan, who'd waited patiently for Dap to finish his catalog, repeated his earlier question. "So, did any of these servants gossip at all about that time before you came, about Lady Randal being abused by her husband?"

Dap shook his head. "I can't say that they did. And old Margery would have known for sure if any of that was going on. She never talked about it. And I think she probably would have, at least to us fellow servants. Mind you, I did hear a rumor about that treasure the friar mentioned. That came from Thomas, the groom. He knew a lot about the old lord's comings and goings and where his horses had been. He claimed he's seen Lord Stephen leave the manor one morning with a full saddle bag and came back with it empty. He didn't know what was in that bag, of course, but he imagined it might be riches of some sort. So that rumor was alive."

Alan sighed. "It might be worthwhile to talk to some of the servants that were in the household at the time of the murder. But they are all dead, you say?"

Dap pursed his lips in thought, and returned to counting on

his fingers, until he reached a certain point and aid, "Sarah, the nurse. She's still alive. Living retired somewhere in Southwell, I believe, in a cottage Lady Randal set her up in for her old age. Her and that David fellow, but who knows where he's gone to?"

"Right," Alan said. "Maybe it would be worth finding this old nurse and speaking to her?"

"It would if we thought that the murder of the *old* Lord Randal had any connection to the murder of *our* Lord Randal," Little John said, bringing everyone back to the point at hand. "But what if it ain't? Why should the one have anything to do with the other?"

Tuck shrugged. "It would if we could connect the same motive to the same murderer. And if, perhaps, Lady Randal *is* that killer…"

At that, a huge commotion broke up the parley as Thorvald burst into the clearing along with half a dozen of Robin's other men. A young religious, wearing a mask and dressed in the black habit of a Cluniac monk, sat in Thorvald's cart with him, while Will Scathelock, one of the oldest and most level-headed of Robin's meinie, walked behind the cart leading a gentle palfrey and surrounded by young Donald of Doncaster, Wat o' the Crabstaff, Skipper Haakon, and John the cook's son.

"So you've caught one, have ya?" Much the miller's son greeted the newcomers with a half-toothless grin. "I don't know—this one looks like just a common brother. Not likely to have much of a purse on him."

"'E 'asn't," Thorvald answered, acting as spokesman. "Barely two farthings to rub together, this one."

"Then why did you bring him here?" Friar Tuck wanted to know. "What part of 'rob from the rich, give to the poor,' don't you understand?"

But Thorvald was not in the mood to banter. He reached

over and yanked the mask off the young monk's face, and the lad blinked large green eyes when exposed to the sunlight once again. "This 'ere is a Brother Philip from Lenton Priory in Nottingham. 'E's connected with the Church o' Saint Mary the Virgin there, an' 'e's on 'is way ta Peveril Castle." This last bit of information drew a few grunts of interest from the assembled group, at which Thorvald poked the monk's arm and said, "Go on, lad, tell 'em what ya told me. An' don't worry. Every man 'ere is a servant of Countess Lydia!"

Brother Philip's eyes grew even larger, which Alan a Dale would not have thought possible. Thorvald, of course, was speaking nothing but the truth, for Lady Lydia Peveril, Countess of Chesterfield, had long ago appointed Robin and his men her personal Foresters—a position that had no actual duties since she had barely any forest on her lands, but it did provide a certain protection from the authorities, as long as they were somewhere near Peveril Castle. The outlaws' summer camp, where they were settled now, was unfortunately a long way from that fortress.

Brother Philip seemed about to burst into tears as he bobbed his head from one side to another, scanning the faces of the outlaw band and looking doubtful as he considered the dwarf's claim. Alan could see that the slight little monk was trembling, and his heart went out to the lad. He stepped toward Thorvald's cart and, reaching up, laid a hand on the young monk's knee, which made Philip jump a bit. But Alan said in his kindest, mildest tone, "Don't worry, brother. No one here is going to hurt you. Just tell us what we need to know, as Thorvald says."

But even this would not have worked had Ellen not followed her husband to the cart and added her own hand and voice to comfort the frightened lad. "It'll be all right," she whispered, and at that Brother Philip, in a sudden rush of courage, replied in a shaky voice:

"I'm charged with bringing an urgent letter to the Countess Lydia from Lady Maude Peveril."

"From the Sheriff's wife?" Little John cried, his interest piqued.

"P....p...precisely," Brother Philip stammered. "She says that the Countess must receive this letter," and with that he reached into his habit—Alan noticed his hands were not tied—and pulled out a sealed piece of parchment.

Friar Tuck stepped forward and immediately snatched the parchment from the monk's hand. "Sealed by Lady Maude's Peveril seal." After a moment's thought, he jerked his head toward the trembling monk and snapped, "Do you know what's in it? What's the urgent matter she needed to inform the Countess of?"

"N...no, no," the trembling monk shrugged. "I only know that Lady Maude told me it was a matter of life and death, and I must get the message to the Countess with all possible speed."

"If she was in such great haste, why did she entrust the letter to you?" Will Scathelock asked. "You were just ambling along on this little palfrey when we picked you up. It would take you at least another day to get to Peveril Castle. Couldn't she at least have provided you with a stronger horse for the journey?"

"Not only that," Alan a Dale went on before Brother Philip had had a chance to answer, "but truly, I mean no offense, you are one rather frail brother coming down the Great North Road without company or protection of any kind. What was she thinking sending you, by yourself, on this life-and-death mission?"

"I know, I know," Philip said, looking slightly overwhelmed but holding out his hands as if to calm the questioners. "She chose me because I make a regular visit to Peveril Castle on behalf of my priory. It was founded by the Countess's great-grandfather, I believe, and she still gives us regular support. Of course, as you say," and here he looked straight at Alan, "I am always accompanied by a few of my brother monks, but this matter Lady Maude thought so urgent and secret that she wanted nobody else to know I was going. She did not think I would be in danger from…from outlaws like you…because I am carrying no riches. She also wanted to keep my mission a secret from her husband, so she could not be seen loaning me one of her husband's stouter stallions. It was better that I leave Nottingham unobserved," and here he looked at Will Scathelock, "than that I be waylaid by the Sheriff or his men."

"That's it, then," Friar Tuck said, breaking the seal on the letter. "If this matter is as important as you say, then we need to know what it's about."

Tuck unfolded the parchment and began to read. He read quickly and silently, wanting to get to the bottom of this mysterious crisis as quickly as possible, while the rest of the band watched him in an agony of suspense. Realizing this, Tuck held out a calming hand as, continuing his perusal of the letter, he murmured soothing words to the others, "Yes, it's just news about Robin's being accused of the murder…no, nothing here we didn't already know…something about some friar helping the Sheriff with mapping skills. I wonder what that's about?"

"Can you tell whether she wrote this before or after Robin came to see her?" Little John asked, then turning abruptly to Brother Philip asked, "Did she give you this today? This morning? This afternoon?"

"Early afternoon," the young monk replied. "I've only been riding for three hours or so."

"Well, perhaps we should…" the friar began, then stopped and froze, his mouth open and his eyes bulging. Then he looked up and gazed into each of his listeners' eyes. Then he said, "She…

she comes to the end of the original letter and closes it, but then she adds a hasty postscript that explains why she wanted such speed and secrecy for the letter. My friends, this is what Lady Maude writes: 'Postscript in haste: They have captured him! He is a prisoner in Nottingham Castle. Please hurry, my Lady, your influence may be the only thing that can save him! Come yourself! Now!' And that is where she ends. Robin is in the Sheriff's hands!"

The assembled group exploded in shock and horror. Word spread immediately throughout the camp and in a moment Arthur Bland, Sir Palomides, Jock of Barlborough, and the entire outlaw band and their women were surrounding the friar, demanding to know what was to be done now. Two dozen voices continued to talk over one another until Little John's booming voice called everyone to attention.

"This babble ain't getting us anywhere," he boomed. "Now every second may count while Robin is in the Sheriff's clutches. We need cool heads and wisdom to prevail as we think what we are to do."

"Lady Maude has got a point," Will Stutely said, looking around for agreement. "The Countess may have some sway with the likes of Gisbourne and Oxenford, but she's not likely to be of much use at Peveril Castle. And I'm afraid our little Brother Philip here on his gentle palfrey is not going to reach our Countess before the Four Horsemen of the Apocalypse arrive."

"Right," Thorvald agreed. "I can take 'im an' the letter too in my cart, but I don't know that'd be any faster."

Sir Palomides, who had been listening in silence to this whole long scene, stepped forward and laid a calming hand on Thorvald's shoulder. "Your offer is bold and generous, friend Thorvald," the Moor said, "but I believe everyone will agree this is a task that calls for my own action. You all know," he continued, addressing the whole assembled group and turning to take them all in, his hands stretched palms outward as an orator might speak to a crowd, "You know that my great destrier Zulfiqar is the strongest and fastest mount in Sherwood. He is the fastest method of getting me and that letter to Countess Lydia. And I shall bring my sword, my shield and my helmet to deter any of the Sheriff's deputies or Gisbourne's guard from stopping me on the road. And I shall leave now unless I hear someone raise an objection."

He heard no such thing—only Much the miller's son running toward the horses shouting "I'll saddle Zulfiqar and bring him!" Followed quickly by Will Scarlet's shout of "I'll run to your tent and get your arms and helmet!" just before he took off in that direction.

There was a look of welcome relief on the faces of Little John, Friar Tuck, Stutely and most of the others, until Alan a Dale cautiously raised an issue: "This is all well and good, and I agree wholeheartedly that Palomides should take on this task. But even if the Countess leaves the hour he arrives at Peveril Castle, it is likely to be three days before she is in Nottingham. And as I am sure Will Stutely will remember, executions can be arranged very quickly under Gisbourne's watch." All the band nodded grimly at that, remembering Will's own narrow escape from the hangman when he had been in Robin's position not so many months before.

"Then what do you propose," Friar Tuck asked. "Or are you merely pointing that out to depress us all?"

"No, no," Alan said. "All I am saying is that we must not abandon the quest to discover who Lord Randal's actual killer is. If we can discover that quickly, then we can confront the Sheriff with the evidence publicly, and he'll have to let Robin go free."

"Gisbourne does everything in secret," Stutely objected.

"He'd never agree to a public meeting with anyone like us. And he won't care about evidence because the trial will take place behind closed doors. Only the execution itself will be public. And it will be soon."

"Let me see what I can do," Sir Richard said. "Gisbourne and the Sheriff will have to meet with me. I'm a nobleman and a landowner. If they do not do so, I shall stand in the public square in Nottingham and call them out for the cowards and caitiffs they are."

"Tell them you will present evidence of Robin's innocence in open court when called upon," Alan said, warming to the idea. "Do so where the people of the city can hear you."

"Even if you can get them to delay pronouncing Robin's fate for just a few days, it should be enough time for me to bring the Countess to confront them," Sir Palomides added.

"I shall take Dap here as my attendant," Sir Richard continued. "He has steady nerves and a calm hand, and he will impress them with his account of his master's death. Implicating this Lady Eleanor may well be enough to at least cast doubt on Robin's arrest, certainly enough to delay things."

Dap nodded his tacit assent to the knight's decision, and there was a general mumbled agreement among the men, though Alan cautioned, "Perhaps that may be our initial strategy, but I still maintain that Lady Eleanor is a very unlikely killer. Perhaps, after all, Lady Randal *did* kill her son, for the same reason she killed her husband, whatever that may have been. Or perhaps we'll discover, once we have time to examine it, that the murderer was someone else completely."

"It's too bad Wulf has run off and disappeared," Dap said. "He could help to verify my own account if he came along with us to speak to the Sheriff."

"Disappeared?" Friar Tuck asked.

"Yes, after Lord William's death, Wulf sems to have left Randal Manor. He was suddenly nowhere to be found," Dap said.

"Grieving over the loss of his master?" Tuck probed.

"Wulf? Wulf you say?" Sir Palomides called out as he hauled himself into Zulfiqar's saddle while Much held the great beast. Will Scarlet had appeared with his shield, bearing his coat of arms, *Chequy argent and sable*—essentially a black and white checkerboard, and Palomides hung it across his shoulders. Then, sheathing the sword Will had brought him, he asked, "You mean the young lad who kept looking for mushrooms while you were here?"

"What are you saying...mushrooms?" Alan a Dale responded.

"Yes, didn't you see?" Palomides said. "He kept searching the ground on the edges of the clearing, and whenever he saw a mushroom he'd snatch it up and put it in the pocket inside his tunic. Not a very good judge of them, I'm afraid," Palomides shook his head. "I'm an expert on spices and garnishes of all sorts for cooking, as you all know, and this Wulf lad was picking a number of very questionable varieties of the things. But I must be off! See you in three days, if not sooner!" the Moorish knight cried as he shook Zulfiqar's reins and let the great horse take off as fast as it could through the trees.

"Mushrooms," Alan said to himself, thoughtfully.

CHAPTER SIX

Deep in the bowels of Nottingham Castle, Robin Hood lay battered and exhausted on a pile of straw that was the only furniture in his narrow cell. He was actually grateful that it was his feet that were chained to the wall rather than his hands, because it enabled him to lie down in relative comfort on the dirty straw. His eyes were blackened, his nose bloodied, and his lips swollen from the brutal pounding his face had taken from the guard with the ragged scar, whose fists were broad and solid, and who beat him whenever he failed to answer questions posed him by the Sheriff or Gisbourne—which was, unfortunately, most of the time.

Robin had steadfastly refused to answer questions about the number of followers he had in his band, the amount and location of any treasure he had stowed away, the identity of any spies he might have in Nottingham. He had no followers, he worked alone, he told them. He had no treasure stored away— what he had not spent he gave away to the poor (and that was not far from the truth). He had no spies in Nottingham, he told the Sheriff, then added as an afterthought, "Except your wife, who tells me things whenever I swive her!" That was, of course, the most truthful thing he told his inquisitors, and the one they were least likely to believe, thinking it a mere taunt and insult. Robin smiled inwardly at this while Scarface landed a roundhouse punch on his left cheek that cost him two teeth.

"I'm innocent of this charge of murder," Robin kept repeating, so often that it became like a refrain to the rhythm of his beatings. The Sheriff merely laughed at his protest.

"Fool. We don't need a confession from you. We can easily convict you without one," John of Oxenford sneered. "But answer our questions and we can make your death swift and painless. Beheading rather than a slow and painful hanging. Just tell us what we want to know: Where is your outlaw camp?"

Robin tried to evade this question as best he could. Twice he had given answers that seemed absurd. "In the caves under Nottingham Castle," he told them first. Next, he said, "Within the walls of Lenton Priory." They had left off questioning him for several hours after that. Robin guessed that they were actually checking out those locations to see whether he had told the truth. When they returned to his cell Sir Guy had angrily told him that they knew he was lying, and threatened to hang him forthwith, without more ceremony, if he did not tell them the truth immediately.

When Robin realized that Sir Guy and the Sheriff had actually followed up on his claims, he pretended to break down and reveal the real location of the outlaw camp: in the woods outside of Barnsdale. He hoped that his two tormentors would send some of their deputies the sixty miles to search the woods, a task that would take a good four days, and perhaps leave him in peace for that time. They would certainly never believe him again, and Sir Guy would probably make good on his threat to hang him as soon as they found he'd been lying, but Robin thought if he could postpone that eventuality, and save himself four days of beatings, there might be time for his friends to mount a rescue. At any rate, putting off the execution kept him temporarily alive, and where there was life there was hope.

So far his plan seemed to be working, at least for now. It had been quite some time since his last interrogation. In his windowless dungeon, he had no idea whether it was day or night, and the cell was lit by ample torchlight at all times. Still, it felt like a full night had passed since his last beating, and Scarface had even brought him a dinner, or breakfast, of stale bread and moldy cheese, with a cup of what looked like ditchwater. Robin noticed a bandage tied around the guard's right hand, and smiled inwardly with satisfaction, realizing that that last roundhouse punch had perhaps broken a bone in Scarface's hand. But thinking of that, Robin was reminded that his jaws were quite sore, which made chewing painful. Still, he had forced himself to eat to keep up his strength. And so it was something of a surprise when his cell door opened to admit a man he'd not seen before, robed in the white habit and black cloak and hood of a Dominican friar. He carried a satchel hanging from his cincture, which contained several rolled parchments and a round metal object, and after he entered he sat cross-legged on the floor of Robin's cell—just far enough from him to remain out of the outlaw's reach—to look him straight in the eye.

"Good morning," he began, and Robin felt an inner surge of satisfaction that he'd been right about the passing of the night. Still, of course, he wondered what on earth this strange friar could want with him at this point. Clearly, he was in league with the Sheriff and Sir Guy, but Robin felt that he must have his own motives for coming to question him like this, and without his two masters.

"Good for who?" Robin asked, his voice croaking from his cries of pain the previous day, and from his thirst. "And what do you want of me? Your monastery need a contribution, is that why you're popping in here while two great bullies are taking a break from pounding me to a pulp?"

The friar's face twisted upward into a smile, and when he smiled the wrinkles at the corners of his eyes and the sides of his mouth crinkled and stood out in deep creases. It was a round, ruddy face, hard beaten from the weather, suggesting a man who had lived out of doors for much of his life. His eyes were a piercing dark color, nearly black, so that it was hard to distinguish his pupils from his eye color. And the eyes did not participate in the smile the rest of his face assumed. There were streaks of gray in the hair around his tonsure as he reached up to throw his hood off his head, and Robin was soon drawn to the most notable feature in the calm face that looked at him across his cell: The man had the thickest, darkest, bushiest eyebrows Robin had ever seen.

"Save your quips for someone who cares," the friar said. "And don't waste my time with them. I'm a busy man. Now listen: My name is Friar Bungay. I want to show you some things." And with that, the friar reached into his satchel and brought out one of the rolled parchments he had brought along. He unrolled it and held it up before Robin's face. It was perhaps two feet square. In the torchlight, Robin could see a colorful drawing in the shape of a brown and green circle, surrounded and occasionally pierced by areas of blue. Looking more closely, Robin could see parts of the drawing labeled with the names of exotic countries, cities, and seas.

"Have you ever seen one of these before?" Friar Bungay asked. Robin shook his head. "It is what is called a Mapamunde," the friar continued. "A chart of the world. It is an imaginative projection of the shape and scope of all the world's land mass— all three continents—with as much detail as we can include from our current state of knowledge. You see that at the top of the map, the eastern portion, the continent of Asia is depicted, with the lands of India and Cathay and so on. At the bottom of the map, the western half, the two smaller continents of Europe and Africa are presented. You see our island of England here pictured at the far western part of Europe? The three continents in this landed hemisphere were settled by the three sons of Noah—Asia by Shem, Europe by Japheth, Africa by Ham—as is well known. This streak of blue between Europe and Asia is the great midland sea, the Mediterranean, and here, precisely in the middle of the map, at the apex of that sea where the three continents meet, is Jerusalem. God's holy city, at the very center of the world."

"This is all very interesting," Robin said with an uninterested yawn. "But why are you telling me all this? Have you decided that I cannot go to my hanging without this vital knowledge about Mapamundes? Or did the Sheriff send you here to bore me to death, and save himself the expense of a hanging?"

The friar's face crinkled in another of his insincere smiles as he answered, "Please don't interrupt. I'm building to something important for you to know, but I have to begin with these preliminaries so that you will understand." And with that he rolled up the Mapamunde and returned it to his satchel, patiently removing another roll of parchment as he did so.

He unrolled the second parchment gently and carefully, displaying it for Robin's view. This page was about the same size as the previous one, though this one was more rectangular than square, wider than it was long. But it had the same sorts of colorful areas and Robin could see small pictures of things like Nottingham Castle and Lenton Priory drawn near the right edge of the map. Hills, rivers, and certain holy wells and shrines Robin knew of in the forest were pictured as well, though the farther the items depicted were from Nottingham, the sparser were the elements pictured. Robin noticed that Creswell Crags, which had been his company's winter headquarters, were marked on the map. But the area around their current hideout and the Great Oak Tree was currently blank.

"You see, the same concept that produced the Mapamunde can be adapted on a more local level. And for much more practical use," Friar Bungay said. "This, you see, is my current project." Now Robin stood up, moving as close to the friar as he could before his leg irons stopped him. Friar Bungay continued: "By the time this is done, the Sheriff's deputies and I will have been over every square foot of Sherwood Forest. And we will have found your camp. Oh, yes, there is no escaping it. We will be able to locate the precise point of your camp, because this map is drawn to scale. Do you know what that means?"

"I don't know what any of this means," the prisoner answered. "Except maybe that you love to hear yourself talk."

The friar's eyes crinkled again but he ignored the comment as he reached once more into his satchel, pulling out a metal implement that Robin recognized as an astrolabe. "Scale means that a particular distance on the map corresponds exactly to a particular distance on the earth. On this particular map, I've drawn it so that one inch on the map corresponds to one mile in the physical world. Half an inch is half a mile, one eighth of an inch is a furlong, and so on. Do you know what this instrument is?"

"I remember seeing the old king's sage use something like that once. Used to find the positions of stars, aren't they? So what's that to me?"

Eyes crinkled. "Yes an astrolabe is used for that purpose, it is true. But I have found that it has other valuable functions as well. Because knowing the positions of the stars will tell you precisely where you are on the earth's surface, it can tell you precisely where you are in Sherwood Forest. And it can be used to measure the depth of wells, the height of towers, and the distance of one particular place—Nottingham Castle for example—from another—let us say your camp. Have no doubt, Robin Hood, we will find the exact location of your camp soon whether you tell us where it is or not. My two unscientific friends, the Sheriff and Sir Guy, are simply wasting their time trying to beat that location out of you."

"And you've told them that?" Robin asked.

The friar shrugged. "They don't always listen to me. But you would be wise to do so."

"And why is that?" Robin asked in a voice tinged with irony. "You going to tell me how I can escape this prison?"

The eyes crinkled, and Friar Bungay answered in a flat voice, "I personally don't care one way or another whether you live or die. It's all one to me. But I'm trying to demonstrate to you the absolute certainty that your camp cannot remain hidden from the Sheriff's men for long. Our surveying of the forest and my mapping it in its entirety will make it impossible for your outlaw band to hide, run as they might. Your band can move its camp, of course, but it can never be moved to a place that will be unfamiliar or hidden, that is not on this map. Do you understand that point?"

Robin thought that perhaps the friar was a little too confident. Having seen the map itself, Robin knew that the location of the outlaws' camp was not yet covered. But what if they moved to one of the areas already mapped? The Sheriff's men and this pompous friar would be spending a good deal of time mapping the areas that were still blank on the map, and it would be months before they circled back to explore the sections of the forest they'd already mapped. And by then the outlaws could move to another section of the forest mapped much more recently. They could keep dodging the Sheriff's efforts to capture them, perhaps indefinitely, using such a simple device.

He did have to admit, though, that Friar Bungay's project was getting the guards and the deputies off the roads and into the actual forest for the first time. It did make it far more likely that they might stumble upon the outlaws' encampment. And Robin felt a need to get back to Sherwood as quickly as he could to warn his men what was happening, Unfortunately, he was stuck in this cell waiting to be hanged, so his options were somewhat limited.

Robin sighed and looked into the friar's dark, penetrating black eyes. "Look," he began. "You've obviously got some reason for telling me all this, so stop playing these games and say what it is you want from me."

Robin's demand was met not with another crinkle but this time with an exaggerated lift of those weighty eyebrows. "Ah," the friar said. "Now we come to it. I think I have convinced you that it is futile for you to try to protect your base camp. And so I want you to tell me precisely where your encampment is. It would save me a great deal of time, and it would impress Sir Guy and the Sheriff that I was able to extract from you by peaceable means what they could not get through violence."

Robin scoffed. "And why should I do that? Betray my friends in order to make you look good? Have you lost your wits along with your eyebrow trimmers? What would there be in it for me?"

"Well," Friar Bungay began thoughtfully. "It would save you at least several more days of beatings for one thing..."

"You're missing my point," Robin interrupted. "I'm taking those beatings because I *won't* betray my fellows. I could have already told the Sheriff my band's whereabouts if I just wanted to stop the pain. But they're going to execute me anyway—by hanging or beheading, as you so gently reminded me—so why not prolong my life by refusing to give them what they want from me?"

The eyes crinkled again. "You didn't let me finish," the friar continued. "I remind you, I am the one drawing the map. I was going to say that, if you help me, I can pinpoint your camp on the map somewhere far from its true location. And furthermore, I can use what influence I can to lobby for a public trial for you on these murder charges. You are innocent, everyone knows it, and cannot be convicted in open court. And even if you were, there will certainly be a good number of your men at the trial in disguise, and they well have a much greater chance to rescue you."

Robin began to rub his chin in thought, then winced in pain at the touch of his own hand on his bruised jaw. "So what good does it do if you fake the location of our base? Gisbourne's guards will go to the false spot, and know you faked it."

"Not necessarily. I'll simply tell them that your fellows must have become concerned that our search was closing in, and quickly moved camp. It buys your men some time, anyway. As I said, the map will make it impossible for them to hide in the future. But they would be safe for now, and with an open trial you may even be saved. And even if Gisbourne and Oxenford do suspect I tricked them in some way about the site's location, the fact is I don't intend to be staying in Nottingham indefinitely. Once you help me with what I ask, I'll soon be gone."

"Help you with what?" Robin asked, frustrated. "What is it you think I can do for you?"

"You can help me find a particular spot in Sherwood that I and my crew of deputies have so far been unable to locate. Of course, they don't know that's what I'm trying to uncover. No one does. You see, I have no interest in finding your camp. But this search for you gave me the opportunity to talk Gisbourne and the Sheriff into giving me a large crew of men that can help me search the forest. And what I'm truly interested in finding is a place that looks like this."

And with that the friar reached once more into his satchel and brought out a small, blank fragment of parchment and a small inkhorn with a quill pen attached. Quickly he began to sketch a crude drawing of a low treeless hill, one that Robin could see was shaped like something man-made rather than something natural. Perhaps an old barrow from Roman times or even before. At the edges of this mound the friar drew three large stones, and seemed careful to place them in very precise positions around the mound. Robin recognized these as boundary stones. Now the friar held the quick makeshift drawing up so the prisoner could see it plainly.

"I know that you and your men know Sherwood Forest better than any other man alive. So tell me, Robin of Sherwood, are you able to identify this particular place? The picture is not a perfect map, but what does it look like to you?"

Robin, of course, recognized this mound immediately. And he knew it was barely a mile west of the outlaw camp at the Great Oak. It was the place that was called Thynghowe, a hill that his comrade Skipper Haakon told him had been a meeting place for the various petty chieftains during the Viking age in this part of Britain. But he was not about to tell Friar Bungay any of this— not yet anyway.

"It's possible I know such a place," the outlaw answered. "And that I might be able to tell you where it is. But why on earth would I? How am I to know you're not just trying to get me to betray my friends so that you can capture them all and look like a brilliant hero to that numbskull Sheriff and that base liver-eater Gisbourne? And you expect me to trust you, just like that?" Robin snapped his fingers. If this were the ideal scene in his head, he would have stalked out of the room at that point. Unfortunately, his leg irons prevented such a dramatic exit, but he crossed his arms and turned his head away instead.

Not really anywhere near as effective, he told himself.

Friar Bungay's mouth turned up slightly in one corner. "That, sirrah, is precisely why I urge you to point out the location of your camp to me. You show me where it is, and immediately, here in your presence, I will mark it in a different place on this map. This *is* the map I will be showing Gisbourne and Oxenford. That is the best I can do under the circumstances to demonstrate my good faith. Are we agreed then? Will you point out the outlaw encampment?" And he held the map out within Robin's reach, so that the outlaw could take it from him and point to the spot.

Robin narrowed his eyes as he looked into the friar's face, trying to detect the least hint of mendacity there. Here was a man admitting to him that he fully intended to mislead and betray his employers. Why should he show any compunction at the betrayal of an imprisoned stranger? Yet what the friar was holding out to him was more than tempting. An open and public trial? The deliberate misleading of his enemies as to the location of his hideout? Those were benefits worth taking a risk for, though Robin was uncomfortable that the risk was not his own but his fellow bandits', who could be set upon without warning if the friar was lying to him. It occurred to Robin that it might be wise to test the friar, to give him a false location for the camp and see what his reaction would be.

"All right," the outlaw said. "I'll trust you then. There's too much at stake here to do nothing." He took the map from Friar Bungay's hand and pointed to Creswell Crags, the outlaws' winter camp that they had abandoned months before. "Here is where we were encamped when I left my company."

But in answer the friar slowly shook his head and his eyes crinkled with amusement at Robin's pathetic attempt to trick him. "You can see that the Creswell Crags area is already filled in with some detail on the map. That means I and my men have already been there, searching the ground. We did find some evidence of an encampment there some time ago, but no one is there any more." He clicked his tongue and shook his head again. "This will not work at all if we are not truthful with one another."

At last Robin decided he must, after all, commit to this offer, at least to the extent of risking his meinie's location. They would be found eventually anyway by the friar's relentless surveying of the forest, and this opportunity might, after all, buy them some time if the friar was honest. "All right ," he said at last. "I'll take this chance with you. But I warn you that if you betray us, one of my men—someone with the strength of Little John, or one of our great bowmen like Will Scarlet or Jock of Barlborough, will put an arrow right between your eyes to avenge me. And believe me, with those eyebrows of yours, that would be an easy target."

Friar Bungay nodded, assenting to the conditions, and Robin held out the map to him and pointed directly to the blank space on the west side of the map where the clearing of the Great Oak lay. "There is our camp," he said. "With a large clearing at the foot of a great oak tree, hundreds of years old. And a clear brook running a furlong way down a slight slope to the south."

The friar nodded again, studying the blank spot as he took the map back from Robin. First he took a small knife from his satchel and careful scratched out his previous drawing of the hill and boundary stones, as if he wanted no one else to ever see that drawing. Then he took his quill and ink, sat down cross-legged on the floor of the cell, and began to write quickly on his map of Sherwood. He wrote on the east side of the map and farther north, halfway between Nottingham and Worksop.

"There," the friar said rising from the floor and waving the map in front of Robin's face. "Just as I said! This is the map I shall show Gisbourne and the Sheriff. So as I said, you gave me the location of your camp, I deliberately suppressed that knowledge to mislead your enemies. I am a man of my word. Now, if you would give me..."

But Friar Bungay, carried away by his own ego, had carelessly wandered too close to the chained Robin, and the outlaw made a sudden grab for the friar's hood, drawing the struggling cleric closer and into his powerful grasp. He had the friar's back to his chest, his left hand twisting the friar's arm behind his back, his right arm hooked around Bungay's neck, rendering him helpless.

Immediately realizing that any struggle on his part would only result in the pressure increasing around his throat, the friar held himself very still, and spoke slowly and reasonably to the prisoner. "If you believe that I can set you free, I'm afraid you are sadly mistaken. I have no key to unlock your leg irons. I have no weapon on my person that you can take to threaten me or any of the guards that might come. And if I call now for the guards, they will not take kindly to your imprisoning me. If you think that you might hold me hostage till they unlock you, how will you escape? You still will have no weapons and they will. They'll cut you down before you reach the door, and save Oxenford the trouble of trying you."

"And none of that will matter a whit to you if I break your neck here and now," Robin whispered menacingly in his ear. "You've addressed me as if I were a peasant and a halfwit since you entered my cell. Now you listen to me: It is I, not you, who have the upper hand here. You've tried to convince me you can be trusted because you made your markings on a bogus part of a map. But it was an exchange in which I first provided you with information and waited to see if you would follow through. It is an exchange in which I have no power, and am at your mercy. But this second exchange will be different. What you want most of all is for me to tell you where this mound is with the three boundary stones. And if I give you that location, I simply have to trust that you will take these vague steps you suggest to set me free. It's not good enough."

"Then...what are you saying?" Friar Bungay choked out as the pressure increased on his throat. "You're right, I need that information. What is it you want of me?"

"This time *you* need to make the first move," Robin told him. "I will give you the location of that barrow on your scrap of parchment, *after* I am a free man."

He could feel the cleric stiffen. "But I can't guarantee..."

"Then neither can I," Robin answered.

After a short pause, the friar's head moved up and down as freely as it could in that powerful grip. "All right," he said. "I'll do what I can."

"And when I have what I want," Robin told him. "I will give you what *you* want." And he let the friar go.

CHAPTER SEVEN

"Mushrooms!" Alan cried when Sir Palomides had galloped off. "And we have Palomides' expert knowledge that those were mushrooms of a particularly harmful variety. I knew Lady Eleanor could not have been guilty of this crime. This Wulf must have put some of his mushrooms on the plate with the fried eels and killed his master! We should have thought of this before, but sometimes the servants get overlooked."

Dap made no response to this last comment, but did agree with Alan's assessment of the dinner of eels. "Yes, he had the opportunity," he commented calmly. "I remember distinctly that I brought in Lady Eleanor's plate to her, and Wulf followed with Lord Randal's. He could easily have placed some of those mushrooms in Lord William's food when my back was turned. And it would explain why he has not been seen since that day. His flight is a good indication of his guilt, isn't it?"

"People like to say that, but it isn't always true," Friar Tuck said. "But in this case, it seems pretty likely. So it looks like we may have already solved this case, doesn't it?"

"It does," Sir Richard pronounced decisively. "And that is how Dap and I will present it to the Sheriff. We'll bring up the name of Lady Eleanor solely to give context to Wulf's villainy. And if anyone there is so churlish as to impugn Lady Eleanor's honor, I shall remind them that the lady staunchly maintains her innocence, and that Wulf's fleeing from the scene of the crime does much to suggest his guilt. Dap, let us be off!"

Will Scarlet had brought out the horses on which Sir Richard and Dap had arrived, and the pair of them started off toward Nottingham. Meanwhile Little John and Will Stutely, each with an arm around the shoulders of Brother Philip, were steering him over toward the Great Oak to sit and have a light dinner with the rest of the outlaw band, while they were eager to return with him and a small party in disguise to Nottingham, to keep an eye on the progress of Robin's murder trial. But first they had some serious planning to do.

* * *

When Sir Richard and Dap trotted into Nottingham, they left their mounts at the sign of the Prancing Pony. Neither of them was particularly familiar with the city—Dap had been there once in the company of Lord William to see a man about a hawk he wished to purchase, Sir Richard perhaps once a year in his younger days for tournaments and the like. But it was not difficult to see the walls of the recently erected stone fortification, replacing the original motte-and-bailey construction, on the highest point of Castle Rock, rising above the crossing of the River Trent.

"Yonder lies the castle," Sir Richard said, nodding in its direction. "If we're going to see the Sheriff, I expect we'll find him there. If not, this Gisbourne fellow will probably be there. Either of them will be appropriate persons to hear our evidence." Dap merely nodded, and they began the trek uphill to the castle itself. The bustle of the city was an unusual experience for Dap, who was fascinated by the variety of shops along the road—here a wine merchant, there a goldsmith, here a carpenter, there an apothecary, and here and there a tavern with ale and meat pies on display. And the people! The streets were crowded with carts bringing vegetables or leather goods for sale, monks and nuns from nearby houses, royal guards in the charge of Gisbourne, women shopping at the various shops, servants in livery rushing here and there to do their masters' bidding. Sir Richard was oblivious to all this: His only interest was in reaching the castle as quickly as possible to confront the Sheriff of Nottingham and to save Robin Hood if he could do so.

It was less of a walk than Sir Richard had anticipated, and the hill sloping to the castle was less steep, and before he had finished musing about what he was going to say to the Sheriff, he was at the castle gate, and one of the guards, in the black and gold livery of Sir Guy of Gisbourne's servants, was asking him to state his business.

"Sir Richard at the Lee, to see the Sheriff," Sir Richard had told him.

"Right, then, this way, sir," the guard replied courteously. Dap blinked a few times. There really was a significant difference in the way nobles were treated in their dealings with men like the Sheriff.

They followed the guard across the castle's middle bailey to a door leading into a kind of lesser hall where another guard stood at an inner door. "Sir Richard at the Lee to see the Sheriff," the first guard told the second, who nodded and then nodded to Sir Richard, saying, "I'll announce you, my lord," gave a stiff bow and then turned on his heel and entered the door. He popped his head out again quickly and told Sir Richard, "Right. The Sheriff will see you now. Please follow me, my lord."

The knight strode into the hall where he saw the Sheriff beneath an arched window, rising from a large wooden chair at the far end of the room, which was about thirty feet square. He was a squat and portly man of some fourteen stone, with a belly that preceded the rest of his bulk as he moved forward to greet Sir Richard, leaving behind the two clerks who sat with quills poised above parchment at a long desk that was perched on the dais to the side of his chair. While the Sheriff bowed and greeted the knight courteously in his gravelly voice, Dap stood to the side, his hands behind his back, and looked around the room. Large woven tapestries in bright red and blue covered the walls to his right and his left, the one on his right depicting Joshua at the Battle of Jericho, blowing the trumpets that would bring down the walls; the one on the left Christ's entry into Jerusalem with the mobs strewing the street before him with palms. Dap, beneath his chiseled face and stern demeanor, was far from slow-witted, and decided that the tapestries were depictions of good government—Joshua bringing theocracy to Jericho, Christ claiming the throne of David in Jerusalem. Reassuring for the Sheriff's visitors, Dap mused, this suggestion that John of Oxenford's graft and corruption were divinely sanctioned.

He watched the Sheriff's insincere smile that turned his mouth up at the corners amid his gray-streaked brown goatee. He watched him rubbing his hands together in a kind of oily anticipation of what this local nobleman might want to see him about, and how he might turn whatever it was to his own profit. Ostentatiously dressed in a fine blue samite jerkin over improbably red hosen, Oxenford seemed to Dap something of a bloated fop whose opinion of himself far exceeded the opinion of everyone who had ever met him.

"It's not often Nottingham knows the pleasure of your society, my Lord of Verysdale," the Sheriff began. "And come to see *me*—I must say I'm quite flattered by your visit. What is it I can do for you, Sir Richard? Whatever is in my power you shall have, you may be certain of that."

"That is wonderful to hear, my good sir," Richard answered in the same tone of faux sincerity. "I am told you have the outlaw Robin Hood in your power. I shall have *him* if you would be so good as to bring him to me."

The two clerks looked up astounded. The Sheriff gagged and sputtered, and his eyes bulged as if they planned to pop out of his face. His color grew suddenly a dangerous shade of grayish-white as the blood drained from his face and he tugged at the collar of his jerkin as if it had suddenly grown too tight for his neck. Then without a word he spun on his heel and stalked back toward the dais, which he soon mounted and sat back into his chair, his color now changed to a violent ruddiness. Finally finding his voice, he addressed the knight.

"The villein who styles himself 'Robin Hood' is charged with murder and will remain in our dungeons," the Sheriff rasped. "I cannot simply release him on your say so, whatever your rank, *my lord.*" This last he pronounced with a bit of irony, as if he doubted the legitimacy of Sir Richard's title if he were so base as to request the release of a known thief and poacher, whatever may be his culpability in this murder case.

"Robin Hood is no villein, sirrah, He is of good English yeoman stock—like yourself, as I understand, master Sheriff," the knight answered, foregrounding Oxenford's own social status.

The Sheriff, his face growing even redder until it seemed on the verge of bursting from within, now hurled himself back down onto his chair with an angry plop. "Whatever you say, Sir Richard, I must keep the outlaw in my cells until his trial and execution. All the evidence points to his guilt in the murder of Lord Randal, and I intend to keep law and order in my shire. And that means hanging the murderer."

"Evidence?" Sir Richard cried out. "You haven't even looked at *any* of the evidence. I have, thoroughly. And my companion here, Lord Randal's falconer, was with him at the meal served at his sweetheart's, Lady Eleanor's."

"The young lord ate with Robin Hood's brigands earlier in the day. The outlaw is far more likely to have killed the lad than is his own paramour," the Sheriff claimed. "This second meal is merely a red herring."

"Eels, not herring, are what killed Lord Randal, sirrah," Sir Richard countered. "Or rather, poison mushrooms mixed with those eels. Dap's fellow servant, the dog boy Wulf, is the one who poisoned his master thus. Is that not so Dap? You were there."

"I can tell you," Dap began, "that Lord William's hawks and his hounds all died within an hour of having eaten those same eels. And it was scarcely an hour later that Lord Randal died in the same way."

"So you say," the Sheriff said. "But it remains that Lord Randal ate with a known criminal that same morning. And the boy's own mother…"

"Knows that her son died after eating a meal at Lady Eleanor's house, and believes you have arrested the wrong person," Sir Richard said. "Indeed, nearly everyone *knows* you have the wrong man imprisoned. You probably believe so yourself, but have imprisoned Robin simply because you have a grudge against him."

John of Oxenford fumed. He was thwarted by Sir Richard's rank in responding as he'd have liked to the knight's challenges, and sputtered a moment before realizing he could foist responsibility for Robin' incarceration onto another's shoulders. "Say what you will, my lord, but once having arrested the culprit, my own authority over him is done. He is now officially in the charge of Sir Guy of Gisbourne, the king's representative in this region."

Not to be put off by such an obvious dodge, Sir Richard used the opportunity to push for what had been his true objective all along. He knew the Sheriff would never willingly give up his prisoner, but wanted to force Oxenford to try Robin in open court. "So Sir Guy is to be judge in this case, then?" Sir Richard began. "Then I and Dap will be present to give our evidence before the court. And when precisely will this trial take place?"

At this the two clerks looked at one another in surprise and foreboding. They'd never heard of such demands being made in Nottingham since Oxenford had taken the reins as Sheriff. They waited to see what the outcome would be.

"Sir Guy is a busy man," the Sheriff said, thinking he might still deflect this attack. "I'm sure he will hear the case by and by, when he decides the time is right."

"The time will, of course, be soon, and it will be cried through the town, I am sure," Sir Richard insisted. "You may recall that a speedy and public trial is the right of every freeborn Englishman. Which Robin is. Or does English common law no longer hold sway in Nottingham? If that is the case, I am sure the king would be quite interested to hear it."

There was a significant pause before the Sheriff responded, in a defeated growl, "Right. I will consult with Sir Guy and the trial will be set. And it will be announced throughout the city. Now if that is all, Sir Richard, I have my own work to do," and with that he gestured toward the still speechless clerks.

"That is all," Sir Richard said, nodding to hide the hint of smile that flickered across his face. "Good day to you, master Sheriff." And with that he turned on his heel and strode out the door, followed by an admiring Dap, who glanced over his shoulder curiously at the defeated Sheriff.

"And a good day to *you*!" Oxenford snarled, without much courtesy. "And good riddance," he added under his breath. Then he sighed. How was he going to explain this to Sir Guy?

* * *

At the foot of the Great Oak, Little John and Will Stutely had convened with Friar Tuck, Will Scarlet, Thorvald, Jock of Barlborough, Much the miller's son, Davy of Doncaster, John the cook's son, Will Scathelock and a few others to decide on a course of action that would put them into position to help Robin Hood escape the gallows at Nottingham if other options failed and they were forced to stage a rescue. The hapless Brother Philip was pressed into service for advice or information about the workings of Nottingham Castle.

"When I was Sir Guy's guest," Stutely began, "the cells were all below ground level, so there was only a thin strip of a window high in the wall, that barely let in light. Is that still the arrangement there, Bother Philip?'

"I...uh..." the monk stammered, "I don't know. I have never seen the dungeons myself. What rumors I've heard describe them much as you have, so..."

"Who might be granted access to the inner rooms of the castle, would you think? Shall we disguise ourselves as nobles from beyond Nottingham, aristocrats Gisbourne or the Sheriff are unlikely to have ever met, come to town to witness the comeuppance of the notorious outlaw Robin Hood?"

"Um...I can't say," Brother Philip spluttered. "I don't know that either of them has a wide knowledge of nobility beyond the shire..."

"That's not likely to work, though," Will Scarlet said. "It's hard to pull off something like that. There's just too many ways we could give ourselves away as not belonging to the gentry. And though Oxenford's unlikely to know his arse from his elbow, Gisbourne is nobility himself, and could detect us pretty easily."

"What about a group of mendicant friars that, say, you've run into on your excursion, Brother Philip?" Friar Tuck suggested. "Could we make our way into the castle with that kind of ruse?"

"Mmm, not sure," Brother Philip hesitated. "They'd wonder, wouldn't they, why you'd seek housing in the castle instead of coming to the Priory with me, or stopping at some other religious house around Nottingham."

"And you're not going anywhere near the place, Friar!" Little John's voice boomed. "You think anybody in that castle, let alone the Sheriff or Gisbourne himself, would fail to recognize you after your phony 'last confession' of Stutely when we rescued him? And the same for you, Will."

"Now, John..."

"I mean it, Will. Every one of those guards will recognize you, no matter what you do to your clothes or how you hide your face. We can't take a chance on you being recognized."

"Well if we're thinking that way," Friar Tuck pointed out, "then you yourself can't be one of the party, either. You remember how many guards you laid out during that rescue, and how you were arrested yourself? You think they're not going to recognize someone of your size coming into their castle again?"

Little John looked frustrated but cast his eyes to the ground, knowing that Tuck's point was indisputable.

After a moment, Thorvald raised another suggestion. "Now 'ow about we try somethin' altogether different?" he began. "A travelin' troupe o' entertainers? If I come into town drivin' my cart, dressed in some kind o' 'arlequin getup, I'll look like a jester or acrobat, just what they expect from someone my size sad to say. But I bring with me Davy boy there, an' 'e challenges all comers to a wrestlin' match, right? An ol' Jock, the finest archer in England, an' 'e puts on 'is own show, maybe a challenge as well, right? Will Scarlet an' Much an' John the cook's son 'ere can come up with some mummin' or mystery. Too bad we ain't got Sir Palomides nor Alan a Dale neither to 'elp us with a ballad or two, but the six of us ought to be enough to provide a little distraction but be few enough to avoid a lot o' suspicion. What do ya think? Brother Philip, is that somethin' that might get us in?"

The young monk looked down and scratched his tonsure, "Well," he began, "I...uh...I'm not too sure, but I don't think that's too bad of an idea. I mean, there are often entertainments of one kind or another by companies that pass through the town. Even the authorities might welcome a group of performers if people are coming into the city for a trial, if there is one. It would help keep the crowds from getting too rowdy."

"Ha!" Will Scarlet exclaimed. "Maybe it'll be in Robin's interest to help the crowd get rowdy. We can probably handle that as well!"

"Right," Little John concluded, clapping his hands. "Then it's decided, unless anybody's got any objections: Thorvald will lead Davy, John, Scarlet, Jock, and Much into Nottingham town and pose as wandering players, and infiltrate Gisbourne's fortress so as to bring aid to Robin if it becomes necessary. And Brother Philip, you'll accompany them back to Nottingham, and you'll be our liaison to Lady Maude herself, and be on hand in case she or our spies has to get a message back here to us. Right?"

"M...m...me?" Brother Philip stuttered. "But I...uh..."

"Right!" Thorvald and Scarlet interrupted him.

"Right!" Davy and Much chimed in.

"Right!" Jock and John the cook's son agreed.

"R...r...right," Brother Philip mumbled, with a bit less certainty.

* * *

Zulfiqar was a strong grey Andalusian stallion sixteen hands in height, with the powerful and heavy physique of what knights called the Great Horse, bred for use in jousting and in tournaments, in which Sir Palomides had excelled in the old days. The horse was not made for speed or for long journeys, but his strength and endurance gave Palomides the confidence that he could reach Peveril Castle by early morning at the latest, following the wide Great North Road most of the journey. That is, if there were no long delays on the way.

The horse was just settling into a brisk trot that Palomides thought he could keep up for at least a few miles before resting a bit, when one of those delays appeared to be looming about a furlong ahead of him. Six mounted armed men, wearing surcoats on which were emblazoned the sable lion rampant on a field of gold—a crest Palomides recognized as belonging to Sir Guy of Gisbourne himself—had formed a line across the road in front of him. Obviously, they had seen him coming from some way off and had staged this ambush. Palomides sighed. He'd left his chain mail corslet and coif back in his tent at the Great Oak. Less weight for his horse, and more comfortable for himself. Only now, he was wishing he'd worn it. But he did have his sword and shield, and he brought out his helmet, which he had borne before him on the saddle. At least it would protect him from any head wounds, and it would disguise his color as well. He didn't have the time to engage in the kind of ignorant questioning that often arose when he encountered unsophisticated Englishmen who had never seen a Moor before.

The helmet in place, Palomides swung his checkerboard shield before him and grasped it with his left hand, to protect his body as well as display his colors. With his right hand he drew his short sword from its sheath and held it high, so that the waiting guards could have no doubt that he was armed. Zulfiqar, veteran of the lists, responded unerringly to the squeeze of Sir Palomides' knees that urged him forward.

The horse's trot turned into a canter and the six guards broke their formation, each of them unwilling to be the target of this armed knight's gathering charge. The head guard held up his hand uncertainly, calling out, "Stop! In the name of the king's guard!"

"Gisbourne's guard you mean!" Palomides cried as he passed between the troops, none of whom drew a weapon to challenge him, "Else why are you wearing his colors? I have urgent business, and have no time to stop for your foolish prattle!" This last he had to call loudly over his shoulder, as he'd passed the guards' post without having to use his sword.

Six guards from Sir Guy of Gisbourne's Nottingham Castle were left staring after the departing Zulfiqar with mouths dumbfoundedly gaping. After a few very silent moments, the fat one called out to his captain. "Jack, do you suppose we ought to go after him?" There was a good bit of grumbling from the other guards, who wanted no part of tangling with a skilled knight with a war horse and his own coat of arms blazoned on his shield.

The one called Jack answered in a slow, thoughtful drawl. "No...no, I don't think so Hogbody. Better let him go than hinder him, I mean, rushed and harried as he be. A noble knight like that isn't likely to know anything about where a group of thievin' bandits is liable to be camped, is he?"

The guard nicknamed "Hogbody" shook his head. Like almost every other idea one could think of, the idea of this knight's knowing Robin Hood's secret camp had never occurred to him.

And Sir Palomides, by this time half a mile beyond Gisbourne's guards, slowed Zulfiqar's pace and smiled. If every obstacle he faced on the road to Countess Lydia could be overcome so easily, this quest would be a walk in the park.

* * *

Thorvald's cart was barely large enough to hold himself and Will Scarlet in the driver's seat, with maybe one or two passengers in the cart itself. Brother Philip accompanied them riding his own gentle palfrey, but they had agreed that they should bring no other horses aside from Millie, Thorvald's sturdy chestnut mare, to pull the cart. But Much, Jock, Davy and John the cook's son were all coming along, which meant that they would have to take turns walking to make it easier on the horse, and that would certainly slow them down somewhat. But if they were trying to pass themselves off as a poor traveling band of performers, it would look suspicious if they arrived in Nottingham with several expensive mounts. Brother Philip left them at the city walls to amble his way back to the monastery, promising to keep faith and contact Lady Maude as soon as he had checked in with his superiors in the priory. But the outlaws, dressed in old brown or gray tunics and hoods, rolled—and walked—into town, through the city gates, and, after asking directions of a passing servant on High Street, pulled up directly in front of the Sheriff of Nottingham's own house.

"Will, come with me," Thorvald said. "The rest of ya, stay with the cart."

And with that he climbed down and made his way purposefully to the Sheriff's front door. Will Scarlet, not quite sure about this and wishing he'd been consulted beforehand, trailed his mate as Thorvald stopped at the door and pounded on it. In a whisper, Will asked, "What exactly are we doing here, Thorvald? You've thought this through, have you?"

The dwarf had not time to answer before the door was thrown open by Anna, the Sheriff's cook and serving woman, who looked straight ahead and then, startled, looked down into the face of the little person at her door.

"May I help you…sir?" the woman said, hesitatingly.

"Is the lady of the 'ouse at 'ome then, my good woman?" Thorvald asked in his most courteous voice.

"She…*may* be," Anna replied, uncertain as to whether to commit her mistress to seeing this crew of what appeared to be beggars at her door.

"Tell 'er it's Thorvald the Dwarf and 'is Amazing Revelers at 'er door. I'm sure she'll want to see us right quick! Remember the name now, ducks? What is it then?"

"Thorvald the Dwarf and His Amusing Regulars," Anna sighed and, closing the door, said, "Wait here."

"Close enough," Thorvald shot back before the door thudded shut.

"Just what do you plan on doing here?" a frustrated Will Scarlet asked. "What makes you think she'll let us in? And if she does, what then? You've brought us right into the lion's own den. You want to end up in a cell with Robin?"

"Keep yer 'osen pulled up, Scarlet," Thorvald answered calmly. "First, this is the Lady Maude we're dealin' with 'ere, an' ya know she's a protector of Robin's from way back. It's 'er as what wrote that urgent letter to the Countess to come to Robin's aid. So she's on our side, dummy, and ain't about to turn us in to that oaf of an 'usband she's got. Second, she'll meet with us because she's going to recognize the name 'Thorvald' and know it's Robin's men 'oo are out 'ere an' not some wanderin' group o' performers, even though that's what I'm 'avin' 'er maid tell 'er we are. And third and last, my lad, we need 'er to give us a legitimate place in this town. We can say we've got license from the Sheriff 'imself ta perform in Nottin'am, if she gives us a letter ta that effect. So the guards an' the Sheriff's men won't bother us, see?"

"Hmmph," Will Scarlet responded. "That plan's actually not half bad. Maybe there's a working brain inside that hoary head of yours after all. Would have been nice if you'd shared your scheme with the rest of us before bringing us here, though."

"Couldn't," Thorvald admitted. "I didn't actually think of it till we were already in front of the 'ouse. But better late than never, I always say."

At that the door reopened and Anna, scowling down at them, said, "All right then, follow me," and led them into the receiving hall, where Lady Maude Peveril sat in a large wooden chair in a sparsely furnished room. Maude addressed the servant, "You may leave us, Anna." And then added, "In fact, why don't you go to the market square and pick up some fresh vegetables if you can, for the Sheriff's supper tonight."

Anna obediently threw a hood over her hair and grabbed a small basket before leaving the house, grumbling audibly to make unmistakable to her mistress her displeasure at this sudden unlooked-for errand.

"So," Maude began, "now that the prying ears are out of the house, what on earth is this 'Thorvald the Dwarf and his Atrocious Ramblers'? What are you doing here?"

"I gave yer servant the name 'cause I knew you'd at least recognize 'Thorvald the Dwarf.'" Thorvald told her, not bothering to correct the rest of the mangled name. "We're 'ere in disguise to keep our eyes on what's 'appening with Robin,"

"And to help with his escape if it comes to that," Will Scarlet added. "We intercepted your messenger and saw your letter to Countess Lydia. We've brought Brother Philip back and sent Sir Palomides to the Countess—he has by far the fastest horse, and is least likely to be waylaid by guards on the road."

Maude sank into her chair in a posture of great relief. "Thank God," she mouthed. "But why the performing freakshow?"

"We want people to know us as just some innocent acrobats in town to entertain," Will explained. "People will know who we are, but won't be suspicious of us."

"Basically, we're 'idin' in plain sight!" Thorvald added.

CHAPTER EIGHT

When Little John and the others had retreated to sit around the Great Oak and plan their invasion of Nottingham, it left Alan a Dale and Ellen by themselves at the edge of the camp. Alan sat down, his back against another oak, and a pensive scowl on his face. Ellen, who could read his moods like portents of the changing weather, sat down and looked at him questioningly, placing a hand on his knee. Without warning she tickled him through his hosen and said in the funny, high pitched voice she used when trying to jostle him out of a dark mood, "Where shall the hand go next, my pretty one?" And she snorted through her nose like a snuffling beast.

"Ah, Ellie," Alan said, not in the mood to play. "Something's not right here, don't you see?"

"So you don't think our fat friar's assessment that 'This case is solved, praise Jesus!' is correct, then?" she responded. "Why not? It seems pretty clear this Wulf fellow poisoned his master and ran off, don't you think?"

"Oh, I think we can all agree on that part. But think about it, Ellie. What's the servant's motive? Why, after years of serving this master—who was, by all accounts and by our own brief dally with him, a kind and easy master—why would Wulf suddenly decide to kill him? Was William going to dismiss Wulf from his service? Had he done some unspeakable wrong to Wulf or his family or his sweetheart? Did Wulf want to rob his master and run off? How could he do that with Dap and Lady Eleanor there? He ran off all right, but there's no indication he robbed William. No, unless we know *why* this happened, we can't say this case is solved."

"Well, you've convinced me," Ellen said. "But then, I've always been easy for you. To convince, I mean. But what if Wulf had no motive at all? What if he was only acting as the tool of someone else who wanted Lord Randal dead? Someone who hired Wulf, or otherwise convinced him, to commit this crime and then to flee Nottinghamshire?"

Alan nodded, as if this was precisely where his own thoughts had led him. "Right. And until we find out who that person was, this murder is far from being solved."

"We have enough to exonerate Robin," Ellen agreed, "but not enough to give Lord William justice."

"And I want very much to secure justice for him," Alan said. "He was a good man, and one who wanted to marry his beloved in spite of what his family may have thought about it."

"Sounds like you are looking for justice for yourself," Ellen said wryly.

"Not a bit of it," Alan insisted. "I have no family—lost my parents years ago in the old king's war, as you well know. It's *your* family that wanted to prevent our marriage. So...no similarity at all!"

"No. Clearly," Ellen agreed, or pretended to. "So what are we going to do about this injustice?"

"We?" Alan raised his chin and his eyebrows in surprise.

"Of course we. You don't think I'm going to let you tackle this quest for justice by yourself, do you? With a potential murderer at the end of it?"

"That's precisely why I don't want you helping me," Alan

countered. "You think I want to see that pretty little face looking up at me from a funeral bier?"

"And what about your face?" Ellen asked. "It's a lot less pretty, but I've gotten kind of used to it."

"Didn't you make a vow to love, honor and *obey* me? Well you're not coming with me, and that's my final word!"

"And didn't I make a vow to cleave unto you for better or worse?" Ellen argued. "Well, this is the worse, and I'm cleaving."

Alan knew Ellen well enough to know that she had made up her mind and he had as good a chance of changing it as he had of stopping the sun from setting. "So, I misspoke before. That was my semi-final word. Here's my final one, which you *will obey!*" He spoke as sternly as he was able, but he knew she saw through that. "You are to help me out in this investigation, but you're going to be damn sure you don't get killed. Is that clear?"

"Perfectly," Ellen agreed, and folded her hands in her lap in a pose of perfect obedience. "So, where do we start?"

Alan scratched his head, then suggested, "We look for Wulf?"

"Well," Ellen mused. "His fellow Dap didn't know where he'd got to. Who else can we ask?"

Alan shrugged. "All I can think of is talking to Lord Randal's family again. He was employed in that household. Maybe they know something about him. Or maybe one of the other servants does."

"Then that's probably the best place to start, I suppose," Ellen agreed. "But won't they just think of you as a servant yourself? Why would they talk to you?"

Alan, whose gittern was still slung across his back, fingered the strap and answered thoughtfully, "They will probably remember me as the minstrel who sang at Lord William's funeral," he told her. "Perhaps I'll tell them I left Sir Richard's service and set out for greener pastures, and see whether the new Lord Randal wants to hire me. They'll talk to me then. And I'll tell them I've run off with you…you were a kitchen wench in Sir Richard's castle…"

"What's wrong with Lady in Waiting?" Ellen wanted to know.

"Sir Richard's got no wife or daughter, so that's not going to work. And besides, what would a noble lady be doing running off with a minstrel?"

"'Fine," Ellen conceded. "How about I'm the girl who keeps the chickens? Is that above a kitchen wench?"

"It is if you say it is," Alan agreed. "So that's our cover story. While I talk to the family, why don't you talk to the servants, and see what you can find out about Wulf from them?"

"Fine," Ellen said. "But let's get something to eat for now. And let's set off in the morning. If we leave now it'll be dark before we're halfway to Lord Randal's manor. And I don't want to chance being on the road in Sherwood at night. I hear there are outlaws."

* * *

Alan had initially found it a fairly easy task to ingratiate himself with the Randal household. He and Ellen had shown up on the doorstep of the Randals' manor house and when he'd asked to see the master of the house, the servant told them that the master was out, but that the mistress would see them. And so he and Ellen had spent a pleasant hour with old Lady Randal, who was more than happy to welcome the man whose voice had shown her son's soul the way to heaven. Lady Joan, as she begged Alan to call her, was not long in telling Ellen, Sir Richard's former chicken-wench, how her lover had provided her with the only consoling moments she had spent these past two weeks. When Alan told her he had left Sir Richard's employ and set out on his own for greener pastures, and had brought his new wife along as well in hope of finding a position for her, the old woman had actually cracked a smile. And when Alan had offered to play for his supper that evening as a kind of test case, with the stipulation that if the family liked him well enough and he liked the family in return, they would take him on and Ellen as well, Lady Randal had agreed and they had struck a bargain. "You will have to deal with Geoffrey though—the new Lord Randal as is—to make your employment final," she told him. "He is now the master of the household, you know."

"And do you think he'll be willing to give us a place here, then, Lady Joan?" Ellen asked.

The old lady shrugged. "He's touchy and taciturn these days," she admitted. "No doubt all the extra responsibility that's been heaped on his shoulders since William's murder. But the fact is, we're down a couple of servants since that time, so it may be there's room for you two."

Alan's ears pricked up. This was just the opening he was looking for. "Oh are you? I mean, I know that Lord William's falconer, Dap, came over to join Sir Richard's household."

"Yes," Lady Joan shrugged again. "He came to us and told us he felt he could no longer work here without Lord William. Too painful, the memories. Said he needed a new start, and that Sir Richard was willing to give him a position. Well, I can understand that. And Geoffrey is less interested in falconry than William was."

"But you said there were two servants you'd lost?" Alan pressed.

"Yes, that dog-boy of William's has gone as well. That boy named Wulf. Didn't have the courtesy to come and talk to us about it, as Dap did. Just disappeared. Run off I shouldn't wonder. My stars, it's really hard to get good help these days.

Their mothers don't raise them right, that's what I say."

"So," Ellen asked, clarifying Lady Joan's words, "this Wulf fellow has gone, and you have no idea where he is now?"

"Don't know and don't care," Lady Randal replied. "Gone with the wind. Gone to live with the wolves, like his name suggests, as far as I know."

"I see," said Alan. "Pity." He wondered whether it would be wise to bring up the rumor that made Lady Joan her own husband's murderer, but ultimately decided against it. If it had any bearing on the current case at all, it would suggest the possibility that Lady Joan was behind her son's murder as well, and had hired Wulf to poison him at his lover's home. But since the lady had shown no reluctance to bring up Wulf's name, and no interest in his whereabouts, Alan rated that possibility as highly unlikely, and decided to move on.

"Well, I have other things on my agenda," Lady Joan said in a concluding tone. "Stroll around the grounds a bit until suppertime, minstrel. And you, girl, come with me and I'll introduce you to the servants!"

"Ellen," said the "girl" under her breath. "The name is Ellen."

* * *

Dinner at Randal Manor had been a rather dismal affair. Throughout the meal, even when Alan was playing, Lord Geoffrey was as aloof and unwelcoming as he had appeared after his brother's funeral. Lady Joan had been a bit animated when she had announced the planned minstrel's entertainment, and the young Lady Anne had clapped her hands together in glee at the idea. But the new lord's mood had blighted the proceedings, and there were no guests at supper beyond the immediate family, so there was nothing to liven up the occasion from the outside.

Perhaps Alan's choice of songs had contributed to the soberness of the occasion. He had begun with the well-known ballad of Sweet William and his Bonny Barbara Allan, followed by his own rather recent gruesome composition telling the story of the girl Meggie and the severed head of her lover Sweet Willie. Not the most cheerful of songs, and Alan was all ready to end with a rollicking jolly ballad of Robin Hood when he realized with a start that this was not the time and place for such a story—this family had been led to suspect Robin Hood in the murder of their son and brother, and though they all seemed to have focused their suspicions on Lady Eleanor instead, Alan was still hesitant to introduce the bandit into the dinner conversation, since he wanted to make sure nobody at the manor associated him or Ellen with the outlaw band. And so he ended his performance rather lamely with the wistful lyric

> *Western wind, when wilt thou blow*
> *The small rain down can rain?*
> *Christ, that my love were in my arms,*
> *And I in my bed again!*

The family only looked puzzled over that snippet, though the elegiac tone of the words was certainly clear. Lady Anne applauded with some emotion after that, and Lady Joan clapped politely for a moment, but Lord Geoffrey rose from the board, cleared his throat, and said without ceremony, "You play well, minstrel, but rather dolefully, and the last thing we need at our table these days is a tragic muse. Thanks for this evening. You can have supper with the servants. But we won't be needing your services after tonight. Can't really afford to take on another servant right now anyway. Now I can't sit around making merry. I've got responsibilities to attend to."

And without more ado, he stalked off to look at his account books.

Lady Joan, with a wan smile, shrugged her shoulders and added, "Oh, I *am* sorry master Alan. I suppose I got it wrong earlier. But the ballads were well sung. I'm sure you won't have any difficulty finding employment elsewhere. And now I'll leave you as well. Anne dear, perhaps you can show our minstrel guest the servants' quarters where he can sup himself, won't you? Good evening, sirrah." And off she went as well.

The fair Anne, who like her mother had dressed for supper in an embroidered gown and hidden her ginger hair beneath a white wimple, waited until Lady Joan had left the room and then smiled, her green eyes twinkling, and began her wonted chattering that Alan had expected after her behavior at the funeral.

"Be at ease, Master Alan," she began. "I see no reason for you to eat with the servants. Be seated here at our table and I'll call Roger to come in and bring you a trencher with meat and gravy, and a flagon of our spiced claret wine—I don't think you'll find a better anywhere, and you must be dry after performing those tunes. I really liked the 'Barbara Allan' one, you know. Such a sad story. Such a hard hearted girl, that Barbara Allan. You won't find me acting that hard hearted, I can promise you that. No, no, don't deny me good minstrel" (Alan had just bowed slightly in prelude to begging her not to bother, and insisting he join the servants in their meal), "I will not take no for an answer. Oh Roger! Roger! Oh there you are" (the cook's server had just poked his head in the door), "quick now. Bring Master Allan here a plate and some wine, will you? That's a good chap."

"Lady Anne," Alan began, "Please, I…"

"Now, now, you're not allowed to say me nay, you know. Courtesy requires you must do what a lady demands, and despite your lower class, you should be taking lessons from your betters, else how will you ever get on in aristocratic courts as a resident minstrel, for heaven's sake? Sit, sit, sit!" the young lady demanded, and Alan sat, completely vanquished. "Now there you are," the girl continued, standing over him like a master at some monastery school, about to drill him on his exercises. "I was curious to hear what my mother said to you about being wrong earlier. I understand she is the one who hired you to entertain for supper—and really, I'm abashed at the fact that there were only the three family members for super tonight, but that's just the way it worked out. We have several guests coming for tomorrow, and I suppose if Geoffrey had been less stingy he would have hired you for that party. I'm sure it's what mama had in mind when she booked you for this evening. She intended to test you no doubt, to see whether you were to be hired for the larger event. I could see that she would have been glad to have you but Geoffrey put his foot down on *that*, didn't he? Well no matter. Now what was I saying?"

"Um…" was Alan's dazed response.

"Oh that's right, I was asking you what my mother meant when she said she was incorrect earlier. Ah, here's Roger with your dinner. Just leave it Roger, will you? Good lad."

Roger, who at a burley forty years was hardly a lad, dropped a trencher and a mug of claret at Alan's place at the table, grumbled something resembling "Ma'am" and disappeared again from the dining hall. Alan, thankful for something to do with his mouth, since he wasn't going to use it for getting a word in edgewise any time soon, tucked in gratefully. He really was hungry and thirsty after his performance.

"Well?" Lady Anne demanded looking crossly at Alan, who had just realized there had been a lull in her monologue. He thought for a moment, and then remembered she'd asked him a question.

"Yes, right," he began. "Lady Joan suggested to me that the household might well be able to afford to give two new servant positions to my...my paramour and me. Obviously, Lord Geoffrey's estimate of the household purse differs from Lady Randal's."

"But we're poor as church mice in our little family," Lady Anne seemed to agree with her brother. "Whatever gave mama the notion that we had oodles of money to give away to new servants?"

"Well she said that because you'd lost the two servants recently, there may be room for us to join..."

"Oh *those* two," Lady Anne broke in, wrinkling up her nose as if the food on Alan's trencher were five days spoiled. "But they weren't house servants after all, they were my brother's falconer and his dog boy. Dap I suppose served well enough, and was useful to have around, even if he *was* expressionless and dull as ditchwater. But that other one! Surly as they come. No, I won't miss him a bit now he's run off to seek his fortunes elsewhere. Always hanging about mooning over me like a lost puppy. I mean, did you ever hear of such a thing? As if I would countenance such unseemly behavior. I wouldn't have him in the house. Nor mother neither. I'm quite happy to see him gone. But no, those two were not house servants. There's no room in the household to replace them, not with the pittance Geoffrey has got in his purse."

"Pardon me, my Lady," Alan said as Lady Anne paused momentarily to take a breath. "Did I not hear you say at the funeral that Lord William had left all his gold and silver to you? If the household is in severe monetary straits, and since you live in the household, oughtn't you to perhaps contribute a bit of that money to the upkeep of the place? To pay servants, for instance?"

"Oh, you think to cajole a position out of me then, do you?" Lady Anne responded, feigning a kind of affronted benevolence that had done all it could and yet was faulted for not having done more. "I have very little. Very little. My brother William left me what he had, but what he had, once we'd scoured the manor house and any coffers he owned, was far less than I was led to expect. Believe me, he had led me to expect there was something...well, never mind all that, suffice it to say I've been rudely disappointed in this whole affair. So no," and here she gave a mirthless little laugh, "don't think you're going to wheedle a living out of *me*, sirrah."

"That was hardly my intent, my Lady. I was merely..." and here Alan was cut off again, but this time not by Lady Anne but rather by his own wife, as Ellen had suddenly appeared in the doorway from the kitchen. She was dressed and appeared ready for the road, and she said, "Husband, I've just been informed by our host, Master Geoffrey, that we are not to be given any sort of position here in the manor. Though he was not so churlish as to deny us shelter here overnight, I have no wish to impose upon the hospitality of this house longer than necessary, and I suggest we leave now, while there are still a few hours of daylight left where we can make our way to a welcoming inn or tavern, where perhaps you can ply your talents again and bargain for a room for the night."

"And in good time, too," Lady Anne responded huffily. Alan was at a loss to figure out what he had said or what had occurred to cause the sudden change in her favor toward him. She called her servant Roger and told him to show the guests out, and he and Ellen were ushered to the door without more ceremony.

Ellen, following the time-honored advice that, in polite society, one should always respond to people *as if* they had said or done the courteous thing, managed to ask Roger before the door shut on them, "Please thank your master and mistress for their kindnesses to us this afternoon, and tell them how much we enjoyed their pleasant company!" She got no reply beyond the sound of the heavy oak door closing.

"Well," she said, gazing up at Alan with a sparkle in her clear blue eyes, "that is one strange household."

"We'll have to exchange the stories of our separate dining experiences," Alan said. "But come now, Ellie, we've got a good walk ahead of us." They had, of course, brought no horses, since if they were indeed a poor itinerant minstrel and his mate, they'd have been unlikely to own a horse. But Sir Richard at the Lee's castle in Verysdale was only a few miles from the Randal Manor, and though they knew Richard was currently in Nottingham, they were sure that, as members of Robin Hood's band, they would be welcome there.

"So did you learn anything useful from that strange trio before we were so decidedly shown the door?" Ellen asked.

"Useful?" Alan considered. Then he shrugged. "Who can say at this point? I learned that Lord Geoffrey is cold, moody, and downright unfriendly. Or maybe it's not unfriendliness so much as it is arrogance? Maybe he just doesn't like associating with social inferiors like us."

"Or maybe he's got secrets he doesn't want anyone to know about. Like just why his brother was murdered."

"Well if that's it," Alan replied brushing away a low hanging beech branch that hung over the narrow road toward Verysdale, "he's keeping those secrets locked up pretty tight. As for his sister, she's awfully annoying with that perpetual-motion mouth of hers. She was very friendly, in contrast, but then toward the end quite suddenly seemed to grow angry with me and nearly pushed me out. I didn't understand it at all."

Ellen paused a moment, stooped down and picked a few deep purple Michaelmas daisies from along the side of the road that lay in full sun. She began absently weaving their long stems to make a garland for her hair as they walked, and as she contemplated what Alan had told her. "People talk a lot when they are nervous," she said. "Perhaps Lady Anne was nervous because she, or the rest of the family, had something to hide. What had you been talking about right before she grew angry?"

"Well, I know I was trying to get her to open up a bit about the servant Wulf, and I said something about there being two open positions for servants in the household, since Dap and Wulf had both left. And suddenly she seemed defensive and said they had no money to pay us and I should stop trying to get money out of her and leave."

Ellen let a small smile light up her face. "Well," she said, "maybe the family really doesn't have much money, or she doesn't want to part with it. But that sounds suspiciously like an excuse. If she was warm and friendly up to that point, it may be she was trying to flirt with you. That could have made her nervous and might be behind the chattering. And perhaps your mentioning that you had a woman with you who also was looking for a position stopped her little coquettish act right in its bloody tracks."

Alan stopped and twisted his face into a frown of disbelief and surprise, mixed with a touch of gently-stroked ego. "Am I that irresistible to the weaker sex, then?" He asked, fishing for a spousal compliment.

"Not so much the weaker sex, perhaps, as the weaker *mind*," Ellen said without batting an eye. "But did you find out anything new about our friend Wulf and his relationship with the family?"

Alan shrugged again. "Only that no one seems to have been overly fond of him. Both Anne and the old Lady Randal—the only one of the family who seems the least bit normal to me— dismissed him as a kind of nonentity in the household. No one seems to know or care anything about him."

"Yes," Ellen said. "I found similar attitudes among the servants when I ate with them. He had no friends among them, and nobody seemed to know much about him, or could suggest anyplace he might have gone when he left here."

"Well, this trip has been a classic dud," Alan complained. "We know no more than we did when we started."

"Oh, I wouldn't go so far as to say that," Ellen said, a teasing tone in her voice. "You haven't heard from me what *I* learned yet."

"No?" Alan said, raising his brows to their natural apex. "And what did you learn from the servants, dear?" He asked perfunctorily.

"We got into the rumors about old Lady Randal and her husband. And I got the directions on how to find Sarah, the children's old nurse, where she lives now in Southwell. If we can believe the servants—and you usually can—this old Sarah knows more about this household than anybody alive, more than all three Randals combined. Let's pay her a visit, shall we?"

CHAPTER NINE

L ady Mary of Winchester rode with her long blonde locks secured under a St. Briggita's coif, which capped her head and held her hair in place in a cloth bag at the back. She was mounted astride a strong bay rouncey, her leather boots in the stirrups and the skirts of her simple woolen gown hiked up to give her legs some freedom. She wore a brown cape and hood, but the hood was thrown back and the cape draped behind her on the horse's back. It was a long ride to Nottingham and she cared little for her appearance. All she cared about was arriving in time to save her beloved Robin Hood from the gallows.

Her mistress, Lady Lydia Peveril, Countess of Chesterfield, was dressed more fashionably in an olive-green gown of fine linen with which she had somehow managed to cover her legs well past the tops of her own riding boots. A royal blue cape billowed out behind her, its hood covering her head, where her own hair was swathed in a white silk veil embroidered with gold threads, which was held in place by a barbette around her chin. Her own mount, a beautiful black Andalusian mare, trotted in front of her at a pace Lady Mary feared her own mount would have difficulty keeping.

But it was Sir Palomides' powerful war horse that was setting the pace. The knight had arrived just a few hours before and, having delivered Lady Maude's plea for help, presented his own arguments as to why it was imperative that the Countess drop everything and immediately make the long ride back to Nottingham Castle. There was not a moment to lose. The outlaws' experience with the Sheriff of Nottingham's justice after Will Stutely's arrest had given them a sour foretaste of just what Robin would face in a court of the Sheriff's devising: a foreordained verdict, a sham of judicial proceeding in which the accused was found guilty in absentia and without legal representation, followed by immediate execution. And without someone of worth and rank to advocate for him, that would be Robin's fate, even to the point of execution in private, without witnesses.

The Countess had been doubtful as to how much weight her voice would carry on its own but upon hearing that Sir Richard at the Lee would also be using his influence on Robin's behalf, the Countess agreed. Palomides, allowing a scant two hours to rest and refresh himself and his horse, had urged Lady Lydia to travel as light as she possibly could and to take only a single retainer rather than her whole household, as that could only slow them down. The knight wanted to arrive in Nottingham by the following day—the third day after his own departure.

Lady Mary, who had been well known to Sir Palomides since before the fall of the late king, had insisted on accompanying her mistress and would brook no denials. Known to her friends as "Maid Marion," she had been smitten by the gallant and notorious outlaw from their first meeting, and while there were serious impediments to their love culminating in anything so socially acceptable as marriage—they were of two widely differing classes, for one, and then of course there was the whole king of the forest bandits thing—she was still ready to risk her life and reputation in his defense. Palomides and the Countess knew there was no talking her out of this determination, and didn't try.

While the Countess rode ahead with Sir Palomides at a fast walking pace, Marion rode behind with Sir Eustace, the commander and senior member of the Countess's household guards, the two of them trying to keep up but gradually falling farther behind. Their horses were simply not as fine or as fast as Lady Lydia's or the Moorish knight's, and so they did the best they could and made conversation between themselves. Sir Eustace, well past his prime in his mid-fifties, was far less of a deterrent than Palomides to would-be bandits or, significantly more dangerous, Sir Guy of Gisbourne's guards. Still, he was another sword to support the doughty Moor, and Marion knew him to be as brave and faithful a retainer as could be found in Nottinghamshire.

Sir Eustace was taller than average and sat bolt upright in his saddle. His eyes were hazel and his hair a salt-and-pepper shade of gray, though his full beard was pure white and trimmed back so as not to hang down out of his helmet when it was necessary for him to wear one. They were all hoping that it would not become necessary to do so on this journey. Yet Sir Eustace still carried a shield, on which was blazoned the Peveril family crest: three sheaves of wheat argent, or silver, on a field azure. Accordingly, he also wore the silver and blue livery of Lady Lydia's household.

Marion had been lost in her own thoughts for the first part of the ride, letting her mind range back to her first brief dealings with Robin—Robin Kempe as he was then called, when he was chief of the old king's castle guards. Then years after the king's fall, she had run into him by accident as Robin Hood, captain of the outlaws of Sherwood. Well, "run into him" was something of a euphemism. His men had captured her and her companions with the intent of robbing them. *Had*, in fact, robbed them, Marion now recalled with some irritation. But he had in the meantime flirted with her shamelessly, and kindled something in her that had bloomed and flourished ever since. And when in gratitude for their rescuing her from kidnaping, the Countess had named Robin and his men as her official foresters, essentially taking them under her protection (without, in fact, actually requiring any service from them), Marion hoped to see far more of him. That, alas, had not transpired. But that fact had not lessened her affection for him. And to have him now held in a dungeon by his keenest enemies! She was not sure she could hold up, and her imagination saw her beloved hanged, or broken on the rack, or killed even more gruesomely. She began to grow faint at these fancied horrors.

Beside her Sir Eustace had cleared his throat and Marion realized he had been doing so off and on for several minutes. Apparently he wanted to say something but was hesitant to break her reverie.

"Oh, Sir Eustace, forgive my failure in courtesy," Lady Mary addressed the venerable knight. "I was truly lost in thought. But I would converse with you now with pleasure." Anything to channel her brain in a less frightening direction.

"My Lady, I merely wanted to ask if you are comfortable?" Sir Eustace said with gruff voice but tender heart. "Would you not, perhaps, have preferred a side saddle on such a long ride?"

Marion scoffed. "*Those* things. How does one even balance on such things? I can see myself falling forward onto my face in the mud if I urged my horse to move faster than a gentle trot. It would take me a week to get to Nottingham, and we've got to get there in time to save my...to save Robin."

Sir Eustace's hazel eyes danced for an instant, amused by the image of the Lady Mary falling in the road. But his face sobered quickly enough in empathy with her. "My Lady," he said, his head bowed toward her deferentially. "If your intent is to keep secret your love for the outlaw, I'm afraid you have failed miserably.

You cannot keep the love from your eyes whenever they gaze upon him, or your excitement from your limbs whenever you anticipate his presence. I doubt if there is a single servant at Peveril Castle who is not aware of your attachment."

Marion, abashed by Sir Eustace's frank comments, tried to brush them away. "Nonsense," she said, the flush in her face belying her words. "Robin has been very helpful to the Countess, and to me, in the past, and so we must both be very concerned about his imprisonment and anxious for his safety. That is all. I cannot, as you well know, love one of his class. If I am to love— or to marry—it must be someone with noble ancestry."

"Of course, of course," Sir Eustace agreed, backing off slightly and sitting more upright in his saddle, breaking the intimacy they had momentarily achieved. He rode in silence for several minutes until, unable to maintain that mask of indifference any longer, he spoke to the point again, though this time less directly.

"There are precedents, you know," he began. "There is a story going around saying that the young Marquis of Saluzzo in Italy has taken to wife a peasant girl, can you imagine?"

Marion snorted. "I can well imagine what his *subjects* think about that. To be ruled over by an heir sprung from peasant blood? Heavens, what next?"

"There's even an emperor from Byzantium I heard of who married an innkeeper's daughter," Sir Eustace added. "Of course, she ended up poisoning him, they say, so that might not be the best example," he deadpanned.

That actually brought a smile to Marion's face, despite her concerns. She teased the knight, "So how do you know about Byzantine emperors?"

"When I was a young man, I traveled to the Holy Land on a crusade," Sir Eustace confided. "It gave me a good deal of time to learn about Constantinople and its rulers."

"Truly?" Marion asked, taken aback. "You? On crusade?"

"Well, as I say, I was much younger," Sir Eustace modestly responded. Then after another few moments' silence, he continued. "I was the second son of a noble house—my father was lord of a manor on the coast of East Anglia. With nothing to inherit, I was drawn to the holy wars, hoping, I suppose, to win some wealth or even some land there if we were victorious. Of course, we were not."

"No," Marion mused. "They never are. At least in my lifetime. But I suppose you did enrich your soul in the Lord's service."

"Well, that is what the priests tell you. I can't say my soul felt any more enriched than it did before I left. I can't say killing Moors as noble as your Sir Palomides there made me any holier. But no, the true reason I went on crusade was to impress a certain young Countess, hoping to astound her with my martial skills and make her father willing to bestow her on me in marriage."

"So you were in love with her?"

"I was not," was Sir Eustace's startling reply. "I wanted the lands and title she came with. No, in fact, the woman I was truly in love with was a commoner who lived and worked in that Countess's castle." Sir Eustace sighed.

"A commoner?" Marion blurted out, incredulous.

"Indeed. Her name was Abigail. She was a servant in the Countess's employ, and helped her dress, brought her dinner, was at her beck and call. When I visited the Countess, I did so out of duty and necessity. But what I truly looked forward to was stealing moments of love, of ecstasy, with my beloved Abigail in some deserted room or corner of the castle. I looked forward to marrying the Countess because it would mean I would always be near my Abigail."

"Why didn't you simply marry the servant girl?" Marion asked. "It's easier for a man. You could have chosen whoever you wished. You had no inheritance to worry about. Women of the noble class must wait on their father's decisions as to whom they are allowed to wed. The Countess could not have married you. But the servant girl could have."

"And followed me on an itinerant life of wandering from court to court to find service with some great lord?" Sir Eustace replied. "It would have been no life for her. She had security where she was. At least I thought she did."

"What do you mean?"

Sir Eustace sighed again, this time a deeper and more heartfelt sigh that seemed to drain the strength from his body. He slumped forward on his horse and then began his answer. "While I was on my crusade, the Countess's castle had been attacked and sacked by a large party of Vikings who'd been sailing along the coast of East Anglia and saw that castle as an easy target. In truth, it was not well defended. Everyone in the castle was killed. My Abigail had most certainly been—" he struggled for a courteous way to say it—"meddled with before her throat was cut." His voice broke and he could say no more for several minutes. Marion said nothing. She blinked away her own tears and gave Sir Eustace space to resume his narrative at his own leisure.

"I did not expect to be telling you all of this now," the knight apologized. "Even my Lady the Countess does not know all of it. But I tell you this as…as a kind of warning. A story with a moral, let us say. To act on my love, no matter what others may have thought, no matter about class or ambition, was my truest course, I realized too late. There is no sadder feeling than too late. And I have felt that feeling for thirty years."

Taken aback by this confession and exhortation from Sir Eustace, Lady Mary felt faint on her horse and stopped to take some deep breaths. As she did so, Sir Eustace whispered to her. "I'll say no more after this, my Lady. But let me simply say: You have no father. You have no uncles. No family at all any more, and no property or manor whose inheritance you will be responsible for. If you choose to say yes to the outlaw, who is there shall say you nay? Not the Countess, it seems to me. Let us rescue your outlaw, and then see where your heart lies. Isn't Robin Hood's whole way of living a rebellion against social status? Remember the popular adage: *When Adam delved and Eve span, who was then the gentleman?* Think about it."

* * *

Lady Maude Peveril sat in her husband's office in Nottingham Castle, her arms crossed defiantly across the bodice of the embroidered kirtle she wore over her blue silk chemise. She was angry, staring at the Jericho tapestry and wishing Joshua would come to Nottingham with his trumpets and bring the walls of the castle down on her husband's head, and take with him hatchet-faced Sir Guy of Gisbourne as well.

"Lady Maude, I cannot concede your argument. You seem to be assuming that the law exists at the whim of the peasants, whereas in fact it exists for the sole purpose of keeping the peasants from transgressing the boundaries established for them by God, through his Regent the king, and the king's agents, which is to say, myself and those of my class and position." Gisbourne delivered his lecture while standing, as if he were a learned master at the university. Vain as any peacock, he strutted back and forth between the two sides of the dais on which Maude and her husband sat, his dark flowing locks streaming behind him like the unfettered hair of a maiden. Maude looked into the Sheriff's eyes and saw them gloss over. She knew he would just as soon yield to her request to try Robin Hood in open court, but was continually being prompted by Gisbourne to deal harshly with the outlaw to set an example. And Gisbourne's arguments were much better informed than Maude's were.

"You say that the artisans and merchants of Nottingham, and the peasants roundabout, would be discontented if the villein were put to death in a court untainted by public sympathy," Gisbourne continued. "How is that justice? Justice must be disinterested and transcendent, like God Himself. The emotions and sentiments of the masses of people are prejudicial. If I am to judge—and as the king's representative here I must be the judge—then I must do it unswayed by the voices of the ignorant rabble."

"Yes, yes, but Sir Guy, it is not merely the common rabble lobbying, as my wife says, for the outlaw to be judged in open court," John of Oxenford maintained. "It is, as I've told you, the nobleman Sir Richard at the Lee as well, who strode boldly into my hall here and demanded a public trial. Says he has evidence of the outlaw's innocence and demands the right to testify. Says Robin Hood is a yeoman of the shire and as such is guaranteed an open and public trial by his rights as a free-born Englishman according to English common law. Whatever *that* is."

"This is nonsense," Sir Guy scoffed. "Who would presume to tell God that He must submit deliberations on justice to the common view? And isn't the king the same as God? And am I not the same as the king in Nottingham? This argument is pure poppycock. Besides, what is one nobleman's opinion worth, when I can assure you that dozens of barons and prelates—the Bishop of Hereford for one—are demanding Robin Hood's execution?"

"The Bishop of Hereford!" Maude spat. "That oily tongued oligarch! He's had a grudge against Robin Hood for ages. And you say you don't want to be prejudiced by the opinions of others? What hypocrisy. You mean you don't want to be prejudiced by people with whom you disagree!"

Sir Guy glared at Maude with eyes that would have burned holes into her skin for an instant until a quiet "ahem" from the rear of the dais, at which Gisbourne's new cartographer Friar Bungay had been sitting recording the meeting for future reference. "If I may, Sir Guy?" he began tentatively, a fixed smile on his lips and the corners of his eyes crinkling.

"By all means," Gisbourne answered expecting support from the friar against the Sheriff and his stubborn wife. "What is your learned opinion on this matter?"

Friar Bungay cleared his throat again, stood up, and came to the front of the desk at which he'd been writing. "I must agree with Lady Maude, I'm afraid," he said, at which Sir Guy blew out an angry breath and Lady Maude smiled coyly, looking down at the floor. "What this Sir Richard at the Lee contends is quite true. There is a new spirit abroad in the land, and it begins chiefly with the barons, that holds that no nobleman nor any freeborn man in the commonwealth may be imprisoned without due process of law, including a public trial and, in most cases, a trial by jury. As I say, it is not a concept originating in the 'common rabble' as you call them, but among the nobles themselves. It ensures that the king—or his officers, Sir Guy—may not impose flagrantly arbitrary and capricious sentences on individuals. It places the law itself above the king."

Sir Guy rankled. He found the concept revolting. The people must be held in check by an iron hand. Otherwise you got chaos, not a peaceful commonwealth. You got outlaws running free in Sherwood, blatantly defying the law and their social betters. You got, in short, Robin Hood. But this man, this Friar Bungay, had proven himself an invaluable ally in recent days. His learned skills in the area of mapping the terrain were making his search for the permanent camp of the bandits easier and easier. And this friar had been able to wheedle a confession from Robin Hood about where that camp was, a spot halfway between Nottingham and Worksop that Bungay had pinpointed on the map that very afternoon. Gisbourne had every intention of sending the better part of his guard to that precise location tomorrow if possible. But if he had to keep the guard in Nottingham to provide security for a public trial of the outlaw, it would delay their deployment elsewhere. So he was not yet ready to concede defeat on this point.

"Come, come, Friar Bungay," Gisbourne answered. "Can you show me a single noble here in Nottingham or roundabout, aside from this radical anarchist Sir Richard, who is willing to say a good word about this villein Robin Hood? Can you?"

At that point one of Gisbourne's armed guard strode into the hall and stood at attention, drawing Sir Guy's notice by calling out, "My lord?"

Annoyed, Gisbourne answered, "Well? What is it?"

"There is a Countess Lydia of Chesterfield at the door, demanding entry, and demanding that you turn over to her the prisoner Robin Hood immediately."

* * *

When the Countess of Chesterfield stormed into the Sheriff's chamber with her three companions, it was with the single-minded purpose of saving the life of her friend and one-time savior Robin Hood. The outlaw's attachment to her household as her official "forester" was essentially a legal fiction: It enabled him to claim her protection, even though the only time Robin spent at Peveril Castle or its grounds was when Lady Lydia invited him there for a feast. And it hardly protected him from prosecution for crimes committed outside of her jurisdiction. Or at least it might not. Lady Lydia was about to find out.

"Sheriff," she demanded, ignoring Oxenford's and Gisbourne's awkward attempts at courtesy in their greetings to her—as well as their manifest surprise and apprehension at the sight of her sturdy Moorish companion. "I am given to understand that you have taken into custody my servant, Robin Hood, and have imprisoned him without trial and without my being informed of his arrest. This is highly irregular, and violates my prerogatives as a peer of the realm. Am I not to have the right to maintain justice in my own manor? I demand that you bring him to me at once, and let me be the judge of my own servants!"

Lady Maude had perked up noticeably at the news that her cousin had arrived, and now felt a surge of relief, and of pride as well, that her message had reached the Countess in time to bring her to Nottingham. The fact that she had brought that little blonde hussy Lady Mary of Winchester with her undercut Maude's joy somewhat, but she could pass over that for the moment, for Robin's sake.

The Sheriff was dumbfounded and could only respond with a few inarticulate burbles. Sir Guy, however, was not about to be told his business by a woman, peer of the realm or no, and made his position quite clear. "Lady Courtesy," he began with precise correctness. "We were unaware that the outlaw Robin Hood had a formal connection with any English noble, let alone yourself. However, that does not protect him from crimes that may be committed outside of your jurisdiction, and the murder of Lord Randal took place at a manor within the jurisdiction of Nottingham. Accordingly, the Sheriff here made the arrest and I, as the king's official representative in this city, will serve as judge in this case."

"Oh will you indeed?" the Countess came back at him. "You think the king's commission to man the fort here gives you that authority?"

Sir Guy shrugged. "Martial law. There is no recognized local government here outside of the castle, and so it falls to me to see justice done."

"Then see to it!" the Countess demanded. "Justice in this case demands that the prisoner be well treated, not thrown in a dungeon where he may be brutalized by your guards, Gisbourne!"

Sir Guy reddened, not from shame at his rough treatment of the prisoner, but at the Countess's omission of his title when she addressed him, as if he were a servant of some sort. The Sheriff, cognizant of his own complicity in this affair, began to babble again with unintelligible excuses. But Lady Lydia continued:

"And of course the trial at which you pronounce your just verdict must be public, as justice also demands."

"And witnesses who have evidence to bring before the court must be heard as well," Lady Maude added, to ensure Sir Richard's testimony, and that of the servant Dap, would not fail to be brought forth.

"Precisely!" the Countess agreed. "As my cousin Lady Maude points out, all evidence needs to be examined. Now where is my forester? I demand to see him immediately to ensure he is not being mistreated."

"My Lady," Gisbourne answered, stubbornly holding his ground but feeling blindsided by the revelation that this Countess was close kin to the annoying wife of this buffoon of a Sheriff. "You cannot expect to examine the cells of Nottingham Castle, a royal fortification, without the consent of the king himself!"

Throat-clearing again from the back of the dais, once more the scholarly friar stood up, his eyes crinkling and his ponderous eyebrows moving up and down in anxiety over speaking once more before these exalted personages. "If I may interrupt again, Sir Guy," Friar Bungay interrupted, "I think you will find that a peer of the realm may command, in the name of the king, such a privilege, particularly since she outranks you in terms of the social hierarchy." And after a moment's silence, the friar added, "My lord."

Sir Guy's haughty manner eased somewhat, as it might in one who can see that he has lost a battle but has no intention of losing the war, and he relented on this point. He beckoned to his guard, who had not left his post at the door, and addressed him clearly, "Jack, take Lady Peveril to see the outlaw Robin Hood in his cell. But only the Countess. Her retinue, such as it is, must remain here." And with this his eyes surveyed with undisguised contempt the young blonde girl who seemed nearly overcome with emotion, the old knight who was obviously well past his prime, and the freakishly dark-skinned Moorish knight who must have taken up with this Countess because no one else would employ him.

"Before that happens, Sir Guy," the Countess continued. "I need your promise of the free and open trial of my servant. And I need you to set the precise day, time and place of the proceedings." On this she would not budge.

Having already yielded the lesser point, Gisbourne gave in on the greater as well. If everyone was going to push him for this open trial, then let it be. The judgment would still be his. And he told the Countess, "Very well. An open trial will take place here, in this chamber, the day after tomorrow, at the hour of nones. Let it never be said that the king's justice is..." and here he tried to remember what Friar Bungay had said, "arbitrary and capricious. Now go, my Lady, and visit your outlaw."

Having said that, he leaned forward to speak confidentially into Jack's ear, "But make sure somebody cleans him up first. Make him look halfway decent at least."

"It'll be hard to disguise the bruises, my Lord," Jack responded in the same low tones.

Gisbourne pursed his lips. "Well," he said, scowling in concentration. "Make sure the light isn't any too good in the cell, anyway."

Jack bowed slightly toward the Countess, and said, "Please follow me, my Lady." But before he led her out of the room, Lady Lydia took a small bag from Maid Marion, intended for delivery to Robin's cell.

CHAPTER TEN

Thorvald the Dwarf and his Amazing Revelers were causing quite a stir on the lawn outside Nottingham Castle. They'd set up an eye-catching array of entertainments designed to attract the attention of the crowd of onlookers that thronged about the castle on the morning appointed for the public trial of the notorious outlaw Robin Hood. There was a carnival atmosphere about the town, due to the celebrity status of the defendant. The greater part of the assembled masses thought of Robin as a kind of counter-culture hero for the laboring classes, and if they did not know of specific instances of his generosity to their own neighbors had at least heard legends of such deeds. And all of these believed that Robin would be acquitted of the charge of murder since, as it naturally followed from his reputation, he could not be guilty.

Thus Thorvald and his revelers had been busy from the moment they had set up at prime, and had grown busier as the morning wore on. And although immediately after setting up they had been hassled by two of Gisbourne's guards (whom they nicknamed "Pudgy" and "Grungy," for obvious reasons), the permit composed and sealed by Lady Maude had done the trick, and for the rest of the morning they were tolerated by the authorities, who had more things to worry about than a group of itinerant players.

On one side of the green, a space of lawn had been roped off where David of Doncaster demonstrated his wrestling skills. Thorvald himself acted as a kind of barker for David, shouting to the assembled crowd, "Come on, you brawny he-men of Nottinghamshire! Try your luck with the Doncaster Destroyer! He may look young, but he's never been beaten! For one small penny, you can buy yourself a chance at winning this fine longbow—" and he held up a well-made six-foot bow of aged yew with a flaxen string. It was David's own bow, but he was fairly certain he was not putting it at risk. His likely challengers—city apprentices, or farm laborers given a holiday because of the unprecedented interest in the day's events—were likely to be inexperienced and over-confident in their own strength. And David knew they were no match for his skill and experience. And so by this time, he and Thorvald had racked up well over a shilling in winnings.

Across the lawn, Jock of Barlborough, was giving a demonstration of archery such as few in that crowd had ever seen. With Thorvald's cart as a backdrop, Jock was shooting cups of ale out of the hand of brother Philip from a distance of twenty yards. The young monk had kept his word. He had shown up that morning to serve as liaison between the outlaws and the Lady Maude, who would be inside the castle at the trial. He was to move back and forth between the lady and the Sherwood men, to report on the progress of the judicial proceedings and to keep the men posted in case they needed to mount a rescue attempt. But in the meantime, before the trial began, he'd been persuaded to help Jock with his demonstration. To Philip's chagrin, that "help" was to collect wooden tankards from the various outlaws, tankards from which they had just chugged the ale, and hold them out by their handles so that Jock could get a bead on them and shoot them out of his hand. "Don't shake so much, Brother Philip," Jock kept murmuring to him. "It mucks up my aim!" While this was going on, Much the miller's son was circulating among the spectators, finding scoffers who were willing to bet on the outcome of each shot. Much knew that Jock would never miss at that distance. But the spectators didn't know that, and Much was raking in far more than the wrestling show was making.

But Will Scarlet was drawing the largest crowd of all. On a makeshift stage raised a few feet above the ground close by Thorvald's wagon, Will was performing a series of conjurer's tricks he'd learned as a boy from an itinerant juggler who had spent a few nights in his small town. Will had started by magically making an egg dance in the palm of his hand without touching it—a trick that involved a hollowed out egg and a fine strand of long fair hair affixed to the eggshell by a drop of white wax tied around the finger of his free hand. He followed this up by cutting a long piece of rope in half and then magically restoring it to its original length—which he did by using a bit of sleight of hand to make the audience believe he was cutting his rope in the middle when in fact he was really cutting it near the end, and when he "restored" the rope, no one noticed it was just a little bit shorter than it had been. Then Will asked if there were any member of the audience who was completely fearless. A number of young men, hoping to impress some young woman or other, volunteered, and Will chose a tall, muscular fellow with an iron looking jaw and long blond locks. For this trick, Will held a lit candle between his fingers, secretly holding a palmful of incense ground into dust.

"Are you ready, fearless fellow?" Will asked his volunteer.

"Ready for whatever *you* can do!" the fellow responded, earning a cheer from the crowd for his bravado in the face of the conjuror. Will raised the hand with the candle toward his lips and blew at the incense dust, which caught fire and flew through the air straight at the volunteer's face. The fellow yelped in fear as he saw the flaming sparks flashing toward him, but they disappeared quickly and never burned him at all, and the fearless volunteer slunk back into the crowd, abashed, while the audience applauded Will's sleight of hand.

But Will's favorite trick involved making coins disappear and reappear. To make this work as desired, he had John the cook's son planted in the audience. John who looked like one of the simple spectators himself, was called on by Will to donate a coin from his own purse to help demonstrate the trick. John pretended to be reluctant to part with a penny from his purse, but finally did so at the urging of others in the audience. Will took the coin, made a few magic signs over it, snapped his fingers, and the coin disappeared, to the astonishment of the audience and the chagrin of John, who whined that he'd lost his coin. The coin had really disappeared up Will's sleeve, of course. But then Will astonished his onlookers even more by pulling a coin out of John's ear—which had come, of course, from up Will's other sleeve. But it happened that this coin was a sixpence, to the delight of John and the other onlookers, several of whom volunteered to donate a coin next. Of course, the next coin—a shilling—disappeared, only to be replaced by John's original penny. This process was repeated several times, and occasionally Will allowed an audience member to exchange a sixpence for a shilling, but generally the audience were losers in the transactions, and Will had made several shillings' profit by the time the trial had begun in the castle.

* * *

When the notorious bandit Robin Hood was led into the hall that had been set up as his courtroom, he was unencumbered by any irons on his wrists or his feet. The Countess Lydia had demanded that these be removed, since they would have given onlookers the false impression that Robin was a criminal. She had further brought Robin a change of clothes, so that he appeared not in the Lincoln green livery of the outlaws of Sherwood—clothing that was bloodied and soiled from several days of imprisonment and the gentle questioning of Gisbourne's guards—but in the silver and blue livery of members of the Countess's own household. His hosen were gray and his tunic a soft azure blue embroidered with three sheaves of wheat in silver thread.

Thus when Robin appeared in the hall, if it were not for the two guards who held him gingerly by each arm, he looked no different from anyone else in the courtroom. The Countess, Sir Palomides, Sir Eustace, and a pale and anxious looking Maid Marion stood in the front row of spectators. Robin had eyes only for Marion as she stood directly facing the dais on which he was made to stand, at the right side of the seated Sir Guy. To the left of them the Sheriff and Friar Bungay sat at a desk, Bungay acting as clerk so that there would be a record of the trial. Robin locked eyes with Marion, and tried by his expression to silently reassure her that all would be well, somehow.

Also in the front row sat Lord William's family—the new Lord Geoffrey Randal, his weeping mother, and the young Lady Anne, who had been provided with stools out of respect as the family of the deceased. On the other side of them stood Lady Maude, feeling a bit miffed that, after all she had done for Robin, the outlaw was making eyes at that little blonde minx Lady Mary. And to Maude's right were Sir Richard at the Lee and Lord Randal's former servant Dap, who were eager to be called as witnesses in this affair. And finally, at the end of the first row and happy to have three bodies as a buffer between her and the victim's family, stood Lady Eleanor. She wore a simple mourning dress of black-dyed wool, and behind her wimple and veil she was clearly weeping.

This front row of spectators was flanked on either side by members of Gisbourne's guard, some of whom were also stationed at the doors of the hall. Behind the first row most of the gentry and a number of the artisans of Nottingham were packed, while others crowded around the doorways and even larger crowds waited for news on the lawn outside the castle, where they were being entertained by Thorvald the Dwarf and his Amazing Revelers. And as Robin was being led to the dock, Brother Philip was making his way through the crowd to join Lady Maude, from whom he expected to take messages back to Thorvald and his troupe.

"This court will come to order!" Gisbourne began in his most pompous voice. "This is the King's court, and any disorder will not be tolerated. My guards are here to keep order, and have instructions to eject anyone causing any sort of disruption in the proceedings. Now then," and on that note he turned toward the accused. "You, sirrah. We know you by your popular pseudonym of 'Robin Hood.' I charge you to state for the record your full name."

"I am called Robert fitz Ooth of Locksley," Robin answered with a straight face. Marion closed her eyes with exasperation, while Maude smirked, recognizing the aristocratic-sounding alias that Robin used when he was in the mood.

"Well then, Robert fitz Ooth of Locksley, you have been charged with the murder of Lord William Randal, whom you did poison…" (at that an obviously cautioning cough came from the neighborhood of Friar Bungay, and Gisbourne corrected himself) "whom you are alleged to have poisoned at a meal served at your outlaw camp in Sherwood. How do you plead to the charge?"

"I am pure as the soul of a new-born babe," Robin answered, much to the amusement of the majority of spectators, who tittered at the plea.

"Note that the prisoner pleads not guilty," Gisbourne said, glancing at the friar and the Sheriff. Then, since Sir Guy had ignored the Countess's plea for a trial before a jury of Robin's peers on the grounds that they would probably find him innocent, and had therefore refused to allow any advocate to conduct a defense of the accused, Gisbourne began to question the prisoner himself. "Now then Locksley," he began, and Robin needed a moment to recognize that it was he who was being addressed. "Do you admit that you did in fact feed Lord Randal and his two servants on the day he died?"

"The three of them were our guests at dinner, yes," Robin answered. "All three left with full bellies and very healthy constitutions."

"But he died shortly thereafter!" Gisbourne cried, as if clinching his case.

"As, I learned later, his dogs and hawks died as well. And we fed neither hawk nor hound in Sherwood."

Gisbourne looked irritated at the response, and cautioned Robin, "You, sirrah, are here to answer my questions, not to go off on your own tangents. Tell me why this lord and his men were eating this dinner of yours."

"Some of our men had met them on the road," Robin explained, "and thought that they looked hungry." It did not seem to be the place to bring up the robbery. And Robin's response brought another ripple of laughter from the spectators.

Sir Guy, feeling he was losing the sympathy of the audience—if he had ever had it—glared at the spectators and warned, "I won't have this court turned into a jester's stage. Any more disturbances and I'll have my guards clear the place!" Countess

Lydia scowled and pointed a finger at Gisbourne threateningly. Clearing the court would break his promise of a public trial, which was Robin's only chance. Gisbourne shot the next question at Robin through gritted teeth: "Tell me, Locksley, what was the poison that killed Lord Randal?"

"Since I did not give it to him, I cannot say. Perhaps if you were to examine the hounds and the hawks who died after eating the same things he ate at the meal he had later, you could answer that question yourself."

Sir Guy's hatchet face clouded again and he seemed on the verge of cautioning Robin a second time when Countess Lydia stepped forward and called out, "Gisbourne!" Sir Guy blinked, appalled not only by the Countess's interruption but also by the audacity of the woman in omitting his noble title. But aware that as a peer of the realm she outranked him, he could not very well deny her.

"There are men here who witnessed Lord Randal's death," she continued, "and who have information as to who really killed him. Are you going to waste more time with this charade, or are you going to examine the facts of this case?"

Gisbourne reddened from the base of his neck to the edge of his scalp. There was nothing he hated more than to be made to look a fool before witnesses—in this case the whole patrician society of Nottingham. But he could not risk proving himself an incompetent judge as well, so against his own inclination and bias, he called Sir Richard to the stand.

* * *

"And as soon as Sir Richard testified, the game was up [pant, pant]. It was clear to everyone that Sir Guy could never find Robin guilty on the facts of the case, and if he simply ignored the evidence and pushed a guilty verdict through anyway, every person in that room—the family, the girlfriend, the gentry of the shire, the Countess herself—would recognize the decision as…now what did Lady Maude tell me…? Oh yes: 'arbitrary and capricious,' that was it [heave, pant]."

Brother Philip, badly winded from his run, was relaying the news from Lady Maude's side back out to the lawn where Robin's men remained entertaining the crowd, and was beaming in satisfaction at being able to bring them the good news. David, Jock and Will Scarlet were continuing their entertainments, but Thorvald, John, and Much had gathered around Philip to hear his report.

"So Sir Richard testified and that was it? They let Robin go? Where is he?" Much the miller's son, hungry for answers, was impatient with how long it was taking Brother Philip to serve them.

"Oh no," the monk replied. "Sir Guy wanted everything corroborated a hundred times over. So Lady Randal gave the evidence that Lord William had come home very ill, that his hounds and his hawks had already died, and that he suspected he was poisoned at Lady Eleanor's house, since the animals had died after eating the leftovers from his plate there. Then Lady Eleanor herself was questioned, and she said yes, she had served the eels to Lord William, but had no reason to want him dead— she had planned to marry him, she swore. And she explained how Lord Randal's own men had served the meal. Then the falconer Dap came to the stand and talked about serving the dinner at Lady Eleanor's house, and how the dog-boy Wulf had brought in Lord William's meal. So then that Moorish fellow who runs with your band, the black knight, said he had observed Wulf collecting poisonous mushrooms at your encampment on the day Lord Randal died. There was a sigh of relief from Lady

Eleanor at that point, and some outcries of anger and chagrin from the Randal family, crying about what a brute Wulf was for betraying his master. The girl Lady Anne was especially vehement in her vitriol against Wulf, saying she'd like to chop up his own mushrooms and stuff them down his throat if she ever saw him again."

"So *then* they let him go?" Much repeated.

Brother Philip held out his hands palms down as if to say, be patient, I'm coming to that, and he continued: "The Sheriff himself spoke out then—Lady Maude said she knew he would, since to let things go on any longer would make not only Sir Guy but also himself look like fools before the whole town, unable to admit the truth even when it was biting them in the arse—and the Sheriff says, 'It's obvious now that the murderer is this dog-boy, this Wulf, who has turned on his master and killed him and, as I understand from the Randal family's reaction, has run off.'

And the new Lord Randal, this Geoffrey Randal, says, 'He has, and no one can say where he's gone.' And the Sheriff says, 'Then my men will make it their priority to track down this killer and bring him to justice. I'll give them that task after this trial is ended.' And Lady Maude said under her breath, 'Notice he doesn't say how *long* after. Sometime around Saint Never's Day, I'd wager.' And after that, Sir Guy simply said the court was adjourned. And Lady Maude sent me out here to bring you chaps the glad tidings."

Now Much squinted at Brother Philip, weighing what the monk had just told him. "So, yer saying you never heard Sir Guy pronounce Robin as innocent, or order him to be released, is that what yer tellin' us?"

Brother Philip looked perplexed, and began to babble, "Well, I...that is, Sir Guy...I mean, I'm sure that he...well why wouldn't he...? I mean, he must have done. Later. But Lady Maude...she wanted me to bring you the...the good news right away...so I didn't stay."

"Understood," Thorvald responded. "But now you've delivered it, we need you ta get back in there, Laddie, an' come back to us when ya've learned what they've done with Robin. If 'e's not released, 'e's gonna be needin' us to rescue 'im. Go now."

Brother Philip nodded and, having just recovered his breath, turned heel and ran back to the courtroom.

* * *

The courtroom, now returned to its status as lesser hall of the castle, was nearly empty by the time Brother Philip got back to it. The Randal family was just coming out of the door as Philip reached the entrance, and they were snapping at one another like distressed dogs. When would they get justice for their kinsman? When would the Sheriff's promise to seek the murderer Wulf begin, or was he simply making promises he couldn't keep in order to stave off any complaints they might have about the shoddy way this affair had been handled? And Wulf had been gone for what? Well over a week now? He could be in London by now. Or even out of the country. How could he ever be found? How could William rest in peace with his killer on the loose and unpunished?

Brother Philip could sympathize with this family. How frustrating it must be to learn that the man responsible for the murder of their son and brother was free and escaped, with only the incompetent and venal Sheriff to rely on to track him down. But all those thoughts were driven from his mind as he stepped into the room.

The first thing he saw was Robin Hood, wearing chains on

his legs and his hands, being roughly shoved from the room by five armed guards in Gisbourne's livery. Sir Guy and the Sheriff had already left the room, and Robin was being followed slowly by Friar Bungay, whose head was bowed as if in prayer. Philip's mouth gaped in shock and horror, and then he saw Sir Palomides, Sir Eustace, and Maid Marion on one side of the room in animated conversation, Sir Richard, Lady Eleanor, and Dap on the other side in an attitude of defeat and despondency, with Countess Lydia and Lady Maude clutching one another's hands in the center, the Countess weeping and Maude comforting her cousin, while looking as if she would burst into tears herself at any moment.

Philip made straight for Maude, forgetting all courtesy in his bafflement and blurting out, "What's happened? How could they take Robin back to the dungeons? Wasn't he proven innocent?"

"Innocent of the murder, yes," Maude answered. "But we did not reckon on the depths of treachery in Gisbourne's heart. Yet I must admit, his depravity does not surprise me. It's my own husband's at which I am astounded. I suppose he has become all the more perfidious by association with Sir Guy."

"But...I...I don't understand," the monk said. "What have they done?"

"Dismissed the charge of murder," Lady Lydia said between sobs, "and then ordered Robin's re-arrest on the charges of robbery and poaching the king's deer. And they are likely to hang him for that if they can get away with it. Oh Maude, my dear, I *should* have come with a show of power. I thought speed was of the essence, and I thought my influence would be enough to free him. Now I see that Gisbourne sees himself as petty king of this region, and will answer to no one. But by all that is holy, I *will* break his power. Let him beware that I don't break his *neck!*"

CHAPTER ELEVEN

When John of Oxenford had called for Robin's re-arrest after he'd been acquitted of murder, the outlaw had stood a moment dumbfounded, but quickly shook off his stupor and tried to run. But he'd been surrounded by five guards, and despite Robin's landing a few significant punches, he was finally subdued and put into irons. It was a soul-killing reversal that the Sheriff had not had the courage to announce before the gentry of Nottingham that had gathered in that hall, and so had waited until they had emptied the chamber. Oh, they would hear the news of Robin's arrest all right. But away from the heat of the moment, which after the exonerating evidence would almost certainly have resulted in a spontaneous uprising against the arrest, those same nobles would be less moved to take any action in a situation that really did not concern them personally. And so no one was around to object to Robin's new arrest beside the Countess and Sir Richard and their small groups. And what could they do against so many armed guards?

Perhaps Sir Palomides and Sir Eustace might have combined with Sir Richard to put up a defense, if any of them had realized initially what was going on. But by the time they recognized Robin's danger, he was already in irons and being rushed off the dais, and two more guards were standing between them and the five who were leaving with Robin. And violence at that point may well have put in danger Lady Lydia, Lady Mary, and possibly Lady Eleanor as well, who was still in the chamber. Lady Maude, as the Sheriff's wife, was probably safe, though putting her in a cell overnight might do a lot to tame the boldness of her spirit, at least from her husband's point of view.

And so Robin was forced back down the corridor leading to the castle dungeon. They brought him back to his same cell and dragged him inside, hooked his iron chains to the stone wall and made to leave, but not before Scarface, his right hand still bandaged, fetched Robin a roundhouse punch on the cheek with his left hand. "Just for good measure," he said, and spat at Robin's feet.

"Now, that's probably unnecessary," soothed Friar Bungay, who had followed them all into the cell.

"What d'ya mean?" Scarface grumbled, holding up his bandaged right hand like a trophy. "Look what he did to my hand! I got to get some of my own back."

"Hurt your fist with his face, did he?" Bungay replied, then tsked his tongue at them and shook his head. Then, loudly clearing his throat in an authoritative manner he said, "I need to stay here and question the prisoner for a while. You all can go back to your duties."

"Gisbourne didn't give us any orders to that effect..." began Jack, the officer in charge.

"That's *Lord* Gisbourne to you," Bungay snapped. "He left it up to me as to when I wanted to do the interrogation," he explained, assuming the role of quasi-commander. The guards had seen him coming to the dungeons in order to question this prisoner before, and the friar assumed they would take his word for it now.

Jack shrugged, grumbling to himself, "Sure, don't tell us anything. We're only the guard after all." Then more loudly he answered, "All right, Master Friar, you can have him. Boys, let's go back to the lesser hall and make sure those stragglers leave the place. We certainly don't want any of *them* walking around the castle unattended."

But as they turned to go, Friar Bungay stopped Jack. "Before you go, you'd better leave me the keys. I don't want to get locked in here, and I don't want to leave the door unlocked when I leave with *him* inside." And on the "him," Bungay nodded toward Robin as if the outlaw were Satan himself chained in Hell.

"All right," Jack answered, handing the ring of keys over to the friar. "But be careful with that one. He's a slippery devil, he is."

Robin held his tongue as he and Bungay waited for the guards to leave, but when the door had clicked shut the outlaw burst out in anger and frustration. "'Oh, don't worry your pretty little head,' says the clever friar. 'Leave everything up to me,' he says. 'I'll get you off this murder charge,' he says. 'You can trust me,' he says. Well I trusted you, and look where it's got me! Right back in the same cell, and not a chance to get off on *this* charge. 'Cause guess what? I'm guilty as the devil himself of robbery and poaching. And there's plenty of evidence—all the Sheriff's got to do is call in any of the pillars of society I've robbed over the years. I thought Lady Lydia would save me," and with that he paused and looked at his silver and blue garments, "but all she did was dress me in her livery, so I'll go to the gallows as her servant and not as a free rebel of the greenwood."

"Stop ranting and listen to me now," the friar said, keeping his voice low. "We may not have much time, and besides, one of those goons may be listening at the door for all I know. You had your public trial, didn't you? You were in fact found innocent in the case of the murder, weren't you? How on earth could I have predicted that that bumbling Oxenford would arrest you for another crime before you'd even left the court after your *first* trial? So stop blaming me for what didn't happen and start trusting me for what I still may be able to *make* happen." He took a breath. "So. You promised to show me on my map the precise location of that hill with the three boundary stones."

Robin scoffed. "I told you I'd show you that after I was a free man!" Holding up his chained wrists he asked, "Do I look free to you?"

"Not yet," Friar Bungay answered, his eyes crinkling momentarily in amusement. Then he held up the ring of keys. "But you're about to."

* * *

Lady Mary of Winchester was inconsolable in her grief. "I've never loved before," she managed to gasp out between tears. "And if Robin is taken from me, I never shall again. I care nothing about the difference in our rank. Nothing in life is worthwhile for me if he is not part of it." On that note Sir Eustace gave a grim smile and nodded to her with understanding.

But it was Sir Palomides who answered her. "My Lady," he began, "that is the true love of which troubadours used to sing. Of which I *myself* used to sing. And which I myself used to feel. When my beloved Isolde was cruelly taken, I mourned without ceasing. Even though I knew she was not mine and would never be mine, I shed bitter tears and vowed that I would never love again. That life was no longer tolerable. But I survived. Look on me now. Would it have been better if I had yielded to my grief and died of a broken heart? I went on. I have remained as doughty a knight as I ever was. I have lived a worthwhile life. And who knows? It may even be possible for me to love again." With that he glanced at the Countess, and then went on. "But

Robin Hood is not a lost cause. There still may, there still must be some way to free him. If nothing else, I will bring his entire meinie here to storm these walls. They'll not let their captain die without a fight."

"Well I for one have not been in love in that way, and I'm not about to leave myself open to such grief as you're talking about without putting up a fight," Countess Lydia said. "I've said I won't have my authority challenged by an upstart crow like this Gisbourne, and I won't have them abusing my retainers with impunity without putting up a fight. Now here's what I propose to do: I'm going to London."

"London?" all three of her companions exclaimed.

"That is where the new king, this Constantine, has his court. He'll see me—he has to, I'm a peer of the realm. And I'll tell him what's going on here, and the kinds of abuses that are being carried out in his name by these arrogant scoundrels. I'll bring back a royal pardon for Robin. Perhaps I can even get him to rescind Gisbourne's authority and appoint some new castellan for Nottingham. But I need to start now."

Sir Palomides considered the plan, and then objected. "My Lady, give me this commission. Write a message to the king and give it to me to deliver. I can make better time on Zulfiqar, and we certainly must recognize that they will want to execute Robin speedily. It is a long way and arduous for one of your delicate..."

"I'm not so delicate as all that," Lady Lydia snapped. "You think just because I'm a woman, I'm not up to the journey? The Great North Road is wide and well maintained between Nottingham and London. And my horse is a good one. Besides," she looked frankly at Palomides. "You think the king will deign to meet with a Moorish knight when he turns up at court? You'll be lucky he doesn't throw you in prison, as an outlandish foreigner."

Palomides looked abashed, but he could not argue with the Countess's logic. Still he persisted, "Then you must allow me to ride with you. You're sure to need protection on the road, and whatever you say about your own fortitude, you are not trained with sword and shield as I am."

"And I," Sir Eustace added, bowing deferentially. "You shall not go without me, my Lady."

Maid Marion, her weeping quenched and her resolve redoubled, added her own voice. "I can't see that I can do much good here, with Robin locked away. I'd like to come along with you as well, my Lady. I know Robin better than anyone, I'd wager. Even you, Sir Palomides. Perhaps there are things I can tell the king about his character that others could not."

"It's settled then," the Countess declared. "Let's pick up our horses from the stable and ride."

* * *

"Well that feels better," Robin told Bungay after the friar had unlocked the fetters that had bound his hands and feet. "But," he added, rubbing his wrists to coax the blood back into them, "I'm still hardly free, am I? Even if you get me out of this cell, how do I escape the castle itself? As you so persuasively put it the last time I had the pleasure of your company, I can never make it to the castle gates—I will have no weapons and the guards *will*. How did you put it? 'They'll cut me down before I reach the door, and save Oxenford the trouble of trying me,' Wasn't that it?'"

The friar's eyes crinkled. "Indeed it was. And it was completely true. But I was talking about what would happen if you tried to escape by yourself. Yes, the armed guards patrol all the passageways in the castle. But there is another way, and I can show it to you."

Robin still hesitated. "And I should trust you why?"

The friar shrugged and his massive black brows shot high on his forehead. "Why would I risk my own life unlocking you if I didn't intend to take you all the way to freedom? Listen: There are tunnels underneath this castle. The hill it's built on, this Castle Rock, is made of sandstone. You know what that is?"

"Of course," Robin said. "You think I'm a complete imbecile?"

"Not complete," Bungay said. "Sandstone is about the softest stone there is. Easy to dig into. There have been man-made caves and tunnels through this hill since the Norsemen first occupied the area, hundreds of years past."

"And you can get me into one of these tunnels from here? Without the guards seeing?"

"I made sure of it," Bungay answered. "There's a trapdoor leading straight into a cave right here in the prison wing—I believe they actually have dungeons down there as well, though they're disused now."

"All right," Robin said. "Let's not waste any more time. Get me into those tunnels and if they catch me again, it's my own bloody fault."

"First let's do this," Bungay said, beginning to pull off his black Dominican robes. "If you are dressed as a friar, no one will pay any attention to you once you get out of the castle. The guards will be looking for Robin Hood, not a religious. Take my habit, and give me that livery of yours. I'll just be another anonymous servant of your Countess Lydia. We can get away more easily that way."

"We?" Robin responded.

"Of course," the friar answered. "You think they won't know who let you go? I've got to say goodbye to this place as well, and disappear."

Robin saw the sense in this and quickly stripped off his silver and blue livery and donned the friar's robe and hood while Bungay pulled on Robin's tunic. "That's it then," he said. "Let's go!"

But Bungay still was not moving. He shook his head and produced the map of Sherwood he had just taken from the inner pocket of his habit. "There's one more thing. You think I'm doing this out of the goodness of my heart? Show me on this map where the hill with the boundary stones is. That's what I need from you. And then we'll put this place behind us for good."

* * *

"So it's that sniveling little snake Wulf that I have to thank for destroying my hopes of a future life with my beloved Lord William and for ruining my own reputation," Lady Eleanor complained as she walked out of the castle in the company of Sir Richard and Dap. She spoke through tears, but seemed determined to rise above her grief. She was tired of crying in public. "Strange. I never thought the little weakling had the gumption to carry out such a thing. Or the brains to plan it."

"My Lady, that has been the general feeling among those who knew the facts of the case," Sir Richard answered her. "And nobody can give a plausible answer to the question *why* he would do such a thing. Dap here worked with him for some time, and cannot fathom it."

"Nor can I," the lady agreed. "But in fact it seems he did it. Was there some unspoken grudge between him and his master, Dap? Did they quarrel about his duties...or his pay?"

"He was paid as much as any of us in that household. Which was always too low. But compared to the rest of us he was no worse off. And I never saw him quarrel with Sir William."

"Nor did I," Eleanor agreed. "Though I can certainly believe you were paid little. That family are a penny pinching lot. I always felt Lord William might have been more munificent, but his mother and siblings would have objected. Oh well, this Wulf's motives will, I suppose, always remain a mystery."

"Perhaps," Sir Richard agreed without conviction. "But there is another strong possibility: Wulf may have had no particular reason to want Lord Randal dead, but he could have easily been suborned to commit the murder by someone else—especially if he was paid a sum that seemed grand in comparison with his own meager earnings."

Lady Eleanor stopped and looked on Sir Richard with bulging eyes as if such a thought had never occurred to her. "Yes…" she replied tentatively. 'I see what you mean. And that family! I wouldn't put it past them!"

"Wait," Sir Richard answered with a skeptical shake of his white locks. "You're saying you think that one of Lord Randal's own family might have paid to have him killed? *Why*, for God's sake?"

"It's easier to find motives there than in poor old Wulf," Lady Eleanor said. "Why, they would have killed him just to prevent him from marrying me. I was too low born for them. They thought he should have a princess or a Countess. Or at least someone with a vast fortune in gold or lands. And that, I assure you, is not me."

"And who among them would you think the most likely to take such decisive action against William's marrying *you*?" Sir Richard asked.

"Well," Lady Eleanor answered thoughtfully. "I know that Lady Randal was most vocal in her hatred of me. She nagged William unceasingly about it, he told me. But she'd never contrive the death of her own son. Lord Geoffrey, though—he was as against the match as his mother. And he stood to inherit the title, didn't he? If anyone in the family had the most to gain by William's death, it was Geoffrey."

"Geoffrey was not so ambitious," the tight-lipped Dap disagreed. "But preventing you marrying William I can see. But why spare *you*, if that was the motive?"

"Exactly!" Sir Richard cried, fascinated with this new approach. "Why should Wulf only kill his master? If you were the motive for the murder, why not kill you as well? Or *instead*?"

Lady Eleanor shook her head. "Wulf didn't have a chance to use his poisoned mushrooms on me. He was assigned to bring Lord Randal's food. He couldn't have poisoned mine as well without Dap seeing him, since Dap was bringing my plate. Besides, I would have noticed the mushrooms, since I had cooked the eels myself and hadn't added them to the pan."

"But did he know he was taking Lord William's plate when he picked it up?" Sir Richard asked. "Or was it decided on the way from the kitchen to the table?"

Dap stood still and thought. Then, without changing expression, he answered, "As I recall, it was on the way in to the table. I said, 'I'll serve Lady Eleanor and you serve the master.' And so it was."

Sir Richard furrowed his brow in consternation. "Then we really don't know," he said, "if Wulf intended the poison for Lord William...or for *you*, my Lady!"

* * *

They groped their way along the narrow tunnel, touching the wall as they went to keep their balance and to judge the direction the tunnel might be leading them. Friar Bungay had grabbed a burning torch from its holder near Robin's cell in the prison, and held it before them as they moved, while Robin followed him, unsure of where—or if—they would be coming out. But Bungay claimed he had tested this before, and knew where the tunnel led, although he admitted that there was a great maze of tunnels in this Castle Rock, and he must concentrate so as not to take a wrong turn and come out in the guards' own headquarters.

The darkness, the closeness, and the heat of the tunnel made Robin wonder if he wouldn't have been better off staying in his cell. Now that he had revealed the location of the boundary stones to Bungay, how could he be certain he could trust the friar? But surely Bungay was taking a great risk with his partners, the Sheriff and Sir Guy, by taking Robin from his cell. He needed to simply take a deep breath and trust. But how take a deep breath when he could scarcely breathe in this stifling tunnel? And how trust when he feared at every step that the tunnel would cave in upon him and bury him alive?

But just when he felt he could not stand one more moment of this oppressive darkness, Bungay's torch lit up a wooden door in front of them. And with the lifting of a drop latch, the door opened—with a little shoving on Bungay's part. And it opened onto the castle lawn, near where Thorvald the Dwarf and his Amazing Revelers were still entertaining.

Jack and the guard with the scar had fulfilled their lord's command to ensure that all the spectators remaining in the lesser hall were forced out of the castle and had followed them out the door and onto the lawn. They stood for a few minutes watching the entertainments, in particular David of Doncaster's wrestling exhibition for they were standing close to the cord that ringed that designated area. But looking past the wrestlers, Jack saw two figures emerge as if from the side of the hill. One of these was dressed as a Dominican friar, with black hood, and the other in the silver and blue livery he had last seen on the limbs of the prisoner Robin Hood. Was it possible, he considered, that Friar Bungay, the trusted adviser to his master Gisbourne, had actually led the prisoner to escape? He recalled with a sinking feeling that he had entrusted the friar with his keys. Quickly he elbowed Scarface and said quietly, "Don't make a fuss that will excite the crowd or they'll get away, but look at those two men over there."

Scarface tensed and rasped hoarsely, "Is it the outlaw? And that treacherous friar?"

"It may be," Jack said. "Follow me!" And with that he stepped under the cord and into David's wrestling ring.

But it's not to be assumed that the guards were the only ones on the castle lawn who had seen the pair of escapees emerge from the tunnel. Brother Philip had just made his way back through the crowd, having been sent by Lady Maude to inform Robin's cronies of the dire turn events had taken, while she herself had gone to track her husband down and berate him for his duplicity and cowardice—"As if that's going to make any difference," she added mournfully. And just as Philip had reached the wrestling ring, he noticed the fugitives leave the tunnel. He quickly motioned to David to look at the escaped men, upon which the wrestler immediately recognized Robin, though he didn't have time to wonder why his captain was dressed as a friar and someone else was running away in Countess Lydia's livery. Philip quickly skipped off to inform Thorvald, and from there the word reached each of Robin's men in turn, before Jack had even stepped into the ring.

But when he did—"Aha! One of the castle guards is bold enough to enter the ring with me!" David cried, and the crowd around the ring swelled immediately, the many burghers of Nottingham and yeomen and laborers from the surrounding manors surging forward in the sincere hope of seeing one of Gisbourne's bullies put in his place. "Well let's see what you're made of then, shall we,

Master Guard?" With that David grabbed him by the collar in his right hand and the hem of his tunic in the other.

"That's not what I am…" Jack began, but David quickly fell back onto the ground, dragging Jack along with him, and rolling back, flipped the guard backwards so that he turned over onto his front side, his face in the dirt. Jack was stunned, and made an effort to rise, but David had quickly leaped onto his back and pushed the guard's face further into the earth with his left hand while twisting Jack's right leg high up toward the back of his head with his right.

Scarface, confused at what was happening to his comrade and angry that Jack's protestations of, "Get your bloody hands off me you great oaf! I'm with Gisbourne's guard!" were falling on deaf ears, decided he must take steps to end this travesty. He'd come as far as the space between David's wrestling ring and Jock's archery display, and there, his back to Jock, he drew his sword from his scabbard and barked an order in the direction of the wrestlers.

"You're to cease and desist this wrestling immediately! I order it in the name of the king! And the Sheriff! And Sir Guy of Gisbourne!" When no one paid any attention to his orders, he raised the sword over his head in a threatening posture and gave one last command: "If you do not stop now I will be forced to take action against you!" But as long as David held Jack enmeshed in his grip, Scarface was stymied, fearing to strike lest it be Jack who came off the worse.

Nor had the guard given any heed to what was going on behind him, where Jock had bet one of the bystanders half a crown at two-to-one odds that he could disarm the oblivious guard with a single arrow. And so while Scarface shifted his weight from one foot to the other, holding his sword aloft and peering at the wrestlers, waiting for an opening, Jock had notched his arrow, taken careful aim, and let fly. The arrow struck the sword hilt one inch above Scarface's bandaged hand, and the terrified guard dropped the weapon as if it were a venomous adder. One of the adolescent boys in the crowd snatched up the sword and ran away with it before Scarface could catch him, or even get a good look at who had pilfered the weapon.

Now Scarface wheeled in anger, but by the time he'd determined that it had probably been Jock who'd disarmed him, the archer was back to shooting tankards out of the hands of some of the bolder volunteers from the audience. Scarface turned back to stare in the direction he'd seen the silver-and-blue-liveried servant scampering off to, and thought he saw the figure disappear toward the city gates. He called to Jack that they must move on, but David Doncaster called out to both of them, "I let you leave this ring only after you acknowledge that I've beaten you…"

"Mm…mmahmmih! Nnn eh mmi ah!" Jack sad as loudly as he could, though his voice was muffled by the ground into which David was shoving his face.

Seeing his opponent's difficulties, David grabbed Jack by the hair and lifted his head up, addressing him calmly, "What was that? I didn't quite catch it…"

"I acknowledge it! Now let me up!" Jack growled, spitting out clumps of dirt as he did.

"And the second thing is, you owe me a penny! That's the price of trying a throw with me, and we've been charging anyone stepping into this ring a penny all day long! You can't expect special treatment just because you're a member of the guard, now can you? So cough it up, sirrah!"

Jack sighed. David now held him upright and had his shoulders pinned and his neck pushed forward in a full nelson hold. "How can I find a penny while you've got hold of me like this?" When his eyes rolled over to Scarface he ordered, "Give this lunatic a penny and let's get moving!"

"Right!" the other guard replied, tossing a penny from his purse into the ring. "We need to get after those fugitives! I saw one running toward the gate just a moment ago—we should still be able to catch him." Jack leaped out of the ring and the two guards began to shove their way through the crowd. They immediately saw coming towards them two other guards—Pudgy and Grungy—and Jack called to them that they were to shut down this carnival and clear all of these people out of here. The two newcomers, weapons drawn, began to order David and Jock to pack up their paraphernalia and close down.

So intent were they on that task that they, like their fellows Jack and Scarface, missed the phenomenal final magic trick performed by Will Scarlet.

During the excitement, Thorvald had recognized Robin immediately despite the black Dominican cowl that shadowed his face, and thinking quickly the dwarf had weaved his way through the crowd and grabbed his captain by the arm. Fearing he'd been spotted, and coiling to spring out in flight or fight if necessary, Robin had looked around quickly and, seeing no one at eye level, knew instantly who had seized him. "Don't speak, Robin, and don't struggle!" Thorvald whispered up to him. "Just come wit' me an' follow my lead. We'll get you out of this!"

Without a word the man in the friar's habit let himself be led back through the crowd to the site of Will Scarlet's magic show. "Come now," Will was barking to the onlookers. "Who's got the courage to volunteer for my final illusion of the day, the one that may put your very existence in jeopardy?"

That sounded to the gathered crowd like something of far more consequence than a dancing egg or a disappearing coin. And the audience members who had earlier been cheering the luck, good or bad, of their fellows, now looked at one another abashed, no one being ready for the kind of challenge Will was proposing. But momentarily a gruff voice full of years floated up to them: "I got 'im right 'ere! Look no further, Master of the Revels, 'ere's your volunteer now!" And with that word a befuddled-looking friar was shoved up onto the low platform that served as Will's stage. Scarlet stepped forward and grasped the Dominican's other arm, saying for the sake of the crowd, "Ah, it'll make my day to show what I can do to a preaching friar, of all men! Come right this way," and with that he swung the friar around to stand center stage looking directly out at the audience. "And stay exactly on the spot I put you," he added in a murmured aside to the brave volunteer.

"Now watch closely," Will called again to the onlookers in his barking voice, "and marvel at my powers!" Will let go of Robin's arm, reached down to pick up a rather large blanket from the platform, and then threw it over Robin's head, more than covering him completely from pate to boots. "And now watch closely ladies and gentlemen and prepare to be astounded. One…two… three…*Evanescere!*" And on that powerful cry, the onlookers all saw the blanket that covered the friar collapse suddenly to the floor, and believed that the spell may have immediately struck the Dominican down. At the sudden gasp of shock that reverberated among the witnesses, Gisbourne's two guards leapt onto the low stage and snatched the blanket up, but there was no one and nothing underneath. Now quickly discerning that perhaps this friar was the person Jack and Scarface had been seeking, Pudgy and Grungy quickly broke down the makeshift stage, guessing that the friar had somehow crawled under the boards so as not to be seen. But there was nothing under the stage at all. Unlikely as it seemed, the friar had vanished without a trace.

CHAPTER TWELVE

It was about three miles from the Randal estate outside of Halloughton to the town of Southwell, and Alan a Dale and his wife Ellen traveled the distance in less than an hour. Neither of them was familiar with the town, though they knew it was under the governance of the Archbishop of York, and that the prelate kept a residence there, which he visited only occasionally. What the town was famous for was its minster, which housed the remains of Saint Eadburth. Eadburth was the daughter of King Ealdwulf of East Anglia, and had been the Abbess of Repton some four centuries earlier. Her relics were held in the minster and were the objects of veneration for pilgrims traveling to the site. Eadburth was renowned for her pious life and acts of charity, and her relics were deemed to have a beneficent effect on those who prayed to her.

In the small village that grew up around the minster, the Randals' old nurse Sarah had retired to spend her last years, on the expectation that she might be cared for in the minster if she became too feeble to live on her own. It was hard for Alan to reconcile Lady Eleanor's characterization of the family as particularly miserly with this charitable treatment of the one long-term servant who had survived to old age, but Ellen assured him that, according to the Randals' cook, from whom she'd gotten her information, the small house had been a legacy bequeathed Sarah by the father, old Lord Stephen, who had also given the minster a generous donation on the condition that they provide a place of refuge for the nurse in her dotage.

"There seems to have been a pretty close relationship between the nurse and old Lord Stephen," Ellen told her husband. "The cook hinted that maybe this Sarah was the old man's paramour, and maybe that's why Lady Randal did away with her husband. If that's really how he died."

"Which I'm still not convinced of by any means," Alan said. "But there does seem to have been something that connected them. Lord Stephen was unusually generous to her. There's no rumor that he made provisions for any other servants in the house, is there?"

"Not at all," Ellen answered. "For the most part, the servants I talked to had the same opinion of the Randals' generosity as Lady Eleanor did: that is, that they have none. Oh, the servants all had good things to say about Lord William, and they were really sorry to see him go, because they anticipate some real stinginess among the Randals who are left."

"Then it sure doesn't make any sense for one of the servants to have killed off the only one in the family who was likely to treat them with any favor," Alan said.

"You mean Wulf?"

"I mean whoever persuaded Wulf to do the murder doesn't seem likely to have been a servant."

"Well, maybe we can find out now," Ellen said. "From the way the cook described it, this looks like it must be the house! Last house on Southwell Gate before the minster itself."

They stood before a very common looking cruck house: Like the handful of other houses along the street, it was a building with a wooden frame and a thatched roof. It had a heavy oak door, and a few unshuttered windows high on the walls. The wooden frame itself was plastered with a waddle-and-daub mixture of straw and mud, probably mixed with a little manure for good measure. The house was perhaps twenty feet square, and if it was anything like similar homes he'd been in, Alan assumed it would be a single room with few furnishings.

"Well," Ellen said, taking in the sight. "Lord Stephen didn't impoverish his family leaving *this* to the nurse."

Alan, whose childhood had been a good deal humbler than Ellen's had, shrugged. "It's no worse than most peasants live in. Just because your family happened to own two acres and a horse doesn't mean *everybody* does."

"Yes, we actually had *three* rooms," Ellen said. "And a lean-to for supplies. But owning a bit of our own meant that my father wanted to sell *me* off to the highest bidder. So being better-off than other peasants only meant that as a daughter I personally had a worse time of it. I'd have been free to choose any poor sot I wanted if I'd been just as poor a sot as them."

"And you did get to pick your poor sot after all, as it turned out, thanks to Robin and the lads. But let's see if this Sarah is home, shall we? Let's see if she answers a knock!"

It was several moments after Alan's vigorous rapping that the woman cautiously opened her door a miniscule crack. "Your business?" came a rather quavering voice from within.

"Um...excuse us, madame, we're sorry to have disturbed you, but might you be the woman called Sarah, who was late a servant in Lord Randal's household?"

"Who's askin'?" asked the quivering voice again.

Alan was a bit nonplused at this wary response, and looked at Ellen, who simply shrugged. "Well, uh, my name is Alan a Dale, and this is my wife Ellen. We, uh, are come from the Randals' manor in Halloughton," he said with perfect honesty. "We're looking into the murder of Lord William, and are trying to find out who was behind the crime."

"I don't know nothin'," came the feeble answer, and the door slammed in Alan's face.

This time when he looked into Ellen's eyes, they bore an exaggerated mocking look. "Smooth," she told him. "Very smooth. She's afraid to open her door and the first thing you do is talk about murder."

Alan blushed, looking down at his boots. "I yield to your superior knowledge of how to handle old ladies," he told her. "Please, be my guest," and he gestured to the door.

Ellen sauntered to the door with a superior air, and began by knocking gently and calling in a tender, soothing voice, "Sarah my dear, I've just come from your old gossip, Beulah the cook from the Randals' kitchen. She bade me greet you in her name, and sent me with all of the latest tittle-tattle from the old place. Care to have a cup and a chit chat?"

At that the door flung open and a diminutive elderly lady stood in the entryway with her hand on her hips and a beaming, wrinkled countenance. She wore a dark gray gown of homespun wool with a sleeveless brown linen tunic, and a wisp of her white hair curled onto her forehead from under her white wimple. "Well why didn't ya say so in the first place?" she asked. "Come on in then. Bring your oaf of a husband with ya, if he promises not ta interrupt us."

Ellen threw Alan a victory smirk as she stepped past the old woman into the house, and Alan followed, suitably abashed. There were two wooden chairs inside, a small table, a bedframe with a straw mattress, and a trunk at the foot of the bed. The dirt floor was covered with straw. Ellen sat in one of the chairs, while Alan, assuming Sarah would need the other chair, prepared to stand throughout the interview. Perhaps, he thought, he could lean against the stone fireplace in the corner, where were a few plates and cups and cooking utensils. Sarah placed three of the wooden cups on the table and filled each of them with small beer from a pitcher that had been sitting on the hearth.

"I don't get many visitors," the old woman began without more ceremony. She handed a cup to Alan, then picked up the other two and sat down next to Ellen, handing her a cup as well. "Once in a blue moon somebody from the old place will visit—Beulah or Hazel the seamstress or even, maybe once a year, Lady Anne herself rememberin' her old nurse. But it's rare. Nobody else in that household that I know any more. Anyway, you see why I'm loath ta answer the door—and even more loath ta invite anybody in. I'm as defenseless an old spinster as any you're goin' ta find. Got ta take care of myself 'cause nobody else will!"

"Well, now, somebody has taken care of you all right, it seems," Ellen said in a conversational tone. "Set you up in your own small house near a fine minster, where they've agreed to care for you when you get old."

"Old-*er* you mean, deary," Sarah corrected her. "Though I'm not yet ninety, which the priests say was the age of my namesake, Sarah in the Bible, when she had her first-born. So I'm not despairing yet of finding a husband!" And with that she laughed at her own joke with a kind of light, tinkling laugh that fit her small frame and had an almost musical quality to it.

"But surely someone valued you enough to set you up this way in your retirement. Beulah told me it was the old master himself, old Lord Stephen."

"Oh, aye, it was him all right," Sarah answered. "'For years of faithful service ta his family,' he wrote in his will. And they *were* faithful years. Them kids had more ta do with me than with their mother. Not that I'm complainin', that's just the way gentle folk do."

"Yes," Ellen said. "But still, it's an unusually generous thing to do…"

"Especially for *that* family," Sarah agreed. "Ever since the old man died, they been cuttin' corners and pinchin' pennies. I said they had only the two servants left that I knew from my time there. Well that's mainly because the others left for better-payin' positions, and many of them as left was never replaced."

"And when did you leave?" Alan asked, forgetting himself, as Ellen gave him an admonishing look. But Sarah, now comfortably in her nattering mood, waved off Ellen's look and answered: "Five years it's been. Lady Anne had reached the marriageable age of twelve, and they reckoned my services were no longer required, so I was put out ta pasture."

"But surely you could have been kept on for several more years, at least until the girl actually *was* married off," Ellen suggested.

"Could have, sure," Sarah said. "But I was gettin' on you know, and didn't move fast enough ta please the mistress of the house or young Geoffrey. Lady Anne might have kept me, but the other two convinced her they could save money by lettin' me go, and Lord William was never willin' to fight all three of them at once, so he agreed."

"But the cost of your maintenance at the house must have been negligible," Alan protested. "Certainly less than this house…"

"Oh the house was already paid for, and the endowment to the minster," Sarah explained. "So they're not out anything for my upkeep here. They were saving pennies by lettin' me go, but pennies mean more ta them than people."

"But that was not the case with Lord Stephen, I take it?" Ellen asked, trying to steer the conversation back to Sarah's relationship with her former master.

"Oh no," the old woman insisted. "Lord Stephen was a good

master and a generous man. Maybe too generous. I suppose I first began ta hear about the family's money problems just before he died. Seems he spent more than he brought in from his lands."

"And yet he still paid for your retirement home..." Ellen prodded again.

There was a pause in which Sarah looked at Ellen through narrowed eyes, until she finally sighed and responded. "All right, Miss Ellen, I can see where this is goin'. Beulah probably shared some of the gossip with you from that time, didn't she? See, I know what people were sayin'. Once they knew Lord Stephen had set this up for me, they all assumed the worst. That I served him as a lot more than the children's nurse, is that what you're implyin'?"

Ellen reached out and touched the old woman's arm. "I don't mean to imply anything, and I've no wish to insult you or to bring up uncomfortable memories. But you must admit the gift was an unusual one."

"Aye, that it was," Sarah agreed. "But I was never Lord Stephen's leman, no matter what the old biddies at the manor say. But I'll tell you what it was," her voice suddenly took on a confidential tone and dropped to a loud whisper. "Shall I tell you what it was?" She asked, leaning forward.

Ellen's face lit up, all ready to share confidences, and leaned forward herself, replying, "Yes please! What can you tell us?"

Continuing in a whisper, though there was certainly no one who could possibly have overheard the conversation, Sarah continued: "Lord Stephen as ye may have heard, had been a crusader. He fought in the company of Guy of Jerusalem against Saladin at the Siege of Acre. When he came back, he was a changed man—more broodin' and prone ta meditate upon his mortality. But a rumor had started—I don't know where, but the servants were all abuzz with it within a few weeks of his return—a rumor that the old man had brought back a treasure with him from the Holy Land, a treasure of incalculable worth. The groom Thomas even claimed he saw Lord Stephen coming and going with bags full of gold. *That* was balderdash, of course."

"Indeed," Ellen answered. "We heard rumors even now about that treasure, and how nobody had ever found it after the old lord died."

"Oh aye, ya would sure have heard that," Sarah said. And she went on frankly, "And no doubt ya also heard the rumor that Lord Stephen's wife killed him for the treasure. Lies, all of them, lies."

"You don't give any credence to the talk about Lady Randal killing her husband, then? For any reason?" Alan pursued.

Sarah scoffed. "Ah, no doubt you've heard that the lady had a lover and so wanted her husband out of the way. Or maybe even that Lord Stephen had a lover—happen it was me, you're thinkin'—and that's why she killed him. Well I'm tellin' you, and I saw everything that went on in that house, that Lady Randal had no cause that way to murder Lord Stephen, and no more would she have killed him on account of the treasure. She never talked about that treasure at all. The children, oh, sure, they thought it would be a great lark ta be rich, and pestered the old man about it every so often. Why, when Lady Anne does visit me, she still brings it up. But Lord Stephen never acknowledged the rumor. Never said it was true. Just old wives' tales, he'd say to everybody. Everybody else, I should say. For me, he had a different story."

"What are you saying?" Alan pushed. "There really *was* a treasure? And Lord Stephen told you about it and nobody else?"

"He trusted you more than he did anyone else, even his own family, is that it, my dear?" Ellen asked in more soothing tones, trying to soften Alan's strident goading.

"That's it precisely deary," the old woman said. "He always said he couldn't trust the children not ta squander the treasure foolishly, and he couldn't trust Lady Randal to resist the children's urgin'. Me, I'd been with his family since he was a boy himself, and he knew I could have no designs on the money, since I didn't stand to gain anythin' from it. So he bound me to a pledge of silence, and he entrusted ta me a sealed parchment, which he said contained the specifics of where the treasure was hidden. No one would think ta look among *my* meager possessions for the key ta riches beyond imaginin'. But they might not hesitate ta rifle through his own things. Anyway, I was ta keep the parchment and keep quiet about it, and in return he would give me this house and status within the minster, as you've heard."

"So that was it," Ellen breathed and sat back in her chair, now speaking again in her normal voice. "And you never told anybody about this? Not even after Lord Stephen's murder?"

"I'd taken an oath never to breathe a word. To my thinkin', the master's death did not release me from my promise. This is the first word I've uttered about it in, oh, must be fifteen years."

"And why have you chosen now to renege your oath?" Ellen asked, puzzled and a little awed at Sarah's determination. "And why reveal all this to *us*?"

"Because accordin' ta your pushy husband there, the young Lord William's been murdered, and nobody seems to know what it was about. If it was about this bloody parchment again, then I'd be aidin' and abettin' the murderer wouldn't I? Withholdin' evidence, innit?"

"What do you mean, 'about the bloody parchment *again*'?" Alan pressed. "You're saying that Lord Stephen's murder was definitely over the parchment?"

"What else?" Sarah said, and shrugged.

"But if that was the case, my dear, then why didn't you reveal the parchment's existence at the time?" Ellen asked.

"Well, the murderer had to be somebody in that house," Sarah explained. "And if they killed *him* for it, they would have killed me too for it, wouldn't they? If they'd known I had it."

"Makes sense," Ellen agreed. And after a moment's pause, she took up the thread. "But you say you're sure the mistress did not kill her husband."

Sarah shook her head. "Poor woman didn't have it in her. She loved Lord Stephen and her grief for him was not feigned, I'da seen through it in a trice if it was."

"And the children, we were given to understand, were away from the manor house at the time?" Ellen said.

"Right. Visitin' their mum's family they were."

"Then," Ellen ventured, "who is it you think killed the old man?"

"Well, had ta be one of the servants, didn't it?" Sarah said, matter-of-factly. "I mean, stands ta reason. The lady got a lot of attention from the local magistrate, bein' the only one sleepin' on the second floor and all, but there was never no evidence linkin' her to it. No blood. No motive. No nothin'. So they just dropped the case as unsolved. But one of the other servants could easily have slipped upstairs, done the deed, and slipped back downstairs while everybody else was sleepin'."

"Sarah," Alan said, a thought striking him suddenly. "The servant that became Lord William's dog-boy, Wulf. Had he started working in the manor house at the time of the old lord's murder?"

Sarah wrinkled her brow, calculating. Then her face cleared and she said, "Oh no, I remember the lad you're talkin' about. He didn't start until maybe five or six years later, I'm sure of that."

"Besides," Ellen said, addressing Alan, "if this all happened fifteen years ago, as Sarah has said, then Wulf would have been only, what, seven years old at the time?"

Alan nodded. "You're right, of course. It just would have tied things together so neatly..."

"So here's the most important question in my mind," Ellen continued. "Have you still got this parchment that Lord Stephen put into your hands for safe keeping? And if so, may we be vouchsafed an opportunity to see it?"

But even before Ellen had finished speaking, Sarah was shaking her head and sighing. "No, no, it's gone. Long gone."

"Lost?" Alan asked. "Or stolen?"

"Here's how it was," the old woman explained. "The morning after Lord Stephen was found murdered, by the groom Thomas and Lord Stephen's personal valet, David, I checked my own belongin's. The parchment was still there. So I was convinced that whoever had killed the master hadn't found out from him where the key to the treasure was. And after the murder things went on in the manor house much as they always had before. So gradually I got ta thinkin' I'd been wrong in assumin' one of the servants was the killer. Maybe it had been someone, some old enemy from his crusading days, who'd entered the house in secret and did him in."

"And what changed your mind?" Alan asked.

"About a month or so after the murder, one of the servants, the East Anglian David, told the mistress that he couldn't live on the reduced wages she'd been forced ta give him since the master's death, and that anyway he'd decided to go off and become a religious if he could find a house that'd take him. So she told him ta go with her blessin'—she was only too happy ta be rid of a servant who wasn't really needed any more. And off he went."

"So...?" Alan asked, not quite seeing where this was going.

"Go on, my dear," Ellen encouraged her, knowing the point was coming soon.

"Well it struck me that David found the body—if he'd rushed to the corpse and grabbed it, feigning sorrow over the death, it was the perfect way of hiding the blood that might have been on his clothes from having done the murder the night before in the first place. And then I looked through my belongin's again."

"No parchment," Ellen concluded.

"No parchment," Sarah agreed.

"And yet you still didn't go to the authorities, after you were certain who the murderer was?" Alan exclaimed, exasperated.

But Ellen understood far better than he did. "Magistrates aren't interested in penetrating the mysteries behind crimes. Only in finding someone to blame. Sarah hadn't volunteered what she knew when the crime was fresh. Coming forward then would have only laid suspicion upon herself. They weren't going to go in search of this David, long since disappeared and out of their jurisdiction. Sarah would have been an easy victim to blame as an accomplice, and they'd have felt justice was done."

Sarah nodded sadly, and Alan shrugged, considering what he knew of people like the Sheriff of Nottingham and the kind of justice he'd just tried to enforce in his accusations of Robin.

"So there it is," Sarah ended quietly, her voice returning to the quavering soprano they had first heard through the door. "If knowing what I know about that earlier murder can help in any way ta expose the killer of the young lord I'll be satisfied. William was always good ta me, and he had his father's best qualities: courtesy, sociability, generosity—much more than any of the rest of that family. I'm very sorry he's dead. Very sorry indeed."

"It's hard to say how much it'll help," Alan mused. "I suppose there's no reason to think of Lady Randal as a suspect any more.

And if this David killed Lord Stephen and stole the parchment, then what reason would he have to kill Lord William?"

"But it does suggest a motive for William's murder," Ellen ventured.

"How so?" her husband asked.

"Well, nobody knew about the theft of the parchment, did they? If somebody thought there was a great treasure still unfound, and thought Lord Stephen might have passed the knowledge of his treasure's location to his eldest son, wouldn't that be a motive?"

"Of course," Alan agreed. "And there's another possibility. Suppose this David couldn't figure out what the parchment was telling him, and decided to come back to William thinking the son would understand better?"

"But why poison him?" Ellen said. "Except maybe as revenge for William's refusing to help him…"

"Or, if he'd approached William about the parchment, to silence the one person to whom he'd revealed his murder of the father?"

Ellen threw up her hands. "All this speculation is getting us nowhere. Especially since we don't know where this David is or what he looks like…"

"Round faced fellow," Sarah said. "Very dark eyes, almost black they were. Had an irritatin' manner of crinklin' up his eyes and the corners of his mouth when he smiled, which wasn't much. Really thick, black eyebrows. If you ever saw him you'd always remember him by those eyebrows."

CHAPTER THIRTEEN

When Robin fell through the trap door it was as much a surprise to him as it was for the admiring crowd, who all gave Will Scarlet a rousing ovation when he picked up the blanket and found nobody under it. Much the miller's son, waiting on all fours beneath the low stage, quickly repositioned that door and ushered a scrambling Robin into another door, this one leading directly into the sandstone tunnels of Nottingham's Castle Rock. Much showed Robin where to crawl to enter the tunnel, then dropped in with his captain and shut the well camouflaged door behind him, John the cook's son waited just inside with a torch that he had lit moments before just inside the tunnel. Scrunching down in the narrow confines of the passage, he said "Follow me!" And began moving in a direction Robin thought must be away from the castle itself.

He quickly took after John with Much behind him following in single file, and the miller's son chattering away as if they were out for a Sunday stroll. "We found this tunnel last night," he said. "It was when we were lookin' over the lay of the land out there, figurin' as to where we was gonna set up our three carnival games. John took a torch and followed it ta see where it came out. Comes out several hundred yards down and just outside the walls of the city, near a dirt path that connects ta the Great North Road as far as we could tell. So we decided to set up the magic stage over it, and we already had a trap door in the stage for just that same disappearin' trick Will pulled off with you. 'Ya never know,' says Thorvald. 'Somebody might need ta make a quick getaway.' A' lo an' behold, it hath come to pass, eh Robin?"

"That it hath," the outlaw said. "But seriously, I can't tell you how glad I was to see you boys out there. And twice as glad we didn't have to fight our way out of Nottingham. No telling who might have got hurt in that. And with the Countess and Lady Mary on hand? Things might have gotten very, very unpleasant."

"Oh don't I know it!" Much agreed. "I might've even gotten blisters on my fingers from all the arrows I'd've had to shoot saving yer sorry hide."

"Sorry!" Robin exclaimed, cut to the quick. "I happen to value this hide of mine pretty highly!"

"Yeah, but have ya ever had to peddle it? It'd make a pretty thin coat. Maybe a pair of kid gloves, if nicely tanned first."

"A poor thing but my own," Robin agreed. "And somewhat the worse for wear after the beatings I got in that place."

Much turned serious. "Truly Robin, are ye all right? No bones broke or anything?"

"A few less teeth," Robin admitted. "Another night in that place and I'd look like you, Much my lad. But how far does this thing go? Where'll we be coming out?"

"You'll see yerself in a minute," Much answered. "We're almost there."

At that very moment Robin heard a light "thunk" from just ahead, for John had come up against the trap door that led out of the dark tunnel. As he pushed against it, a beam of light nearly blinded Robin, and in a few seconds all three of the outlaws had scrambled out into the fresh air. They were indeed at the foot of the hill, and outside the city walls. And there, on the path right before them, was Thorvald parked in his cart.

"Thorvald, your ugly face right now is just about the most beautiful thing I've ever seen," Robin breathed out with a sigh of relief.

With subdued laughter and congratulations, David of Doncaster, Will Scarlet, Jock of Barlborough, and Thorvald himself welcomed Robin, but whisked him into the bed of Thorvald's cart and covered him with Will's blanket and some of the other paraphernalia they had quickly dismantled when the guards had shut down their carnival. They were taking no chances on anyone recognizing the fleeing friar whom the guards had chased on the castle lawn. Thorvald the Dwarf and His Amazing Revelers had decamped quickly and driven down here in the cart while Robin and the others were making their way through the tunnel, and had arrived just in time to meet them at this end. "But let's keep things as quiet as we can," Thorvald warned. "We don't want bystanders to see anything but a troupe of players leaving their last entertainment, on their way to the next!"

And so, with Robin safely hidden and Much and Jock in the cart itself, making sure that Robin stayed completely covered by the blanket, Thorvald, with Will beside him, drove the cart casually toward the Old North Road. John and David, having drawn the short straws, trudged alongside on their way to Sherwood Forest.

* * *

A carpet of reddish-brown leaves had begun to decorate the clearing around the Great Oak where the outlaws of Sherwood kept their summer camp. Robin Hood, now free of his friar's disguise, was back in Lincoln-green attire and seated comfortably on a leafy cushion at the foot of the huge tree. He was conducting an important meeting of the bandits and was circled by all his meinie, who filled the clearing. He first thanked all who had helped in his escape from Nottingham Castle, and had barely finished doing so when he was interrupted by Friar Tuck.

"Robin, speaking frankly, I feel that I have to say this: You were being reckless, and not for the first time, in making this visit to Nottingham, when all the forces of the law and the crown were weighed against you. You got yourself captured, and you nearly got yourself killed. And aside from leaving your men leaderless, you put at risk the lives of all those—Thorvald and Scarlet and Much and the rest—who came after you to save you. Need I remind you what the book of Proverbs says? 'A wise man feareth, and departeth from evil; but the fool rageth, and is confident.' I want your word right now, given freely here before all of our band, that you will not be so foolish as to put yourself in this kind of danger again."

Robin set his jaw and glared at Tuck. He knew there was some truth in what the friar was saying, but what was he supposed to do? Sit here in Sherwood and twiddle his thumbs? "I admit there was a bit of rashness in my visit," he conceded. "But Tuck, you've done things yourself that were dangerous. Can I sit in Sherwood eating venison while others do my work for me? I felt we needed to know what they were saying about my guilt in Nottingham, and saw no surer way of finding out than visiting with the Sheriff's wife, the horse's mouth as you might say."

Once again, Robin had barely finished when the largest man in the clearing boomed out his own answer in support of Tuck: "There were a hundred other ways to discover that, if indeed we needed to discover it," Little John argued. "You picked the most dangerous, the most imprudent choice. Tuck is right. It's for your own good I'm saying it, you need to promise 'never again.'"

"Ah, John, you'd turn on me too, would you?" Robin answered, somewhat taken aback to have his two closest lieutenants aligned against him. "Sure, there may be other ways of discovering this or that, but thumbing my nose at danger is the most fun way, now you have to admit it!"

"Fun for you might be a bloody nightmare for the rest of us," Will Stutely argued. "Look, when I was taken by Gisbourne's guards, and went to hang, many of the rest of you risked your lives to save me. But I didn't get myself arrested through my own rash actions, and the ones who took the chance to save me did it out of love and comradeship. I wouldn't have put their lives on the line if I could've helped it."

Robin could see where this was going, and it wasn't in his direction. "All right," he conceded. "Maybe I was reckless. Maybe I shouldn't endanger the rest of you with my own rash adventures."

"Swear you won't go to Nottingham again, disguise or no, without suitable protection," Tuck said, pushing his advantage.

"I swear it," Robin said, "if that's what'll make you all happy. I swear by the blessed Mother of God, who you know I hold most dear!"

"That's settled then," Tuck said, as Will, John, and many of the others nodded in satisfaction, and as Robin thought to himself, "And I hold the Virgin most dear because she is all-forgiving, so when I break my vow she will shake her head, say 'tsk tsk,' and clasp me all the tighter to her bosom." Because if they thought he was going to curtail his occasional visits to Lady Maude, well, they had another think coming, that's all.

"But to be fair," Robin continued, "none of you was forced to storm the castle to get me out. The one I suppose I owe the most thanks to is a Dominican friar who was serving as a kind of geographical advisor to Gisbourne and the Sheriff. Fellow by the name of Friar Bungay."

"Bungay? What kinda name is that, I wonder?" asked Much the miller's son.

"Village in East Anglia, I believe," Friar Tuck said. "Must be where this Dominican hailed from. But why do you say you owe him these thanks?"

"It was he who unlocked my shackles, who opened my cell door, who led me into the tunnel and out again to safety. Why he even exchanged clothes with me so that I'd be better disguised as a mendicant friar."

"He sounds like a saint!" Friar Tuck exclaimed. "Just the sort of selfless charity one would expect from a holy friar!"

"Well, it wasn't quite so selfless," Robin corrected. "Actually, he promised to help me on condition that I would show him on a map the location of the Thynghowe, the old Norse meeting place with the boundary stones not far west from our camp."

"Why would he be so interested in that place?" Skipper Haakon wanted to know. "No one uses it any more. There's nothing there but the stones."

Meanwhile Much turned to David of Doncaster and asked "What's a map?" David shrugged.

"I didn't ask, and I didn't care," Robin answered Haakon. "I was a bit concerned about my own neck at the time. But now that my neck is a bit safer, let me tell you all something else this friar told me. He had been helping the Sheriff and Sir Guy to carefully map all of Sherwood Forest." Much and David looked at one another in confusion. "What that means," Robin continued, noting several of his men looking at him with blank expressions, "is that he was creating a chart, a careful picture of every inch of Sherwood, drawn perfectly to scale, so that any one of the Sheriff's deputies could find his way to any exact spot in the forest. It is only a matter of weeks if not days before they find this spot, and know exactly how to get back to it.

What I'm saying is our hideout is not secure."

This was greeted by a very uncomfortable buzz among Robin's listeners, the gist of the mumblings reaching Robin's ears being, "So what do we do about it?"

"This means we will need to move camp again," their captain told them, and to the groaning that met those words he added, "We can return to Creswell Crags. What I learned by looking at Friar Bungay's map is that his men have long since finished mapping that area and so, since they didn't find us there, they are continuing to look elsewhere in the forest. We move there, and it will be a good long time before Gisbourne and his guards look for us up there again. So let's begin to get our things packed up. Thorvald, I hope you'll make your cart ready to transport some loads back and forth. Ellen, do you think you could organize the women to start packing things up?"

"No, I don't think so," Ellen answered, refusing to take the question as it was intended, as rhetorical.

Robin, taken aback, paused in the orders he was giving. "You…what? What do you mean, Ellen?"

"What I mean is, we're forgetting something here. You've been cleared of the murder charge the Sheriff laid on you, and that's wonderful. But we still haven't figured out who was behind the murder of Lord William Randal. Yes, we know that he was poisoned by his servant Wulf, but we haven't found out who Wulf was working for when he killed his master."

"And why is that our concern now?" asked Arthur Bland, the burly former tanner who had joined Robin's band after losing a fight with Little John. "Robin's safe. We're in danger and need to move camp. I'm sorry about Lord Randal, but it's not our job to investigate murders."

"No," Alan a Dale spoke up. "That is the Sheriff's job. And look how well he does it. We do have an interest in this murder. We entertained Lord Randal the day he was killed. He was our guest and was killed on his way home from our camp. And I personally talked to him long enough to think of him as a friend. He deserves justice, and if I can give it to him I will do so. Ellen is right. We need to find out who was behind Wulf's treachery. If Lord William is going to get justice, it's going to have to be from us."

Will Scathelock, the middle-aged yeoman archer whose maturity often led Robin to leave him in charge when he and Little John were away from camp, spoke in slow and reasoned terms: "We cannot neglect our own safety, and so we cannot delay our preparations to move camp. But I agree with Ellen and the minstrel that we have some responsibility to Lord Randal's memory. So I propose this: Let me take charge of the move to Creswell Crags, and let Thorvald assist me. Alan and Ellen may take charge of the investigation, as they have been most involved in it so far, and perhaps Robin and Tuck and some of the others may want to assist them. And let us take care of both of our responsibilities."

There was much nodding among the outlaw band, and Friar Tuck voiced the majority opinion when he said, "Yes, I believe as a group we can actually walk and scratch our cullions at the same time. But I believe what Alan is saying, that we do have a moral obligation to complete this investigation of Lord William's murder. We *are* our brother's keeper. Why don't we hear what Alan and Ellen have discovered while the rest of us have been focused on freeing Robin?"

"Well," Alan began. "We did talk again with the members of Sir William's family, and we also spent a good deal of time with the Randals' old nurse, Sarah. And we are quite sure that we know who killed the old Lord Randal, Lord William's father."

"And it's not Lady Randal herself, as we were led to believe?" Robin said.

"Not at all," Ellen answered. "Sarah identified one of the servants at that time, a certain David from somewhere in East Anglia. Said he had killed this old Lord Stephen after forcing him to reveal where his great treasure was hidden. Seems Sarah had been holding a piece of parchment that revealed the hiding place. Well, this David had covered his crime by pretending to find Lord Stephen's body, and later had left the Randals' employ—he said in order to become a religious. But after he left, Sarah realized he had taken the parchment."

"That does seem to solve the old man's murder," Friar Tuck agreed. "But what does it have to do with Lord William's death? Is this David person still in the area?"

"I don't know where he has been these fifteen years," Alan said. "But I'm sure he's in the area now. Listen: Sarah told us that you could always recognize David by his black bushy eyebrows. Once you saw him you'd never forget those brows, she told us. Well, Friar Tuck, you'll remember this. At Lord William's funeral, there was a Dominican friar attending the service. He didn't speak to any of us, but he acted as one of the pallbearers. And he disappeared soon after the interment. But one thing that was easily recognizable about him: He had great bushy eyebrows."

Robin stood as if thunderstruck. Then he cried, "Bushy eyebrows you say? A friar? That's…that's Friar Bungay, the cartographer who freed me from Gisbourne's prison!"

"What's a cartographer?" David whispered to Much, who shrugged.

"No, that's far too great a coincidence," Friar Tuck said. "Things like that only happen in stories."

"Not so far-fetched," Alan reasoned. "Consider: This David of East Anglia is obsessed by his master's treasure. So obsessed that he kills him after forcing him to admit where the clue to his treasure is hidden. He steals that clue from the nurse Sarah and then goes off to see if this clue, this parchment, will lead him to the riches. But what if this parchment is a map? And what if it's drawn in such a way that only Lord Stephen would have been able to read it? But David doesn't give up. He decides to educate himself. He joins the Dominicans not because he has a vocation but because he wants to learn, and they are the most learned group he knows of."

"That sketch of Thynghowe that he showed me," Robin mused. "It must have been copied from that parchment map he stole from the nurse. His whole scheme of mapping all of Sherwood was a grand plan to find the place where Lord Stephen buried his treasure."

Much the miller's son pricked up his ears at that. "Say, if we know that this treasure is there, why don't we try to beat this friar to it and keep the treasure fer ourselves? *With* a half of it going to the poor, as always..." This last he added when he saw Friar Tuck's brow begin to lower with righteous anger.

Will Stutely piped up at that. "Well, now, we'd be digging all over that hill without Lord Stephen's map to tell us where to dig. But if we do send a party over to Thynghowe and wait for this Friar Bungay to show up, we might persuade him to share with us..."

"Or more importantly arrest him on suspicion of the murder of Lord William as well as Lord Stephen," Ellen added. "Have we forgotten already that we're trying to catch the killer and bring him to justice for the sake of Lord William?"

"Exactly," Robin agreed. "We need to focus on the primary goal here, to catch Lord Randal's killer. Who is, let's not forget, *not* Friar Bungay but the servant Wulf. If we can find Wulf, we can force him to tell us who put him up to poisoning Lord William. So, we know that Friar Bungay killed Lord Stephen for the treasure. I guess we're assuming that was the motive in killing William as well? We know that Bungay and Wulf were both servants in the Randals' household. Is that the connection? Was Bungay in the house when Wulf started? Did they become friends, and did Bungay come back and get Wulf to partner with him in murdering William?"

"No," Alan answered, "They didn't know each other as servants, Bungay left the Randals' employ years before Wulf got there."

"And besides," Ellen added. "If the killers thought that William knew where the treasure was, and wanted to get the information from him, why would they poison him? With no chance to force the truth out of him?"

Robin slapped his forehead. "Mary, Joseph and all the saints, you're right. The motive had to be something else."

"And that means that the *murderer* may be somebody else," Ellen concluded.

That stopped the conversation for some time. Friar Tuck shook his head and said, "It may be, it may be. But we are pretty certain that this Friar Bungay has at least killed once before. He must therefore be at least considered as having killed once again. For what reason, we do not know. Remember he was seen at Lord William's funeral, which meant he was taking a very personal interest in the death of his old master's son."

"I agree," Alan a Dale said. "We need to go and visit Father Timothy at the parish church in Halloughton, See what he knows about the unusual visitor who acted as pallbearer in that ceremony."

"Yes, I agree we should do that," said Ellen, with a touch of impatience. "But our most important task is to find Wulf."

Alan nodded, but said with some regret, "I did talk to the Randal family, and none of them could give me any idea of where this Wulf may have disappeared to. And you yourself talked to the other servants. No clues."

Robin sighed. "Not much to go on there then. And his fellow Dap had no idea where he might have gone. Is there anyone else, anyone at all, that ought to be questioned about him?"

Everyone looked glum for an instant, before Little John made the suggestion, "Lady Eleanor? I suppose she was one of the last to see the dog boy before he slipped away, wasn't she?"

"It couldn't hurt," Alan agreed. "We've tried everyone else."

"Well let's do this then," Robin said, taking charge. "Friar Tuck, can you and Alan go and visit Father Timothy, and see if you can learn from him what Friar Bungay was doing there at the funeral? And Ellen, if you can stand being away from your husband for a brief time, why don't you go and visit Lady Eleanor? I have a feeling she'll talk to you more readily than one of us ruffians."

"She'll need an escort, though," Alan objected. "With a couple of known murderers tramping about Sherwood, I don't want her going off by herself."

Robin considered for only a moment and then responded, "You're right, of course, Alan my lad. And your Ellen is so valuable a personage in our little community that I won't entrust her care to just anyone. I'm so caught up in this pursuit of Lord William's killer, especially since it may involve my own deliverer, Friar Bungay, that I don't think I can stand to the side and think about other things while you all are poking into this mystery. I will volunteer to accompany Ellen on her visit to Lord Randal's paramour, if she will have me! I'll carry my sword and my bow, and I'll venture to say she couldn't have a more capable protector. What say you to this offer, my Lady Ellen?"

Ellen bowed to the outlaw captain with mock courtesy and replied, "How can I say no to such a gallant offer? After which she uttered sotto voce, "And you'd better behave yourself, or you'll need protection from me!"

Robin held up his hands and vowed, "I swear by the Virgin herself that my intentions are pure as the driven snow. Now, Much, Will Scarlet, bring us out some horses. We should make these inquiries quickly. The more time we lose, the more opportunity for these killers to escape!"

Alan a Dale was not amused by Robin's banter, and his grim face made that clear. He kissed his wife farewell for the moment and, reassured by her tenderness, rode off with Friar Tuck.

Robin, oblivious of having caused anyone discomfort, went on speaking generally about the frailty of women and, at the same time, the irresistibility of their charms. Having never met this Lady Eleanor, he suggested, he was eager to see the paragon Lord William had chosen as the vessel to keep his holy love. "She must be one of the great beauties of the age," he said as he and Ellen mounted and started off. "With Lord William out of the picture, maybe I should have a go at her myself!"

CHAPTER FOURTEEN

"Oh so you think because this happened in my house that I must be allied with this servant, Wulf? You're still trying to make me guilty of my own love's murder?" Lady Eleanor was not welcoming to this small delegation from the outlaws of Sherwood. She had not received Ellen and Robin courteously, and had no intention of answering their questions passively, if at all.

"Believe me, I understand your reluctance to talk to us," Ellen soothed. Lady

Eleanor's reaction to Robin Hood's arrival at her home had been nothing less than frantic. She had been quite vocal in putting the blame for Lord William's death on the outlaw leader, chiefly in defense of herself. When he showed up at her door, she could think of nothing but that he must want to exact some kind of revenge on her for her outspoken attacks. When Robin agreed to wait outside while Ellen spoke with the lady, she agreed to at least hear what Ellen had come to discuss with her, and invited Ellen to sit with her in her private solar on the second floor of the manor house.

"Have you been wrongfully accused of murder by your own fiancé's family?" Lady Eleanor came back. "If not, then you don't understand it!"

"Well, I *sympathize* with it," Ellen corrected. "And here is what I *do* understand: I understand the difficulty of making a satisfactory marriage when one's family is against it. I know that Lord Randal's mother and his siblings were against his marrying you, and hoped he would wed someone with more lands and a bigger dowry. I know how painful such things can be."

"You?" Lady Eleanor looked doubtful. "You're a simple peasant woman, living in the forest with a band of outlaws. What could you possibly know of such things?"

Ellen bit back a few fiery words, camouflaging her growing resentment with a perfectly lovely smile, and then said, "My father is a free small landholder, not unlike your own. Like you I had no significant lands or dowry, but I was young and pretty and my father insisted that I marry a rich landowner who was old enough to be my grandfather."

Lady Eleanor, moved by Ellen's sincerity, grew softer in her attitude. "I know such marriages are common. My own father was weighing similar possibilities for me if Lord William would not propose."

"Fathers think they are helping their daughters when they do such things," Ellen said. "The old man, probably a widower, teaches the young girl how to be a wife. Then he dies and leaves her a wealth of goods and land, and she is free to marry whoever she likes. And often it develops just that way. But often it does not; the old man is a bully or the lady dies bearing the dotard's heir. Or both."

"I can't imagine a lonelier, more hellish existence. I don't think I would want to live. But that possibility is still there for me, now that my true love is dead."

"It was in fact Robin Hood himself who saved me from that fate," Ellen continued. "He and his men broke up my wedding in favor of my own true love, Alan a Dale, who became one of Robin's band, and I became his wife. So I'm telling you, we are not here to trap you or to judge you or to trick you. My husband performed for Lord William when he dined with us, and he was so impressed that he offered to take Alan into his household as a servant. That is why we have been so eager to pursue his murderer, and try to bring that murderer to justice."

"And his murderer was Wulf of Brinkley. And you want to track him down," Lady Eleanor finished the thought.

"That's true," Ellen said. "But try as we might we haven't been able to think of any possible reason for Wulf to kill his master. Can you? Without a motive, we can't help thinking that there was someone else behind the murder, who persuaded Wulf to poison Lord William—perhaps with money or some other promise. And the only way to find out who that might have been is to find Wulf and get him to *tell* us who that might have been."

Lady Eleanor scowled in thought. "To answer your question, no, I can't think of a reason why Wulf might have wanted to kill my darling William. I mean, I never saw him happy—he was always something of a surly fellow. Never friendly to me or anyone else I ever saw. I thought he might just be very shy—some young men are—but he didn't even seem to like his dogs much. Not happy in his work, but that's not a reason to kill your employer. He could have simply taken off if he wanted to quit his job."

"*Riiight...*" Ellen said thoughtfully, drawing out the long vowel. "So you didn't know him well enough to give us any guess as to where he might have gone after he did take off?"

"I didn't," Eleanor answered, scowling some more. "But now that I think about it, one thing William did tell me about Wulf was that he seemed to have developed a fondness for William's sister, Lady Anne. Too shy to talk to her, I guess but always mooned about with his mouth hanging open when she came anywhere near him. I would think that if he had a choice, he wouldn't have taken off at all if it meant leaving for good the far-away lady who was out of his reach."

"Well, a cat can look at a queen, I've heard it said," Ellen answered. "But it seems after all he *has* absconded."

"But my guess is he is not far off," Eleanor continued. "He's not intrepid enough to leave the country where he's always lived and start all over again. I wonder if it would be worth your while to talk to Lady Anne herself. See if she's heard from him. Of course, Anne won't talk to me, none of the family will. They never wanted me and now they never have to have me. Isn't that nice for them?"

Ellen ignored the last part of that comment, and said, "We have talked to Lady Anne. She says she doesn't know anything about where Wulf has gone, and doesn't really care." Eleanor could not suppress a little eyeroll at that information. Then Ellen asked, "Well if we are not able to find Wulf himself, can you think of anybody who had some grudge against Lord William? Anyone he didn't get along with?"

"Outside of his own family, you mean?" She joked. Then she added more seriously, "No, no one he ever mentioned."

"He ever mention an old servant named David from East Anglia? Or a certain Friar Bungay?"

Ellen thought a moment and shook her head.

"What about the legendary Randal treasure?" Ellen continued. "Did Lord William talk about it? Did he ever hint that he knew the place where old Lord Stephen, his father, had hidden his vast riches?"

Ellen laughed at that. "Oh, William mentioned his father's hidden riches once or twice, but only to joke about it and say he wished his father hadn't been such a miser, because the family could use the money now. And yet he never acted as if his own funds were small. Just like him to offer your husband a post and damn the expense. But if he knew where the mythical treasure was he never let on. I think he just thought of it as an old rumor that didn't have any truth behind it."

"I see," Ellen said. Then, after a moment's thought, she told Lady Eleanor, "I can't think of anything else to ask you, my Lady. I thank you for your help. I do hope something you've said might help us find Wulf himself, or the person behind the murder. But…" she hesitated, then reached out to take Lady Eleanor's hand in her own, "before I leave you, please allow me to tell you how truly, truly sorry I am for your loss. I know I would be devastated by it, and I suspect that is how you are feeling, my dear, though you show your toughness to the world."

At that word Lady Eleanor broke down, slumped forward, gripped Ellen's offered hand in both of her own, and allowed the tears to pour. Between sobs she thanked Ellen for her kindness, and then added, "You are truly the only person who's expressed any kind of sympathy for what I'm going through. Everyone else simply assumed I was guilty, or was only sad that I was robbed of the chance to marry above myself. The only other sympathetic ear I've found was that minstrel who sang at my beloved's funeral."

Ellen blinked, momentarily surprised, and then said, "Him? Oh, that was my husband."

Lady Eleanor blinked in her turn, and then responded, "Of course it was."

* * *

The deep shadows of the small Romanesque church of Halloughton darkened Father Timothy's fine features as he sat, head bowed in perplexed wonder, examining the filigreed silver reliquary in his hand. "What was it doing in the grave?" his weak voice asked the unresponsive air.

But it was Alan a Dale who answered. "I definitely recall hearing a metallic 'clank' when the two dogs were dropped into the grave in their shrouds. Since one of them is split open, we can see that it was deliberately planned. Somebody hid the reliquary in the shroud in order to come back and dig it up later."

"But why, then, would he leave it at the graveside after he'd taken all the trouble to bury it and dig it up again?" the priest went on. "It just doesn't make any sense."

Friar Tuck guessed, "Perhaps he had just gotten it out when he heard you approaching, and rather than be caught in the act, dropped his prize and ran off."

"But it would have been just as quick to keep the reliquary and run off with it," Father Timothy objected.

"Unless," the friar continued, "he had left the object at the side of the grave and gone to pick up his shovel to start refilling the hole, and you interrupted him at that point? Then it might have taken him too long to come back and pick it up before running off..."

"But you're assuming that the thief was caught in the act," Alan insisted. "We don't really have any reason to believe that, do we? Father Timothy, just tell us as carefully as you can exactly what happened when you arrived at the church this morning. We've just had it in bits and pieces so far."

The priest took a deep breath and said, more calmly now, "Yes, I suppose when you walked in here I seemed almost incomprehensible with distraction. Look: This is how it happened. I was coming across the lawn from the rectory just as the sun was rising, to sing the office of prime. It was still dark enough that I did not notice until I was in the church yard itself that during the night someone had dug up Lord Randal's newly made grave. I did not see anyone in the vicinity of the grave, and although it was dark, I think I would have noticed someone slipping away through the shadows. That does not mean the robber did not see *me* as I was coming. I suppose he could have run off some time before I saw the open grave. But if that is the case, I would think he'd have had plenty of time to grab the reliquary."

"So it may well be that this desecration was all done in the darkness before dawn, well before you made your way to the church," Alan thought out loud.

The priest shrugged, then continued: "When I arrived, I saw that someone had dug up his grave, and though they had left Lord Randal undisturbed in his casket, they had ripped apart the shroud in which one of his greyhounds was buried with him. The remains of the dog himself were not tampered with, but next to the shroud I found this reliquary—although it too seems to be undisturbed, and the thief has left it behind. It's a great mystery, but I am glad to see the relic returned."

"I take it you missed this from your sanctuary only after Lord Randal's funeral?" Friar Tuck concluded.

"Indeed," Father Timothy answered, "it was the very next day that I discovered the relic of the tooth of Saint Edmund, King and Martyr, had gone missing from its niche in the church wall. I assumed it must have been stolen—for surely you know there is a traffic in relics, though generally those are false. And there would have been no way for a thief to establish the authenticity of that tooth if he had simply stolen it. He may have found, after stealing it, that he could find no buyer, and this was his elaborate means of returning it."

"But why on earth would he bother to go to all the work of digging up the grave if all he wanted to do was return the relic, and why rip open the dog's shroud?" Tuck asked.

"He didn't," Alan said with an authority of his own. "He wasn't returning the relic, and he hadn't stolen it. He had hidden it so that only he knew where it was, and he was not retrieving the reliquary but rather something that he had hidden *in* it. Something he wanted nobody else ever to find."

"How can you say all that? How do you know?" Father Timothy asked, his face blank.

"No, I see what he means," Friar Tuck said. "It's the only logical explanation of all this. The thief took the reliquary, but didn't want to keep it. He only wanted to make sure nobody else found it and found what he'd hidden inside."

"So tell me, how often do you open up the reliquary? For cleaning or whatnot?" Alan asked.

Friar Tuck looked at Father Timothy and both of them burst out laughing. "Never?" the priest replied tentatively. "It's certainly not something regularly done. The reliquary itself is dusted when the church is cleaned, but no one opens it. The relic is sacred. It would be sacrilege to let the relic be touched. It is meant to be looked at through the window of the reliquary."

"Then if someone were to hide, say, a small item inside the reliquary where it could not be seen from the outside, no one would be likely to find it until that first someone came back and claimed it?" Alan pursued.

"It could be done," Father Timothy shrugged. "It would be a sacrilege, but it could be done."

"The only question I have," Alan pondered, more to himself than either of the two clerics, "is just how long this particular item was hidden inside that silver case."

"I think my young colleague and I are thinking along the same lines," Friar Tuck told the priest. "A valuable piece of parchment may have been hidden inside this reliquary for some fifteen long years, or it may have been placed there only within the last few weeks."

"You have definitely lost me, I'm afraid," Father Timothy

said. "And I certainly can't give any opinion on what might have happened in my church so long ago. I think you are aware that I have not been in this parish fifteen months, let alone fifteen years."

"But you *can* tell us this, Father," Alan said. "At Lord Randal's funeral, there was a strange Dominican friar here, a fellow with very prominent eyebrows who stood in the back during the service and in the end helped carry the casket out to the graveyard."

"Yes, yes, Friar Bungay that was," Father Timothy said.

"You know him?" Tuck asked. "He's a regular visitor to Saint James?"

"Oh not at all," the priest answered. "I had never seen him before the morning of Lord Randal's funeral. But he turned up that morning around terce, said he was a Dominican from the Blackfriars Priory in Derby, but was currently working as a scientific advisor for Sir Guy of Gisbourne at Nottingham Castle. I told him he was welcome and asked if he had any particular reason for stopping, and he said that he understood there would be funerary rites for Lord William Randal on that day. I said he understood aright, and that he was about an hour early if he wanted to attend the service. He was content to wait, and he proceeded to take a comfortable seat in the sanctuary and tell me the story of his life."

"Indeed?" Tuck asked. "Anything interesting in that story?"

"Plenty, now that I think about it. He told me that he had been in service with the old Lord Randal, he that was Lord Stephen, and that he'd known the young Lord William when he was yet a boy. And he'd come, he said, to pay his respects in honor of his old master. Said he'd volunteer to help as pallbearer if needed as well, so I quickly agreed to that—sometimes I'm prevailed upon to help with that back-breaking task myself, and I'm none too fond of it."

"I don't blame you," Tuck answered. "But you said there was something interesting about his story? What were you thinking of?"

"This Friar Bungay mentioned that he had a soft spot in his heart for Saint James. Said that he'd stopped in the church for help the night after he'd left his service at the Randals' manor, and he'd had a long conversation here with my predecessor, old Father Mark. Said he wanted to be schooled and learn Latin and all the liberal arts, and natural philosophy and the like. His master, he said, had just died, and his master had been on a crusade and knew much of the world. Said he wanted to learn about the world and how to read maps and such things."

Alan looked meaningfully at Tuck when he'd heard that.

"And Father Mark advised him to join the Dominicans?" Alan suggested.

"Didn't have to," Father Timothy replied. "He said he'd already thought about a vocation, and that's why he'd left his service. But Father Mark encouraged him. And he said that since then, he's actually been to Paris to the University, and learned from all the expert masters there. But he'd always remembered this church through the fifteen years since, and remembered Father Mark fondly. And this is the interesting part, he remembered being impressed by our little reliquary of the tooth of Saint Edmund, because Edmund was a king of East Anglia, and that was where he was from, from the town of Bungay."

"And that didn't pop into your mind when you saw the relic had been stolen?" Alan asked, dumbfounded.

Father Timothy shrugged. "I never thought of it again until just now, when you asked me what he'd said. Besides, he was a religious. Who would have thought he'd steal?"

* * *

On his favorite horse Daisy, Robin was ambling along through Sherwood on his way back to the Great Oak. Ellen rode beside him on a small but serviceable dapple gray palfrey called Bridget, and she was repeating to Robin the things she had learned from Lady Eleanor.

"So the lady could not really give me any very helpful ideas as to where we might begin a search for Wulf," Ellen said. "She said that she really hardly knew him. And that's not surprising, since she may be poor, but she's one of the landed gentry and so wouldn't necessarily pay much attention to somebody else's servants. That's just the way they are. But she did give me some hope that Wulf may not have fled the country altogether. She said that he had a kind of unrequited love of the sister, of Lady Anne Randal. And because of that, Eleanor seemed to think Wulf would stay in the vicinity, if only to be near her even if she never spoke with him."

Robin scoffed. "I have a hard time accepting that possibility. Would anyone with any sense risk the very real possibility of a noose for a completely imaginary love affair? If Wulf hasn't fled this whole part of England by now, I wouldn't give a farthing for his sanity. A few arrows short of a quiver, I'd say."

"Oh, now, how can you scoff at love?" Ellen chided. "When I was a girl, we had many a roving minstrel who'd come to the manor and entertain us with love songs for a free supper. They were wondrous songs, as I recall."

"And that's what happened with your Alan a Dale I suppose, is it?"

Fingers of bright red crept up Ellen's neck and began to blush her face. "Well, I will admit it started that way. Gentle words of love are certainly a good first step for a man intent on wooing."

"But it's so insincere," Robin complained. "Now when I was in the old king's guard, the castle was full of knights and squires prating about *fin amors* in their high courtly style. The lover was always dying of love and his lady the only saving medicine, or weak and imprisoned and the lady's love the only key, or lost on the sea and the lady's love the only guiding star. And she had lips like cherries and eyes like stars and a neck as long and white as a swan's. Can you imagine a real woman looking like that? But the most hypocritical of all was the lover saying how pure and inviolable the *woman* was, and how far beneath her *he* was. But then he'd marry some other woman and he'd end up beating her. Well, not Palomides, of course. He was a prolific poet, and I never doubted the love he expressed for his lady; but then he never married her either."

"So is it love you find laughable, or just the way it's expressed in these poems?"

"Well, the poems for sure," Robin answered. "They lead to some warped ideas. Look at our Wulf, for one. Does he really think that there's some chance the lady of his house is going to someday give him a loving smile, even though he's nothing but a dog boy? But as a servant in a noble house he's heard enough of these mind-warping poems that he thinks someday the woman so high above him socially is going to stoop to his level and give him a loving look?"

"Perhaps," Ellen said thoughtfully. "Or perhaps there is simply the natural feeling of wanting to be near what you are fond of. I mean, look at yourself. It's no secret that you harbor tender feelings toward the Lady Mary of Winchester. Does it make you a fool if she never deigns to return your affection? These feelings are natural, not necessarily caused by flowery poetry."

It was Robin's turn to redden, but he plunged ahead to cover his embarrassment. "Not *caused* by the poetry, but turned into unrealistic expectations *by* it," he replied. "There is in men an inborn urge to couple with women. That's what philosophers mean by 'natural law.' It's basic and honest. If I see a woman who raises my spirits, I approach her with my intentions pretty obvious, and usually she responds in kind. Natural law, you see? I wouldn't have to tell you that your hair was like golden wires and your eyes like crystal pools. I'd simply grab your horse's reins and say, I'm aroused by your fiery spirit and your ample hips, sweet Nell, let's make the Beast with Two Backs!"

This sounded too close to a real proposition to Ellen, and she pulled on her horse's reins and gave Robin a severe blow to his right shoulder. "Oww!" He exclaimed. "A simple 'no' would have sufficed!"

"You'll speak courteously to me, Robin Kempe, or you'll be returning to camp alone, and you can explain to my skilled archer of a husband why I left you on the road." Ellen's chin was thrust forward in a defiant posture, and her blue eyes were flashing.

"I take your point," Robin answered, rubbing his shoulder and pulling a long face. "It was only banter."

"It was banter with an underlying purpose, and you know it as well as I do. Robin Hood, just because many women throw themselves at you, because they are enamored of the mythical bad boy you represent to them, it doesn't mean you should expect *all* of them to do so, or assume freedoms that they do not grant you."

"But I was just…"

"But me no buts. You may scorn courtly love, but courtesy is not to be sneered at. Those you interact with must all be treated as people of worth. And that means all women too. And while we're on the subject…"

Robin had just opened his mouth to reply, but was cowed by this last opening.

"This regular fornication with the Sheriff of Nottingham's wife. You're compelled to it by 'natural law,' I suppose? Despite her marriage vows?"

"Well..." Robin said, "they're not *my* marriage vows."

"Have you considered what Lady Mary's reaction might be, if she knew about your antics? If you really *do* love her, doesn't that constitute an unspoken vow of your own, to seek carnal pleasure with no one other than her?"

"But natural..."

"Natural depravity. That's what your 'natural law' is. It is the law of beasts. And men should be better than beasts." Ellen said this with an unmistakable period, as if she had done with the subject for good.

Robin, however, feeling wronged or at least misunderstood, was not willing to drop the subject altogether. He had just opened his mouth to respond to Ellen's reprimand when he saw her eyes, looking beyond him, grow wide with shock. Unable to speak, she pointed over his shoulder at something they were approaching at the side of the road. Robin looked in the direction she indicated, and saw what looked to him like a pile of dirty gray and brown rags at the edge of the wood. Then he noticed that there was a dark reddish stain in the midst of the gray. Bringing Daisy to a halt, he handed her reins to Ellen, dismounted, and stepped cautiously over to examine the clothing.

When he was within a few steps of the pile, he realized with certainty that it was in fact a body. There were boots showing at the foot, and tangled hair visible at the head. The corpse was clearly lying on its face. Ever so gently, Robin used his own boot to turn the body over onto its back. Both he and Ellen sounded a simultaneous gasp.

It was Wulf.

CHAPTER FIFTEEN

Robin and Ellen entered the Saint James churchyard in Halloughton just as Friar Tuck and Alan a Dale were preparing to leave it. They were as astounded to see the desecrated grave of Lord Randal as Tuck and Alan were to see the body of the dog boy Wulf slung across the back of Robin's horse; here Robin had placed the corpse when he and Ellen decided to bring it to Saint James, the closest church they could think of, for immediate burial. Robin led Daisy while Ellen rode beside, mounted on Bridget. Wulf had been dead for several days, and though the weather had been cool in Sherwood in mid-October, it would be a kindness to Wulf's remains to inter them as quickly as possible.

As the four riders met in the churchyard, Friar Tuck quickly answered the newcomers' question about the disinterment of Lord William's dog and of the stolen reliquary. Robin was not surprised at the dogged determination of Friar Bungay to keep the secret of old Lord Stephen's treasure to himself and to find it despite any claim the rest of the Randal family had to those reputedly untold riches. But though they were all certain by now that Bungay was guilty of murdering the father, it was not at all clear that he had anything to do with poisoning Lord William.

And what about the murder of Wulf?

Ellen revealed what she remembered from Lady Eleanor's comments about the dog boy. It turned out the lady had been quite correct in assuming that Wulf would not have traveled far from the lands he had lived in all his life. When she mentioned that Lady Eleanor believed Wulf would stay close because of his affection for Lady Anne, Alan remembered how Anne herself had alluded to the servant's apparent feelings for her. That much, at least, seemed incontestable, coming from two so very different sources.

Father Timothy helped ease Wulf's remains down from Daisy, and laid him on his back, looking for the cause of the fellow's death. It did not take long to make that determination: a single stab wound, straight to the heart, most likely from a knife—it was not wide enough to be from a sword.

"Difficult to tell much else from that body," Friar Tuck declared. "Looks like crows have been at it. And it's rained since the fellow expired. So I don't imagine you noticed any tracks or any other evidence where you found the body."

"No, nothing," Robin said. "But that stab wound does tell us something."

"What's that?" Father Timothy asked.

"It tells us Wulf knew his killer and was on friendly terms with whoever it was. There's just the one wound, and there's no wounds on his hands or arms, none that I can see anyway. It looks like he didn't fight, but let his killer walk right up to him and stab him to the heart. He never saw it coming."

"Wulf knew his killer, was friendly with his killer," Alan mused. "And who would he have been friendly with who also had the best motive for killing him?"

"The person who talked him into killing Lord William," Ellen answered immediately. "What if he was meeting his co-conspirator in secret there on the road, away from any village or manor, to collect the promised payment for murdering his master?"

"Of course," Alan agreed, and speculated further: "Suppose they'd agreed to meet just at that spot on what would have been, what, a week after the murder, at a certain time of day."

"Or night," Ellen corrected, "when Wulf couldn't have seen the knife coming."

"He's expecting a purse full of gold or precious jewels or whatever," Alan imagined, "reaches out and receives instead a knife in the chest."

"This all sounds likely," Robin agreed. Then added, "So Wulf wasn't staying around this neighborhood because he wanted to be close to Lady Anne, as Lady Eleanor suggested. It was to meet his partner and collect his payment."

"So he met his collaborator, who killed him so he'd never be able to tell anyone else who had *really* been behind Lord William's murder," Friar Tuck conceded. "Have we established any connection between Wulf and the Dominican friar, Bungay? Might he have been the one to conspire with him, perhaps promising him a share in Lord Randal's father's treasure?"

"As far as we know, Bungay had never met Wulf. He'd left the Randals' service long before Wulf began," Alan reminded him. "And we don't see how the poisoning could be connected with the treasure, either."

Tuck nodded, then after a moment added, "But what I still can't understand is why the killer didn't remove Wulf's body somewhere else and bury it , or at least hide it. Why leave it at the side of the road?"

"Someone surprised him and so frightened him off before he was able to hide the body?" Father Timothy suggested.

"Then why wasn't the body found right away, by whoever frightened the killer off? Tuck asked.

"If it was dark," Timothy continued, "perhaps the person who happened on the scene didn't even see the killer sneaking off, and passed right by the fresh body without noticing it in the dark."

"Maybe," Tuck said, in an unconvinced voice.

"*Orrr...*" Ellen said, stretching out that final *r*, "the murderer was not strong enough to move the body."

After a moment of silence, Alan cried out, "A woman!"

"Yes, yes, that I can see," Friar Tuck agreed.

"Wulf was not that large of a chap," Robin said. "Certainly many women would have been able to move him. But if it were a woman of relatively small stature and dainty...someone like..."

"Lady Anne!" Alan cried out.

"Of course!" Ellen agreed. "If it's true Wulf would have done anything for her, she's the one most likely to have talked him into killing Lord William. Say she promises him not riches but her favors for the small service of poisoning her brother. And he comes to that secluded spot the following week, expecting a liaison. Is that the sort of thing likely to appeal to his natural desire, Mr. Robin Hood?"

Robin, still smarting from her earlier comments, answered brusquely, "If by her 'favors' you mean a roll in the hay, then I think it a most likely scenario."

"But hold on," Friar Tuck said. "I admit everything you are saying is plausible, but what possible motive would Lady Anne have for murdering her own brother? I mean, I might believe that the brother, Lord Geoffrey, had a motive, since he was first in line to inherit the title and lands. But what resentment could this Lady Anne have against William that would provoke her to kill him?"

"Money," Alan said decisively.

Everyone else looked at him questioningly. "Every time any of us has talked to her, she's made some kind of complaint about the family's not having enough wealth. It's kept her, she claims, from marrying Sir Peter of Verysdale, or at least that's what we've been told. And Lord William was well aware of her feelings. It was to her that he left all his gold and silver. Geoffrey got the land and the manor house, and his mother the cattle, but Anne got the cash."

"Do you suppose she actually knew that he had made his will to that effect?" Ellen wondered. "And wanting a significant dowry that might make the difference in her marriage plans, decided to hasten his death, with the help of her hapless admirer, Wulf?"

Alan shrugged. "It's a motive," he said.

"Well, it all fits," Tuck said. "The question now is, what do we do about it? We don't have any legal authority to arrest Lady Anne on suspicion of murdering her brother. We don't even know if any of our speculations are actual facts. And it isn't as if we can simply go to the Sheriff and explain our suspicions."

"When have we ever needed 'legal authority' to do anything we thought best?" Robin said. "There are more ways into the woods than one. We can surely think of some way to get the girl by herself and put the difficult questions to her."

"Well that might be…" Alan began, and then stopped abruptly as he saw approaching six men on horseback, followed by a horse-drawn cart, all bursting through the trees into the churchyard with the speed of dire purpose. He had to blink a few times before he realized that it was Sir Richard leading the group, flanked by his son Sir Peter and servant Dap. Behind them on horseback rode Little John on his great horse Bishop, Will Stutely, and Jock of Barlborough. Thorvald, of course, was driving the cart, in which rode Will Scarlet and Much the miller's son.

"Message came…to Verysdale…from Lady Maude…" Sir Richard was trying to tell them the trouble but was so out of breath from the vigorous ride that his son took over.

"Lady Maude sent us a message through Brother Philip," Sir Peter explained. "We were closer to Nottingham and easier to find than your camp. She says that the Countess Lydia is in danger. Gisbourne has sent twenty of his guard to waylay her on the road—and assassinate her."

The stunned group in the churchyard sprang into action as Robin called, "The horses! Quickly!" Alan and Friar Tuck ran to fetch the horses they had ridden in on, which were still saddled and tied to tree branches at the edge of the yard.

"There is truly no time to waste," Will Stutely added. "The Countess is returning from London on the Great North Road with Marion. Palomides and Sir Eustace are guarding them, but against twenty guards they have little chance."

All business and taking charge, Robin ordered, "Thorvald, you take Ellen and Friar Tuck back to camp. Will and Much, you grab their horses and ride with us. We'll ride south as quickly as we can. And don't spare the horses," he cried as he mounted Daisy and galloped off, not bothering to look back to see if his orders were being carried out.

Those already mounted—John and Stutely, Jock and Dap, Sir Peter and Sir Richard—galloped after him, while Ellen and Tuck climbed into the cart that Much and Scarlet had just vacated. Alan, who had been slower to mount, fell in beside Scarlet and cried, "But why is Gisbourne intent on killing the Countess?"

"She's been to London to see the new king," Will Scarlet answered. "Rumor has it that she is bringing a writ from the king that relieves Gisbourne of his office and orders him to abandon Nottingham castle to the king's new castellan. On no condition does Gisbourne want that order to reach Nottingham."

"Then we must ensure that it does!" Alan exclaimed, and spurred his horse into a gallop.

* * *

The four riders were coming north at a slow but steady pace. Their horses had been pushed harder than they were comfortable with, and the quartet were content to give their mounts a bit of leisure, despite their anxiety about what they were returning to.

Countess Lydia, wimpled and dressed in a simple blue homespun gown she had purchased in London so as not to draw attention to herself on the road back to Nottingham, was fuming silently as she rode next to Sir Palomides. The Moor, sensitive to the lady's agitation and its cause, tried once again, for perhaps the hundredth time on this homeward journey, to assuage her restless edge.

"My Lady, we have been less than four days about our journey. The horses must rest or they will fall dead beneath us, and we shall never reach Nottingham in time."

"Four days is time enough for Gisbourne to have passed sentence on my faithful servant Robin, and to have hanged him as well!" was the Countess's rejoinder. "And then this whole quest will have been in vain!"

"You forget that Robin Hood has many friends, even in Nottingham," Palomides said. "Sir Richard at the Lee is no small advocate. Robin even has an ally in the Sheriff's wife. Surely she will have something to say about this matter. And if worse came to worst, he has Little John and the rest of his meinie, who will not suffer him to be hanged while they live. Remember how they rescued Will Stutely from hanging, despite Gisbourne and his thugs."

"Well," Lady Lydia mused, patting the leather purse hanging from her belt, in which she carried a parchment order sealed with King Constantine's own signet ring. "Sir Guy will have little to say about this or any other matter of law or state when we arrive in Nottingham and present the king's proclamation in open court." Indeed, despite her curiosity she had not dared to break the king's seal on the missive she bore. For one thing that would have brought into question the authenticity of the order. Thus, though they had the king's word that the document relieved Sir Guy of his royal appointment to Nottingham Castle, Lydia had no clue as to whom Constantine had appointed as Gisbourne's successor.

If Lady Lydia was visibly fretting in her saddle, Maid Marion was audibly grieving in hers. As the company drew closer to Nottingham, the dread of what they would find there cut deeper and deeper into Marion's soul, like a nail being driven into a coffin lid. It had reached the point where she could no longer hold back the flood of tears that poured from her eyes, and there seemed nothing Sir Eustace could do to soothe her pain.

"Lady Mary," the old knight tried again. "Robin is nothing if not resourceful. He has escaped greater threats than this one, and come through laughing and swaggering like the cock of the walk. No prison run by the likes of Gisbourne can hold a fellow of his quick wits! I swear, he was not made for the hangman's noose but rather for the marriage knot, if you'll have him! Mark my words!"

"Oh Sir Eustace," Marion wept, oblivious to his comforts. "He will die. He will die without ever knowing how I loved him."

At that moment Sir Eustace's sympathetic eyes looked beyond Marion and suddenly grew wide in surprise and horror. Marion glanced behind her and saw eight armed and mounted guards emerging from the trees at the edge of the road. Suddenly frantic, she lurched back and pulled her horse in the opposite direction, only to see eight more guards coming, swords drawn, from the other side of the road. Behind them two more mounted and helmeted soldiers were closing in from the rear, and another pair of chain-mailed riders were sitting on large destriers, blocking the road before them with swords at the ready. The apparent leader of the guards held his helmet before him on his saddle. He had long greasy hair and a jagged scar on his left cheek, and they could see that his right hand was swathed in bandages.

The spokesman made no attempt at courtesy. The hawk does not greet the rabbit with pretty words before swooping in for the kill. He noticed that both ladies were dressed in the same simple blue homespun disguising the rank of the noble peer, and so demanded, "Which is the Countess of Chesterfield?" Receiving only silence in reply, he added, "Surrender her to us and the rest of you can go your way. We only want the Countess."

"Gisbourne," Lady Lydia whispered to Sir Palomides. "He knows what I'm carrying and wants to stop my mouth before I reach Nottingham. Take the parchment..." she began, reaching for her purse.

But before she had finished her thought, a voice behind her cried, "I am the Countess Lydia of Chesterfield. Your quarrel is with me, now let the others go!"

But the Countess could not abide the idea that Lady Mary should sacrifice herself to save her mistress, and cried out even louder, "My faithful attendant pleads nobly, but she is lying. I am the Countess Lydia Peveril!"

Scarface paused, momentarily flummoxed. He looked from one lady to the other, expecting to determine by their attire which was the servant and which the peer of the realm. Then, unable to distinguish and with an indifferent air, issued the command, "Kill them both!" And the rest of the guards rushed in to obey the order.

Palomides swung his checkerboard shield onto his left arm to protect his armorless body, and unslung his arming sword with his right, and in less time than it took the first four guards to cross the space from the forest edge he had knocked from their mounts a pair of them and was whacking away at the other two. While he was as skilled with that short sword as any man in England, oh, how he wished for a jousting lance of the sort with which he had unhorsed four challengers in the space of a minute in the days of the old king. Out of the corner of his eye he saw Sir Eustace gamely trying to fend off a like number of guards with designs on Lady Mary, and despaired of giving help to either of them. He had confidence in his own prowess in dealing with four or five attackers, but twenty might be too much to hope for, and as they had surrounded the small band of travelers, he did not know how he could possibly keep all of the assassins away from the Countess herself, let alone the mistress of her chamber, even with the valiant help of Sir Eustace.

The Countess, for her part, was doing her best to keep her palfrey directly behind Palomides' great war horse, the better to keep some distance between her and the hired killers. And to sell herself as dearly as possible, she had drawn her own long dagger and held it before her to menace any guard who came close. If this was to be her last stand she would not go down meekly.

Lady Mary had actually left her own horse and had climbed behind Sir Eustace in his saddle. It had been Eustace's idea— he reasoned that he could protect her better if he didn't have to worry about being separated from her and her mount. And he continued to back the horse away from his attackers, forcing them to come at him from the front rather than sneaking behind him to get at Lady Mary. But he knew it could not work for long against so large a force of the enemy. His defense, and that of Sir Palomides, could only be seen as a forlorn hope. But if they were to yield, they were turning Lady Mary and the Countess over to certain death.

By this time Scarface himself had fastened his helmet and entered the fray. Seeing Sir Palomides in dire straits, beset with six battling guards, Scarface determined to dispatch the doughty swordsman once and for all. Approaching the valiant Moor from the rear as cautiously as he could, with a tight-lipped smile he raised his sword high with his bandaged hand and paused momentarily, girding himself to bring it down with all the force possible upon the knight's exposed skull.

At that moment he dropped the sword, his hand groping toward his throat, from which the point of an arrow had suddenly sprouted, having entered through the back of Scarface's neck. His eyes opened in shocked surprise, which was the last sensation he felt before he dropped from his horse into utter blackness.

Fifty yards up the Great North Road, Jock of Barlborough knelt in the dust, notching another arrow to his bowstring. His elimination of Scarface had been the work of a few seconds. At this range, he could not miss, and he took aim now at one of the other guards dogging Sir Palomides, who stood his ground like a chained bear bedeviled by a pack of curs. Meanwhile Will Scarlet, his quiver full of arrows in the road before him, began to rain down deadly shafts on the crowd besetting Sir Eustace.

Their captain fallen, Gisbourne's guards began to fall into disarray, and when four more of their number fell, from arrow shafts or, distracted by the archers, from sword thrusts dealt by Palomides or Eustace, two of the guards decided to charge the archers, but as they did so, the thunder of hooves coming up the road announced the arrival of the main body of Sherwood outlaws, with Robin and Sir Richard leading the way with swords at the ready. Little John, more at home with his quarterstaff than a sword, rode straight into the fray surrounding Sir Palomides and Lady Lydia and, quickly dismounting, began to flail his staff about until he had broken the legs of three of her attackers so that they fell from their saddles, moaning in the dust and unable to stand. The rest of the Countess's attackers—of whom there were but three left on horseback—backed off from the berserking giant to regroup at the roadside.

But no one fought as grimly as Robin Hood. He might have been more deadly with his bow, proving perhaps even more formidable than Jock or Will, but having left it in camp for his visit to Lady Eleanor's, he had to settle for his sword. He was fighting for the love of his life, and at no time did he ever anticipate so sharply the pang of loss his heart would endure if anything were to happen to Lady Mary as he did at that moment. After some minutes striking in tandem with the valiant Sir Eustace, he became aware suddenly that Sir Eustace had ceased to resist. Accordingly he fought even more savagely, wounding five of Marion's attackers and skewering one completely on the point of his sword, so that the few that remained retreated from the fray.

By now four more guards lay dead in the road along with their commander, the man with the scar. Ten others lay incapacitated by wounds, including the three whose legs were broken by Little John's onslaught, three more felled by arrows, and four slashed or stabbed by sword thrusts. Some of these looked as if they might prove fatal. Only five guards remained on horseback, and these gathered warily together at the side of the road, beaten and bewildered, searching one another's eyes for a clue as to what their next steps should be. They were all tired, and none was unscathed by slashes or deeper wounds. Sensing their indecision, Robin took charge of the situation.

"Throw down your weapons if you want to live," he called from Daisy's back in the ringing voice of a warlord. Little John was standing before him, facing the guards and brandishing his staff. On either side of him stood Jock and Will Scarlet, their bows drawn with arrows pointed straight into the group of guards. Without a second's more delay, five swords dropped clanging to the ground. Will Stutely dismounted and ran in front of the guards' horses, gathering the dropped weapons, while Much the miller's son and Alan a Dale scampered among the fallen, confiscating their weapons as well. At this point Robin glanced toward the Countess Lydia, whose privileged rank gave her the status of the true decision-maker here.

The Countess moved her horse beside Robin's and quietly told him, "I am far less distressed than I was, since my greatest fear on our ride from London was that we should arrive too late to save you from a hanging. But relieved as I am, I must still get to Nottingham with my charge from the king, and I apparently need a larger escort."

"We are at your service, my Lady," Robin answered her with all the courtesy a yeoman might muster. "What about these?" and he gestured toward the guards, mounted and fallen.

"Let them live if they can," the Countess answered, this time in full voice as one in command. "But we cannot leave them the means to attack us again. And so here is what we will do: The five of you," she addressed the trembling group on horseback, "may keep your own mounts, and five more. The rest of your horses we will confiscate. You can take care of your wounded and let them ride with you or walk back to Nottingham. You can bury your dead here, or transport them back to Nottingham Castle. But we will take all of your weapons and half of your horses, to preclude any attempts to follow us and ambush us again. Now I suggest you dismount to see to your dead and wounded. We will continue with all due speed to the city...."

But the Countess was interrupted at that point by a cry from Lady Mary. At the sound Robin spurred his horse to her side, where she sat behind Sir Eustace on his mount. The knight was slumped forward and was breathing heavily. But he had turned his head to look toward Marion, and addressed her with all courtesy: "My Lady, you have come through the hostility unscathed? Do you have any further need of my services?"

Robin could see the wounds that had slashed the old gentleman's arms, and could also see at least two deeper wounds where blood was oozing from his torso. Tears had begun to flow unchecked from Marion's eyes. "I am unhurt, sir," she answered. "You have rendered your service nobly, and you have my eternal gratitude."

Then in a voice that rose barely above a whisper, Sir Eustace replied, "Good. Then you will not be offended if I rest for a while now." His eyes flickered for an instant toward Robin, and added, "Remember my advice, my Lady, when you remember me." And at that word the knight slipped from his saddle and fell to the earth. He was dead.

* * *

Sir Eustace's death cast a gloomy pall over the ride toward Nottingham. The old retainer's body was laid gently over the back of his horse, his hands and feet tied together to prevent his slipping once again into the dust of the road.

But their circumstances would not be improved by taking time to grieve. Robin knew neither he nor any of his men should be seen entering Nottingham. He would be easily recognized as, almost certainly, would Little John and Will Stutely. Scarlet, Jock, Much and Alan could as well be identified by their Lincoln green clothing, and so it was decided that the bodies of seven slain or wounded guardsmen must be stripped of their chainmail corslets and their helmets. The Norman style nasal helmets would cover enough of the center of the outlaws' faces as to make identification more difficult for the casual observer, and the chain mail would cover their green livery. And indeed, it would appear as if Countess Lydia were being escorted into Nottingham by Gisbourne's own guard, so that no one would be likely to interfere with them, either on the road or in Nottingham itself, until the Countess had delivered the king's orders.

All this time Jock, John, and Scarlet kept watch on the five mounted guards, taking turns as one changed into the armor while the other two kept Gisbourne's men at bay. Then the Countess, Lady Mary, and Sir Palomides mounted three of the confiscated horses, determined to give their own beasts a lighter burden. Palomides led Zulfiqar behind him, for he would put the great destrier in no one else's charge, while Robin led Marion's mount and Dap the Countess's. Then, flanked by Sir Richard at her left hand and Sir Palomides at her right, Lady Lydia led the company on the road to Nottingham, her head proudly erect as if she were leading a royal progress. Bringing up the rear were Dap and Jock, who was leading Sir Eustace's horse, bearing his master's remains.

Robin, escorting Lady Mary directly behind the Countess and her fellow nobles, could not remain silent, though the lady's countenance drooping with sorrow made it clear she was in no mood for conversation. "Marion," he began familiarly, "forgive me for interrupting your reverie. I know you are shocked and saddened by the events of this day. Sir Eustace was a good man…" at this his companion sobbed. "But never did his virtue shine more brightly than on this day. And I will honor his memory forever because I know he died saving the life of the woman I love most in this world." Then Robin, so completely unaccustomed to confessing his emotions sincerely and without irony or skepticism, did something else that was highly unusual for him: He blushed from his hairline down, though the phenomenon could scarcely be seen in the shadow of his nasal helmet.

And Marion, turning over in her mind what Sir Eustace called his "advice"—that she should love wherever her affections bloomed, regardless of social status, gave Robin a tight-lipped nod, acknowledging his words. It was as much as she could do on this mournful day, but she determined to act more definitively another time. Sooner rather than later, she told herself.

* * *

Alan a Dale found himself riding beside Sir Peter of Verysdale in the train of horses following the Duchess of Chesterfield to Nottingham. Under normal circumstances, Alan would have hesitated to address one of the younger gentry like Sir Peter familiarly, but having just fought beside him in mortal combat, Alan thought it would probably be fine to chance it. "I admired the way you handled yourself in the fight back there. Knightly skills are a wonder to watch," Alan began. In truth, he'd been so busy himself striking and fending off blows that he hadn't noticed Sir Peter's chivalric talents at all, but he had a particular reason for conversing with Sir Peter, and thought this might be a prudent and effective way into a conversation.

Sir Peter flashed Alan an amused grin. "If you saw any strokes I landed, it must have been out of the corner of your eye. We were all kept pretty busy by the strength of those guards."

"True," Alan acknowledged. "but truth to tell they were simply mercenary bullies like Gisbourne himself, fighting simply because they like having the power to make others submit to their masters' will. Robin, John, Palomides, Sir Richard, poor Sir Eustace, and yourself fought with a vigor and ferocity that comes from defending your friends and the things you love.

That's what made us successful against a much larger force."

"That and the element of surprise. And a lot of arrows," Sir Peter said, and he and Alan both laughed softly. "But I will always be grateful to Sir Palomides for rescuing me as he did from those assassins in Iberia," he continued. "And to tell you the truth, I do still harbor feelings for the Countess Lydia. I live in hope that one day she will decide that administering her lands on her own is more difficult than it need be, and start looking seriously for a partner. And here I am!"

Alan nodded. "I do recall your partiality toward the Countess," he replied, glad to seize this easy opportunity to question Sir Peter about his relationships. "But I was under the impression you had moved on. Did I not hear rumors that you might be considering a match with Lady Anne Randal?"

Sir Peter laughed again, this time a bit more heartily. "With Annie?" he said. "A rumor is all it was, I assure you." Then seeing Alan's dubious expression he went on. "Oh, Annie is a nice kid, for sure. We've been friends since she was a toddler. We lived on neighboring estates, you know, and often got together with the family. Annie used to follow me around—I must have been six or seven years older than her—and got so she thought of me as her favorite brother. She certainly confided in me a lot more than she did her own brothers. After I'd been fostered for years at Horsley Castle and became a knight, and I returned home to Verysdale, she took up with me right where we'd left off."

"But she never entertained ideas of marrying you?" Alan probed.

"Oh, I suppose if my father and Lord William had settled on the idea, she'd have agreed to it. But I think her brother hoped to marry her into some richer noble family. And for that matter my father wouldn't have minded my marrying into wealth either. Neither of our estates is very lucrative."

"Oh, I've heard about that too," Alan replied. "Say, what about that great treasure her father was supposed to have left? Did she ever talk to you about that?"

"Ah, I'd heard that rumor too. But Annie didn't believe in those stories at all. She always said if her father'd had a big treasure, he'd never have left his family so poor. And I figured she was probably right."

"So," Alan mused, mostly to himself, "she had no interest in the treasure, and she wasn't set on marrying you..."

"Not at all," sir Peter continued. "Fact is, marrying me would have been like marrying her own brother. And she certainly knew I was devoted to the Countess. We really didn't have secrets from each other."

"Yes, I recall seeing you and her conversing privately at her brother's funeral," Alan said. "What was she talking to you about then?"

"Oh, this and that," Sir Peter answered. "She was devastated at the loss. She really had a lot of hopes for her brother. Hopes that he could give her enough of a dowry to net her a rich husband. That's really what she wanted, she was always so worried about her family's dwindling wealth."

"Did she have anybody in mind in particular?" Alan probed.

Finally, a light coming into his eyes, Sir Peter asked, "Say why are you so interested in Annie anyway? How does any of this concern you?"

Alan had expected the question. "I assume you know from Sir Richard that we've been involved with trying to find Lord William's killer," he began.

"But we all know that his servant Wulf poisoned him, don't we?"

"Yes, but we are certain that Wulf could not have been acting alone. He had no discernable motive. And he appears not to have fled Sherwood, but to have stayed around despite the law's condemnation. We think he was planning to meet his co-conspirator again, perhaps to be paid for his crime."

Sir Peter whistled. "Interesting, but what does it have to do with me, or with Annie?"

Alan swallowed, having finally come to the significant point. "This Wulf fellow was apparently enamored of Lady Anne. We thought that if anybody could have gotten him to kill his master, it would have been the young woman he admired so much."

At that Sir Peter let out a loud guffaw. "Annie? Conspire with Wulf? That's truly absurd. She couldn't stand the little blighter. Gave him absolutely no encouragement at all. Never spoke with him if she could avoid it, and she almost always could. Oh no, no. She despised the little beast. She made a point of knowing nothing at all about him. Could never have told you where he was from or anything like that. No, you've definitely got it wrong there, sirrah." And with that he continued to laugh robustly.

Alan sighed. It had been quite an eventful day. They'd discovered important news about Friar Bungay and his murder of the old Lord Randal, but that brought them no closer to finding out anything about Lord William's death. They had managed to rescue the Countess and Maid Marion, but had lost Lady Lydia's favorite retainer. And now, it seemed, all their work in finding evidence that led them to suspect Lady Anne of murdering her brother, and her admirer Wulf, seemed to be crumbling into dust. It looked like he and Ellen would have to start building a new case all over again.

CHAPTER SIXTEEN

L ady Lydia Peveril, Countess of Chesterfield, approached the gate into Nottingham Castle on one of Sir Guy of Gisbourne's own horses, escorted by Sir Richard at the Lee on her right hand. Lady Mary of Winchester followed close behind her, flanked by Sir Peter of Verysdale on her left and Sir Palomides on her right, mounted on another of Gisbourne's rounceys and leading his own great war horse. Robin had slipped back, making a group of seven outlaws dressed as nasal-helmeted guards and corseted in chainmail. Robin, not at all anxious to land himself in Gisbourne's dungeons once again (particularly without a Friar Bungay to show him the way out), was taking an uncharacteristically cautious approach. He hoped only to blend in with the others, riding anonymously in pairs behind the nobles in military fashion. Dap was the last rider in the group, and he was leading a string of riderless horses, on the first of which the body of Sir Eustace was borne.

The guards at the castle gate, unaware that their commander had secretly sent a force to murder this noblewoman specifically to prevent her entering the gates of Nottingham in this manner, let the company in without question when the Countess announced that she had come from the king with papers specifically intended for Sir Guy of Gisbourne's eyes.

Once they were inside the castle's outer bailey, they were met by several grooms who took their horses to stable, and Sir Peter took charge of Sir Eustace's body, asking that it be brought to the chapel and given the appropriate rites, explaining that they had been beset by bandits on the way, and that the Countess's close retainer had been killed. In the meantime Lady Lydia strode purposefully toward the castle's great hall, accompanied by Marion, Richard and Palomides. Their strategy was a confident, businesslike manner that expressed to any onlookers that this group belonged here and were carrying out essential duties in a competent manner. No one was going to stop Lady Lydia until she had confronted the lord of the castle.

The seven armed outlaws followed Lady Lydia down the long passageway that led directly into the great hall. Each had a hand on the hilt of his sword as they looked about them, alert for any sign of intended violence against the Countess. Robin moved swiftly but cautiously along the wall on the right of the passageway, a wall lined with several very large tapestries. He was just passing a wall hanging depicting Judith with the head of Holofernes when a hand shot out from behind the tapestry and grabbed him by the hem of his corslet, yanking him behind the arras and into what he quickly realized was a hidden and dimly lit alcove. And he was looking directly into the dark smoldering eyes of Lady Maude Peveril.

"I see my warning was in time to save your precious Countess," the Sheriff's wife was whispering as her arms moved around his neck and pulled his helmeted head toward her face. She was dressed in one of her simple everyday gowns, unornamented but woven of a fine linen reaching to her feet, Her luxuriant auburn hair was flowing free around her shoulders, and she added, "But you! Why on earth would you put yourself in danger by coming here again?"

"Maudie, it was a very close thing. We were very nearly too

late, and had a devil of a fight to save them…"

"Them?" Maude repeated, her left eyebrow shooting upwards.

"The…the Countess and her entourage, you know," Robin realized it may not be good manners, or even safe, to talk to Maude about how hard he had fought to save Marion. "And I'm here to keep protecting them. I didn't think anybody would recognize me dressed as a guard like this…"

"You think *I* wouldn't recognize you, no matter what kind of disguise you wore? I knew it was you just from the way you walked. Oh Robin, tell me the truth. You came here because you wanted to see me, didn't you? You wanted to thank me for getting that message to you."

This thought had never occurred to him, although now that she mentioned it Robin thought it was probably the right thing to do. "Of course," he told Maude. "That was certainly *one* of the reasons for coming here, as well as, you know, protecting the Countess as I said."

"Then why don't you show me some gratitude?" Lady Maude whispered hotly into his ear, which she suddenly licked and then pressed her mouth against his, giving her tongue free rein. When she paused for a breath and drew back her head momentarily, he answered, "But Maude, the truth is I'm just exhausted—worn out from fighting Gisbourne's twenty guards. I just don't think I'm up to it."

With that Maude's hand reached down beneath his chain mail and caught hold of Robin's manhood, which immediately responded to her touch. "Oh my," she giggled. "You must not be *that* tired. This little fellow is certainly up to it!" And with that she was lifting her gown up to her waist and pulling him toward her by that same organ. "You know I'm not the kind to take no for an answer," she whispered again, helping him pull off his mail with her other hand.

And Robin, carried away by what he had called the "law of Nature," pressed Maude's body against the wall of the alcove, spreading her legs and lifting them over his forearms while he held her bottom with both hands, giving in to the lady's urgings and thumping her into the wall. But though his body fell mechanically into the act urged upon him, in the back of his mind he thought of Maid Marion, and momentarily felt some guilt in this consummation with another woman. But stronger than his remorse for the act was his desire for Marion herself, and his frustration with the idea that he would never have her in this way because of the differences in their status. And so rather than looking directly into Maude's fierce eyes, he closed his own and imagined Marion's face looking at him, and making those sounds that were coming now from Maude's throat, in the throes of her own ecstasy.

When it was done, Robin felt a prodigious letdown, almost as if he had been prepared for venison and had been served a pottage of oats. On previous occasions, he'd always felt exhilarated after a romp with Lady Maude. Now he simply felt lost. He could not get the thought of Marion out of his mind, and somehow he knew that from this point on it would be forever thus. He let out a confused sigh.

Maude seemed not to notice the change in him. The sigh she interpreted as exhaustion. "Well you kept up your end of the bargain well enough, but you do seem to have tired yourself out," she remarked as she let her gown slip back to the floor and arranged her flowing hair as best she could without a mirror. "Your blood was up, I'm sure, battling all those guards, but a bout with me is guaranteed to wear you out."

"Always, my dear Maudie," Robin answered with a false bravado, straightening out his hosen and grabbing his mail coat. "I think you could wear out a bull."

Maude gave a short laugh and said, "Well I don't intend to try. Your horn is all I can take. Now I'm off—you follow in a few minutes. It won't do to be seen coming from behind this curtain too close together!" And with that she blew him a kiss and, taking a cue from the Countess's entrance, strode from behind the arras with a confident step.

* * *

Lady Mary had entered the great hall with the Countess and her entourage, but when she looked around she did not recognize Robin under any of the nasal helmets that surrounded her mistress. When she asked Little John and Will Scarlet whether they had seen Robin, both shook their heads and looked wonderingly around. Then she asked Dap.

The servant had come in behind the others, having handed off his burden of Sir Eustace's corpse to Sir Peter. And following behind, he had seen one of the armored guards accompanying the Countess duck behind a tapestry. "There was a woman holding a man's severed head," he told Marion in his blandest, tone. "I can't be sure it was him. I can't really identify any of the outlaws with their mail and helmets on. But if he's not here, it was probably him."

Maid Marion lowered her brow in concentration and, it must be said, with a little bit of pique. The man had just escaped from the dungeon in this very castle, where they would have hanged him if he hadn't found a way out. And now he'd broken off from the safety of this group and was galivanting around the halls of the place on his own? What could be done with such a fellow? Wait till she found him. She'd teach *him* to put her through this worry, just see if she didn't!

At that point Lady Lydia, who it turned out had walked into

an empty hall, told her guards to go out into the castle environs and compel anyone who seemed to be above the rank of churl into the great hall to hear a proclamation from the king that concerned all of them deeply. "Try the lesser hall," the Countess told them. "That seems to be where Gisbourne tends to hold court when he's at home."

Typical, Lady Mary smirked. The easiest thing would be for the Countess to simply move to the lesser hall herself with her entourage, but making the others come to her was a very conscious assertion of her power. Marion decided to use this opportunity to leave the hall herself, and search the neighboring corridors of the castle for her mislaid Robin Hood. The words of the late lamented Sir Eustace were ringing in her ears: "To act on my love, no matter what others may have thought, no matter about class or ambition, was my truest course," he had told her. And thinking of Robin's danger if he were recognized within the palace walls, she thought of Sir Eustace's further warning, "There is no sadder feeling than too late." She would track Robin down if she could.

Six disguised outlaws left the great hall, followed immediately by Lady Mary of Winchester. Lady Lydia squinted in puzzlement as he saw her lady in waiting depart, but shrugged, assuming she had gone with the guards to help summon the officials of Nottingham to her lady's will. But Marion broke off from the others almost immediately, and retraced the steps of the entourage, looking for the arras with the severed head upon it. She'd taken only a few steps along the nearly deserted passage when she met the Sheriff's wife, smoothing her skirts around her legs and shaking her auburn locks, still running a hand through them to help straighten them.

"Oh Lady Maude!" Marion exclaimed, reaching a hand out to touch the lady's elbow in a familiar greeting. "How fortuitous to have run into you!"

Maude nodded toward Marion, avoiding her eyes and murmuring, "Lady Mary of Winchester! What a surprise to see you here again. I...I had not heard that you had returned. Is the Countess with you?"

"Indeed," Marion said. "We've only just arrived. My Lady is in the great hall, where she has summoned the Nottingham court to wait upon her. She bears an important missive from the king that she says she cannot be delayed in delivering."

"Truly? From the king?" Lady Maude replied with feigned incredulity. Had she not been the one who had sent the warning to Sir Richard about Gisbourne's intended ambush of Lady Lydia as she returned from the king? But obviously no one had informed this prim little twit who had been responsible for saving her life. But she supposed that was all right. It meant Robin hadn't had any private intimacy with her since the rescue. Maybe they weren't so close as she had feared. But she only added, half in jest, the phrase so many people in the north were repeating of late. "Who *is* the king these days, anyway?"

Marion smiled politely and answered, "If you were to visit his palace in London, surely you'd have no doubts that Constantine truly is in charge, a worthy heir to the late king. Please, attend on my Lady in the hall, and perhaps you'll find your husband and bring him with you. The king's proclamation should have significant import for him in particular."

Maude nodded and passed on, muttering, "I'll find him if I can" as the stiff leather heels of her shoes echoed along the passageway.

Marion's brow furrowed as she puzzled over Maude's strange demeanor, but she had walked only a few more steps along the corridor when she saw on her left the large tapestry on which was depicted a victorious Judith, bloody sword in one hand and holding the bloody head of Holofernes by the hair in the other.

She looked for all the world like a triumphant David returning from battle with the head of Goliath, and Marion could not resist stopping before the arras to admire it for a moment.

But as she was doing so, an armored form emerged from behind the tapestry, hurrying out in the direction from which Marion had just come and pulling a nasal helmet back over his head. Marion blinked a moment registering what she could see of the face, and then cried out in a mixture of relief and frustration, "Robin!"

As he recognized the voice and turned gingerly in its direction, the outlaw's shoulders hunched upward in the posture of a boy who's been caught with his hand in a cookie jar, and he opened his mouth to speak but was preempted by a torrent of words from Lady Mary. "Have you gone completely out of your mind? What on earth are you thinking, wandering about in this castle by yourself when it's full of people who…" now her voice lowered to a whisper, which still had the effect of shouting, "Who want to see you hanged? Where just days ago your execution promised to be a grisly popular entertainment for the entire city? You disappeared and worried me half to death, and here you are, sauntering out from behind a tapestry in Gisbourne's own entry hall. What's behind that tapestry anyw…" and in the middle of that sentence, the second shoe dropped in Marion's head.

She looked over her shoulder to catch a glimpse of Lady Maude disappearing in the direction of the lesser hall. When she turned back to him, Robin's look of chagrin was recognizable even on a face obscured by his helmet. Nor was the helmet sufficient to cover the crimson blush that had sprung into his face. Robin cringed, expecting a tirade of red hot anger to explode from Marion's gaping mouth.

But instead he only heard her whisper, "Oh I see." Nodding, she repeated. "Yes. Now I see." And with that she turned and, holding her head high like the aristocrat she was, made her way decidedly but without haste back toward the great hall.

Robin, too mortified to follow or to utter a word in his own defense, stood as if bolted to the floor, alone in that dark corridor. And Ellen's words came back to him like Jeremiah's to the Jews of old: "Natural depravity. That's what your 'natural law' is. It is the law of beasts. And men should be better than beasts."

* * *

By the time Robin had finally gathered himself and come into the great hall, he found it packed with dozens of people, many of the clerks who peopled the city's bureaucracy; several of the nobles of the county who were in the castle that day; a few clergy who had business in the castle, including Brother Philip, whom Robin recognized, in town on some business for the Cluniac brothers of the Church of Saint Mary the Virgin; and of course most of Gisbourne's actual guards, at least of those that remained.

Lady Lydia stood on a dais that was raised along one of the great hall's inner walls. Though still dressed in the simple blue gown she had ridden in from London, her figure and her demeanor were imposing enough to leave no doubt as to who was in control of this situation. She was flanked by Sir Richard and Sir Peter, with Palomides and the six other outlaw-guards ranged on both sides of the dais for her protection. At one of the doors into the hall Robin noticed the servant Dap, and decided it might be a good idea to stand guard here at the other door. One never knew when he might need to exit, or prevent someone else from exiting.

Marion was not on the dais. It worried Robin that he could not see her.

He did, however, see Lady Maude, standing at the burly

Sheriff's right hand close to the stage. The hatchet-faced Gisbourne stood at the Sheriff's other side, and directly behind him Robin recognized Jack, captain of Gisbourne's guards, who seemed puzzled by the fact that he did not recognize any of the armed guard that stood around the Countess.

Lady Lydia was holding up a sealed parchment letter and calling for the crowd to quiet itself. This, she seemed to indicate by her waving it, was the reason for which she had asked them to assemble. As the crowd noise subsided, she cleared her throat and announced with a voice projected from her diaphragm, "I have here a proclamation from our good king Constantine, whom I have just now returned from visiting in London. As anyone who examines it can see, this is the king's own seal, and has not been broken, so that you will understand this missive comes directly from him and has not been altered or tampered with in any way. This proclamation, I have reason to believe, is composed in Latin, and therefore I am asking a member of the clergy present to examine the letter and verify the seal, and then to read it and render it into English for the rest of the assembly here."

At that there was some grumbling among the audience, with the clergy present looking cautiously at one another. Undertaking to translate this letter promised to land the volunteer in a very sticky situation with Sir Guy—or with the Countess, depending on what the letter said and how it was received. So there was no immediate response to Lady Lydia's request. She looked vainly among the crowd for a few moments, until her eye landed on Brother Philip, and she smiled broadly.

"Brother Philip! You are a Cluniac monk of nearby Lenton Priory, correct? An honest man of God with no conflict of interest in any affair that concerns the relationship of Nottingham Castle to our reigning King Constantine, is that not so?"

Brother Philip, whose priory administered the Church of Saint Mary the Virgin, certainly did have a prior connection to the Peveril family, who had chartered that church, but that perhaps did not enter the Countess's thoughts, and if it had entered Brother Philip's, he repressed it accordingly, and answered in his usual quavering voice, "Uh, no, my Lady, I mean, Your Grace... that is, Lady Courtesy."

"And can we say you are enough of a scholar to be able to translate Latin on sight?" the Countess demanded.

"Um, passable, my Lady...Courtesy, passable," Brother Philip stammered.

"Then Brother Philip of Lenton Priory, I charge you with the task of coming to this platform and opening the king's proclamation, and announcing to this audience the import of the royal message. Come up here. Now!" she added the last as the young monk hesitated tremblingly before complying with her command.

After scrambling onto the dais, the monk stood abjectly before the Countess and received the letter from Lady Lydia's own hand. "First read the seal," she told him, "and confirm it to be from the king."

Brother Philip squinted at the wax seal, trying to focus his eyes as the parchment shook in his hands. "Yes" he said after a moment's hesitation. "The seal bears the words 'Constantinus Rex,' denoting the parchment to have been sealed under the king's hand. And it is, as the Countess has declared, unbroken."

"Then please, Brother Philip, you be the first to break it and to peruse the contents of the letter."

Philip nodded and unsealed the parchment, unfolding it and reading the text in his trembling hands. His eyes widened more and more the further he read in the document, until his mouth gaped open as well and he was so taken by the contents that he forgot his timidity and stopped shaking, but looked up at the Countess in amazement. "And do you know my Lady, what this letter contains?"

The corners of Lady Lydia's lips turned upward as she nodded and answered, "I have an inkling. Please, Brother Philip, translate for us the king's command."

Brother Philip lifted his head and perused the letter, translating from the beginning in a voice that gained confidence as his reading continued:

> *His excellency Constantine, by the grace of God king of the English, to the lords and ladies of Nottinghamshire, Greetings!*
>
> *Whereas we are informed by impeccable witnesses of the egregious abuses of power engaged in by our royally appointed castellan of Nottingham Castle, Sir Guy of Gisbourne, viz.:*
>
> *Firstly, his undeserved oppression of the yeoman Robin Hood, forester of the estates of the Lady Lydia Peveril, Countess of Chesterfield, in his refusal to release the said Robin Hood after the latter was exonerated in open court and his intent to hang the said Hood for poaching offenses, when no statute allowing such a punishment exists in our realm;*
>
> *Secondly, for dressing the royal guard of Nottingham Castle in the livery of his own estate, thereby usurping the powers and privileges held solely by the Crown itself;*
>
> *Thirdly, for profiting by illegal acts committed by city and county officials of Nottingham in the unwarranted and unapproved taxation of persons*

traveling through Nottingham on the king's
highway;
*   We therefore command that the said Sir Guy*
of Gisbourne be immediately stripped of his
position as commander of the royal garrison at
Nottingham, and of all powers accruing thereto.

At that point Brother Philip broke off reading, and a great commotion began among the assembled crowd. Some shouted appalled disbelief, some lifted cries of relief and thanksgiving, some murmured in anticipation of what Sir Guy's reaction would be, and whether the Countess could possibly enforce the king's proclamation in the face of guards loyal to their commander.

These latter listeners did not have long to wait before Gisbourne made his first move. He had clearly determined to brazen it out, and scoffed at the Countess's letter. "What is this poppycock? Clearly this Lady of Peveril, for the sake of her felonious servant Robin Hood, has had this letter forged for the sole purpose of trying to drive me from office. Balderdash I say! This smacks of treason against the king's own appointed official. Guards, get her off that dais and put her in the dungeons! We'll find ways to get to the truth behind this conspiracy. Guards! Arrest her I say!"

But his guards, twelve of whom were there in the great hall, looked at one another in confusion. Though they were hesitant to believe the Countess's letter had come directly from the new king, they were cautious about disregarding such a missive, attested to by a noblewoman of the stature of Countess Lydia. Besides which there were seven guards and three doughty knights on the dais with her, all of whom had drawn their swords upon Gisbourne's protest, clearly intent on defending the Countess and her monastic interpreter. Several of the guards looked to Jack, their company captain, but he too was manifestly confused, especially as to why the guardsmen on the dais, dressed in the armor and helmets of his own company, had sided with the Countess without any order from himself. He met the eyes of several of his men and almost imperceptibly shook his head. The guards did not budge.

Momentarily stymied, Sir Guy took another tack, exploding, "So I am to be stripped of my command, am I? And just who does your bogus king suggest be installed in my place? Hmm? That should give us a clear picture of who is behind this outrage. Perhaps Richard at the Lee? Or his callow son? Sycophants of the Countess's? Go on, Brother Philip. Tell us who is to be installed in my office, and we shall know this travesty for what it is."

At that word, Brother Philip's eyes retuned to the parchment and he read on:

> As regards the office of the deposed Sir Guy of
> Gisbourne, we hereby command that in his
> place shall be appointed our long-serving officer
> in that same city, the current shire reeve of all
> Nottinghamshire, the honorable John of Oxenford,
> who shall keep his current position as Sheriff,
> but at the same time will also take on new
> responsibilities as castellan of Nottingham Castle
> and commander of the royal guard of that fortress.
> And to this we put our signature by our own hand,
> and our royal seal.

"And with that, it ends with a flourish, and the name 'Constantine' writ large, I presume in the king's hand," Brother Philip needlessly concluded.

This last revelation was greeted with a stunned silence. Countess Lydia herself had not foreseen this development and appeared shaken to the core. And it was hard for Robin and his men to triumph in Gisbourne's downfall when it simply meant Oxenford's rise to greater authority. But it was hardly six of one, half a dozen of the other in the eyes of Sir Guy and the Sheriff. Gisbourne seemed puffed up by a bit of hope in hearing the name of his proposed successor. "Sheriff!" he called across the crowd that stood between the two of them in the hall. "This letter turns out to be far less onerous than it first appeared. Surely you and I can work this out in conference. Let us adjourn to some separate closet and discuss these developments by ourselves. It may be quite easy to comply with the letter of the law in the case of this proclamation, but to maintain the spirit of the current status quo."

Now Jack and his guards turned their attention to John of Oxenford to see how he would answer. Indeed, if one talks of spirit, they had already subconsciously transferred their allegiance to the Sheriff, whom they had always obeyed in any case, and they knew his answer now would determine their future loyalty.

Oxenford himself was wavering. He knew that when the king wrote of Gisbourne's dividing the spoils of Nottingham's inordinate taxes on those traveling the Great North Road, it was his own graft that Sir Guy was party to. But what the king didn't know wouldn't hurt him—that had been the Sheriff's philosophy for years, and with Gisbourne out of the picture there would be no one with whom to share the ill-gotten loot. On the other hand, it was good to have a partner and fellow conspirator in the ongoing war with the bandits of Sherwood. Especially one with a noble title. He'd hate to lose that kind of close ally. Drawn both ways, he glanced at his wife.

Lady Maude, who had no love for the condescending thin-faced knave who commanded the king's guard, and enamored of the idea of moving into Nottingham Castle from her smaller current residence, raised her eyebrows at Oxenford, rolled her eyes around the spacious great hall, and gave him a knowing smirk. And the Sheriff said, "Guards, arrest Gisbourne for treasonously resisting the order of the king!"

But Gisbourne was not to be caught napping. In one swift motion he had produced a long poignard from a sheath on his thigh and, with his free hand, had snatched a woman from the surrounding crowd and was holding her in front of him, the dagger at her throat. From where he stood, Robin could not make out the lady's face, but a glimpse of her blonde hair plunged his stomach into his boots, and a glimpse at the simple blue homespun gown she wore made him sure: It was Marion Gisbourne he was using as a shield.

A cry of anguish exploded from the dais as Lady Lydia cried, "Don't approach him! Please! That's my most trusted lady!" And with that cry Jack held up his hand to stay the guards from pursuing the retreating Gisbourne.

Meanwhile Sir Guy was backing out of the hall, his knife playing about Lady Mary's jugular. "That's right," he murmured. "You all stay put and the lady keeps her pretty white throat unscathed." Robin was tempted to push his way through the crowd to reach the withdrawing pair but hesitated at the thought that if Sir Guy even glimpsed him approaching, he might slash Marion's neck. So he stood poised for a moment, then thought he might be able to slip out his own doorway and make his way around to the other side to come upon Gisbourne from behind.

He had just begun to put his plan into action, slinking noiselessly outside the hall toward the other open doorway, when he heard more screeches from within the hall and saw Gisbourne struggling with another figure. Sir Guy's left arm was tightly holding Marion's neck but he was swinging the dagger in his right wildly at the figure of Dap who, having been standing on guard at that door, had tried to wrest the knife from Gisbourne's hand from behind. "Get away or I'll gut her like a pig, I swear I will!" Gisbourne was shouting, while women screamed in the hall and Jack's voice could be heard ordering, "Stay back! Don't endanger the woman!"

Dap danced in front of Gisbourne as he tried to turn down the corridor and Sir Guy, thrown off his concentration by Dap's feints toward his knife hand, alternated between pointing the knife toward the lady or the master falconer. Robin was now sprinting toward the unsteady, struggling trio, trying to decide which of them to tackle: He was annoyed with Dap for putting Marion in greater danger, but it was Gisbourne who was the greatest threat and should not be allowed to escape. But he couldn't be sure he would not be endangering Marion if he charged into Sir Guy, who even accidently might slash her with the knife if tackled so suddenly.

And so it was Marion that Robin slammed into, grabbing her about the waist with both arms and propelling her several yards from Sir Guy and onto the castle's stone floor, where she lay stunned with Robin on top of her. Sir Guy had made a great swipe with his knife in her direction, but had missed completely, though Dap, making an unsuccessful grasp for the dagger, was seriously slashed when his hand clasped the knife blade itself.

Gisbourne sprang away immediately, racing at full speed through the corridor toward the castle's front gate. Jack commanded the guard in the hall to pursue their former commander, and they emerged one by one from the doors to the great hall, having to maneuver through the crowd within. And when they did pursue their quarry through the passageway, they were impeded by other guards who, having been guarding other parts of the castle, had missed the revelation in the great hall, and were following the orders of the fleeing Gisbourne to prohibit the others from arresting him.

There was thus a good chance, Robin realized, that Gisbourne would get away. But that was secondary, he thought as he lay on the castle floor atop the tackled Marion. Maybe she would be grateful to him after this, he thought hopefully. Maybe she would forget, or ignore, his earlier misstep with Lady Maude.

A loud harumph came from under Robin's mail corselet, and he rolled over to give Lady Mary some air. "Now if you'll remove yourself from my pinioned legs, I may be able to lift myself up," she announced.

Robin leapt to his feet and, with the humblest possible courtesy, offered the lady his hand. This she spurned, and boosted herself from her prone position with her own arms. Standing but disheveled, Marion straightened her gown, smoothed her hair as best she could with her hands, and, turning her back on Robin, stalked back into the great hall without a word.

Or, Robin thought, maybe she's not feeling so forgiving after all.

CHAPTER SEVENTEEN

The oaks all about them were losing some of their tawny red, and the beeches many of their golden bronze leaves as, three days later, Alan a Dale and his Ellen rode their palfreys along a path through Sherwood that led from the Great Oak clearing, now deserted, in the direction of the Randals' manor house and Verysdale. With them rode Sir Richard at the Lee, caparisoned as a knight in arms, for Alan and Ellen believed that they needed an unmistakable authority figure to accompany them on this particular errand. Besides, the rest of Alan's comrades had all moved north by now, and he and Ellen would be following them soon. But resolving this particular issue was important to them.

The woods were pleasant and the weather quite warm for late October and Alan, always happy to listen to a fellow singer, delighted in the yellow breasted chiff-chaff as it cheeped its own name from the surrounding trees, or the rusty breasted wood nuthatch whistling from above. But Ellen felt compelled to chat with Sir Richard, for courtesy's sake, and the knight was happy to follow suit.

"So there has been no trace of Sir Guy since he fled from the castle after Lady Lydia delivered the king's order?" she asked Sir Richard, since he'd been part of the deputation that had scoured the woods around Nottingham after Gisbourne's escape.

"We think he found his way out of the castle—and the town

itself—by making use of those tunnels under the fortress, those same passageways through which Robin escaped," the knight answered. "He knew the castle better than anyone and had probably made himself very familiar with those dark places. He was a sneak by nature and I'm sure the tunnels appealed to him because of their potential for concealment. He most likely made good use of them in the end. We searched them, and then we searched the city and the surrounding forest. We found no sign of him," the knight answered. "And we made a very thorough search. Fortunately, we did not come too close to the outlaw camp around the Great Oak. But it *could* have gone that far."

"Fortunately, that camp has been abandoned and all the lads removed to the winter camp at Creswell Crags. Thorvald and Friar Tuck were leading that migration just days before your search."

"Yes," Alan put in, ignoring the birds for the moment. "And Robin's gone up there to meet them with Jock and Scarlet and the rest of the boys who took part in the Countess's rescue. Which seems strange to me. I would have thought he'd have gone with Palomides to escort Lady Mary and the Countess back to Peveril Castle. Instead he sent Little John with them."

"That was odd, wasn't it?" Richard agreed. "Usually he's very careful to safeguard any venture Lady Lydia and Lady Mary undertake. I suppose he was anxious to make sure all of his meinie were safe. And he did send his most trusted lieutenant in Little John, after all."

Ellen made no comment on this. She was fairly confident she had noticed some coolness that had grown between Robin and Marion, but did not want to be responsible for starting any uncomfortable rumors. So she decided to change the subject. "With Gisbourne out of the picture, do you suppose the Sheriff will continue to search for Robin's camp with the use of that careful map Friar Bungay created?"

Alan shook his head. "The map was mainly Gisbourne's obsession. The Sheriff is certainly no friend of Robin's but he doesn't think things out long range. He makes quick decisions and doesn't react until someone pokes him."

"That may be true," Sir Richard said. "But the Sheriff also knows that their double arrest of Robin after he'd been acquitted in court was the chief reason for Gisbourne's fall, and he doesn't want Robin's name to come before the king again any time soon if it's attached to his own. So he's willing to let things flow along as they will for awhile. For that matter, he was very lukewarm about our search for Gisbourne. No doubt he wasn't eager to bring his former ally back to Nottingham in chains."

"Especially since that ally knows that the Sheriff is just as guilty as himself of those things for which the king deposed Gisbourne," Alan suggested. "Why should he want an embittered former accomplice back in town, spreading all kinds of stories about the man now holding his former rank?"

"But I wonder where Sir Guy could have gone," Ellen mused, tilting her head and squinting her eyes in thought. "Does he have a family estate of some kind, that justifies his use of the title of 'Sir'? Has he gone back there? Or is he simply hiding in the forest somewhere? There's a lot of forest, and a lot of places to hide, as we all know."

"Quite so," Sir Richard agreed. "But it seems unwise for him to stay in the woods alone, where his mortal enemies have their own secret abode. If I were him, I'd certainly make my way back to wherever his family hails from."

"But where is that?" Ellen persisted. "And does he have a sizable and powerful family? Could they raise a significant force to come back here and retake power by violence? The king's presence here, as we've clearly seen, is in name only, and maintained solely by those who, like the Countess and yourself, Sir Richard, choose to use their own influence to keep the peace."

"Gisbourne is a small village in West Yorkshire," Sir Richard said. "And there is a small manor there with a lord. And perhaps Sir Guy is a younger brother of that family. But he never claimed that was the case. To my knowledge, Gisbourne's roots are uncertain. He merely appeared one day with some two score guards and orders from the new king to fortify Nottingham Castle. For all we know he was simply a brigand who took advantage of the chaos after the old king's fall to make himself captain of some free company of mercenaries, and convinced the new king to knight him and establish some kind of royal presence here in the north. But that's just a guess."

"If what you say is true," Alan said, "then he has no family to return to. No reason to leave the woods. And every reason to form himself a new free company to rival our own."

"Now, this is all speculation," Ellen said. "We don't know what's true, or what's possible. There's no sense worrying over a future we can't possibly know."

"True enough," Alan conceded. "But I'll say this: We haven't heard the last of Sir Guy of Gisbourne."

"I suppose not," Sir Richard conceded. "But speaking of fugitives, I wonder what ever became of that Friar Bungay, after all? Last seen hightailing it into the forest after sneaking Robin out through the tunnels. We found no sign of him either when we searched the forest. But then, we weren't looking for him."

"No, you wouldn't have been," Allen agreed. "The Sheriff would just as soon have him gone as well. I suppose he knew an incriminating thing or two about the intrigues in that castle."

"But Friar Bungay is guilty, we've agreed, of the murder of the old Lord Randal," Ellen protested. "Shouldn't someone be pursuing him in the name of justice?"

"It's a crime that's what, fifteen or sixteen years in the past?" Sir Richard said.

"But it's still murder," Ellen argued. "One of two murders that family has had to accept. Shouldn't Lady Joan, at least, have the peace of knowing that her husband's murder has been solved and the culprit brought to justice?"

"But what is the real evidence of that murder?" Sir Richard asked. "A lot of hearsay from old servants like the nurse Sarah? The strange affair with the reliquary in the churchyard? Besides, Bungay truly is a friar. An ecclesiastical court would have to try him, and he won't face the noose."

"*Yesss*," Ellen said, drawing out that last sibilant. "Besides, Friar Bungay is certainly not the same person he was a decade and a half ago, when he committed that crime. He's made something of himself. Joined a religious order, received a fine education. Even helped our good friend escape hanging. Perhaps there is justice in his transformation."

"But is it a change from a wicked life to a virtuous one?" Alan asked. "Isn't it just his greed for that treasure that led him to that vocation, that education, even that charity toward Robin which was just a *quid pro quo* for Robin's showing him where that hill he was looking for was?"

"So he's changed, but it's his sin that changed him, not his conscience," Sir Richard agreed.

"I suppose," Ellen replied dreamily. "But I've heard Friar Tuck say many times that God has a way of bringing good out of evil, and by that means confounds the devil. Maybe in the case of Friar Bungay the devil has been confounded after all."

"Maybe," Alan agreed, unconvinced. "But look, here we are."

As they rode into a large clearing in the forest, they stopped in front of a modest waddle-and-daub manor house. "The scene of the crime," Sir Richard remarked, gazing up at the building.

Had the house belonged to a landowner with more considerable wealth or influence, it would likely have been built of stone, or at worst solid oak timbers, rather than the cheaper network of interwoven sticks packed with clay that comprised its walls. Perhaps, too, it would have been surrounded by several outbuildings, instead of the one barn that housed the family's three cows, two horses, and flock of chickens. There were also a few acres of oats and barley beyond the barn, where the trees were sparse and a plow could till the soil.

The house itself was two stories high, perhaps eighty feet wide and forty deep. Alan had seen similar houses, and guessed that the family's private rooms were on the second floor, while the doors at the front of the house would open into a large hall, on one side of which might be a small family chapel, at the other a dining room, beyond which would be a pantry and a buttery and then the kitchen itself. A wooden stairway would lead up to the private solars upstairs, below which there were likely to be a few storerooms. These houses were always quite similar.

The visitors dismounted. Sir Richard looked about, apparently with the expectation that some livery boy would appear to stable their horses. But Alan knew better, and tethered his horse to the lower branch of a small ash tree standing before the house. Ellen did the same and Sir Richard, shrugging, did so as well. He stepped boldly to the large wooden doors at the front of the house, with Ellen and Alan in his wake, and pounded heavily on those doors with a mailed hand.

Nothing happened.

Showing a hint of impatience, Sir Richard again pounded on the door. This time it opened and an ancient servant poked his head out and started a bit at the sight of a fully armed knight and two attendants waiting at the doorstep. "They don't get many visitors here, looks like," Alan whispered to Ellen as the servant blinked ill-naturedly.

"Master ain't at home," the hoary-headed porter rasped with no apparent attempt at courtesy. "Mistress is in a sick bed upstairs. They're not receiving visitors, thanks all the same."

And with that the fellow began to shut the door, but Sir Richard stopped him with a word: "We're not here to see either of them, but rather the Lady Eleanor. Please announce us at once, if you please, sirrah."

The gatekeeper gave an aggrieved sigh and flung the double doors open wide, saying, "Wait here in the hall while I fetch her down, then." He turned his back on the guests and walked to the stairway, leaving the three visitors to follow behind and shut the doors themselves. As they stood unattended in the hall, Alan looked about. The interior of the house was exactly as he'd expected. There to the right was the dining room. It was at that table that Wulf and Dap had served those fried eels to Eleanor and Lord William, bringing them in from the kitchen beyond the buttery down a narrow hall he could see off the dining room. From that kitchen he could hear a few more servants clanging a few pots and pans around. Perhaps there were a few other servants, maybe one to tend the chickens and one to milk the cows, one last servant to help with the plowing. But it was a small household by any standards among the gentry. Looking at things as they were, Alan was not surprised that the Randal family thought Lord William should seek further afield for a wife.

She came down the steps in the same black gown she had worn at Robin's trial, though it seemed to fit her a little more snugly today. She descended with a stately air that might have led onlookers to guess her a princess or duchess at the very least. Her russet hair was free to float like a wraith around her fair face, and her dark eyes peered at the visitors curiously. What more could you people want of me, they seemed to be asking. But as she reached the foot of the stairs, she greeted them courteously. "My Lord Richard! And Ellen, my good friend, and the sensitive singer as well. Please, come sit at my dining table. Clive!" She called to the octogenarian butler. "Bring our guests some wine, will you please?"

As Clive stalked into the kitchen, apparently indignant that these visitors were causing him to do some work, Lady Eleanor ushered them into the dining room, where they sat facing each other at the high table.

"Now then," Eleanor began. "Why have the three of you come to see me again? Something more about my dear William's murder? This is becoming so tiresome. Why, oh why do you keep tormenting me so with it? I've told you all I know. Why has no one found out the killer yet? Has no one found that culprit Wulf? Find him and he can be forced to tell what he knows. To tell which of that horrible Randal family paid him to murder my dearest love." And with that she barely stifled a sob, and tears began to form beneath her long lashes.

"My Lady, we believe we are very close to solving the murder," Alan told her. At that she sat up straighter, and her eyes opened wide. But Alan continued, "You apparently have not heard, though, that Wulf has been found."

"Found?" Lady Eleanor seemed quite surprised, then regained her composure. "Then surely he has told you who was behind the plot to kill Lord William. Is that what you've come to tell me?"

"I'm afraid not," Alan replied. "He was in no condition to speak when we found him. He was quite dead at the time."

Lady Eleanor gave a great horrified gasp and covered her face with her hands. It was, Alan decided, a somewhat exaggerated reaction. "So he can never tell us who the true murderer was!" the lady lamented. "It seems we will never find the killer now."

"Don't be so sure," Ellen answered. "His body told us a great deal. He was stabbed at close quarters, and he showed no sign of having been in a struggle. He obviously knew his killer well and felt no need to protect himself at their meeting. We're quite certain that the person he was meeting with was his co-conspirator. Probably he was expecting a payoff from that person—whatever it was he'd been promised for pulling off this killing. And that person killed him, to ensure he could not reveal the other's role in Lord William's murder. You were right. Wulf never left the area, even though he was the chief suspect in the murder. He couldn't leave before being paid."

"And he got paid. In full," Alan concluded.

By now the ancient Clive had brought out a flagon of wine and set cups before the three guests as well as his mistress.

"For a while we followed the lead about the old servant David, out of East Anglia, who almost certainly killed the old Lord Randal," Ellen continued. "He turned up recently as a friar in the service of Sir Guy of Gisbourne, We thought he may have conspired to kill the young master over the whereabouts of the famous treasure Lord Stephen was supposed to have brought back from the crusades. But we really couldn't figure out a sound motive or even an opportunity for the friar to have killed Lord William. So he was out."

"And we're grateful to you for giving us the whole family of surviving Randals as suspects," Alan continued. "You gave us motives for all of them. But we ruled out Lady Joan. No convincing motive there. As for Lord Geoffrey, he did get the manor in Lord William's will, but we haven't been able to find that he gets any enjoyment out of his new position, or that he ever even wanted it."

"As for Lady Anne," Ellen went on, "she did get what gold and silver there was in Lord William's hands, which was not a great deal. It's true she would like a larger dowry in order to be married, but she never thought her brother had any more hidden away anywhere. She never believed in the treasure. And we have the word of Sir Richard's son, Sir Peter, that she was never interested in him as a husband."

"Too much like brother and sister," Sir Richard interjected, speaking for the first time. "It would have felt like incest to her." And with that the old knight shuddered.

"So we have you to thank for allowing us to eliminate all of the Randal family from our possible suspects," Alan said.

"Well if that's true," Lady Eleanor said, somewhat flustered. "Who's left? You say you are very close to finding the murderer. Who do you think it is?"

"Oooh," said Ellen, drawing out the long vowel, "it's you, my dear."

* * *

Lady Eleanor reared back as if someone had struck her in the face. Her eyes grew large as juggler's balls and she gave a sharp bark of laughter. It appeared she was completely astonished by the accusation. Then she lowered her brows and with eyes like slivers she gazed into the faces of each of her three guests. "You're not joking, then?" she said after a moment. "Have you gone completely mad? I've told you William had promised to marry me. What motive could I have to kill him? I've told you I barely knew Wulf's name. How could I conspire with him? You people are reaching for straws. But I won't be insulted in my own house. Clive!" she called, then turned back to her visitors. "I'll have him show you the door. This interview is at an end." And with that she began to rise from the table.

"Wulf of Brinkley," Ellen said quietly. When Eleanor

responded only with a questioning look, she continued. "That's what you called him. It struck me as odd. No one else in this entire investigation—not even his fellow servant Dap—has known anything at all about Wulf's background."

"Even Lady Anne, " Alan added, "whom you tried to get us to suspect, knew nothing at all about him. Sir Peter, who you tried to get us to believe was Anne's choice of a husband, said very specifically that Anne knew nothing about Wulf, *not even where he came from.* He stressed that. And yet you, who claim to have barely known the fellow, knew he was from Brinkley."

Lady Eleanor scoffed. "And what of it? I suppose it must have come up in some conversation I overheard sometime—"

"Conversation between whom?" Alan pressed. "Wulf never talked about where he came from. Dap didn't know, and didn't think Lord William knew either. So what conversation would this be? A conversation between you and Wulf himself perhaps?"

"I told you I never spoke with the churl," Eleanor insisted. At that point, Clive had come back into the room and asked what he was wanted for. "Oh yes, uh, would you mind pouring the wine for us, Clive?" Eleanor asked, backing off from her threat to have her guests chucked out—and the fiction that the elderly Clive would be able to do it. The servant gave a long-suffering sigh that probably could have been heard as far off as Brinkley and splashed wine into the four cups before stomping off, offended at having been disturbed.

The pause in conversation had enabled Lady Eleanor to regain her composure and, she hoped, control of the situation, as she pulled out the ring that hung from the chain around her neck. "And this?" she demanded. "How does your imaginary scenario incorporate the fact that he gave me his signet ring as a pledge to marry me?"

"*Is* that a fact, though?" Ellen asked. "Dap, who's the only person connected with any of this who has no reason to lie, claims he heard you and William arguing about something, and he thought it had to do with your wedding in secret. He seemed to think that you were against that arrangement. Why would that have been?"

"It was a small disagreement only," Eleanor said, waving off the question. "Like every bride, I wanted the affair to take place at the church door before all the town. And I wanted a wedding feast afterwards. I deserved that much from that miserly family."

"But before that day, as we understand it, Lord William was not willing to marry you at all, because of his family's objections," Ellen said. "I would think such a concession would have made you happy."

"Happy? Why? He insulted me by such a proposal. I had no dowry, so he would not use his money to let the world know I was worthy to be his wife. While he was sitting on that huge treasure of his father's! The skinflint!"

"The treasure?" Alan said, surprised it had come up again. "You knew about that, then? But we were given to understand that Sir William knew nothing about it. That he believed it was simply an unsubstantiated rumor that had circulated around his father."

"Oh, he pretended not to know. But Wulf told me he was sure William had papers showing the whereabouts of..."

"Wulf!" Alan exclaimed. "You just said you barely knew him. Barely spoke with him. Yet you were gossiping with him about this treasure?"

Lady Eleanor suddenly looked flummoxed. She clearly had not considered the import of her last statement. And she babbled, "Well, it was just a chance conversation that happened...once before that day...only once did I talk to him that day when the treasure came up..."

"Which I guess must have been the same conversation in which he told you all about his early life in Brinkley," Alan said, not without irony. "Odd that that would come up in a conversation about a crusader's treasure."

"It did, I swear!" Lady Eleanor cried, tears forming at the corners of her eyes. "We talked *one time*, and he told me those things, and I never thought about them again. So why would I want to kill Wulf?"

There was silence for a moment while each of them considered what had just been said. Then Ellen said quietly, "No one has accused you of killing Wulf. But the fact is Robin Hood and I found his body not two furlongs from this house. It would have been quite easy for you to have arranged to meet him there, and then to have killed him, since he was the only witness who could have connected you to this murder."

"But I *didn't* murder my William, I tell you. Why, oh why won't you believe me?" And now the tears were running freely down Lady Eleanor's face.

"Here's what I think," Alan said, unmoved by the tears, and finally free of the lady's charm that had so blinded him to her guilt from their first meeting. "I recall Lord William's telling me you had been schooled for a time at the Minster in Southwell. Now Southwell is just a stone's throw from Brinkley, out there fourteen or fifteen miles northeast of Nottingham. I think you actually had met Wulf while you were there, and befriended him. He'd have been a few years younger than you, probably worshipped you when he was a boy. I think you got him the position with Lord Randal yourself—your lover wants a dog-boy, you know a poor peasant lad from Brinkley that's good with dogs. And so you have an instant spy in Lord William's house, and he can tell you all about what the family really thinks of you."

Eleanor sighed. "I did know Wulf, it's true. I didn't tell the whole truth about that because I knew you'd suspect me of conspiring with him—and I was quite right about that, now wasn't I?"

"The ring," Ellen said, taking a different tack. "A signet ring. You told us it was his pledge of love. But that seems a strange gift. If he was going to give you a ring, why not one with a precious stone or jewel set in it? Surely Lord William had rings of that sort in his family. If he had proposed marriage to you that day, wouldn't he have brought such a ring with him?"

"You know yourself that it was his experience there at the outlaw camp that morning that inspired him to ask me. In fact, it was your own close relationship that encouraged him."

"Yes," Ellen agreed, "but if he truly intended to propose, would he not have stopped at his own home—it was not far out of the way—to pick up an appropriate ring and bring it with him to your manor?"

"It was a spontaneous decision," Eleanor cried. "He decided at that moment to propose…"

"But why would he make that decision so suddenly, when he'd all but given up on the idea beforehand?" Ellen insisted.

"Because I was *with child*, don't you see?" Eleanor cried, and the tears began to flow again, perhaps more sincerely this time.

That revelation was enough to stir Sir Richard to speech for just the second time. "Oh, I see. Lord William, having begat a child on you, was concerned for the child's legitimacy and so decided to do the courteous thing, and wed you despite your lack of dowry."

"Of course," Lady Eleanor said, tossing her russet hair.

"I don't think so," Ellen persisted. "You *thought* that's what he'd do, you even counted on it. You wanted to give birth to Lord Randal's legitimate child, so that he would be heir to the great fortune that you and Wulf suspected he was sitting on. But he refused. That argument Wulf and Dap overheard wasn't you wanting a formal wedding and feast to celebrate, it was about William refusing even to engage in a secret elopement that you'd already talked to Father Timothy about. I believe he gave you that signet ring for his child, so that if the child ever came to him in need, he would provide for it. But it wasn't a pledge for you. And that's why you killed him."

"You and Wulf must have had a signal," Alan continued. "He knew you were going to spring this pregnancy on Lord William at that meeting, and you'd planned the murder if things did not go your way. That's why he was collecting the mushrooms that morning. So what did you promise Wulf to get him to go along? Did he expect to get a share of the treasure? You must have figured you could lay a claim on it for your child by presenting the ring. Or did Wulf do it merely for the promise of your gratitude and a bit of *belle chose*? Is that what you promised in order to get him to meet you for his appointment with death?"

Deflated, Lady Eleanor sprawled on her chair, hanging her head and weeping now without restraint. She picked up her cup of wine and downed it in a few short gulps. "You've got all the answers," she addressed Alan. "Why bother me anymore?"

At that Sir Richard, hearing his cue, said, "Is that a confession, my lady?" Lady Eleanor only shrugged. Richard rose from his chair and formally announced, "Lady Eleanor Franklin, I am arresting you for the murders of Lord William Randal and of his servant Wulf. Of Brinkley," he added that last with a sly half smile.

Alan relaxed and blew out a sigh of his own. He was exhausted from the exchange, and considered Lady Eleanor a worthy adversary in the debate that had finally revealed her calumny. And his mouth was dry. He, too, picked up a cup of wine and brought it to his lips to quench his thirst.

The cup was knocked violently from his hand by a swift swat from Ellen's arm. Alan looked up, puzzled. Ellen caught his eyes and then glanced down to the other side of the table, where Lady Eleanor lay writhing on the floor. A kneeling Sir Richard was trying unsuccessfully to revive her, and after a few moments all her movements ceased. She was dead.

Ellen sniffed the wine in her own glass, then scrunched her face in revulsion. "Foxglove," the herbalist in her recognized. Thus, at the same dinner table, another servant had brought in another poisoned course, this time proving fatal to another of an ill-fated pair of lovers, united now in death.

"Well," Sir Richard said finally. "*That*, I take it, is a confession."

"*Yesss*," Ellen said thoughtfully. "But it's too bad she had to take the child with her."

CHAPTER EIGHTEEN

With the detritus of a great banquet lying on the boards before them, Alan a Dale and Ellen lifted their cups of wine and tapped them together before downing them, in mutual congratulations on a job well done. Across the table from them, the falcon master Dap said in his clipped, detached style, "So in the end, Lady Eleanor chose suicide. Afraid to face the hangman? Or wanting to avoid the public shame of a trial? She was a proud one, that I'll say for her."

Alan shrugged. "The wine was intended for us, I've no doubt about that. She'd killed her lover in a similar way, and she'd stabbed her cohort Wulf with no compunction at all. Like Wulf, we were another encumbrance to her getting away scot free."

"I'll not say you're wrong," Dap responded thoughtfully. "But if she'd planned to kill you to prevent the truth from coming out, why kill herself instead when she was quite sure you'd found her out? Wouldn't that make her want to stop your mouths all the more? And if they were stopped, she'd have had no reason to drink the poison herself."

"You're thinking like a man," Ellen said, setting down the flagon of hypocras, a spiced wine Countess Lydia had imported from Montpellier in Occitan. "Lady Eleanor was with child. That was the chief thought behind every decision she made. She hoped, even expected, that Lord Randal would wed her and give the child his name. She counted on it. Indeed, he had been reluctant to marry her beforehand because of his family's objections to her poverty, and she'd been unable to get him to commit to using the treasure she was sure he had access to in order to fund the marriage. She may even have given herself to him with the intention of becoming pregnant and thereby forcing his hand."

"Then why kill him?" Dap asked.

"He wouldn't marry her. And he wouldn't commit to using his secret treasure, or even admit to having it. So she was pregnant and she was going to be abandoned by the man responsible. You were right when you said she was proud. She was too proud to let Lord William get away with treating her that way."

"Then why kill herself?" Alan asked, putting down his own glass after enjoying a swallow of his own sweet wine.

"It wasn't the shame of a public trial that she feared," Ellen continued. "Or the fear of the hangman. She could have pled her belly—women do it often to escape the noose. The child is innocent, so the mother may be pardoned. No, it was the shame of being a woman with a child and no husband to show for it that she couldn't bear to face."

"So she could bear the guilt of what would have been four murders, if she'd succeeded with us, but not the shame of being an unwed mother," Alan mused. "It's a cockeyed moral compass that, wouldn't you say?"

"Thinking like a man again," Ellen pronounced, giving her head a slight shake. "There's a grudging admiration for murderers, especially those who kill to protect their honor or their family name. A romantic glow about the proud man— or woman—who kills for vengeance, or to redress an insult or injury. But the woman who has yielded her maidenhead without the benefit of clergy, and is saddled by God with a child to proclaim her dishonor to all the world? She can never live down her disgrace. And she'd be an outcast in a hostile world without a protector. No. Lady Eleanor had considered well her options."

"But I don't understand why she would have been so convinced about Lord Stephen's treasure," Dap said, pulling on a different thread of the conversation. "It was an old rumor that the family had all disregarded long since. Why would it loom so large in Lady Eleanor's mind?"

"I've been thinking about that," Alan said. "And I think I have an idea. We think Lady Eleanor met Wulf when she was being schooled at the Minster in Southwell and Wulf was a ten-minute walk away in Brinkley. But remember that the old Randal nurse, Sarah, lived in Southwell as well. She's a gregarious sort, and she was a servant in the days before you were there, Dap—when the servants still talked a lot about, and believed in, that mythical crusader's treasure that the old man brought back. It may be that Wulf first heard of the Randal treasure in gossip around the town that had its source in Sarah—or that Eleanor did. Who knows? That may even have been what first drew her to Lord William in the first place. Maybe she was most interested in his treasure after all."

"I think you wrong her there," Ellen began, then without warning grabbed Alan by the knee and began tickling him again, squealing in her high pitched voice, "But the hand wants you to stop brooding over this and pay attention to your own wife, my pretty one!" She began to snort through her nose again but was interrupted by the voice of Lady Lydia, trying to shout above the after-dinner buzz about the dining hall.

"Hearken to me, please all my household and honored guests," she cried from the carved wooden siege at the center of the head table, on a dais in the great hall of Peveril castle. At her right hand, in the place of honor, sat Sir Richard at the Lee and, next to him, his son Sir Peter of Verysdale. Next to him sat her chief lady in waiting, the Lady Mary of Winchester. To the Countess's left sat Sir Palomides and, next to him, Lady Maude Peveril, attending once again by herself, since there would needs be too much social awkwardness should her husband, the Sheriff of Nottingham, take it into his head to accompany her. To Maude's left sat Robin Hood himself, clothed not in his customary Lincoln green but in the silver and blue livery of the Countess of Chesterfield. Little John sat at Robin's left, and Will Stutely next to him on the dais.

"I trust you have all enjoyed the feast, another triumph for the chief cook of Peveril Castle, master Oswald!" There was a smattering of polite applause as Lady Lydia gestured toward the rear of the great hall, where Oswald stood, wearing a well-gravied apron and holding a long-handled spoon. He gave a slight nod in recognition of the applause, then looked down shyly at his feet. "I know I learned a great deal I never knew before about how skillful is Oswald's blending of herbs and spices from our visiting gourmet Sir Palomides, who gave me a running commentary on all this as he sat by my side through the meal." There was some good-natured laughter from those of Robin Hood's men who sat at the low table to the Countess's right, where Alan and Ellen sat with Will Scarlet, Much the miller's son, Jock of Barlborough, and Friar Tuck. They had all had the sort of experience the Countess was talking about.

"My annual banquet for All Hallows' Day seems to be turning into an annual feast of thanksgiving," the Countess continued. "For as you of my household are well aware," she nodded toward the several ladies in waiting, squires and pages who sat at the low table to her left, "I would not be here—would not even be alive—if it were not for the actions of the several visitors who sit amongst us today."

There was more applause, this time more vigorous and heartfelt. The Countess sat in a close-fitted blue samite gown embroidered across her breasts, with pearls stitched into the fabric. It had long sleeves that hung from her wrists to the ground, and she wore a white silk girdle with silver filigree around her waist, a leather purse dangling from it. A golden band kept her hair in place and reminded people of her rank, though her manner made it unlikely anyone was apt to forget.

"It is first my painful duty to remember our beloved Sir Eustace, who fell in the act of protecting the lives of his mistress and her lady," and with this she nodded briefly to Marion, before wiping her eye with a lace napkin she held in her hand. "He served us well and faithfully and was many years in the service of my grandfather and myself. No one can truly replace him, and he will be sorely missed. Let us raise a silent glass to his memory." And with that she raised her own, and everyone in the great hall followed suit, with a few murmured tributes of, "Sir Eustace!"

Robin raised his glass with the others, but he wasn't focused on the Countess's words. His mind was preoccupied with Maid Marion at the moment, as it had been since he arrived at Peveril Castle. He had hoped that in the intervening days since he'd last seen her, Lady Mary might have softened her attitude toward him and might be willing to show a slight inkling of warmth that he might latch onto and nurture into something vaguely resembling forgiveness. But she'd been cold as a winter in the Orkneys since he'd arrived, and had barely given him a glance. And yet as he sat at the table, he could see her talking animatedly with Sir Peter as if he were the most interesting little pipsqueak in the known world. What was Robin to do about this? As he glanced across the hall at the two of them now, the candles in the hollowed out seasonal gourds with which the Countess's people had decorated the hall threw their shadows in long animated distortions on the wall, like the nightmare images that had haunted his dreams since that day she had caught him coming from his assignation with Lady Maude in Nottingham Castle. All right, he had only himself to blame, as Ellen had told him in no uncertain terms. But how long could this go on? Was she seriously interested in this Sir Peter?

Why not? He asked himself. He was young, handsome, and most important of all, someone of her own rank. What could she possibly see in *him*, a yeoman and an outlaw? Face it, he told himself, you're not husband material as far as she is concerned. Fit only to be a noblewoman's plaything? He glanced at Lady Maude, who had been chattering to him from the moment he'd sat down, and who had received his responses of "uh-huh" and "hmmph" as if they were pearls of wisdom. Well, he thought, if Lady Mary was fine with giving him up to Lady Maude, he'd just have to get the most he could out of what she had left him. And he listened now with truly well-feigned interest to what Maude was saying. And he hoped Lady Mary was watching.

"But Sir Palomides, it is to you I owe my life," the Countess continued. "To you and the brave foresters who arrived with Sir Richard and Sir Peter to save me and my Lady Mary from assassination on the road to Nottingham. But chiefly to you, I say, because you fought unflinchingly against overwhelming odds, and, with our dear Sir Eustace, held those brigands off long enough for help to arrive. And for that I can never thank you enough."

"My Lady," Palomides answered modestly in his deep baritone, "when I was made knight by the old king, I swore an oath to defend ladies from oppression, and never to take arms in an unjust cause. In defending you, I did only what I was charged to do at that time and have ever done since. You may consider me at all times at your service, my Lady." And with that he made a humble bow, as best he could while seated next to her.

"Gentle knight," Lady Lydia responded. "Your courtesy does you credit, but to fail to reward you justly for your great sacrifice in my service would certainly do me none. However, I must give this some thought, and try to find a way to show my gratitude in a manner that you cannot help but embrace. In the meantime, Sir Knight, accept my gratitude and know that if I am ever able to do you a service, you need not hesitate to ask."

As Palomides nodded courteously in response, the Countess looked to Lady Maude and smiled broadly. "And my dear cousin, once again I have you to thank for watching out for me in the dark corridors of power in Nottingham. Your timely message to Sir Richard ended in my salvation, pure and simple."

"And I need no more reward from you than your good will, if that is what's coming next," Maude replied, with astonishing self-deprecation. "It's no more than one kinswoman *should* do for another. I am well aware that you, my Lady, are my closest blood kin, and so my loyalty to you is not for sale at any price."

Robin, somewhat surprised by Maude's failure to take advantage of the Countess's munificence, looked at her questioningly, at which Maude giggled and whispered, "It's through her that I've got the keys to Nottingham Castle itself. I haven't even started looking into what mischief I can get into there."

Robin raised his eyebrows in a surprised acknowledgement, then focused again on the Countess, who had finally gotten around to him. "And you, my loyal foresters—Robin Hood, Little John and the rest of you," and she made a gesture taking in the whole group of Sherwood outlaws present. "For a second time you have saved me. The first time was from an unwanted marriage and a plot to steal my lands. This time it was from an even more insidious plot to take my life. I know now that our friendship is as true as steel, and our fates are intertwined forever. Are they not, Lady Mary?"

Marion was startled by this pronouncement, but quickly wiped the surprise off her face and nodded demurely, but without looking at Robin himself, and immediately turned her eyes back to Sir Peter at her side. Robin was so annoyed by the gesture that he barely heard the Countess's next words.

"But I know that in your line of work, you value the coin of the realm above all things, and therefore," she reached down below the board where she was sitting and pulled out a small wooden chest, "I have decided once again to present you with five hundred gold nobles as a token of my gratitude for your preserving my life. Robin, I give this to you in the expectation that you will share it among your merry men."

"And women," Ellen whispered in Alan's ear, at which he smiled and patted his wife's hand.

A raucous cheer went up from all the outlaws present. Robin gaped in surprise, and made as if to speak, but Friar Tuck was quick to step in and, standing, bowed politely to the Countess and said, "I thank you on behalf of our entire band, my Lady, and I assure you that this gift, in the manner of *all* the cash we claim in our little enterprise, will be divided in two, with half going into our own coffers for our band's expenses, and half going to the poor of Nottinghamshire." And another cheer went up, though somewhat more subdued than the first.

"And now," the Countess continued, with a note of finality, "it's time to knit up all this feast with a song, I think," and with that she glanced at Sir Palomides, whose prowess with the lyre was as well known as his prowess with the sword, but Palomides made a gesture of modest refusal and his eyes rolled in the direction of Alan a Dale where he sat at the end of the low table. He passed his lute to Lady Lydia, who held it out in Alan's direction and smiled, saying, "So let me invite Sherwood Forest's resident minstrel to grace us with a ballad from his own broad repertoire!"

And to a smattering of further applause, mainly from his mates, Alan came forward, took Sir Palomides' lute with a quick glance of thanks to the Moor, and walked slowly to a place in the great hall in the center of the vee made by the two low tables, and directly facing the Countess and the others at the high table. He plucked a few strings to make sure the instrument was in tune— Palomides' tuning was impeccable but the journey from the new outlaw camp at Creswell Crags may have jarred the strings. When he was quite ready, Alan announced:

"I know that the rest of you have been most concerned these past weeks with the safety of our gallant captain, Robin, as well as the danger to our sovereign lady, Countess Lydia. But a few of us here present—Ellen and I, Sir Richard and Dap, the falconer, have been involved more directly in solving the mystery of the murder of Lord William Randal. I admit to being almost obsessed by this search, since Lord William had shown me such courtesy and generosity when we met, for the first and last time, on the day he was killed. And so in the past few days I've composed a new ballad to honor his memory in the only way I know how. Here is "Lord Randal":

> "O where have you been, Lord Randal, my son?
> And where have you been, my handsome young man?"
> "I've been to the greenwood; mother, make my bed soon,
> For I'm wearied with hunting, and fain would lie down."
>
> "And who met ye there, Lord Randal, my son?
> And who met ye there, my handsome young man?"

"O I met with my true-love; mother, make my bed soon,
For I'm wearied with hunting, and fain would lie down."

"And what did she give you, Lord Randal, My son?
And what did she give you, my handsome young man?"
"Eels fried in a pan; mother, make my bed soon,
For I'm wearied with hunting, and fain would lie down."

"And who got your leavings, Lord Randal my son?
And who got your leavings, my handsome young man?"
"My hawks and my hounds; mother, make my bed soon,
For I'm wearied with hunting, and fain would lie down."

"And what became of them, Lord Randal, my son?
And what became of them, my handsome young man?
"They stretched their legs out and died; mother make my
bed soon,
For I'm wearied with hunting, and fain would lie down."

"O I fear you are poisoned, Lord Randal, my son!
I fear you are poisoned, my handsome young man!"
"O yes, I am poisoned; mother, make my bed soon,
For I'm sick at the heart, and fain would lie down."

"What d'ye leave to your mother, Lord Randal, my son?
What d'ye leave to your mother, my handsome young
man?"
"Four and twenty milk cows; mother, make my bed soon,
For I'm sick at the heart, and fain would lie down."

"What d'ye leave to your sister, Lord Randal, my son?
What d'ye leave to your sister, my handsome young man?"

"My gold and my silver; mother make my bed soon,
For I'm sick at the heart, and fain would lie down."

"What d'ye leave to your brother, Lord Randal, my son?
What d'ye leave to your brother, my handsome young
man?"
"My houses and my lands; mother, make my bed soon,
For I'm sick at the heart, and fain would lie down."

"What d'ye leave to your true-love, Lord Randal, my
son?
What d'ye leave to your true-love, my handsome young
man?"
"I leave her hell and fire; mother make my bed soon,
For I'm sick at the heart, and fain would lie down."

* * *

The man was breathing hard, whether from exertion or excitement was difficult to say. He was coming out of the surrounding oak forest known within Sherwood as Birklands, and moving out into a clearing that was on higher ground than the rest of the forest, on a roll that rose less than ten feet above the surrounding ground and about twenty-five feet in diameter. Perhaps hundreds of years ago it had been higher.

Over his homespun blue tunic and hosen, he was wearing a fine linen tabard emblazoned with a crest of three embroidered silver sheaves of wheat on an azure blue background. Being seen in the livery of the Countess Lydia Peveril would not raise any eyebrows in this area of the forest. But he carried a pick and a shovel on his back, as if he were a gardener rather than a forester. He also bore a worn piece of parchment, which he stopped now to study, lowering his prodigious eyebrows the better to squint at the map's faint markings and thin Latin script.

He needed first to find the boundary stones. The small mound itself, he had learned, was very possibly an ancient burial site that had been used a few centuries ago as the assembly place for the Norsemen living in that area. More recently it was recognized as the point at which the borders of three different parishes met. Thus the boundary stones for Budby, Warsop, and Edwinstowe should be visible at the edges of the little hill's rolling summit.

His eyes peered to the southwest, and there he spotted the stone, jutting upward at the southwest edge of the circular hill, marked with a W for Warsop. Precisely the spot he was looking for. He stepped toward it and stood just to the south of that marker. His map told him that the precise point he sought would be exactly six feet directly northeast of that boundary stone.

He was a patient man. The fact that it had taken him more than fifteen years to get to this point was testament to that. And he would rather not simply estimate the direction and start digging in the wrong place. He had his astrolabe with him and first used it to determine true north by the position of the sun, then moved the horizontal, protractor part of the instrument so that the ninety-degree line pointed directly north. Then he carefully marked the precise forty-five degree angle to the northeast, dragging his pick along the line in the direction his instrument had told him. The pick handle, he knew, was precisely three feet in length, so it would be a simple matter to measure the distance along that line to the place he should dig.

At that precise point, he drove the pick into the ground, loosening the earth in order to clear it with the shovel. Then he took the spade and began carefully to dig. His precious parchment indicated that he was to dig to the depth of three feet exactly, There, he knew, he would find that priceless treasure he'd been dreaming of for so long.

As he dug, his mind revisited the events that had brought him to this place, and he reviewed them with, he hoped, a discerning eye. He remembered the old nurse, Sarah, and the groom Thomas, filling his head with fanciful stories of Lord Stephen's fabulous treasure, brought back from the east, awakening that unquenchable hunger within him. Who could truly argue that this obsession had damned him? Of course it was true that it led him eventually to confront the old lord and to compel him by force to yield up the secret of this scrap of parchment he carried with him now. And he thought with some regret that he was also forced to kill Lord Stephen, but given his obsession there was nothing else he could have done: The old man knew him and had suffered from his interrogation, and would most certainly have caused him to be arrested and hanged for the offense. Might as well hang for a murder as hang for a beating. And the murder left no witness.

But surely nothing but good had come from his act. He'd been able to commit himself to a life of service to God afterward, finding he had a vocation as a Dominican. First he had confessed his sin of murder and had done long penance, through myriad services among the poor—tending the sick in a Dominican hospital and even serving a stint in a leper house. He had also had the opportunity to become educated with some of the best masters in Britain and even in Paris, becoming learned in grammar and logic and rhetoric, and the sciences as well, concentrating particularly on mathematics, and going on to specialize his knowledge of astronomy and, more narrowly, cartography.

Yes, admittedly he'd always had the end in view of

understanding the Latin script on this parchment, and learning how to read maps and to locate one's position on the globe through use of the astrolabe, but hadn't he also, in his wanderings, heard the occasional confession, preached the occasional sermon, prayed occasionally for the dead? Surely he had atoned for his sin by now. Yes, he admitted to himself, hiding the reliquary in the grave and then desecrating the grave to get it back, those might be seen as blasphemous acts, but surely that was a venial sin, and he'd given himself a number of rosaries to say in penance. And besides, he'd also saved that Robin Hood fellow from an unjust encounter with the gallows. That was an act of charity worth something, wasn't it?

But now he stopped and leaned on his spade, heaving a loud sigh, partly from weariness, partly from melancholy. He had to admit finally that even his confession and expiation of the sins of murder, blasphemy, and desecration of graves could not exonerate him, when his chief sin, avarice, continued to fuel his obsession and had motivated even all of his "virtuous" deeds in the wake of the murder itself sixteen years prior. *Radix malorum est cupiditas*, he murmured as he resumed digging. But of course, he had no intention of repenting that one.

Clunk. He heard it and felt it at the same time, He'd finally reached that three-foot depth and a thrill of excitement flooded his veins as he bent down to clear away the dirt from the metal box his shovel had unearthed. This was it. It had to be. He did feel a sinking in his stomach when he lifted the box from its grave and saw with a jolt how small it was—perhaps eight by ten by four inches. Nor did it weigh as much as he would have expected if the box contained a significant treasure of gold or silver. Still, he thought, it might in fact be full of precious jewels—enough to allow him to live comfortably for the remainder of his life, on land he might purchase with their value. He'd heard rumors, in fact, that the old Randal manor might end up for sale, as the family's wealth seemed to be dwindling. What a triumph it would be if he could purchase that land and live on it like a rich franklin, able to look down upon that same family that had denigrated him as a servant so many years ago.

But that was nothing but dreams, he thought. He must open this box and behold the precise nature of the fortune that was now his. The box was locked, but a few well-aimed whacks with his spade broke the lock and enabled him to pry open the lid.

His abundant eyebrows lifted high into his forehead as his eyes bulged and his face froze in astonishment. The box contained a single item: a three-inch sliver of very old wood.

For a moment, Bungay was frozen with confusion. Then he noticed that, engraved on the inside lid of the metal box, were the Latin words *Verum Crucis*. Then Bungay's face contorted in uncontrollable mirth, and he laughed loud and long until the birds of the forest chirped and cawed in chorus. Lord Stephen's incalculable treasure was a piece of the True Cross.

Or at least it was a fragment of some Middle Eastern tree that some levantine con artist dealing in phony relics had foisted on the unsuspecting crusader who had assumed it must be genuine. For why would anyone be so evil as to lie about such a thing? But Bungay knew enough about the trade in relics to know that if all the pieces of the true cross currently in circulation were gathered together, they could be assembled into a great three-masted merchant ship. How much of his own wealth had Lord Stephan surrendered to bring this scrap of wood home?

The friar understood why Lord Stephen, feuding as he was with the old Father Mark, would be loath to donate his treasured relic to the local parish church. He understood, too, that Lord

Stephen thought of the relic as a great treasure, a spiritual treasure, not an earthly one. He understood that at some point Stephen would have revealed the existence of the relic, at least to his oldest son, but had been prevented by his own murder.

And as he held the small sliver up to the light to get a better look at it, Bungay smiled and gave a frustrated scoff as he understood, as well, that his own long and futile search was finally over. Oh well, he thought, dropping the sliver back into its box. Maybe I can sell it somewhere.

AFTERWORD AND ACKNOWLEDGMENTS

The two great heroic legends to come out of medieval England—the legend of King Arthur and the legend of Robin Hood—differ significantly from one another in many important ways, including their form, authorship, tone, theme, content and audience. The tales of Arthur were told as chivalric Romances in the courts of medieval Europe, and were composed by conscious artists for aristocratic audiences. The ballads of Robin Hood were composed by popular minstrels and storytellers for the common folk, often in a rough and tumble comic vein. There are no great Robin Hood epic poems and no Sir Thomas Malory to compile the Robin Hood story into a single long and complex narrative. What survive are many shorter ballads that would serve as brief entertainments, plus one long (1824-line) story in ballad stanzas, the *Gest of Robin Hood*, comprising seven loosely connected "fits" telling stories of Robin and Little John.

These ballads record separate instances and tell Robin's story in fragments. In the eighteenth century, these fragments were collected, first in Thomas Percy's *Reliques of Ancient English Poetry* in 1765, then more completely in Joseph Ritson's *Robin Hood* collection in 1795. Ritson even included a completely whimsical "biography" of the mythical Robin. In the following century, the most definitive collection of Robin Hood ballads was included by Francis James Child in *The English and Scottish Popular Ballads* (volume III). For today's common reader, a comprehensive collection of Robin Hood ballads is readily available in *Robin Hood and Other Outlaw Tales*, edited by Stephen Knight and Thomas Ohlgren (1997), to which I refer anyone who'd like to read these texts first hand.

Perhaps the starting point for contemporary understandings of the Robin Hood legend is the 1938 Errol Flynn film *The Adventures of Robin Hood*, in which the outlaw hero is a disgraced nobleman, Robin of Locksley, who remains loyal to the absent crusading king Richard the Lionhearted against the machinations of his usurping brother Prince John and his allies, Sir Guy of Gisbourne and the Sheriff of Nottingham.

There are two major departures this film makes from the original Robin of the ballads: First, Robin is pure English yeoman stock in the ballads. He is definitely no nobleman, and delights in robbing those of aristocratic rank and in flouting the authorities who enforce the status quo. But an Elizabethan dramatist named Antony Munday wrote two plays, *The Downfall of Robert, Earl of Huntington* and *The Death of Robert, Earl of Huntington*, which rewrote Robin's story and made him a fallen nobleman.

Secondly, the placement of Robin into the historical period from 1189 to 1199, the reign of Richard I, is the brainchild of Sir Walter Scott, who includes Robin Hood and his men in his novel *Ivanhoe*, which is set during that time. In the ballads, specific dates are rarely given, though the early ones seem to reflect a time roughly in the thirteenth or early fourteenth century. The fifteenth-century *Gest* mentions the good King Edward, but never specifies whether this is Edward I, Edward II or Edward III, which means it could be referring to any time between 1271 and 1377.

Not that Robin Hood is a historical figure in any sense other than as a symbol of the freedom of the common man as opposed to aristocratic or ecclesiastical authority. For that reason I've set my Robin Hood in a kind of Neverland that is a reflection of the high Middle Ages, but under no specific historical king. Indeed, when my characters refer to "the old king," they mean King Arthur, and my Robin is Robin Kempe, former captain of King Arthur's castle guard. Maid Marion is the Lady Mary of Winchester, formerly one of Queen Guinevere's ladies-in-waiting. Sir Palomides, the Moorish knight of the Round Table, has survived the fall of Arthur and lives in Sherwood because, as a Moor, he has not found another noble lord willing to accept him as a vassal. Thus the setting for these novels is the world of the common man paralleling the Romance world of Arthurian legend. This, of course, is a wide departure from tradition in one way, but in this I hope to preserve the spirit, including the political spirit of rebellion, that lies behind the original ballads.

I've made use of those ballads themselves in this novel. The ballad "Robin Hood and Alan a Dale" sung by Sir Palomides is my own modernization (and abridgement) of Child ballad no. 138 (Child Vol. III, p. 173), while the ballad sung by Alan himself in chapter eighteen is a modernized version of the popular ballad "Lord Randal," Child ballad no. 12 (Vol. I, p. 151). The lyric Alan a Dale sings at the funeral in chapter three is a modernized version of the haunting late medieval lyric still popular among folk singers, called "The Corpus Christi Carol." "Western Wind," sung by Alan at the Randals' dinner in chapter eight, is another modernized lyric from Middle English.

While the time period of the Robin Hood novels is far from specific, I have endeavored to fill that world with genuine physical spaces. Thus the castles and religious houses mentioned in the book all really do exist, or did exist in the thirteenth century or thereabout. There really was a powerful Peveril family that owned the castle and its environs, though there was no Earl or Countess of Chesterfield until centuries later. There really are man-made tunnels or caves under Nottingham Castle, which date back to the high Middle Ages. There really is a Thynghowe barrow with its border stones in Sherwood Forest, a mile or so from the Great Oak. As described in the book, it was a meeting place for the Norsemen that lived in the area in the ninth and tenth centuries.

The astrolabe was invented in classical Greece, and in the early Middle Ages became quite important to Muslims who used it to establish the precise direction of Mecca. It spread to later medieval Europe through Muslim Spain, and became a valuable instrument for astronomers, surveyors, and sailors who used it to navigate. Geoffrey Chaucer wrote a treatise on the astrolabe for his fourteenth-century English readers, perhaps the first example of technical writing in English.

There actually was a Friar Bungay in thirteenth-century England. He is immortalized in a popular Elizabethan comedy by Robert Greene called *Friar Bacon and Friar Bungay*, in which the two friars are rival magicians. Roger Bacon is of course the famous Oxford scholar who is credited with developing the scientific method, and whose scientific experiments got him a reputation as a "magician." The historical Friar Bungay was Thomas Bungay, a Franciscan friar and contemporary of Bacon's, who was educated at Oxford and Paris, and who came back to lecture at Oxford from 1270-72. He gained a reputation as an alchemist, and later was a master at Cambridge. He wrote an important commentary on Aristotle's treatise *On the Heavens*. The historical Bungay's scholarly reputation and his interest in the sciences, especially astronomy, made him a good model for my fictional Bungay, but I've made my fictional version far less prominent, and I've named him David and made him a Dominican, so as not to imply he actually *is* the historical Bungay.

CAST OF CHARACTERS

Alan a Dale: A member of Robin Hood's band, Alan a Dale is best known as a jongleur or minstrel who entertains the men with ballads of his own composition, or that he has learned from others. He is also one of Robin's younger followers, and one of his better archers. He is one of the married outlaws, living with his wife Ellen in Sherwood after being married by Friar Tuck. In the present novel, he and Ellen become the chief investigators of the murder of Lord Randal.

Anne Randal: Lady Anne is Lord William Randal's younger sister. She is sixteen and eager to be married, though lack of a significant dowry has made her a bit obsessed with her family's lack of wealth. She is lively and vivacious, and loves to talk.

Arthur Bland: Arthur is a very large and muscular man who had formerly made his living as a tanner. Upon meeting Little John, the huge tanner wanted to test his mettle against the equally large woodsman, and when Little John bested him, he decided he'd rather join Robin's band than keep his former profession, and enlisted with the Sherwood bandits, a few teeth lighter after his skirmish with John.

Dap: Sir William Randal's falconer, who trains his hawks for hunting. The faithful servant Dap is instrumental in finding

Lord William's killer, and later joins the household of Sir Richard at the Lee.

David of Doncaster: David is the youngest of Robin's band, in his late teens. An orphan, David has found a home with the outlaws of Sherwood. Tradition says that David of Doncaster was a champion yeoman wrestler, and he turns that skill to good use in the present novel.

Eleanor Franklin: Lady Eleanor is the daughter of a free landowner whose lands border upon those of Lord Randal. Lord William is considering marrying her, though his mother, brother, and sister all disapprove of the match. She becomes a suspect in his murder when he leaves her home after dining with her.

Ellen: Ellen is the wife of Alan a Dale, and lives with him among Robin's outlaws in Sherwood. She is one of the youngest and most outspoken of the women who live with Robin's men, and is very knowledgeable in herb lore. She is also more intelligent than most of Robin's men, and puts her intelligence to good use in helping solve the crimes in the present novel.

Friar Tuck: Tuck is a Franciscan, though he belongs to no house and lives with Robin and his men in the forest. He does see to the outlaws' spiritual needs, and is licensed to hear confessions, though he does fight at their sides if need be. He is in charge of most of the outlaws' charitable ventures, taking a third of all they take from their rich marks to give it to the poor.

Geoffrey Randal: Geoffrey becomes Lord Geoffrey when his brother, Lord William Randal, is murdered. He inherits the title and estate of his brother, and appears to be overwhelmed and annoyed by the new responsibilities. If he killed his brother to inherit the title, as some believe, he's not happy with his ill-gotten gains.

Guy of Gisbourne: Sir Guy of Gisbourne is the royally appointed commander of the king's fortress of Nottingham Castle. Determined to enforce royal authority in Nottinghamshire, he has vowed to track down the outlaws of Sherwood and hang them. He's most interested in a public hanging of Robin Hood.

Haakon: "Skipper" Haakon is a Norseman and former Viking who, having given up the sea, still manages to keep his hand in the robbing and looting trade as a member of Robin's outlaw band. His seaman skills occasionally come in handy, if any of the outlaws need a boat.

Jack: Commander of Sir Guy of Gisbourne's guards.

Joan Randal: Lady Joan (or simply Lady Randal) is the mother of Lord William, Geoffrey, and Anne, and the widow of old Lord Stephan, the crusader. She is certain her son was killed by his lover, Lady Eleanor, but is a suspect herself, having been rumored to have killed her own husband over his failure to tell her where his crusader treasure was hidden.

Jock of Barlborough: One of Robin's chief opponents in the Nottingham Archery contest (in the second Robin Hood mystery), the impoverished former soldier decided to join Robin's band of outlaws after the tournament. A native of the village of Barlborough, Jock is one of Robin's most mature and reliable men.

John, cook's son: The young son of the cook at the Priory of Wallingwells (in the second Robin Hood mystery), John decided he preferred the life of an outlaw of the woods to working in the kitchen with his father, and is now part of Robin's band.

John Naylor: See "Little John."

John of Oxenford: See "Sheriff of Nottingham."

Little John: Little John is Robin Hood's right hand man. Born a villein on a manor belonging to a monastery, John fled his servitude and became an outlaw in Sherwood. He is tall, strong and imposing, and is in a committed relationship with Will Stutely. When necessary, John goes by the pseudonym "Reynold Greenleaf."

Lydia Peveril, Countess of Chesterfield: Lady Lydia was the daughter and only child of Sir Stephen Peveril and his noble wife, Lady Margaret Le Strange. Her father being deceased, she became the heir of Earl Ranulph of Chesterfield, and is now the Countess. Although she is the target of several noble families who want to marry their sons to her, she has voiced her intention to rule in her own right. She does so in part with help from Robin Hood and his men, whom she also does her best to protect, having named them her own foresters, and thus servants of her estate.

Maid Marion: Robin's nickname for Lady Mary of Winchester. Marion is the chief lady in the entourage of Lady Lydia Peveril, Countess of Chesterfield. Still unmarried in her early twenties, her fellow ladies all call her "maid." Because her noble father lost his estate and has died, she has no dowry to count on, and thus no noble suitors. She is, however, romantically entangled with the yeoman Robin Hood, though marriage seems unlikely due to their difference in social status.

Mary of Winchester: See Maid Marion.

Maude Peveril: Lady Maude Peveril is the wife of the Sheriff of Nottingham. She was a by-blow of Sir Aubrey Peveril, younger son of the powerful Peveril family, and thus a cousin of Lady Lydia, the Countess. She is also an occasional love interest of Robin Hood.

Much, the miller's son: One of the most dependable and longest-tenured members of Robin Hood's followers, Much is a fine archer and a reliable soldier in the outlaw band. He has a mischievous but charming manner, and loves to bring dinner guests with large purses into Robin's camp.

Palomides: Sir Palomides was a knight in the court of the old king (Arthur) before his kingdom's demise. A Moor born in the Middle East, Palomides became a Christian when he joined the Round Table. After that table fell, he could find no other lord in Britain who would take him on as a knight, and chose to join his old friend Robin in his outlaw band. Palomides is known for knightly prowess and valor as well as his culinary skills and his skill in music and poetry.

Peter of Verysdale: Sir Peter is the young son of Sir Richard at the Lee. He was first seen as a love interest of Lady Lydia Peveril (in the first Robin Hood mystery). In this novel, he is a love interest of Lady Anne Randal, and helps his father rescue Lady Lydia.

Richard at the Lee: Sir Richard at the Lee, Lord of Verysdale, has a large estate around the village of Lee that has been in his family for seven generations. Robin Hood and his men helped save Sir Richard's inheritance (in the first Robin Hood Mystery). Sir Richard helps pay that debt in the present novel by warning Robin of his standing accused in the murder of Lord Randal.

Robin Hood: Leader of a band of outlaws in Sherwood Forest. Of yeoman status, Robin's real name is Robin Kempe, and he is the former captain of the guard under the old king (King Arthur). Now he poaches the king's deer and robs rich nobles and prelates on the Great North Road through Sherwood. When necessary, he goes by the alias "Robert fitz Ooth of Locksley."

Robin Kempe: See "Robin Hood."

Scarface: One of the more vicious and ruthless of Sir Guy of Gisbourne's guards, who takes pleasure in beating prisoners.

Sheriff of Nottingham: Robin Hood's oldest and most persistent enemy, the Sheriff, John of Oxenford, is a corrupt royal official who rakes in a good deal of money through bribery and the illegal seizure and taxation of goods that come through Nottingham. He is married to the far from pliable Lady Maude Peveril, and tends to give her a good deal of freedom.

Stephen Randal: The former Lord Randal, father of Lord William, was rumored to have brought back a great fortune from his service in the crusades. He was mysteriously murdered not long after his return from the Holy Land, and the treasure never found.

Thorvald: Thorvald is an old dwarf with a white beard, who formerly drove a cart in which he carried prisoners to execution or other punishment. Later he gave up that trade to become a merchant under the old king, but since the king's fall he has taken to the forest with his old acquaintance, Robin.

Wat o' the Crabstaff: Wat is a part of Robin's outlaw band who was once a tinker, but was convinced by Robin to give up that trade and join the outlaws of Sherwood. A crabstaff is a quarterstaff, which is Wat's favorite weapon.

Will Scarlet: Everyone knows that one of the most popular figures in Robin's band is Will. However, the early ballads do not seem to agree on his last name Thus if you read the early ballads, there seem to be three different Wills in Robin's band: Will Scarlet, Will Scathelock, and Will Stutely, unless of course, they are all referring to the same character. I've made them all different. Will Scarlet is Robin's nephew, one of his younger followers. He wears a scarlet hood over his Lincoln green livery, and has blond hair and blue eyes. He's one of Robin's most loyal men, and one of his best archers.

Will Scathelock: Scathelock, the un-Scarlet, is a tall, lanky, middle-aged member of Robin's crew, known as a reliable and experienced woodsman. He is often left in charge of the outlaw camp when Robin and Little John are away, because of his stalwart trustworthiness.

Will Stutely: Stutely, even younger than Will Scarlet, is generally considered the handsomest of Robin's crew, though a stint in the dungeons in Nottingham did leave a few scars on his face. He is a slight young man with a freckled and tanned complexion and sparkling brown eyes. He is deferential to Robin and courteous to ladies and others, but has a particularly caustic wit when he wants to annoy an enemy. He also likes to use doctored dice to win at Hazzards. And he is a terrible singer. Will is Little John's particular friend, and the two share a tent together.

William Randal: Lord William is a nobleman who loves to hunt in Sherwood. He befriends Alan a Dale after being "invited" to a forest dinner by Robin Hood's men. He is considering marrying his beloved, Lady Eleanor, but poison puts a stop to his plans.

Wulf: Wulf is Lord William Randal's "dog boy," the servant who takes care of his hunting greyhounds (Troilus and Cresseid). He is a surly young servant who leaves the Randal household after the death of Lord William.

ABOUT THE AUTHOR

J AY RUUD is a retired professor of English at the University of Central Arkansas, now devoting much of his time to fiction writing. He has retold the traditional legend of King Arthur for modern readers as a series of Merlin Mysteries, the final volume of which, *To the Great Deep*, was published by Encircle in the fall of 2020. He is the author of the Robin Hood Mystery series, *Sleuth of Sherwood* (June 2022), *Ghoul of Sherwood* (December 2022), an Eric Hoffer Book Award Finalist, and book 3, *Treasure of Sherwood*, published by Encircle in June 2024. He's also written scholarly books, including an *Encyclopedia of Medieval Literature* (2006), *A Critical Companion to Dante* (2008), and *A Critical Companion to Tolkien* (2011), as well as the first full-length study of Chaucer's short poems, *"Many a Song and Many a Lecherous Lay": Tradition and Individuality in Chaucer Lyric Poetry* (1992), a book that was reissued by Routledge in October 2019 after 27 years.

He taught at UCA and chaired the English department for 13 years, prior to which he was Dean of the College of Arts and

Sciences at Northern State University in Aberdeen, South Dakota. He has a Ph.D. in Medieval Literature from the University of Wisconsin-Milwaukee, and is married to the thoroughly awesome poet and novelist Stacey Margaret Jones. He has two more or less adult children, and as many spectacular dogs as grandchildren (four). He has been to all seven continents, is a lifetime Chicago Cubs fan, and dabbles in community theater, where he once played his own daughter's mother. Follow Jay Ruud on Facebook and @GildasOfCornwall on Instagram.

www.ingramcontent.com/pod-product-compliance
Lightning Source LLC
Chambersburg PA
CBHW050025120726
47903CB00006B/1918